Y013349

KU-303-191

the
FORBIDDEN
CITY

ALSO BY DEBORAH A. WOLF

The Dragon's Legacy Saga
The Dragon's Legacy
The Forbidden City
The Seared Lands (2019)

Split Feather

DEBORAH A. WOLF

the FORBIDDEN CITY

TITAN BOOKS

THE FORBIDDEN CITY
Paperback edition ISBN: 9781785651113
Electronic edition ISBN: 9781785651120

Published by Titan Books
A division of Titan Publishing Group Ltd
144 Southwark St, London SE1 0UP

First paperback edition: March 2019
2 4 6 8 10 9 7 5 3 1

This is a work of fiction. Names, places and incidents are either products of the
author's imagination or used fictitiously. Any resemblance to actual persons,
living or dead (except for satirical purposes), is entirely coincidental.

Copyright © 2018 by Deborah A. Wolf. All Rights Reserved.
Map illustration by Julia Lloyd.

No part of this publication may be reproduced, stored in a retrieval system, or
transmitted, in any form or by any means without the prior written permission
of the publisher, nor be otherwise circulated in any form of binding or cover
other than that in which it is published and without a similar condition being
imposed on the subsequent purchaser.

A CIP catalogue record for this title is available from the British Library.

Printed and bound in the United States.

This book is dedicated with love to

KRISTINE ALDEN

the sister of my heart.

DRAMATIS PERSONAE

Ani (Istaza Ani): Youthmistress of the Zeerani prides. Though she has no children of her own, she loves her young charges fiercely.

Daru: A young Zeerani orphan, apprenticed to Hafsa Azeina. Born a weakling, Daru is keenly aware of the thin line that separates life from death.

Hafsa Azeina: Queen Consort of Atualon and foremost dreamshifter of the Zeeranim.

Hannei: Young warrior and best friend to Sulema, Hannei is everything a Ja'Akari should be: bold, beautiful, and honorable to the marrow of her bones.

Ismai: A Zeerani youth, Ismai wishes to break tradition and become Ja'Akari, though warrior status is reserved for females. Last surviving son of Nurati, First Mother among the Zeeranim.

Jian: A Daechen prince and Sen-Baradam of Sindan.

Leviathus: Son of Ka Atu, the Dragon King, Leviathus was born *surdus*, deaf to the magic of Atualon and thus unable to inherit his father's throne. Leviathus is dedicated to his family, his people, and his king, and works tirelessly to maintain the stability of Atualon.

Sulema Ja'Akari: Ja'Akari warrior, daughter of Zeerani dreamshifter Hafsa Azeina and Ka Atu, the Dragon King of Atualon.

TABLE OF CONTENTS

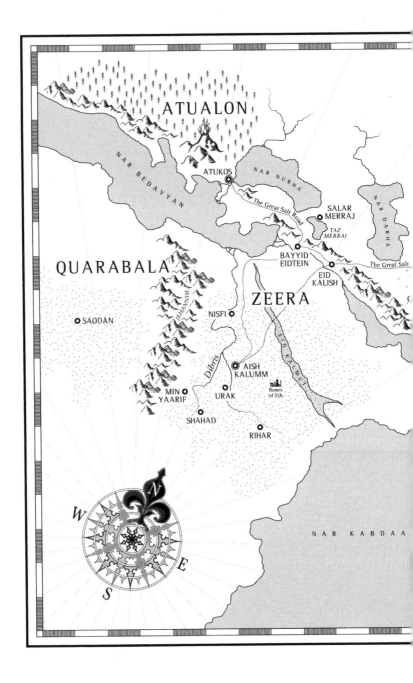

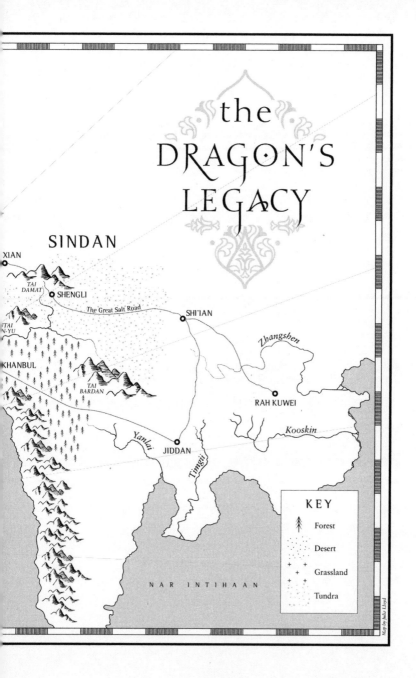

the DRAGON'S LEGACY

SINDAN

XIAN

TAI DAMAT

SHENGLI

The Great Salt Road

SHI'IAN

TAI N-YU

Zhangshen

KHANBUL

TAI BARDAN

RAH KUWEI

Kooskin

Yanlai

JIDDAN

Tinggii

KEY

Forest

Desert

Grassland

Tundra

NAR INTIHAAN

Map by Julia Lloyd

SUNDERED

The wind was born of a twilight lord, playing a seashell flute. Webbed fingers, strong and sure, danced across a smooth shell as they had once danced across the skin of a human girl. She had been delicate and sweet and all things good.

That girl was gone, just as the meat was gone from the shell, leaving only the memory of beauty and faint notes in the wind. But the sea was still the same, and the song was still the same, curling around his heart thick and slow as the magical fog that shrouded the Sorrowful Isles.

Born of sea and sand and the cries of a wounded heart, the wind danced in rage and longing across Nar Kabdaan, the waves of the Sundered Sea rousing to wrath and ruin as they cast themselves, again and again, upon the heartless shores at Bizhan. The waves were born, they struggled, and they died unmourned, one after another like soldiers caught in a dream of war.

The wind was heavy with salt, and the dreams of sea witches, and the tears of lost souls. It struck at the jagged rocks, tore at the sharp grasses like a madman tearing at his own hair. It howled like the voices of a thousand ice wolves buried in fear, forgotten to legend, lost, lost, lost.

The howling woke the half-kin child, because the song of wolves can never truly be forgotten by the offspring of man. The child rose, slipped from his bed, left his mother's hearth behind, and stumbled down the rocky path to the sea.

The moons were faded, half empty.

Because he, too, could hear the howling of the wolves, could feel them singing in the shadows of his heart, the twilight lord put down his flute and swam to shore. He had broken so many laws already that one more could hardly matter.

And besides, he told himself as he slipped through the water,

I wrote those laws. The things that dwell beneath fled from his shadow, and the Two Sisters veiled their faces as he lifted his sleek head above the waves. Eyes wide, the child had nearly reached the water, was so close that the fat little footprints filled with water as he passed, and glittered like abalone shells in the thin light. The wind tore at the veil, at weft and warp of land and magic. It howled and raged as did the storm in his heart, but the moons were thin and weak, and laws older than his held the barrier in place.

He could not pass. He could not...

But the child could.

Just as his dimpled little feet paused at the water's edge, graceful as a mist-dancer poised on the edge of the world, a cry arose. The woman came striding down the path, calling for her child. The mist bowed and kissed her feet, clung to her thin robe in supplication, and gave way before her. Her eyes shone deep and dark as the pools of the dead, and the stars lit her brow like a crown. Slight and sharp as the sea-willow, she was his song of beauty, the very dream of majesty. Her hair was blacker than the shadows, and she ruled the dark wishes of his heart.

The child hesitated, looked back the way he had come, and fell on his fat little rump. His wide round eyes opened wider, and the fat baby mouth pursed into a fierce frown. Before he could make up his mind to cry, the woman scooped him up in her strong brown arms and held him close to her breast.

The twilight lord swam closer, drawn to her as the tide to the moons. Even as his feet touched the sandy shore, even as he shed the sea and his Issuq skin to stand naked in the starlight, yearning for her, hands and face pressed hard against the veil despite the pain, she turned. The waves broke over her feet. The wind sighed through the veil. Wind and water could pass through, but never his living flesh, nor hers, not till the end of Sundering.

The child of both worlds might pass, but his fat little fist was tangled in his mother's hair, and in her heart, as well. The twilight lord looked into his son's eyes—Issuq eyes, eyes of the sea. The boy stared back at him, quiet and solemn and brave as the sky.

Thou shalt not, he thought, and these laws were older than blood, deeper than bone. His heart bled through the veil easy as wind, quick as water, and left the flesh behind.

The woman looked down at the child and cried out, clutching him closer still as she stared blindly into the veil.

She cannot see me, he thought as he pressed harder. *They cannot give her even that much*. Her mouth moved. A blessing for him, or a curse? Perhaps a warning that he should never seek to steal the child. He could not say. Human mouths were such a mystery, and the words, being of the flesh, could not pass to him.

"I will not hurt you," the twilight lord promised. "I will not seek to make him mine." He lied, of course, but she would expect lies from one of the lords of twilight. Even from him.

Especially from him.

She turned her back to the sea and he cried out as grief pierced his heart. Then she paused. He saw the curve of her soft cheek and in that moment it seemed as if she had heard him. There was a quick flash of cold steel. Cradling the child in one arm, she held the other high. In her hand she held a short knife, and a lock of her midnight hair. The wind slapped at her, plastering the fabric to her lithe form. The child laughed with delight. She let the lock of hair fly from her fingers, and paused for another long moment.

Another heartbeat.

Another lifetime.

The wind wept sorrowfully through the veil, bearing the lock. He reached up and plucked it from the sky, the greatest treasure of two worlds. Then the woman walked away. Her steps were slow and seemed painful, as if she walked upon a knife's edge. Yet she never faltered.

Soon she was gone.

He brought the tuft of hair to his face. Sunlight and moonslight and laughter beneath the stars. Webbed fingers closed, tight and trembling, around this last wisp of sky silk.

When the shell flute fell from his other hand, it hardly made a splash.

5

HUNTED

Cold rain fell from the leaves in fat droplets, chasing the rivulets of hot sweat as it trickled down her back.

Akari Sun Dragon rose screaming in the east, but try as he might those hot eyes would never penetrate this emerald gloom. The air was heavy—"thick as fish soup," their father might have said—and Holuikhan fought the urge to suck air in through her mouth. Such would have meant her certain death. She flared her nostrils instead, taking her breath in delicately, lest the shadows she carried rise up and choke her.

The mouth of her bone pipe was close enough to kiss, if she were of an age to be thinking of such things. The leaves ahead whispered, and moved, then parted to reveal the face of her older sister. Anmei was the finest huntress in their village. She wore the forest as another woman might wear a dress. Her bright eyes flashed through the rain, and she pressed her three remaining fingers to her lips.

'*Ware*, she signaled. '*Ware poison.*

Holuikhan clamped her teeth together, again minding her breathing.

Pig tracks, her sister signed, hand movements as graceful as a dance. *Sow. Four young. Come.* She turned away, becoming the forest again. Cupping her hands before her face, she puffed out her cheeks and blew. Air shrieked through the holes where her third fingers had been. A long, loud trill caused the world to go silent.

The forest shuddered as a clutch of chinmong burst from the undergrowth, heads bobbing and clawed hands held tight to their breasts. The alpha female tilted her head at Holuikhan. Red streaks like bloody handprints ran along the sides of its face, and its teeth were yellow-white as it hissed, crest rising and preparing to charge.

Another whistle came from the undergrowth. The raptor shook

water from its feathers in protest, but stood down, and the clutch flowed around Holuikhan like deadly water as they brushed past her to range on ahead. Her lips parted in awe as they passed, so close she could hear their claws scrape against the tree roots, smell the strange spiced-meat musk of their feathers…

"*Sssst!*" Anmei hissed out loud. Her face was furious as it peered from her cloak of leaves. Holuikhan clamped her lips together again, shamed and a little frightened by her lapse. This might be her first real hunt, but the shadows she carried would not be forgiving.

Her sister signaled and the raptors spread out, trilling to one another as they searched for prey. Holuikhan's fingers tightened on the bone pipe, a pretty thing with a belly full of death. Today, for the first time, she held the shadows in her hand. Today in the village a clutch of chinmong eggs was being tended by her younger sister. Some day…

The alpha female screamed, sighting prey. Anmei whistled through her beautiful, maimed hands, calling her raptors to the hunt.

Some day, Holuikhan promised herself for the millionth time, this would all be hers.

The chinmong had pinned a boar—a big boar, the biggest Holuikhan had ever seen—and her hands trembled to the beating of her heart as she raised the pipe to her lips. Bare toes dug into the thick tree roots as she leaned against the hoary trunk of a baobing, the better to steady her shot.

Though she made no sound, and though the thick black sap she had rubbed under her pits and upon her pulse-points should mask her scent, the sooty giant paused in his threats to the raptors and lifted his long, flat head. The oddly pink end of his snout twitched, round nostrils opening and closing like hungry little mouths as they tasted the air. Little red-rimmed eyes flashed in the rising mist and rolled toward her. He had caught her scent. The boar wheeled in her direction, ignoring the calls and feints of the big chinmong.

Time slowed, *slooooowed*. It seemed to Holuikhan that she could count every bristling black hair on the boar's body, and could see the air shimmer around his heavy face as he gnashed his teeth.

I am death, he told her, quite plainly. *I am coming for you.*

I am ready, she answered from her heart. Her hands steadied. She drew in breath through her nostrils, exactly as she had practiced, and crossed her eyes a little bit as she sighted down the length of the pipe. Even as the boar charged, squealing, and the ground shuddered beneath his dagger feet, her lips almost—almost!—touched the knob end of her deadly little weapon, and she blew.

The dart made scarcely a whisper as it left her pipe, the shadow of a shadow of a sound, but it was thunder in her heart as the world stopped.

With its fluff of red down the dart hovered, just at the end of her pipe. The boar floated mid-charge, head down, all four feet suspended above the dark earth like those of an oulo dancer. The forest held its breath.

Suddenly her dart buried itself in the pig's shoulder. He skidded to a stop a hare's jump from where Holuikhan stood, and screamed. He squealed like a man who had taken a spear to the gut, or like a woman who had found her only child drowned in the river. The sound pierced her heart, and tears welled in her eyes even as the boar staggered to one side.

"I am sorry," she whispered, and she was.

The black giant turned heavily around, and in one final gesture of contempt he lowered his head and charged off in the one direction she wished he would not take. Though the pig should have fallen already—she had used the poison from a blue dart frog—Holuikhan could only stand and stare open-mouthed as he disappeared up the old mountain path.

The raptors, tempted beyond their training, screamed in unison and gave chase.

A heavy hand clapped over her shoulder. Holuikhan jumped and squeaked, a very unhunterlike sound. But Anmei just laughed.

Anmei was the prettiest girl in the village, in all the villages around Peichan. When she laughed like this, strong white teeth flashing in her dark face, a crown of ti leaves and her hunter's cloak making her seem as if the forest itself had birthed her, Holuikhan thought she might rival the Huntress herself in beauty.

"Come," she said out loud, the need for stealth long past. "Let us go collect your pig, little huntress."

"If the clutch leaves anything but bones and hair." Holuikhan sighed as she hopped down from the tree root. "Why did he run off like that? That poison was good. I tested it."

Anmei shrugged. "He did not wish to die yet. A fine strong pig. His heart will give you courage." She tapped at her own chest. Anmei's first kill had been a young wyvern. She possessed the heart of a dragon.

"Yes, but did he have to choose that path?" Holuikhan shivered as she looked up the mountain. Even now the mists were rising with the day's heat, mocking her.

"Surely you do not fear Cold Spirit Stream?" White teeth flashed, gentle mockery. Holuikhan shifted her weight from one foot to the other. She slid her pipe into its carrier at her belt, avoiding her sister's gaze.

"The hunters never come this way, do they?"

"Of course not. Everyone knows there are ghosts up there. And you cannot eat a ghost, now, can you?"

Startled, Holuikhan met her sister's eyes, and they both burst out laughing. The sound surprised her, and frightened the forest. When hunters laugh, blood has been spilled. All creatures know this. Then the fit passed.

"Fortunately," Anmei went on, wiping tears of mirth from her eyes, "ghosts cannot eat you, either. Come, come, we cannot just leave him there all alone. It is bad luck to be so… disrespectful." She turned, the leaves of her cloak swirling about her, and disappeared after the pig.

There was nothing for it, then. Holuikhan sighed, steeled her heart, and started up the path to her doom.

❖

The pig had fallen much further away than they had expected. They found him after Akari Sun Dragon had bid them farewell and the moons appeared to light their way. He had run through Cold Spirit Stream, up the mountain trail, down a wide and ancient cobblestone path that reeked of wyvern-mint as they trod upon it, and through the ugly ruins of a pair of mossy gateposts that sat like stone trolls in the children's stories, guarding either side of the road and wickedly determined not to allow them to pass.

Holuikhan gave the gateposts a wide berth—and the side-eye—as she and Anmei crept past them, but they never moved. Not while she was watching them, anyway. The tracks they followed showed the pig's great suffering—here he had fallen and dragged himself, there he had scuffled with the chinmong, leaving a mat of blood, hair, and raptor feathers to tell the tale. His steps were heavy and staggered, and his hind legs dragged at the last. Holuikhan wept to think she had caused such pain. She wiped the tears from her cheeks with the back of one hand.

Such a baby, she chided herself. *Crying over a pig.*

"*Ssst*," Anmei whispered, her voice as soft as mist, "never be ashamed to cry over an animal you have killed. If you cannot feel sorrow for taking a life, you should not be hunting."

The tears came. Holuikhan allowed them to do so, and smiled at her sister's back.

At the last her boar had fought off the alpha raptor—there was no mistaking those long green-and-red feathers—but he had gone down, and a wide smear of gore marked his final hiding place. A heavy curtain of vines, glossy leafed and heavy with green berries, had grown across the path. The pig had dragged himself through this green door.

Strangely, the chinmong milled about on the path hissing, trilling in distress, and refused to pass. Anmei hesitated at the vines, faint lines of worry creasing her brow. She flashed her palm outward, fingers spread.

Stay.

Holuikhan nodded. A girl should be wary of any place that raptors feared to tread.

Anmei stepped up to the vines, peering closely at the leaves, again at the berries, and craned her neck to look high at the branches from which they hung.

No itch leaf, she signed, *no snakes. Safe. Come.* She raised her hands to her mouth and whistled for the chinmong.

The alpha female tilted its head this way, and that way, then shook its feathers as if ridding itself of mites. Its scythe claws dug into the soft earth, and the message it sent was very clear.

Anmei whistled again, sharper. Louder. Her eyes flashed at the raptor's defiance. The big female shook its feathers again, bobbed its head with a strange chick-like peep, then melted away into the forest. The others went with her.

Anmei blinked, and then blinked again.

Holuikhan's mouth fell open. Chillflesh raised the hairs on her arms.

We go? she signed, already rising up on the balls of her feet, ready to run back across Cold Spirit Stream, up the mountain and back down again, all the way to their village without stopping. Raptors were never afraid, even when they should be.

Anmei hesitated and then firmed her mouth. *No*, she replied. *Come.* She pulled aside the vines and stepped through. Holuikhan, not being a raptor, did not have the courage to defy her sister, and so she followed.

It was as if the vines tried to hold her back. Almost before she had fought her way through, a hand clamped over her mouth and an arm snaked around her waist, pinning her arms. She was dragged from the path and behind a hoary old baobing tree, so surprised that at first she forgot to struggle. When she remembered, she tucked her chin to prevent a stranglehold, just as her sister had taught her.

Anmei! she thought, terrified.

Holuikhan kicked back, hard. Her heel collided with her captor's shin, and she was rewarded with a pained grunt.

"*Sssst*," her sister hissed into her ear.

When the shock passed and Holuikhan was able to stop flailing, the hand against her mouth eased up, and the arm around her waist loosened.

Yes, Holuikhan signed, still breathing hard through her nose. *Yes, okay.*

Anmei released her hold and stepped back. Her eyes were as round and white as the big moon, and Holuikhan's stomach dropped. Anmei was never afraid, even when the raptors were.

Then she heard it, a cry that rose up on the winds even as the moons rose over the hunters, the baobing, and the stream of the drowned dead. It was the cry of a human child. Abruptly Holuikhan's feet dragged her forward, all unwilling. Her hands pressed against the rough bark, and she peeked around the trunk of the tree—though she willed none of these things to happen.

Stop! Anmei gestured sharply, but it was too late.

When Holuikhan's mind finally spoke to her of the things her eyes were seeing, she clutched at the ancient tree. It stood at the very edge of a great clearing, ringed with round stone buildings, empty-eyed and crushed like old skulls. Baobing had grown around and into the structures, their roots reclaiming thatch and stone and wood, but not one had ventured into the clearing at the center. Nothing grew there; not tree nor fern nor blade of grass, and Holuikhan knew deep in her heart that nothing from the forest ever ventured forth to peer into the old stone well.

Until now.

It was the perfect setting for a nightmare. A ring of—of *things*—crouched and swayed around the outer edges of the clearing. Manlike and naked, pale-skinned, glitter-eyed, and their limbs shone bright and hard as a night-widow's carapace in the moonlight. They swayed like grasses in the breeze, though there was none to be felt, and they sang in voices high and brittle.

That was not the worst of it. A smaller ring of creatures flowed back and forth around the well...

Witching well, she thought. *Oh sweet Akari, that is a witching well…*

These beings, though almost manlike in their bearing and posture, were less human than the baobing, less human than the pig she had hunted, or the old stone houses. They had extra arms, two sets apiece—corpse arms, she thought, sewn to their bodies as her mother might sew an extra pocket onto an apron. These arms dangled and twitched and moved as of their own accord as the not-men chanted and shuffled round and round in a terrible dance.

The worst of all was a man—or perhaps he had been a man once, when the baobing was a sapling and Cold Spirit Spring was sweet and pure, and bore a kinder name. Tall and proud and still as shadows beneath a dying moon, he was broad of shoulder and narrow at the waist, like the emperor's own soldiers. Something about him, some compelling air, made a part of her that was almost old enough to think of kissing wish that she might creep closer for a better look. The rest of her, the best parts of her, wanted to run screaming into the night.

Her sister's hand closed warm and steady upon her shoulder.

"Let us go," she breathed into Holuikhan's ear, quiet as flower petals on a spring morn. She gave a little tug. "Sister, come away."

Holuikhan meant to, she did. Her fingers let go their hold of the tree's rough bark and she prepared to push away, to melt into the forest with her sister, and never return to this place again. Then the man of nightmares raised his face to the pale moons. He wore a mask of leather scraps and jagged metal and shattered things, and he raised up both arms, as if in prayer. In one hand, the man of nightmares held a weapon, a wicked thing with a half-moon blade.

In his other he held a babe.

Newborn, or close to it, the poor thing kicked its tiny legs and wailed, piteous cries beneath the pitiless moons. Quicker than thought the blade flashed, up and down. The babe screamed, the shuffling priests chanted louder, and the bug-men chittered like soldier beetles scenting blood.

Up, down, the blade flashed, glittering in the moonslight like the bug-men's eyes, and it seemed to Holuikhan that it laughed. Up, down, and the babe stopped shrieking, stopped kicking, stopped. The man of nightmares—

I know you, she thought, *Nightmare Man.*

—brought the tiny, limp body to his mouth, and…

Holuikhan screamed. It was a tiny sound, scarcely a breath, but its echo in her heart was vast. It was this that the Nightmare Man heard. It was this sound that made him look up, mouth dripping, and smile.

"Get her," he growled in a voice as sweet and deadly as mad honey. "Bring her to me. Bring her to me!" The priests stopped their dancing, the bug-men stopped their singing, and as one they turned toward her.

"Go!" Anmei shouted. She tore Holuikhan away from the tree and flung her into the forest, back the way they had come. "Go!" she screamed, and she drew the knife from its sheath at her hip.

"Anmei," Holuikhan cried out. "Anmei, no!"

"Run!" Anmei screamed, even as the first of the bug-men leapt. "Sister, run!"

She ran.

ONE

"Go on." Xienpei handed him a long bundle draped in yellow silk with a heavy red fringe along its edge. She flashed her teeth in the new light, mocking his hesitation. "It will not bite you. Not today, at any rate."

He took the bundle and tugged away the silk, letting it fall upon the floor even as his mouth fell open.

"A sword?"

"A sword, Daechen Jian. It is a virgin blade, still warm from its maker's fires, so take care you do not blood it yet." She took back the weapon, still in its plain lacquered scabbard, and belted it at his waist. "Here, keep this cord tied just so, lest the emperor's soldiers take offense. No blade is to be drawn during the Napua, and no blood spilled. Some idiot always does, and some always is, and if you are that idiot I will leave you to rot in the dungeons. Do you hear me?"

"Yes."

"Yes…?"

"Yes, Yendaeshi." Jian suppressed an impatient sigh and resisted the urge to roll his eyes. His yendaeshi cou ld keep him in his rooms all day, if she was of a mind, and he desperately wished to be free of her, if only for a few hours. "Will the others…?"

"Today the yellow Daechen will walk among us armed. Akari willing, you will not cut yourselves shaving. I assumed you would wish to give your dammati their blades, so the servants will be by later with ten more blades for you."

"Sixteen." Jian kept his face still. "Sixteen have sworn their blood to me."

Xienpei blinked. "Indeed?"

He said nothing. The remaining half-dozen of his bloodsworn

would have to accept their blades later. He would make amends to them in private.

"Sixteen it is, then." She flashed her jeweled smile again, teeth sharp and hungry. "You have been busy, boy." Jian let the insult slide past.

"I would like to get dressed now," he said. "By your leave, Yendaeshi."

"Of course," she nodded, still smiling. "I will have the lashai deliver those swords to you presently. Enjoy the festival while you can, Daechen Jian."

When Jian had finished bathing, the ever-present lashai bound his hair up into a prince's knot and strapped him into a set of yellow lacquered armor. It was lighter than the practice armor to which he had grown used, and newer. It fit him well, though they had to loosen the shoulder straps and the waist was uncomfortably loose. Still, he imagined that he cut a fine and imposing figure, and hoped—not for the first time—that his mother might see him.

She had always loved the festival of flowers, and surely would not pass by this opportunity to pay him a visit. Though the Daechen were discouraged from associating with former friends and family, it was not expressly forbidden.

Jian emerged from the bathing chamber pressed, dressed, and eager to go. He allowed one lashai to belt the bright new sword at his waist, even as there was a knock at the door. Three of the servants entered, bearing the swords for his dammati, and laid them out upon the bed.

There were twenty-two of them.

The Gate of the Iron Fist had been thrown wide, and the bloodstone path scrubbed till it shone. Though none but the daeborn would be allowed to pass through into the heart of Khanbul, the Forbidden City, it seemed as if every man, woman, and child of Sindan had turned out on this day to cram into Supplicant's Square, hoping to receive the emperor's blessing.

It had been years since the emperor himself had come down from his palaces to bless the people, but there was always hope.

The two gigantic stone warriors flanked the gate. The golden one stood, helmeted, arm upraised, while the red warrior knelt bareheaded across the gap, jeweled tears on his face. They were as bedecked with flowers as any of Khanbul's finest citizens. Ropes and necklaces and blankets of flowers had been draped upon the stone giants until it seemed as if their frozen tableau was not a scene of bloody victory and defeat at all, but of romantic love between two great warriors. Perhaps the kneeling man was proposing marriage to the other.

Jian smiled on the inside, and wished them well.

The moat was filled with flowers, so that it seemed as if a person could walk across it. The water was thick with food wrappers and lost hair-ribbons, as well. Here and there a blossom had tucked itself into the wall, between the blades of the vanquished—carried there by the wind, perhaps, or tossed down from on high. Jian watched as a village youth in plain brown farmer's garb snatched the crown from a girl's hair and, laughing, sent it sailing out across the perfumed waters, to land with a splash and a ripple. The girl squealed and punched him on the shoulder, and they shared a laugh.

Jian wished them well, too, though he had more in common now with the stone giants than he did with the village people.

"They look so plain," Perri remarked. His eyes flashed yellow in the hot midsun. "Were we ever like them?"

"Yes," Jian answered, and touched the still-unfamiliar sword at his waist. "And no."

"You are starting to sound like Xienpei," Perri complained. "We are, but we are not. It is always, always this way… except when it is not. The cat is both dead and…"

"Shut up," Jian advised, "or I will toss you into the moat for the zhilla."

"As you say, Sen-Baradam." Perri bowed, laughing. "Though I do not think they would thank you for such a meager feast."

"You *are* kind of bony." Jian stepped onto the Path of Righteousness, setting himself even more apart from the common folk. None but the booted feet of the daeborn were allowed upon the blood-red road.

"Some of these skulls are new," Perri whispered. "Where do you think they get them?"

Jian averted his eyes from the clean white bone. "Not from the Daechen," he said.

One could always hope.

A commotion drew their attention. A girl—a pretty girl with a long face, wrapped in red and pink silks like a plum blossom—was leaning far over the moat. A pair of her friends laughed as they held the edges of her robes to keep her from falling into the bloom-laden water. Her tongue stuck comically out of one side of her mouth as she dragged a crown of blue lilies from her hair and flung it as if she were playing ring-toss in the gardens.

Perri started forward. "She should not do that." His brow furrowed with concern.

It was a lucky toss. The crown of flowers caught a gust of wind and was carried up and over the wide waters. It sailed high and far, arcing down at last to touch the very walls of the Forbidden City, and was caught upon the hilt of a sword.

The girl was transformed. In triumph, she had become a warrior. She shouted, fists in the air, a shout that turned quickly to a high squeal as the fabric of her robe tore. Then there was a weeping sound, a sound that would echo in Jian's dreams for many nights to come. The girl fell forward, toppling down the bank and into the water with a soft splash.

Her friends tumbled like wheat beneath the scythe, laughing.

A pair of guards who had been chatting at the foot of the golden stone giant shouted and ran for the girl, waving their arms. Perri turned to Jian, yellow eyes round as an owl's, mouth open as if he would ask his Sen-Baradam to save the girl.

But it was too late, all of them were too late.

Even as the girl struggled to her feet, raising her skirts with both hands and spitting out a mouthful of wet hair, the waters of the moat rippled. One of the guards flung himself belly down on the upper bank and shouted, red-faced with the effort. His voice was lost in the roar of the crowd. The girl set one foot upon the shore and reached for his outstretched hands.

A fountain of bubbles and ink erupted some distance from the girl, and the many-ridged shell of a zhilla broke the surface of the water, fouling the flowers and the hair-ribbons of lost girls. It rolled so that the creature's bony hood appeared, drawing back so that its mouth and mass of writhing red tentacles were exposed. The thing hissed and spat. Flat silvery eyes as big as shields flashed in the sunlight as it focused on its prey.

Jian opened his mouth, and perhaps he shouted. It seemed as if every person in Sindan was shouting at that moment, and the noise was deafening. The girl lunged forward, and her fingertips brushed those of the guard, but it had been too late for her since the moment she had tumbled into the water.

The zhilla's longer tentacles found her. They touched the foot that was still in the water and curled upward, sliding around her calf and up her skirts like a lover's caress, and she screamed. They all did. Even the emperor's own guard cried out as the girl's hand slid from his grasp, as she gasped and jerked when the zhilla's venom bit into her.

She slipped beneath the waters, lost to them all.

The surface of the moat ceased churning. The guard who had tried to save her was helped to his feet by his companion, who seemed to be yelling at him. They arrested the girl's friends as the crowd milled about, filling the space where they had stood, even as the flowers and ribbons and feast-day trash floated back to cover the place where the girl had died.

"Ah," Perri said, and he closed his eyes.

A low chuckle caught their attention. It was Naruteo, and he twisted his face into an ugly grin at Jian's look.

"Looks like sushi for dinner again, hey?" He laughed. "How many girls have you eaten, sea-thing child? Were they as delicious as that one?"

Perri grabbed Jian's wrist. Only then did he realize he had grasped the hilt of his sword.

"He wants you to draw," Perri whispered. "Look there, Sen-Baradam, he has set a trap for you." And indeed, five or six of Naruteo's bloodsworn had emerged from the crowd and watched Jian with hungry looks on their faces.

Blood thundered in his ears and Jian clenched his fist next to the hilt of his sword. "I cannot blood my blade in his belly," he remarked. "The blood of a coward would ruin this fine weapon."

A fist of guards approached, perhaps scenting trouble between the young Daechen. Naruteo's bloodsworn melted away. Naruteo himself bowed mockingly and turned from the scene, but not without a parting shot.

"We shall see," he told Jian. "We shall discover whose blood runs yellow and whose blood runs red, tomorrow at our Inseeing." And he walked away, laughing. The crowd parted before him, and closed behind him, leaving no indication of his passing.

A crown of flowers hung upon the wall of swords, wilting in the hot sun.

Already forgotten.

The door opened a crack. There was no sound, but the hallway beyond was brightly lit. Jian could not help it. He flinched.

"It is time, Daechen Jian."

He rolled from the woven mat, and on the third effort made it upright. He stood in a puddle of light, blinking away tears and trying not to let his legs shake too much. If his knees gave out he would fall, and if he fell they would just make him stand again. He was not sure he could find the strength.

For days without count he had been down here, in the dark and the cold and the quiet. At first there had been a pallet of straw and a basin for washing, but those comforts had been taken from him. For a while there had been food and water, and then there had been water. Then there was nothing but his heartbeat, and the dark.

"Drink." A figure, dark and blurred, moved between him and the burning light. A cup was pressed to his lips. It felt cool and hard, and smelled of mint. "Drink."

He thought of the winnowing, of the pain that had raged through him, and boys who fell screaming to die in their own shit and vomit. He thought of the wagons, and the greasy dark smoke. He thought of his mother, sitting alone by the fire at night, wondering what had become of him.

He drank. It was tea, nothing more, and it scalded his tongue.

Another shadow fell across his face. "Do not flinch." It was Xienpei. He flinched. "Do not show pain, Daechen Jian, for if you do I will know it. Your failure is mine. Do you understand?"

"Yes, Yendaeshi." He did not.

Then he was seized from every side. Strong hands clamped on his arms, his legs, his ankles. His limbs were stretched out like a skin for scraping, and he was bound into a frame. The door opened wider, and Jian bit his lips to keep from crying out as a mass of shadows split apart to become a pair of lashai bearing arms full of blackthorn vines. Blackthorn was used to scourge the worst criminals, rapists, and murderers, and those who stole from the emperor. The barbed thorns would tear flesh from bone, and if a criminal survived the lashing—few did—they would inevitably die as the wounds fell to rot.

"*Sssst*, little one," Xienpei hissed into his ear. "Be strong, now."

He jerked involuntarily at the ropes when the lashai moved behind him, and again when one of them touched his wrist. As the lashai pinched his flesh hard between thumb and forefinger, he took a deep breath, resolved to show no pain, no fear, no matter what they might do. Whatever they had planned for him, it would be gentle compared to the wrath of Xienpei if he were to fail.

Daechen Jian still had lessons to learn.

When the first thorn pierced his flesh, he grunted and ground his teeth together. It hurt, it hurt, but as he sucked the ragged air between his teeth Jian decided that he could bear it.

By the time the fourth thorn was pressed against his skin, the first had begun to burn. They had started at his wrist, and by the time they reached his shoulder, Jian was twitching uncontrollably and had bitten his tongue so that he was drooling blood. A scream curled in his gut and pushed its way up and into his mouth. He knew he could not stop it.

"If you cry out, Daechen Jian, I will kill your dammati. One bloodsworn for every sound." Xienpei's breath smelled of cinnamon and honey. "And if you faint, if you fail…"

The scream caught in his ribs.

"…I know where your mother lives, Tsun-ju Jian."

The scream became a growl, and the growl a snarl. He turned his face to hers and stared hard into those bright eyes. Another thorn tore through the skin on his back, and he bared his fangs at her.

"Yes," she hissed. "Yessss."

The blackthorn vine curled around his wrist and draped across his arm, around the side of his neck, around his waist and down the inside of one leg. The vine itself was heavy, and warm, and dragged at the thorns embedded in his flesh as if it were a living thing that wished him harm. By the time they started at his other wrist, the pain was a tongue of flame that licked across the surface of every thought and danced to the tune of his heartbeat. He snarled with each new wound, and with each tug at the vine, and bared his teeth whenever any of the shadows loomed too near. The world shrank to a pinpoint of light, and shadow, and pain.

"Good boy," Xienpei crooned as the last thorn tore through his skin. "Good boy."

He drew in long, shuddering breaths, and rolled his shoulders this way and that. The vine dragged at his hide. It itched and burned and stung. They bound him so tightly that he could feel it tear whenever he took a deep breath, so he tried panting through his clenched teeth. It helped, a little.

He had not cried out, and he had not fainted.

He had won.

Xienpei tugged at the vine, and laughed as he threw his head back. "He is ready."

Poles were thrust through rings set into the heavy frame, and thick-set lashai of a type Jian had never seen hoisted him into the air like a pig bound for slaughter. He swayed with the movement, and the pain sang to him, and blood flowed down his arms and back as they carried and dragged him from his cell and into the harsh, cold light. They banged the frame into the door, and into the wall, and dropped the back half against some stairs, and every time they did this Jian would growl, and the lashai would laugh. Eventually they tired of this game. He was hauled at last into a wide circular chamber, and the frame thumped onto the floor.

Jian was in a cool, dark room. The air was dry and held a strange smell, like the fungus that grew on rotting logs, or old seaweed, or tea that had begun to go bad. He wondered, between the waves of bright agony, why they had brought him to this empty place. Then the hulking lashai grabbed the frame, and dragged him around, and he saw.

The bodies of three young girls, just shy of womanhood and as much the same as sisters, sat in three high-backed wooden chairs, facing him. Their small feet dangled a hand span from the floor, and their small hands were folded quietly before them.

Their skin was pale; frost pale, sand pale, drowned-in-cold-water pale. A vine of flowering thorn laced in and among and around them. It sat upon the brow of the first sister, coiled around her head like a maiden-chain. Long thorns had pierced her ears, and dried blood fanned down her neck and across her shoulders, shocking against the white nightdress. The vine was bound around the eyes of the second girl like a sleeping mask, so that she wept a sad and sorry trail of tears. It was wrapped around the mouth of the third sister, piercing her tongue and lips and cheeks, holding her mouth open in a long and silent scream.

Jian wondered if this was to be his fate—left to starve and bleed

23

out, his corpse put on display as a warning to others.

Then the dead girls stirred. As one they turned their ravaged faces toward him. The bound-mouth girl hissed through her wicked gag, and Jian found himself twisting, pulling against his bindings regardless of the pain, like a small creature caught in a trap and facing the knife. When they spoke it was with one voice, a sound that pierced and tore at the air just as the thorns pierced and tore at his flesh.

"What is it, Sweetling?" the blind girl asked. "What has they brought us? Is it beautiful?"

"Can you hear its heart beating?" the deaf girl said. She groped for her sister's hand and, finding it, squeezed. "Is it squealing? Does it fear us?"

"Aaaaaahhhhhh," the pierced-tongue girl hissed. Her breath rattled and knacked through the blackthorn like a long-dead wind. "*Aaaaaahhhhhhh.*"

Jian stared in horror at the three as they twisted and writhed against their cruel bindings, straining to see, to hear, to taste his fear. They were insane, of that he was certain. Their little feet dangled like dead things. The girl with a mouth full of death smiled at him, horribly, and though her mouth cracked and tore, there was no blood.

They are dead, he thought. *Soon I will join them.*

The notion held surprisingly little fear. His mother was his only family, and she would never know. His dammati would be too busy looking after themselves to mourn overmuch. Xienpei would be furious at his failure, but what more could she do to him? Even pain was not so bad, once he grew used to it. Shaking away the remnants of his fear, he let the pain sink into his skin like sunlight, and drank the stink of his own degradation, letting it nourish him as if it were sweet water.

"He thinks he knows fear," the first sister said, "but he has not yet heard the drums of war. He will."

"He thinks he knows pain," the second sister said, "but he has not yet seen the face of despair. He will. He will."

"Aaaaaah," the third sister rattled. "Aaah aaah aaaahhhh."

"Does he pass?" The voice of Xienpei whispered forth from the shadows, weedy and weak. "Will he do?"

The girls twitched and shook like fish too long in the net, and hissed in unison.

"There is mercy in his voice. There is kindness in his eyes. He tastes of fear, of fear, of human fear. Take it away, away, away. Cleanse it of the human filth."

"Does he pass?" Her voice was closer now, and Jian shuddered as anticipation ripped through his skin. "Will he do?"

"Strip him, flense him! Flay him, cleanse him! Tear from him the hopes of the past, that he may face the sins of the future with the heart of a child. He will pass. He will do. If he lives. If he lives." Their voices rose to a mad howl as they chanted in unison.

"Three words thrice shall stay the prince,
"Three names twice shall slay him.
"Three drops once shall bind his heart
"Lest that heart betray him."

Three dead girls strained and strove against their wicked bindings even as hands laid hold of the vines that were wrapped and twisted and bound round Jian's body, and ripped them away from his flesh.

Something in Jian's core tore free.

It used his pain and anger, his fear and fury to shred through the last soft bits of his soul. It reared its head within him, and it roared. It was the roar of the ocean, the song of the sea-thing's child, the cry of a wounded predator. It jerked and strained at the bonds that held him, and pierced the girls with hot and angry eyes, and urged him to kill. *Kill.* Tear and rend and savage until the walls ran with blood, till the floor was slick with gore and offal and his ears filled with the screams of his enemies. Until he was the only living thing in this room, this city, this empire.

The second vine was torn from his flesh, and the beast roared with Jian's mouth. It howled, it sang a song of death and darkness between the stars. The screaming, bloodied muscles of his back bunched, and he strained so that something in his shoulder popped in a flush of wet heat.

The frame shattered.

Chunks and splinters of wood flew in every direction. One corner went end-over-end and struck the blind sister in the temple. It laid her skin open to the bone, and though she did not bleed, she turned her eyeless face toward him and bared her teeth in a mad death's-mask grin, daring him to make an end of it if he could.

The silver-furred beast that had been Jian staggered forward a few steps, raised himself up on his hind legs, bellowing a challenge. Snarling as his gaze fell on the dead things in front of him, the Issuq shook away the last trace of pain from his transformation and crouched low, preparing to spring upon his enemies and make an end to them.

Pain exploded in his head, the stars between the darkness blinding him.

He fell. He fell forever.

Jian woke as he landed on a pallet of straw. His teeth clicked together and his arms flopped like a doll's, waking one shoulder to red agony. He thrashed about like a headless chicken for the space of a dozen heartbeats, until the receding backs of the lashai made sense—and the ceiling over his head, and the bedding beneath him. Never had a straw pallet seemed so soft, or a room so bright and welcoming as these cramped quarters. He was in the Yellow Palace, and the Yellow Palace was in the Forbidden City.

He was weak, and the fear had returned, and he was in more pain than he had ever imagined, back when he was just a boy. He was in one piece, however, stitched and salved and pieced back together like an abused toy, but alive.

Jian, he thought. *I am Jian. A boy, not a monster. It was a dream, nothing more, a dream born of pain and fear…*

"You made it."

Jian turned his head, spurring torn muscles to fresh waves

26

of bright pain. Perri lay on his cot, hands folded over his chest, very still.

"How—" He spat dried blood, and tried again. "How many?"

"Just you and me, so far. You and me."

"Are you okay?"

"No." Perri turned his head slowly. Jian saw that the far side of his face was swaddled in bandages, and that a bright flower of red blossomed where his eye would be. "You?"

"I am alive." *I am Jian.* "What happened to you?"

"Same as you, I guess. They put my eye out when I cried. I guess you did not cry."

"No," Jian said… "No."

"I will never cry again. It hurts too much."

"I am sorry," Jian offered lamely. Then he blurted out, "Good thing you did not piss yourself, I guess."

Perri's mouth dropped open and they stared at each other for a long moment. Jian felt his face flush red and hot.

Then his friend burst into laughter, and Jian could not help but join him. They laughed until their bones turned to water and the air burned their lungs. Until it seemed they would die of it.

TWO

Akari Sun Dragon launched himself into the sky, and the world caught fire.

As the heat of morning kissed the slumbering land a fine mist rose from the sea, to veil the blushing face of Sajani Earth Dragon. It rolled across the outer lands, black and rich, freshly tilled and eagerly waiting the farmer's seeds. It rose up in the streets like an army of ghosts, undeterred by moat and wall and gate, dancing into silent battle with itself, falling and rising and falling again.

Like a war play put on by a troupe of fools.

Sulema stood high above the city and watched it come to life. The mist could not reach her, any more than the poverty and hunger of the lower ramparts might. Any more than the desert's thirst.

I am the Heart of the Dragon, she reminded herself, willing her blood and bone to believe it so. I've come to this city that I might learn to sing the dragon to sleep, and save the world... She stretched her arms out to either side, allowing the fine spider silk of her gown to billow like wings. I am the world's only hope for survival, and the dragon's song courses through my veins. My heart is so light in my breast that it seems as if I might float away with the mist, if not for the crown I wear upon my brow, weighing me down with all the duty of—

The wind blew grit into her eyes.

Sulema ignored it.

Her braids, fashioned by a woman of Atualon and much too tight, pulled at her scalp.

She ignored them.

Her nose itched.

Not even a warrior of the Zeera, trained to discipline since childhood, might ignore an itching nose. Sulema broke free from her pose and scratched. Her shoulders ached, and the small of her back, and the ridiculous golden sandals were torturing her feet.

Daughter of the Dragon, a faint voice sneered. It was her true voice, deep in her warrior's heart where neither the magics of her father nor his shadowmancer could touch her. *Such horseshit.*

"Your Radiance, please," Cassandre implored for the umpteenth time. "*Please* hold still."

"Are you nearly finished?" Sulema sounded petulant, even to herself, as she sighed and resumed her "Most Royal Pose," though the moment was lost. "My neck hurts."

"A royal pain in the neck."

"Excuse me?" She tried to glare at the artist without moving.

Standing at her place by the door, Saskia laughed. *An Atualonian guard would not laugh*, Sulema thought. She had insisted that if she was to be plagued by an arrogance of guards, they would be known as Divasguard and be styled after Sajani—not golden and cold like the Draiksguard. *Then again, a well-disciplined Atualonian guard would have left when I told her to leave, not shadow me night and day like... well, like a shadow.* She would not admit, perhaps not even to herself, that the Zeerani warrior's defiance came as a relief. It was well and good to dream of wielding great power, but not that long ago Sulema had been mucking churra pits. She was not yet ready to rule the world, or even this small corner of it.

Still, she had an image to maintain.

"Pain in the neck?"

"I was suggesting that a massage might be in order later, ne Atu," the master painter said, her face bland, her charcoals scratching furiously across the sheet of parchment in an attempt to capture an image of the king's daughter before she moved again. "A good massage works wonders for a... pain in the neck. Please do not scowl, your Radiance."

Sulema scowled, and at length Cassandre put down her tools. "Well," she said, "I suppose I have enough to work with, after all. Would you like to see, your Radiance?"

"Do not call me 'your Radiance,'" Sulema snapped. At the other woman's crestfallen look, and Saskia's disapproving glare, she added, "Please. 'Sulema' is fine.

"I am sorry," she continued after a moment. "I just… I do not feel well." Where was Loremaster Rothfaust's apprentice with her medicines? Her shoulder had gone numb and cold, and that black tingly sensation was crawling down her arm again. She tried not to think of the fact that the loremaster's medicines were not working as quickly, or as well, as they had in the beginning.

Sulema tried not to touch the pale skin where she had been bitten by the reaver, or notice that a patch half the size of her palm was cool and hard to the touch.

Come to think of it, I spend a lot of time trying not to think these days. Shaking her head to clear it, she stepped down from the short pedestal and walked over to view Cassandre's sketches.

She had never seen a drawing of herself before, and did not know what to expect. She knew what she looked like, or close enough. The water in a well bucket often spoke to her of a girl with an unruly orange frizz the shade of unripened dates—or had until she earned the warrior's braids. Her spotted skin was too pale for the desert sun.

Honey and a sprinkling of spice, Mattu Halfmask had said.

Everyone told her she shared her mother's eyes, hard and golden as a hawk's. She had never cared to reflect overlong upon these things, being more concerned about her seat and the aim of her bow. Thus the image of her own face was a shock to her when she peered over Cassandre's shoulder.

She gasped aloud. There she stood, as real as if Cassandre had stolen her shadow-self and pressed it onto paper, staring out across the jagged lines of a hastily sketched Atualon. The breeze had caught in her hair and she remembered brushing it back from her face. The fabric of the gown was so skillfully wrought in just a few short strokes that she had to touch it… No, the fabric did not feel as soft as the artist had made it look.

"Oh," she breathed. "What magic is this?"

Cassandre went still all over, her eyes sharp. "Magic? Why do you ask?"

"I… it just…" Sulema hesitated, her fingers held in the air over the drawings. They were so real. And yet—

"That does not look like Sulema." Saskia stared at the drawings, as well, and her frown matched Sulema's confusion.

"Pardon me?" Sulema had never seen ice, but she heard it now, crackling through the artist's voice. "Perhaps you can do better?"

"Noooooo…" Saskia drew the word out as she waved toward the sketches. "I mean, they look like her, as she looks now. They just do not look like Sulema. This is some outlander woman, not a warrior of the people."

Ehuani, Sulema thought, *truth*, and her throat tightened. Cassandre had captured Sa Atu, the woman she needed to become, but not Sulema Ja'Akari, the warrior she longed to be. Mattu had warned her, had he not, that everyone in Atualon was wearing a mask of some sort. *And now I do, as well.*

"This is not me," she said.

"*Ehuani*," Saskia nodded and she relaxed. Sulema had not realized the warrior had been tense.

Cassandre pursed her lips, eyes darting back and forth as she considered the images she had created.

"How would you wish me to draw you, then?" It was a deliberate question carefully worded, carefully weighed. Sulema could hear the whisper of words unsaid shushing about the room.

"It matters, does it not?" she asked finally. "Whether you paint me like this"—she held her breath for a moment, and then continued, deciding to trust the master painter—"as I am to be seen, as my father would have me… or as I would see myself?" Her heart pounded in her ears.

Cassandre eyed her in turn. "It matters," she said finally. "It matters a great deal… Sulema."

"Magic," Saskia whispered, and took half a step back from the drawings. "There *is* magic in these, *ehuani*."

31

"*Ehuani*?" Cassandre tipped her head to the side. "You keep using this word. What does it mean?"

"It means 'truth in beauty," Sulema told her, "and though there is much beauty in this work, there is little truth. These do not show me as I am, as I would be. These pictures lie."

"How would you have me draw you?" the master painter asked again, staring straight into her eyes. Sulema stared back, and reached up to rub at her numb shoulder.

This one would have made a good warrior, she thought. "Paint me like one of our warrior women," she answered at last. "Strong and fierce and… whole."

Cassandre's response was a smile as wide and wicked as Sulema's own.

"Good," she said. "*Good*. Put your warrior's garb on, then, but be quick! I do not have all day."

Sulema whistled to herself as she shed the silken garments of her father's people and donned the vest and leggings that she had so reluctantly set aside for this foolishness.

"I notice," Saskia said to Cassandre as she resumed her post by the door, "that you do not deny there is magic in what you do."

"Of course there is magic," Cassandre sniffed as she took up her charcoals and a new sheet of parchment, and as Sulema resumed her place. "It is *art*."

Hours later, it seemed, the dragonstone beneath her feet warmed in anticipation. Sulema dropped her warrior's pose and turned just as Wyvernus strode out onto the balcony. He wore his golden robes of state and carried the Mask of Akari tucked unceremoniously under one arm. His smile when he saw her was so wide, so bright, Sulema could hardly bear to look at him without shading her eyes.

"Ah, there you are, Daughter! I had forgotten that you were getting your sketches done today." He stopped and peered at her. "Ah, you chose to wear a warrior's leathers? That is… interesting." His grin faltered for a moment, but then widened to include Cassandre, inviting her to join in some mischief. "I wonder if I might borrow my daughter for a bit, my dear. If you are nearly finished…?"

Cassandre regarded them both flatly, a dark storm in her dark eyes. "Do you want me to finish this portrait, your Arrogance, or do you not? Perhaps you would prefer to find another painter…"

"There are no other painters in Atualon," Wyvernus protested, "none whom I would trust to immortalize my lovely daughter, at any rate. If this were not a matter of great importance, I would not dream of interrupting you, sweet girl. The very fate of the world…"

"Oh, go." Cassandre brandished her charcoal like a dreamshifter's staff. "Just go. I have enough sketches for now."

"You have the gratitude of Atualon, and her king."

Sulema stepped down from the low pedestal, wincing as her knees wobbled. *Weak*, she thought with irritation. She turned to Cassandre and tried to catch her eye for a conspirator's wink. "My thanks as well…"

Cassandre muttered something rude and rolled up the sheets of parchment as if they were the enemy, while Wyvernus swept Sulema from the room.

He led his daughter down the wide hallway, followed at a distance by Saskia. The inner walls of Atukos lit with joy at his approach and faded slowly behind him, a marvel that still made Sulema smile. *Living stone*, she thought, and she reached out to touch the wall. It flashed gold and red at her touch, and sent a little thrill of welcome tingling along her skin.

"Sajani Earth Dragon loves you, Sa Atu." Wyvernus slowed his steps and tempered his smile, but his eyes were still lit with a boy's anticipation. "These walls did not welcome me until I had been king for a year and a day, but they lit for you at the moment of your birth, and they rejoice now that you are home."

Am I? Atukos was a wonder, but her heart still longed for the Zeera. Perhaps some day Atualon would feel like home.

Perhaps when you have been queen for a year and a day.

Sulema stopped short, staring at her father. "Did you just…"

Can you read my mind? Like a vash'ai? Then, before he could respond, *Can I learn to do this? Speak to people in their heads?*

"Only sometimes," he told her aloud. "Only within the walls of Atukos, and not without effort. It is not so much like a Zeerani's bond with one of your great cats, as I understand it—I cannot read your feelings, your deeper thoughts. It is more like... like watching a fish flash beneath the surface of a pond. There, and then gone again. With a little practice, you should be able to hear my thoughts, as well."

"Only within the walls of Atukos." Sulema's heart fell again.

"Only then," Wyvernus agreed. "And as I said, not without effort. A bond must be forged first, a strong bond of the heart, and even then the magic fails beyond the walls. Otherwise I would have found you—and your dear mother—before those wicked men spirited you away, and I would not have missed you all those years." He reached for her hand.

Sulema did not pull away. Her head spun. *My mother—* but her mind darted away from the thought, as fish from a shadow that falls across their pond.

"So you cannot use this ability to find Leviathus or Daru?" *Or Mattu Halfmask, damn his hide*, she thought. She did not wish her father to know of her feelings, not just yet.

"They are not within the fortress, so no. I have tried." He gave her hand a squeeze. "As I have tried to find your young Mattu." He gave her a sideways look. "I am also aware of certain people whispering in the shadows. You may have heard that I helped young master Halfmask... disappear."

"I had heard that," she agreed, reluctantly. "So... it is not true?"

Her father snorted a mirthless laugh, and let her hand fall. "Not a word of it. Against the parens' will, I spared the lives of Mattu and Matteira when they were small, and I have protected them as my wards ever since. I may not be Ja'Akari like you, my dear..."

Sulema laughed in spite of herself.

To think of her father, a man, as a warrior! Certainly he was a powerful man—powerful enough to keep the Sindanese emperor cowering behind his shining walls, powerful enough to keep Sajani Earth Dragon trapped in her dreams—but he was still just a man.

Not even the greatest of men could become Ja'Akari.

"...but neither am I without honor," he continued. "If I want someone killed, Sulema, I will kill them myself, in the full light of day. If you cannot kill a person beneath the eyes of Akari, in front of your family—and theirs—then you have no business taking that life."

Sulema had always longed for a father's advice, but this was not at all what she had expected.

"Was this what you came to tell me?"

He snorted again. "I would hardly risk Cassandre's wrath in order to wax pedantic. The last time I got on her bad side, she painted me without hair, and look what happened." He passed a hand over his bald pate. "Never meddle in the affairs of artists, Sulema, for they are clever and slow to forget. Those who wield color, or song, or dance, wield a power as great as our own, in their way. It is simply magic of a quieter sort."

"Ani says 'the silent warrior has the sharpest sword.'" Of course, Ani usually said it to shut her up.

"I believe I would like this Ani of yours. I hope to have the chance to know her better." Then he turned slightly. "Ah, Davidian! Good of you to join us."

Imperator General Davidian was red of face and slightly winded, as if he had been running.

"Your Arrogance, it would be easier for me to guard your person if you would not disappear like that." He pointedly did not look at Saskia, who just as pointedly did not look at him, though both their faces reddened. Sulema rolled her eyes. *That* love story was the worst-kept secret in Atualon.

"My apologies, Imperator General." The king grinned and winked at Sulema. "I promise never to disappear again."

Perhaps I am *home, at that*, she thought, returning the king's grin. *He is most certainly my father.*

The Imperator General raised a small golden whistle and

blew into it. A squad of Draiksguard and Divasguard rounded the corner, marching quickstep. None of them glanced at the king, but disapproval rolled from their cloaked shoulders thick as a morning fog.

"We are caught," the king sighed to his daughter. "Now we are in trouble."

Davidian ignored that. "To the grounds, your Arrogance? We have cleared the place of commoners."

"At once, Imperator. Come, Sulema." Wyvernus took her hand again and tugged, much as Ismai had when they were young and he had stolen honey-cakes to share. "I have a surprise for you."

THREE

The moons-haired princess came to Atualon on a ship so vast it was nearly an island.

The dark wood of his belly had been steeped in slaves' blood and magic, and carved with the blind eyes and severed hands of the sea goddess Sitneh. The silk of his sails had been soaked with the tears of the crones who wailed as they wove, speaking of their loves lost to the ocean kin, of husbands and wives and children who had slipped beneath the waves or been snatched into the sky.

Never had she regretted the price that had been paid to carry her to the king she would marry, and why should she? Not a spoonful of the blood had been hers, nor a measure of pain. Neither were the cries of the sacrificed doves, that they might fly up to her high chambers and disturb her passionate dreams.

Oh, but she *had* sacrificed. She had left behind her gardens, and her sisters, and a little white dog, had she not? She might have married the black-bearded king of the river pirates, and laid a dowry of slaves and oranges and river pearls at her mother's feet. He had been handsome enough, that one. She might have married the king of the green lands, far to the west, and brought a bride price of golden wood and golden children. He had been a stern man and too old for her liking, but his eyes were kind and his swords sharp. It would have been a fine match.

Then one of her ladies had slipped an ivory trinket beneath her pillow, a tiny portrait of a flame-haired man with fierce eyes and a wicked grin, and nothing would do but that she claim him for her own. So she did, and here they were, and all the world had paid the price.

Hafsa Azeina had stood atop the Sea Gate, her short hair

whipping angrily about her head and robes billowing as the deep-bellied ships ghosted into view. Bright horns lifted into the sky and pierced the peace with their glad cries. The heavy bells tolled, ropes burning the hands and shoulders of youths who would give their hearing so that the foreign princess might be bid a proper welcome. The great drums rolled, the glad heartbeat of a city called out by wooden instruments dearer than the humans who made them, and played them, and kept them clean and safe.

Young girls danced upon the sea-walls, children who had been purchased as infants and trained their whole lives, crying in the night as their mutilated feet bled through their thin blankets so that a golden-eyed princess who dreamt the dreams might walk down this gangplank and smile as a king knelt to kiss her fingertips.

One of the dancers had slipped and might have fallen to her death had the Mistress of Dance not dragged her to safety by her long, dark hair. That girl had run away not long afterward. She had been caught and eventually sold in Min Yaarif to a man who beat out of her all thoughts of dancing and running.

"I never knew," Hafsa Azeina told her companion.

"You never cared," Basta replied, twitching the tip of her tail in irritation. "Even now, these things do not touch your heart. I can read your dreams, Annu. You would walk this path again, and water it with the blood of the innocent. You would burn the world to have your daughter and keep her safe. You have no regrets."

Hafsa Azeina regarded the sleek cat, too wild, too wise. "I have regrets," she said. "I regret killing you. For that, I am sorry."

Twitch, twitch. "Do not apologize to *me*. In killing your kima'a, you harmed only yourself. I am not the one to whom you owe your pretty words—as if words might wash away blood, or wipe away tears. As if the worth of your words is more than a life, than the least of lives." Her green eyes closed in a slow wink. "You have learned nothing."

"Will you teach me now?" Hafsa Azeina made a slashing motion with both hands, and the scene before them faded slowly away. "It is too late for such things. I am dead."

"You are not dead." The cat yawned, showing her white teeth, her pink tongue. "You are just very, very stubborn. Of all the Annu ever to walk the path of dreams, why must I be saddled with you? It is time for you to wake. Open those eyes of yours, lest I lose my patience and scratch them out. Time to open that dark heart of yours, lest I eat it."

"You may have it, for all I care," Hafsa Azeina said, closing her eyes, as if shutting out the cold and the dark would make a difference. None of it had ever made a difference. The slaves' sacrifice, the fate of a dancer, all the hate or all the love in the world mattered not at all in the end. "I fear you would find my heart a bitter feast."

"You fear?" Basta growled, velvet-sharp voice prickling the air around her. "Hafsa Azeina, fear? Not yet, Dreamshifter. Not yet... but you will."

"Do your worst," she told Basta. "I no longer care. There is nothing left to fear." Hafsa Azeina opened her eyes, closed them, and opened them again. It made no difference at all.

Nothing left to fear? Laughter rippled through the void. The voice was not Basta's. *Nothing at all? I wonder.*

"'Ware, Annubasta!" Basta howled. "Wake, Annu! Wake now!"

"I cannot," she replied, or perhaps "I care not." She was never quite sure. It made a difference, however. A very great difference, in the end. A thousand hands rose up from the darkness to pin her, to hurt her. Hands tangled in her hair. They pinched and clawed at her skin. But she had felt pain before, and horror.

You are in my world now, Dreamshifter, the voice of Belzaleel said, and he laughed. *As long as you remain here, you are mine.* A tongue joined the hands, licking at her skin like wet flame. *Mine. Sleep forever, for all I care.*

"I will not wake," she growled, even as the hands tore away her silken garments and invaded the sanctity of her flesh. Even then. "I am not afraid."

39

Oh, but you will be, the voice purred, thick and wet as hot blood. *You will be.* Teeth grazed against her throat, sharper and harder than a dragonglass dagger.

In the end she screamed.

In the end she was afraid.

In the end she was weak.

She felt heat first—the real, wholesome heat of a hearth fire in the deep of night. She smelled smoke next, the clean, sharp smoke of fruitwood and herbs. Sensations came back to her slowly—the rough rasp of cloth against skin, the redolence of hot tea and cold meat, the cough and scuffle and creak as whatever poor soul they had set to watch over her corpse tried to get comfortable.

She tried to ignore these things, to send her soul back to the void. Eventually her body would tire of waiting for her to return, and it would die. There was no use. She was afraid—afraid to the marrow of her bones, and once fear has touched a dream it cannot be resumed.

I will not wake, she insisted, every bit as stubborn as Basta had said. Eventually, though, her nose itched. One might endure the torment of a netherlord—for a while, at least—but not even she was made of stone.

She sneezed.

Her caretaker—a young boy to judge by the shrieks—fell out of his chair and went crashing around her room in a panic, breaking pottery and who-knows-what in his haste to escape the rising dead. There was no hope for it, then. Hafsa Azeina sighed and opened her eyes, squinting against the dim light.

A pair of brown eyes wide as saucers and with white all around the edges peered at her from a bundle of shaking linen in one corner.

"Boy..." she began.

He shrieked again, his voice rising higher and higher till it was nothing more than a tea-kettle's whistle, and then he collapsed, senseless.

Well, she had tried.

The doors burst open and a flood of humans poured in, stinking of meat and bone and fear, wide-eyed and open-mouthed at the sight of their queen struggling to sit up.

"Water," she demanded. Her voice was a thin croak. She cleared her throat and tried again. "Water. Bread."

Meat, Belzaleel mocked from his iron-chased sheath in the corner. *Heart's meat. Bones to gnaw. Blood to drink...* Her mouth watered at the thought. She ignored it.

"Bread," she said firmly, "then a bath. And for the love of Akari, someone bring me a toothbrush. My mouth tastes as if I have been dead for a month."

The crowd at her doorway moved, not in response to her demands, but because a tall woman with fiery hair shoved them aside and shouted fit to wake the neverworld.

"Let me through, you goat-fucking idiots! Let me through!" A hefty young man fell to one side, and Sulema pushed her way into the room. Eyes as bright and hot as the Zeerani sun found Hafsa Azeina's face, and warmed the bitter shadows of her heart.

"Mother," she said, rushing to her side. She helped Hafsa sit up, then took the boy's seat by her side. Those golden eyes held her own, pulling her the rest of the way home with their heat and hunger, with their love.

Hafsa Azeina's scalp itched and she stank, and her hands were crushed in her daughter's grip—but her daughter was close, her daughter was safe.

That was all that had ever mattered.

FOUR

Daru's stomach was growling again.

Hafsa Azeina's apprentice tried to distract himself from the gnawing hunger, to count his breaths, to feel for a difference—any difference at all—in the smooth stone as he trailed his fingertips along the wall, to trick himself into thinking his eyes were open when they were closed, or closed when they were open.

The utter dark, dark as a shadow's laugh, dark as the inside of a lionsnake's belly, filled the air around him so completely that it seemed to press against his skin and his eyes. Daru longed to reach up and tear it from his face, but the torn skin around his eyes reminded him that he could not.

He longed, as well, to break away from the cold wall that seemed to him to mock his efforts. It was full of shadows, ancient shadows born of ancient malice, and they pressed against the stone like fish pressing against the river's surface, longing to break free and gobble him up, bones, bruises, skin, and all. Yet he kept trailing his fingers along the wall as he walked, and took the smallest shuffling steps, testing the way with his toes just as he tested the air with his nose.

The *throb, throb, stab* of his broken arm reminded him that to run was folly.

For so long the wall was perfectly smooth, with no corners or doorways or seams, no change of any kind. When the break came, Daru let out a startled cry. He muffled the noise almost as soon as he had made it, but not before it drew unwanted attention. So he held his breath and waited, fingertips trembling against the uneven seam in the stone. Counted his long breaths one... two... threeeeee... fourrrrr... and his heartbeats one-two-three-four-seventy. He held his arm very, very still. The least movement hurt so much that sometimes it brought tears to his eyes, and pain attracted the worst sort of shadows.

After a short time the oldest shadows forgot about him, being slow-minded things with long, long thoughts. Then only the smallest remained to pluck at the raggedy hem of his trousers. Those shadows he could deal with. They had been trying to kill him since he was a baby, and he knew their game well.

"Let go," he said to them softly. "Let go of me, or there will be no more music." They let go, chittering in high, distressed echoes-of-voices. One of them patted his leg with its tiny clawed hand, as if in apology. That made him break out in chillflesh from scalp to ankle. If he was so close to the shadows' world that he could *feel* them…

Well, there was nothing to do for it, was there? Nothing but walking, as he had been since he woke in a crumpled and broken heap on the cold floors of what he had come to think of as the Downbelow. Nothing to do but cling stubbornly to life, and to hope, as he had been doing since the day he was born.

The shadows subsided, and his heartbeat slowed. Daru pressed tentatively against the wall. There was a seam there, all right, and a slight depression in the wall beyond. No more than a hair's-breadth change, and probably nothing he would have noticed had he not been clinging to this shadow-blasted wall for longer than he cared to imagine, but it was a change, and therefore the most interesting thing that had happened to him since he learned that boys could, indeed, eat spiders if they were hungry enough.

Not that he intended to tell that part of his tale—not ever, not to anyone. Daru shuddered. Spiders' eggs might be a rare treat, but the spiders themselves were just nasty.

Even shuddering hurt.

The seam ran up the wall to a point just over his head, and arched back down toward the floor. It was a door then, a door for children or very short adults, or perhaps a niche of some sort… Whatever it was, it had been long sealed shut, its secrets well—

His fingers brushed over a depression next to the arch, and a sound like grinding teeth startled a shout from him. Daru stumbled backward, arms flying out to the side in panic. It was sheer dumb luck that made his head, and not his broken arm, strike the opposite wall of the passageway. Even so, the motion was excruciating.

He shuffled back across the passageway, good arm held before his face, eyes open wide as if they could drink in the dark. It had been long, so long since he had seen the sun that he was thirsty for it.

What I would give, he thought wistfully, *to look up and see the stars.* His splayed fingers found the wall and scrabbled across the unyielding stone as he tried to guess where the little door might have—

Something bit him on the neck.

Daru yelled and crumpled to the floor in fright. Of the seven deadliest spiders he knew, he had found six so far in the Downbelow. He flailed and yelled, and the shadows pressed in close at the sound of fear in his voice.

Light flickered to life. It was a pale light and sickly, less full of stars and moonslight now than of dead things and the pale undersides of mushrooms, but it was a light nevertheless. Pakka waved her arms at him in remonstration and chirrrrrupped, "*Pip-pip-preeeeeee-oh.*"

"Oh, it is you," he managed with what little breath was left to him. "Crap and cat bones, sweetling, you scared me!" He rubbed at his neck. "Why did you bite me?"

Pakka stood on the floor before Daru's feet, glowing with her own faint light. The mantid held up her forelegs in what was very nearly a human shrug, and he laughed. The sound was out of place and unwelcome in the Downbelow, and it startled the shadows, but it was good to laugh even as it hurt his lungs.

"Rotten bug," he grumbled, and he rocked forward onto his knees so that he might push himself upright with his good arm. Now that the fright was ebbing, his busted arm was reminding him that it was busted, and his stomach reminded him that he was hungry, and every remaining inch of his body reminded him that boys were not meant to wander lost and alone in the bowels of the earth.

Yet I am no ordinary boy, he reminded the doubts and the hurts and the hungry shadows, lest they get the wrong idea and decide to devour him. *I am stronger than you know*. Still, it was a miserable—

As he pushed to his feet, Daru's fingers brushed against a small thing long forgotten, buried in the dust. He picked it up without thinking, and as he leaned against the stone wall, struggling to draw breath, he held it up in front of his face. It was a disc of cool metal, about as big around as the palm of his hand, and—oh, it was attached to a chain, a very fine, very thin chain. A medallion, then? He ran his fingertips across its surface. There were raised figures there, but he could not tell what they were.

"Pakka, sweetling, can you give me more light?"

"*Peeeeoh*," she answered. Her sickly light flickered and nearly went out.

"Never mind," he whispered, looping the chain about his neck. The medallion was a curiosity, but until he could eat it or drink it or use the thing or find his way out of this place, it would be nothing more. He stooped and held his hand out so that Pakka could climb up to his shoulder. She flew less often now, and seemed more tired. Her carapace, which he knew should be hardening in the sun and taking on its own unique color, was pale as the moons and nearly as soft as leather. Still she scouted for him, and gave him light, and brought him such food as she could manage.

"You are my girl," he told her, stroking her back. "My fine, good girl. I will find our way home, I promise."

Promise, the shadows laughed, pressing close for a mouthful of his breath. *Promise, promise*. One of them, bolder than the others, thickened in the dim light. Daru imagined that he could see eyes, tiny pinpricks of fell light, and a tongue like dark flame darting forth like a snake's. *I promissse*, it hissed at him.

Daru closed his eyes and took a breath, the best he could manage, and held it for as long as he dared before letting it hiss out again between his teeth. He thought of Dreamshifter, of her fierce golden eyes, her strong hands and terrible scowl.

How strong she was, and how she frightened the shadows.

I am stronger than they know, he reminded himself. He opened his eyes, imagining as he did so that they shone with the fell light of the Dreaming Lands, and he scrunched his face up into the fiercest scowl he could manage.

"I am no meat," he reminded the shadows, "not for you."

The shadows fled.

"*Peeeeep-pip-pip*," Pakka said in an approving tone. She began to groom her antennae with her forelegs.

Daru let his remaining breath out in a relieved little *whoosh*, and slumped against the wall. As he did so, his good hand brushed once more against the small doorway. He pushed and it gave way, until it gaped open in the dying light, daring him to enter.

Daru pushed away from the wall, and stepped closer. He might walk through the arched door, if he chose, but Ismai would have found it a close fit, and someone as big as Tammas or Sulema's brother Leviathus would have had to crouch.

"A door for boys?" he asked aloud. Why would there be such a thing, deep in the Downbelow? And who might have made it?

"*Peeeee-oh*," Pakka squeaked, and she clung to his hair. "*Pip-pip-pip*."

"I know," he told her, "but I think we have to."

He summoned his courage, held his breath, and stepped through the little stone door.

FIVE

*R*ed skies at morning, Jian thought, *divers take warning. Soldiers, too, I suppose.* He shifted from foot to foot. Akari Sun Dragon rose in a fury of blood and gold, calling forth steams as rich and red as the bloodmyst. Everyone—from the sailor to the pearl diver to the midwife—knew that such a dawn was an omen of death. But for whom?

The red steam rose, making ghosts of him and his dammati, and in the baneful light his banners hung heavy and still as corpse rags. Sweat rolled down his back and belly. He itched, he stank, and he had needed to piss for some time, but he did not move as the sky caught fire behind him.

Let the light dazzle my enemies, he thought. *Let the red mist give them pause, let the high ground give me the edge I will need to survive this day.* Let the blood spilled be theirs, and not his.

As the sky brightened further, burning the ghostly mist to tattered rags of nothing, it caught in the eyes of his enemies, waiting far below. It caught on the iron bardings and bindings of men dressed to kill, on the red and green and black lacquered armor of those who would bring him down. The red dawn cried for blood.

Not mine, he promised. *Not this day.*

From the northwest there came a flash of white. From the southwest, high in a thick tree, an answering flash of light. Jian raised the heavy wooden sword above his head, thrust it into the sky, and willed the enemy not to see how it shook. A roar came from behind him, and he knew his standard had been raised: a blue issuq against a field of silver, teeth and claws bared in defiance.

The ache in his shoulder as he held his weapon aloft, the sweat stinging his eyes, the way his heart turned in his chest—these were things to which he could cling, reminders that this was no dream.

Real, he thought, wondering. *This is real.* The hoarse screaming of a hundred angry men below him met the tidal roar of his force, and threw it back in his face like jagged rocks denying the sea. *But the sea always wins*, he thought.

With that, he laughed.

Below Jian, the banners of the red bull and the black hare unfurled, and his enemies raised row upon row of blunted pikes. Beside him, Perri lifted a horn to his lips and blew.

Jian lowered his sword…

…and they charged.

"War is a conversation," wrote the great poet and general Zhao Quan, "a question posed by the sword and answered by the shield. Who will live this day, and who will die? Who will write himself into the history books as a hero, and who will be remembered as the villain?"

The skirmish was the decisive last battle of a seven-day mock war. As observed by the senior Sen-Baradam from the comfort of their lacquered chairs, war games were easy—quickly decided and played out upon the soil much as their war tables had suggested the night before.

To those on the ground, burdened by the ill-fitting armor of the yellow Daechen, hampered further by heavy wooden swords and padded maces or spears, it was an eternity of sweat and pain.

Jian lifted his wooden blade time and again, and time and again brought it thudding down onto the helm or shoulder of a red-armored foe, thrust it into the padded belly of a black-armored boy with whom he had once played a game of knives-and-cups. He tripped over the prone figure of a blue-clad ally who had taken one too many blows to the head.

Block a blow from the side… his small shield was as heavy as a boat. Counter, and thrust… his sword weighed as much as a tree, and he could hardly see or hear from the ringing in his head. Someone fell into him from behind, and he pivoted gracelessly so that they might fall without taking him down, as well, neither seeing nor much caring whether it was an ally or an enemy.

For a brief moment in time Jian found himself without an opponent, as his dammati formed a tight ring about him, swords and pikes held outward and screaming defiance. His lookout in the baobing tree signaled again, the little mirror flashing once, twice, thrice.

Jian lifted the small conch shell, hung on a cord around his neck, and blew as his mother had taught him when he was small. It made a clear sound, silver as sea-foam on a wind-lashed day. The call was answered, then answered again as the forces he had hidden away two nights ago threw back their mud-and reed covering and surged up into the fray, scattering Jian's remaining enemies.

The beating of the drums rolled over them all like thunder, signaling an end to the battle—and to the war. Swords were lowered, spears wavered, and though here and there a small knot of combatants still strove to pummel one another senseless, for the most part the combatants pulled away and bowed, or scowled, or shook their weapons and promised that next time, the outcome would be different. Next time.

There would always be a next time, and another, and one after that. Jian slumped, weary to the marrow of his bones, and wanted nothing more than to drop his sword and walk into the river, that he might be washed back to the sea. Such a thought, however brief, was folly. Xienpei would read it upon his face, she always did. He shook it away, sheathed the wooden sword, and bowed to the man he had been fighting, Naruteo's red-clad dammati named… Quing? Ping?

It did not matter.

The boy, who had once laughed with Jian over cups of sour tea, spat upon the ground at his feet and turned away with a grimace.

That did not matter, either.

At least we won, thought Jian. *This time.*

But the day was young, and so was he.

Weariness set in as they trudged up the hill. Generations of war games had blasted it smooth and dead as old bone. Not a tree clung to the riven soil, not an insect buzzed. The only hint of color, of life, came from the war tents of the Sen-Baradam perched on high like a wreath of flowers upon a maiden's head.

Halfway up the hill, just as a blister on his heel burst and bled through his boots, Naruteo and his bannerman passed them at a steady jog. They jostled through the edges of Jian's men, rousing shouts of anger from war-weary throats. Jian's banner dipped as Perri stepped close.

"Sen-Baradam?" He glanced pointedly at the red squad.

Jian shrugged. "Let them pass. The living need not mind the dead." He turned away as Perri laughed, knowing that his words would be carried to Naruteo's ears, and that his rival would hate him all the more.

Let Naruteo hate. Let him love. Jian did not care. It did not matter. They were none of them more than pieces on the emperor's game board, pearls and stones to be set into a sword-hilt or ground into dust. There was no winning the longer game unless the emperor himself could be vanquished.

And even then, Jian thought, *like as not he would be replaced with another just as bad, or worse.* With his paltry new rank, an unblooded sword, and an army of twenty-two dammati, Jian himself could scarce dream of changing the course of his own fate. The best he could hope for would be to get through this briefing and return to the Yellow Palace for a bath, a piss, a meal, and bed, in whichever order he could get them.

Leading his men at a steady pace, ever forward and up, he never took his eyes from the ground until it leveled out, and they stood in the very shadow of the white tent. Then he halted, raised his right fist high, and splayed his fingers open against the sky's pale belly, dismissing them. A low, ragged cheer rose from the ranks. Victorious, his troops would spend the remainder of this day sleeping and eating. They would sing battle songs all the long walk home, unencumbered and laughing at the Red Bulls and Black Snakes, who would be forced to carry the victors' gear and armor, as well as their own.

No few of them would look forward to the embrace of a village girl—or boy—or the obligation-free release granted by those in the emperor's comfort houses. Let them cheer, let them have their comforts; still Jian did not care. It was an empty life, but it was all they had.

As the rest of his troops left, Perri took up a position at the tent's door, near the unmoving form of the White Stag bannerman. Jian nodded to his friend, and forced a weary smile.

"You are dismissed, too, Perri."

The young man set his jaw and said nothing. The wind whipped the sea-bear banner so that it slapped him heavily in the face. Jian snorted half a laugh, and stiffened as a sound came from behind him.

"Dammati." The voice was low and smooth and dark. It was the voice of the forest. "Faithful as stones, and twice as stubborn."

Jian bowed low. "General."

"That was well played, Daechen. A child's game, yet, but well played. You may survive the Yellow Road, after all. Come." A shadow passed over Jian, white boots stepped quick and sure before his downcast eyes. A swirl of pale silk bade him follow, and Daechen Jian, Sen-Baradam of the Blue Issuq, bowed his way into the tent.

Jian had been studying under Mardoni for nearly a two-moon now. Perhaps in another two-moon he might become accustomed to the opulence of the general's tent, lovingly built as his own childhood home—and better furnished. In another year, perhaps, he might be able to share in the easy banter that flowed among the great men who occupied it, strategists and soldiers and scholars of renown so great their names were known even in backward Bizhan. It seemed to Jian, however, that he might spend a lifetime in awe of the White Stag himself.

Mardoni stood across the war table from Jian, watching as the luminist lit her fat candles, one by one, by blowing upon them. Jian averted his eyes as best he could—the Daechen had all been warned against casting so much as a sideways glance at the emperor's light mage. Still his eyes were drawn by the bright runes that crawled across her dusky skin, the odd pale eyes that glowed as if lit from behind, and the faint shimmer of deep violet light that shimmered about her as if she had chosen to clad herself in color rather than drear human clothing.

It might seem worth risking the wrath of the yendaeshi, the Sen-Baradam, even the emperor himself, to sneak a lingering gaze at her naked form, had Jian not seen the consequences of such folly with his own eyes, on their first day in camp.

Eyes.

Jian shuddered, and swallowed bile.

The candles were lit and set in their places around the war table. Mardoni lifted his antlered head, peered at him. One white eyebrow lifted, and the corner of his mouth quirked as if they shared some great joke. Then the man turned his wide dark eyes toward the luminist as easily as if she were an ordinary woman, and he might ask her to dance.

"Zhaoli? If you would, please, my dear?"

The luminist ignored Mardoni's gaze, and his flirtatious tone. Indeed, as she lifted one fat candle in front of her face and stared into the dancing light, her lips pursed and color grew in her pale cheeks in a way that made Jian blush and look away. Then the other candles flickered, and the table in their midst began to glow, and Jian forgot all about naked women and flaming eyeballs as he watched the magic unfold.

Green sparks fizzed and leapt from the candles, to become trees and grass. Blue arced and snaked to become a river, and small figures of flame and shadow became miniature people as they danced into place. The table shimmered and glowed, then with a pop that made his eyes ache and ears ring, a scene burst into sharp relief, a tiny battle played out by figures no bigger than the toy soldiers his mother had bought for him when he was small. No toy had ever been carved with such cunning skill, though, nor could it move like a man. No tree of clay, wood, or grass made of green cloth could ever ripple thus in an imaginary wind.

Jian watched, as awed as he had been the first time he had seen this magic. The day's battle played out before them, and he watched a miniature version of himself order men into the trees and into the mud, watched himself lead men into battle, and had a sudden, uncomfortable thought. What if, at this very moment, he was in fact a miniature version of a much larger Jian, who watched himself watching himself?

His head throbbed with the beginnings of a truly thunderous headache and he wished—not for the first time—that he might somehow slip back into childhood, to a time when candles were candles and toys were toys, and a man's eyes did not burst into flames at the sight of a beautiful woman.

"There," Mardoni said, and he held a pale hand splayed above the tiny battle. "Stop right there." The tableau froze. Tiny Jian stood unaware as a tiny man in red stood behind him, readying his toothpick-sized spear for what might have been a deadly blow. Had the attack been successful...

Mardoni flicked his fingers, and the figures moved again, slow as butterflies on a cold day. Jian clenched his jaw as Naruteo's man thrust the blunted spear toward the back of his neck. Then he blinked to see Perri leap, twisting like a cat, to knock the blow aside. The spear caught Jian's dammati in the side of the head, knocking his helm off and sending him to crash in a heap. As the Bull's man ran off, Jian noted a peculiar hitch to his gait.

"That is Chei!" He pointed. "I thought we were friends... but he tried to kill me." A serious violation of the rules, but one which Jian knew would never be punished.

"That child is not important," Mardoni said. "This one... this is the one you need to watch." He held his hand above the miniature Perri as Jian's bannerman rose and took up the standard, swaying on his feet.

53

"Him? That is Perri. I trust him with my life." It was a revelation. "I owe him my life."

"Ah, a treasure among younglings, then, truly. It is good to have friends, Daechen Jian."

They watched as the figure of Chei ran to Naruteo's side. *I will remember this*, Jian thought. Tiny Perri picked his helm up out of the mud, put it on, and straightened the banner of the Blue Bear. It shamed Jian to think that he had not seen the depth of Perri's loyalty before now. *I will remember this, too, my dammati.*

"It is good to have friends," Jian agreed.

"It is good to have friends." Mardoni bared his teeth in a slow, feral grin. "It would be better to have an army."

SIX

On the third day of the march back from battle, Jian thought about dirt. There was grit that covered your face, even coating the teeth so that every meal you ate was that much less pleasant. Or powdered dirt as fine and soft as the stuff a woman might use to powder her face. Then there was the foul black dirt like small rocks that you might crush with your fingers, but which would work its way between your toes and flay your feet by the end of a day's march. His hair itched with grit, his clothes chafed, and when he spat, he spat mud.

Bath first, he thought.

His stomach rumbled a protest.

Bath first, his mind insisted. Enough was enough. *I am more dirt than man.*

They moved together as a unit, their raised voices a fine harmonic counterpoint to the soft *stamp, stamp, stamp* of booted feet upon the hard-packed earth. No longer did their heads bob like a raft of sea dogs on a choppy sea, nor did they stumble on the verse or the step or trip over their own gear. They had become a living being, like a dragon from the legends, made up of the songs and stories and dreams of all their souls and one true heart.

Jian became aware, however, of a commotion on the far side of the formation, and he signaled a halt. This led to growling among his dammati and soldiers, and it echoed his own distress, for every delay was one more obstacle between his skin and a bath, his stomach and food, his head and a pillow. Naruteo's squad stamped to a halt behind his, shouting insults. They had been forced to march through the dust of their betters, and it had not improved the mood of the Red Bull's troops.

Well, let them grumble. If the Bull wanted to make these decisions, perhaps he should win a battle or two. The thought cheered Jian, and he was grinning as he walked to the source of the disturbance.

The grin faded when he reached the far side of the march. Garid Far-Eyes, one of Jian's steadiest men and the least likely to panic, was round-eyed with worry. Garid was an avian daeborn, and the feathers that served him in place of hair stood up in a tight crest. He saluted Jian, but his hawk's eyes were fixed on the tree line some distance away.

Jian returned the salute. "Trouble, dammati?"

"Trouble, Sen-Baradam." He pointed. "Civilian."

"Where?" Jian squinted, and saw nothing but dirt, sword grass, and trees. "I do not… my eyes are not as good as yours."

"Nobody's eyes are as good as mine." Garid blinked. "But she is not far from here, only hidden. There, by the strand of red bamboo. A girl, I think, and… chinmong? Maybe? Two of them, I think."

Jian brightened. Raptors were precious and rare, the hunters who bonded with them famous for their bravery, and Jian had always wanted to meet one.

"I have never heard of a chinmong hunter this far to the west." He squinted hard, using one hand to shade his eyes against the sun. "I think I see… by that third tree? The shortest one? Yes, there she is, though not the raptors. Can you see what they are hunting? We should not disturb them." Neither did he particularly wish to walk through a field of the tall, cutting grass.

But chinmong…

"The girl stands as if she is wounded, Sen-Baradam," Garid replied. "And the raptors… there are only two of them, not a full clutch, and the bigger appears to be lunging at her." Jian could not see the raptor, but trusted his dammati's eyes. He shrugged off the last of his fatigue and drew his sword.

"To me, then," he said. "Teppei, and Changha'an and Perri, as well. Sunzi, you take command while I am gone. Two raptors, you said, Garid? Are you sure there are no more?"

"I see only two, but they are very well camouflaged," Garid answered. "There may be more." He blinked. "Sen-Baradam…"

"Gai Khan and Hulagu as well, then. Yes, dammati?"

"Sen-Baradam, if I may ask…" Garid blinked again, uncomfortable as an owl at midday. "What is your plan? Do you seek to aid this girl?"

It was Jian's turn to blink. "Of course. What else would I do? Leave her to the raptors? You said she was wounded."

"Jian…" Perri's voice was soft, but his hand on Jian's shoulder was less so. "Sen-Baradam, even if she is a hunter, she has seen that which is forbidden—seen the emperor's daeborn troops at our war games. If she has been watching us train, and she is human…"

"Death," Garid said.

"Yes," Perri agreed. "It is written. Perhaps Mardoni…?" He gestured to where the White Stag sat astride his fine horse, some distance away, still as a statue but watching them, always watching. Jian's heart hurt. It was tempting, to turn this matter over to the older man, to close his eyes and his ears and his heart, but he could not. He was Sen-Baradam, he was Daechen, but he was human, as well—or half, anyway. He had a man's heart.

Perri's eyes were wide. If Jian failed in his duty, his dammati would pay the price, not he. And Perri had saved his life.

"No," he said. "The command is mine, and the duty. Come."

"What will you do?" Garid asked, and he flinched as Jian turned to face him. "If I may ask, Sen-Baradam?"

"You may not," Jian answered. He waded into the tall grass as if it were the sea, never minding the sharp blades that swiped and sliced at his exposed skin, never once looking back to see whether his dammati would follow his orders.

They know their duty, he thought, and gripped the hilt of his sword so tightly it hurt. *As I know mine.*

Walking slowly in the direction Garid had indicated, he chose his steps carefully, and glanced up now and again to make sure that his path held true. The ground was soft and wet beneath his feet, the kind of ground that is pleasant to walk upon but dangerous to troops on a long campaign. He would have to dry his feet well come evening.

And clean my sword, as well. The thought was as slow and difficult as marching through wetlands.

As the path and his troops fell behind him, the ground grew wilder. By the time Jian reached the stand of red bamboo his calves and shins ached, and his ankles were sore from negotiating the tussocks. The grasses grew shorter, and tiny frogs leapt away from his feet at every step. It would be a fine place to hunt birds, Jian thought, or marsh hogs, but all game had gone to ground in the presence of the chinmong.

Garid Far-Eyes had been right. There were two of them, a red-streaked alpha female, crest raised and shaking with outrage, and a smaller brown-spotted male with a bloody broken claw. These were healthy animals, sleek and fit, bearing the blue tattoos that marked them as domestically bred. Bonded animals, then, not wild—but they were most definitely not bonded to the young woman who crouched before them, hands upraised as if to forestall an attack.

She was a young girl, a skinny stick with big hands and feet. Her rough clothing and wide amber eyes marked her out as mountain-born, and clan tattoos on one side of her face declared her *chinmong-hui*. But she was too young to be a hunter—she still had all her fingers—and this half-clutch seemed more likely to hunt her than to hunt *for* her.

The bigger raptor swung its head at his approach and hissed, pale eyes flashing, foreclaws flexing.

"Hey now," Jian said in as soothing a tone as he could manage, feeling stupid even as the words left his mouth. How did one address a raptor? "Easy, there."

"Hssssssst." It was the girl who hissed at him, angry as the raptor had been and every bit as fierce, if not as frightening. "Stop. Go away. You will frighten them." Her words were long and round with the accent of her people, and her voice rough in her throat. Jian stopped, and blinked at her.

"Uh... yes," he said. "I will frighten them."

"No, you will *not*," she replied. "I have been trying to bond them for days, and they only just let me... *ti ma dai!*" she cried angrily as the raptors ducked their heads and sped away, tails whipping behind them. "*Sao ba dan tai shen!*"

Jian's mouth dropped open. He had not heard anyone cuss like that since... well, since his mother had dropped an anchor on her foot.

"You are too young to use such language," he scolded.

"And you are so old?" She stood, brushing dirt from her leggings and not bothering to look at him. "I am old enough to hunt with my... with my... Anmei." Her face crumpled and she wept silently, tears coursing down her face and leaving muddy streaks. "I cannot go home without her chinmong."

Not old enough to hunt, Jian thought, and his heart hurt as he drew his sword. *Yet old enough to die.* "Who are you?" he asked, that he would know what name to use when he begged his ancestors for forgiveness. "What is your name?"

"I am Ionqui Holuikhan, chinmong-hui-hao of Peichan." She straightened her back, and her pale eyes flashed like the raptor's had as she saw his drawn sword. "Are you going to kill me?"

"I must," he told her. "You have seen the emperor's Daechen in training. It is forbidden."

"Ah."

Jian blinked again. Was she not going to beg for her life? The girl wiped the tears from her face with the back of her hand, and faced death more bravely than Jian had ever faced anything in his life.

"My mother will never know what happened to me," she said. "Or to Anmei."

"Anmei?"

"My sister." It was her turn to blink at him. "We were hunting boar, but we found a nightmare instead. She died that I might get away. I should have stayed with her, but I ran." She frowned at Jian. "Why do you hesitate? I will not run. I will not fight. I am unarmed."

He stepped closer, so close he could see the water rising in Holuikhan's eyes, giving lie to her brave words. So close he could see the rents in her clothing where the chinmong had attacked when she had tried to bond with them, so that she might return to her village with honor. His sword whipped out, fast as a raptor's strike, and bit into her shoulder deeply enough to draw blood.

The young girl clapped one hand over the wound and cried out in pain.

"Fall to the ground," Jian hissed between his teeth. "Close your eyes. Do not move. You are dead, do you understand me? You are *dead*."

The girl—Holuikhan—fell to the ground.

Jian stared at her motionless form for a long while. Would the raptors return to her? Would she survive to return to her village?

At long last he turned and walked back to his dammati, head bowed, heart heavy. When he reached the others, Perri stepped forward. His one eye fell upon Jian's bloodied sword, and he nodded, face tight with sympathy.

"Is it done, Sen-Baradam?"

"It is done, Dammati." Jian did not elaborate. He would not lie to his dammati, but he must deceive them in this.

Mardoni on his white horse nodded approval before turning away.

Garid Far-Eyes stared at Jian for a long moment, saying nothing. Then he also turned away.

Nobody spoke with Jian on the long march home, which suited him fine. They thought him a murderer, he supposed, and thought less of him for it, though the blood he was to have shed was for them. It did not matter.

I have done what I could for them, he thought, *and I have done what I could for the girl.*

It was not enough, he knew.

Days later, long after the grit had been scrubbed from his hair and teeth and from between his toes, after he and his men had eaten and slept and eaten some more, Jian stood high upon a parapet, staring out across the rolling hills and the Forbidden City.

Fitful even in sleep, Sindan twitched and moaned with songs

and merriment, and the sound of an occasional fistfight as young men just returned from battle sought to regain their feet and remember who they were in this place, in this life. Some of their brothers came back wounded, or with pieces of their bodies missing. Even in a mock war, such as this had been, some came back wrapped in shrouds, never to drink or laugh again.

Some came back walking and talking like the people they had been, eating and whoring and farting just like every other soldier, but they had left important parts of themselves behind. These were soldiers whose eyes never really saw the people beside them, though those people were beloved. Whose favorite foods had lost their savor and whose tools and toys of leisure were put away to gather dust.

Jian had met no few of these soldiers, hardened veterans of this skirmish or that uprising. He used to wonder where those missing pieces might have gone, and whether anyone might ever retrieve them again. Could a man's soul, so wounded, ever fully heal?

He had volunteered for watch duty, as neither wine nor saqui nor the fleeting glimpse of a red-robed girl from one of the comfort houses held much appeal on this night. In the dark, by himself, he cleaned the lies from his sword.

I should have killed her.

Empire steel was smooth as a baby's skin. It shone like the stars, and his blade had been honed till it could slice a breath in two. Jian sat in the dark, and polished his sword, and after a while he thought of nothing at all.

SEVEN

They rode down together, down through the merchants' quarters and the craftsmen's quarters and the bright manses of the high parens. Sulema's father rode a sooty buckskin of the type common in Atualon—sturdy, deep chested, and coarse to Sulema's eyes.

Her own Atemi, in heat and angry at having been ignored, was being a snake-faced brat. Wyvernus laughed at the mare's prancing attempts to bite his stallion. Saskia, riding close behind Davidian, looked as if she had bitten into a bad lemon. Her own horse, a chestnut mare infamous among the Ja'Akari for her hot heart and naughty manners, stepped placidly as a goat among the heavier mounts.

Anger rolled over Sulema much as fog had rolled over the city hours before.

She would judge me, she thought, *she who left my mother to die, when they were attacked in Bayyid Eidtein…*

She should *judge you*, answered a voice that sounded much like the youthmistresses. *As you should judge yourself. A warrior who cannot ride her horse is no warrior at all.*

Sulema stilled the voice, as she stilled the tremble in her hands and the unquiet doubt that slipped into her heart. *I am Sa Atu*, she reminded the voice—and herself. She dug her heel into Atemi's side, tugged sharply at the bit when the mare protested, and averted her eyes from Saskia's frown. *I am the daughter of a king.*

Atemi whipped her head about and bit her sandaled foot, hard. *She* was the daughter of the wind. A king's blood did not impress her, at all. Shamed, Sulema touched her mare's shoulder in silent apology. Atemi snorted and shook her head, but subsided, and a truce was made.

The rest of the ride was uneventful. They wound through the streets of the lower quarters even as Atualon's merchants began singing of their wares, rousing the citizens of the city belly first. Salted fish and leavened bread, mare's milk and goat's cheese and little sausages sizzling merrily in the coals. Sulema's stomach rumbled like a restless vash'ai, so loudly that her father laughed.

"Have you not yet eaten?" he scolded. "Breakfast was sent to your rooms hours ago."

"First breakfast, yes," she replied. "But…"

Atemi shied violently. A boy some years younger than Daru darted between a pair of carts and onto the wide cobbled road and came to a sudden halt, staring at her with eyes as wide and startled as those of a hare. Sulema grabbed mane as her mare slid to a halt. Davidian's horse jostled them, and he swore.

"Move," he yelled at the boy. "You idiot…"

Wyvernus held up one hand, and the world fell silent.

"Gavvo!" A young woman in bright clothes fluttered forth from a doorway, tripping over half-tied sandals. "Bad boy," she wailed. "Bad boy! You… oh… oh… Your Arrogance!" She collapsed in the street before them, clutching at the boy. "Arrogance," she squeaked again. Sulema darted a look at her father, who looked bemused and… distracted.

"Citizen," he said in a mild voice. "Rise."

The woman rose into a half-crouch, still clutching the boy, trembling so that it seemed as if she might fall all to pieces in front of them.

"Your Arrogance," she breathed. "I am so… Gavvo did not mean… he is only a boy." Then she burst into tears. The boy stood just as he had before, staring at the horses and ignoring the fussing adults. There was something… odd… about him.

"It is no matter, good woman." Wyvernus waved his hand again, as if he were trying to see through a dust storm. "I, myself, have children, and they are often willful." Someone snorted a laugh, quickly suppressed. Sulema glanced sideways at the Imperator General, whose face was a study of innocence.

"Citizen," her father went on, "has this child been tested by the Baidun Daiel?"

The woman went still all over, as still as the boy. "No. No, your Arrogance. Forgive me, he is little, he is only a child…"

"An *exceptional* child, I think." Wyvernus's voice was gentle, but his words rang like iron upon the stones. "He is to be tested today, good woman. This morning." He glanced back at Davidian, who nodded in turn to one of the Draiksguard. The soldier rode toward the woman and child. "My man will accompany you. Good day." He gave heel to his horse and they rode on, a river of steel flowing around the soldier, the boy, and the weeping woman. Her cries rose behind them, a piteous wailing that smote Sulema's confused heart.

She urged Atemi closer to the king's dun. "Father…?"

"He is an exceptional child." Wyvernus sighed heavily and turned his face toward hers. He seemed to have aged years in just a few minutes. "Gifted, and cursed. We will speak of this later."

"But…"

"Later, I said." He frowned in irritation. "No need to look at me like that, Sulema—the boy will not be harmed. It is a king's responsibility to look after every citizen, the greatest and the least, the gifted and the most challenged. *Especially* the most challenged. Do you trust me?"

She hesitated, but dropped her eyes as his frown deepened.

"Yes, Father."

"Then *trust* me. Come, do not let this cloud spoil a beautiful day. I have a surprise for you, a wonderful surprise. Come!" He gave his dun the heel, and its head. The big stallion half-reared, all game and eagerness, and surged ahead.

Sulema saw no choice but to follow.

They came at last to a large clearing. The ground was strewn with broken rock, the earth scorched as if it had been the scene of recent battle. *Very* recent. Wyvernus hopped from his saddle before the horse had come to a halt, and a younger Draiksguard scrambled to take his reins. Sulema dismounted and gave Atemi over to Saskia, offering the Zeerani a grudging nod of thanks. She was still angry, but allowing one of the Atualonians to handle her asil would have been unthinkable.

"Here we are!" Wyvernus clapped his hands. "Lucius, be a good lad, bring me the drawings. We have used this place as a training ground for the troops since my father's father's days," he told Sulema as she joined him, "but I have thought of a better use for it. Ah, here we are, thank you, boy! Well, Daughter, what do you think?"

Sulema blinked as the Draiksguard surrounded them. Lucius and another young man unrolled a long scroll between them. It was marked in blue and black inks, scribbles of script and numbers, and an enormous, detailed drawing of…

"The Madraj?" she asked hesitantly. It was… and yet, it was not. The Madraj in Aish Kalumm served as a meeting place and an arena. It was a simple stone structure, old and spare as the Zeera herself. This was, it was… an elegant monstrosity.

"Leviathus sketched your Madraj for me, and I thought it a fine thing." Wyvernus placed one arm over her shoulders and urged her closer. "Of course, your Zeerani structure would not be big enough to suit our needs, so I have added a stable here…" He pointed. "…and a staging area here… oh, and a pavilion for the family, here… What do you think?" he asked again. "I had meant it to be a birth-day gift for you, but I could not wait."

"It is…" She stopped. "You… could not wait? Father, the Madraj was the work of a thousand craftmistresses, and it took a generation for them to complete." A cloud passed before the sun, and Sulema shivered as a knot of Baidun Daiel rode up on their silent black horses, cloaks streaming behind them like blood in the river.

"Witness, Sulema." Her father's eyes flashed. "Witness the glory of Atualon."

❖

The warrior mages stood in a circle round her father, half of them facing their king, half facing outward, every mask reflecting the brilliance of the Dragon King. Sulema and the guards had absented the field and stood watching from a safe distance as the king donned his own mask, and began to speak. His words became a chant, his chant became a song…

His song became magic.

At first it was a wave beneath her feet, as if she stood upon the deck of one of the dragon-headed ships that had brought her to Aish Kalumm. The earth beneath her feet trembled, and then the sky overhead, and then the heart within her breast as all the world stopped to listen to the Song of the Dragon King. Sajani Earth Dragon herself rolled over in her sleep as the song wound itself into her dreams, begging her favor, flattering and soothing the sleeping beast even as the king stole her magic. A thimbleful, a goblet full, scarce enough to rouse the great beast to wrath and ruin, but more than enough for the Dragon King's purpose.

The song caught at Sulema. She found herself swaying to it, dancing as if to the *thrum-thrum-tharararummmm* of the world's heartbeat and the sun's chorus. She could feel where the music should fall a little, and lift again, rising up, up—

The song faltered.

The Dragon King faltered, his voice going thin where it should have swelled, and a crack rose through his crescendo. Sunlight flashed and trembled. The Dragon King's voice fell, the magic fell…

And Sulema caught it.

Barely trained, she was not nearly ready. Still her chest swelled with air as she had been taught, until she could feel it pressing lightly at her back like a lover's hand. She let her shoulders fall loose and her throat soften as she released one note—one single note as clear and sharp and bright as a sunblade, strong and true as a friend at a warrior's back. She gave of this power freely and without reservation. The Dragon King, scarce missing a beat, grabbed it up and wove it into his own. His crippled magic righted itself, spread its wings, and *flew*.

The ground beneath the king's feet trembled, pebbles and rubble rolling away from him like sand-dae in the wind as the glittering black stone was exposed, smoothing and shaping itself into an odd concentric pattern. All about them rose great columns of black and gold, arches delicate as lace, steps cut with such precision it seemed as if a giant's knife had carved them from butter.

That which rose from the earth was not like the Madraj, unless a fortress might be said to resemble a shepherd's hut. This creation of her father's was a wonder, a miracle, and Sulema's heart leapt even as dust shivered away, leaving the newborn dragonstone glittering and joyous in the morning light. Standing as she did on one edge of the arena, she could scarce see the other side. It dazzled the mind and quailed the heart.

As her father turned to face her, the mask of Akari blinded her. The growling, fitful earth calmed beneath his feet as the Dragon King strode toward her.

The Baidun Daiel sank to their knees. Sulema was overtaken by a sudden weakness and would have fallen, as well, had her father not caught her by the upper arms and held her fast. His eyes behind the mask were bright as stars. This close, she could see how his hands trembled from the effort he had made, could hear the strain in his voice as he spoke.

"Behold," he said, and his words rang out across the gathering like a new-forged sword. "Behold the Sulemnium, a dragon's gift to his daughter." Neither with his eyes nor his words did the king thank her, or in any way recognize what she had done.

Many of those who were there to witness the birth of a wonder wept openly as Ka Atu went to one knee before his daughter. But Sulema did not weep. In her mind's eye she saw herself drawn and painted as these people chose to see her. A king's daughter in fine robes, with jewels in her braids and a song of power on her lips. It was a pretty picture, fit for one of the Mothers' books.

It was a lie. In that moment Sulema thought that perhaps the Dragon King meant not to supplant himself with an heir, but to harvest what power she possessed in order to bolster his own.

It was an ugly thought, one from which she might have turned away—had she not been Ja'Akari.

Nu'ehu nu'ani, she scolded herself, even as her father regained his feet and kissed her on either cheek, even as the people shouted and cheered. *There can be no beauty without truth.*

EIGHT

The hunters came as thieves in the night, stealing through shadowy woods. They came without warning, without hue and cry, without roar or howl or wailing horn or any of those things that presaged killers in the waking world. The Dreaming Lands fell silent at their passing as a hare might freeze beneath the hawk's shadow.

The Huntress's hounds were black as shadows. Crimson tongues lolled laughing between white, white teeth, while eyes gleamed in anticipation of the kill as they ghosted beneath her perch, a river of muscle and fur and death.

As quickly as they came they were gone, and not a leaf mourned their passing. Still the Lands held their breath, the birds held their song, and Hafsa Azeina high in the trees held tight to the hilt of Belzaleel, lest the demon blade cry out to its fell brethren and give her away.

Then came the Huntress. Fair-skinned, dark-eyed, hair glossy as a raven's wing, she wore a crown of bones upon her brow. Hafsa Azeina knew her as only the hare can know the hawk. Death rode beneath her on a dark horse. It scented the wind for her blood, but death had not found her yet.

The dreamshifter watched from her high, green perch as the woman far below her paused. From this angle she could see dark lashes brush her pale cheeks as that fine-boned face turned into the wind, shell-pale lips open just enough to show the pearly glint of sharp teeth. Delicate nostrils flared wide as she tried to catch the scent of blood. Thrice the Huntress had bloodied her prey, thrice she had lost it in the forest, and anger shimmered in the air around her. The furs and leathers of her mismate armor shifted, the bones in her necklace chittered together as she drew in a deep breath, held it…

…as did the Dreaming Lands, and the dreamshifter who had trespassed upon them…

…and then the Huntress let out her breath in an irritated *hunhh*, almost human in her frustration. From the belt at her waist she drew the golden shofar akibra, twin to Hafsa Azeina's own, and sounded it. Her hounds wailed an answer, a long, low, mournful ululation, and the sorrow in that song drew a smile from their mistress. She replaced her horn, gave heel to her dark horse, and was gone as silently as she had come.

In her wake fell a peculiar silence, as if the forest had anticipated bloodshed, and regretted its absence.

The dreamshifter waited.

Then came the tiny noises of birds ruffling their feathers and shifting foot-to-foot as they listened to see which of their fellows would be first to break the concealing hush. Leaves rustled far below as ever-hungry rodents ventured forth from their hiding-holes in search of food, whiskers bristling in alarm, ears swiveling this way and that as they listened for the *shushhh-shushhh-shushhhh* of snakes. Not much had changed, thought Hafsa Azeina high in her tree, for those who were prey. Such was the life of a bird or a rodent.

Or a dreamshifter.

Breath caught in her throat and her hand clamped harder upon Belzaleel's hilt. She turned her head fractionally, and from the corner of one eye watched as a patch of mist formed, darkened, and became Basta. Her muse and conscience, her kima'a, her spirit self.

Her greatest of calamities and foremost pain in the ass.

You might have gotten me killed, Hafsa Azeina scolded, but there was not much heat in it.

Well, you killed me, so it would only be fair. The avatar grinned a cat's grin and settled upon the branch, tucking her paws beneath a black-furred breast. *And what brings you to this shadowy corner of the Dreaming Lands, Dreamshifter? Reeking of blood and fear, some of it your own. Such a heady scent is likely to bring the—*

Basta broke off, blinking slowly. She lifted her face into the wind and scented, mouth open in a needle-toothed snarl.

Are you mad, *Dreamshifter?* she asked at last, her cat's voice thick with scorn. *That one would do more than merely kill you. Do you know whose skin she wears? Have you looked into her hounds' eyes? What game is afoot, that you would hunt the Huntress?*

This is no game, Hafsa Azeina assured her kima'a. *And I am no easy meat.* She half-drew Belzaleel from his bespelled sheath at her hip. *The Huntress has weapons such as can kill any man or beast. Even a wyvern… even a king. If I can but get close enough…*

That one would not lift a finger to help you, *Dreamshifter. Nor do you have half the skill it would take to catch her unawares, demon blade or no. Take Belzaleel from these lands, while you still may. Better to cast that knife into the fires beneath Atukos, better even to bury his blade in your own flesh than bring him* here, *to the Dreaming Lands. In the Huntress's hands, Belzaleel would be a weapon fit to give fell dreams to the Nightmare Man.*

Your need is not so great that you should risk us all. Basta growled and thrashed her tail as she spoke, fur rising in a black nimbus around her head.

My need is dire. Wyvernus has bound my daughter to his will. I fear that he seeks not to train Sulema as an heir, but to use her. As he had used Tadeah. Hafsa Azeina suppressed a shudder at the memory. *I cannot hope to stand against Ka Atu now, weakened as I am and alone. There are weapons here, for those who have the knowledge to find them, and the courage to steal them.*

I know what I am doing, she asserted.

You know nothing, human. Your tiny mind is not big enough to see the long game these immortals play, much less join the game yourself. You are like a bird, trapped in a net of your own making, and your struggles are drawing attention that you do not want. You wish to keep your daughter safe? Stay away from these lands, Dreamshifter. Leave the Huntress to her hunting, leave the twilight lords to their long game, and let us small folk live such small lives as we have in peace.

Basta stood and stretched, arching her back. *The Dreaming*

Lands are no place for you. Not anymore. The bonds you have woven in life are tearing at your soul, tearing it to pieces, and the scent of your pain draws the lords and ladies as to a feast. You draw danger to yourself—but also to your daughter and those of us foolish enough to care for you. She began to mist around the edges, fading even as a false light broke through the canopy of leaves overhead.

And why should I trust your words? Hafsa Azeina asked. *As you say, I killed you once. Perhaps next time you will conspire to kill me.*

Yes, Belzaleel interjected, in a voice that stank of burned stones. *Yes, yes, yesssssssss. Kill her, Annu. Kill them all. Seize the power you were born to wield.* A spasm shot through Hafsa Azeina's hand, and the blade slid nearly free of the sheath.

Kill you? I think... not. Basta's hindquarters and feet had disappeared. Only her head and shoulders floated among the leaves now, eyes bright as stars, tongue red as blood. *It is in my best interest to keep you alive, and a cat will always act in her best interests. Which reminds me...*

The black face, hated and beloved, faded to a mask, to a dream, to nothing. Her parting words laughed through the leaves.

How is *Khurra'an, these days?*

Khurra'an was failing.

Hafsa Azeina knelt beside the vash'ai on the hearth, using a scrap of linen to rub oils into his dull coat. Never had he tolerated being groomed by humans, or even petted, and never before had she considered performing such a task. But his fur was falling out by the handful, and his great silver-and-black mane had knotted so that she had had to chop much of it off.

There was blood and pus on the stones where he had lain for so long, and she wished she had the strength to turn him over. The smell of rot and cat piss burned her eyes.

We were the terror of the Zeera, she thought, dashing weak tears away with the back of one hand. *The mighty would see our eyes in their dreams and despair. Now look at us... half a season in this* blasted city, and we have been shorn like churrim, reaved of our hair and our strength and our glory. *We should never have come.*

Khurra'an slitted one dull eye at her. *If I have lived long enough to witness the Eater of Dreams weeping over spilt blood, then I have lived too long.*

I am a dream eater no longer. Hafsa Azeina pushed the soft moonsilk fluff of hair back from her face, where once glorious sorceress locks had fallen like a shroud. *I am hardly a dreamshifter at all. Neither am I queen of this land… I am not sure what I am, anymore. Perhaps* both *of us have lived too long.*

Perhaps you should stop mewling for the tit like some helpless cub, Khurra'an growled. He pulled his dry tongue back into his mouth, doubtless realizing that lying slack-jawed with his tongue puddled upon the stone robbed him of dignity. *Leave off. Leave OFF, human.* With a great heaving effort, he rolled so that he was lying upright. *I am no cub, to lie supine while my queen bathes me. If I want my ass cleaned, I will lick it myself.*

Hafsa Azeina winced to see the clotted mess of hair and crusted skin that he left upon the hearth.

You should rest…

Should I? Should we? His voice was gentle. *I am Khurra'an, Rhan-an-ar of the Wide-Water Prides. You are Hafsa Azeina, Dream Eater of the Burning Sands. We are the scourge of this world and the next. We will rest when we are dead, Kithren, and not before.*

At his words, something stirred deep in her breast, where long ago she had buried the ruins of a heart. *You are* right, she said at long last. She reached up and began twisting a lock of her hair between her fingers. *But you need to regain your body's strength. I will bring you water, and meat. The heart of a pig—*

Hrunnnn. He laughed, almost, and shook out what was left of his mane, then began licking one foreleg. *Water only. I have gotten weak and soft from eating fat meat, dead meat, killed by a weakling and drained of all vitality. What I need—what* we *need—is the hunt. Tooth and claw, and the flesh of worthy prey between our teeth. Heart's blood and marrow and entrails, my love, and nothing less.* He sent her an image then, the two of them stalking a great blue goat along the sea cliffs.

Hafsa Azeina licked her lips and swallowed. *Worthy prey indeed*, she allowed. *Worthy prey for any strong hunter—but we are weakened, Kithren. Perhaps this hunt is beyond us now. If we hunt such prey, we may well die.* Not even bonded humans knew much about the lives of wild vash'ai, but every man, woman, and child of the Zeera knew that much—a wounded sire who failed to make the kill was marked for death.

Khurra'an stopped mid-lick.

Then we die. His great golden eyes, so like her own, held a world of love—and not the least shadow of regret. A weight she had not known she carried lifted from her then. The bonds of which Basta had spoken loosened just enough to let her breathe.

Life is pain. She had always known this. *Only death comes easy.*

Ahhh, she breathed. *Yes. You are right. Shall we share a bowl of tea, beloved? Shall we join the dance?*

We shall dance, he agreed, showing his massive, bejeweled tusks in a long yawn. *And it will be glorious.*

NINE

The wind roiled eastward across the dunes, rousing them to song. Wind and sand, sa and ka of the desert, fought against each other and their voices grew angry, discordant. The morning sky, which had dawned soft and rosy, shrieked with the souls of hungry bintshi. It raked at them with sand-teeth and fire-breath, and turned the anger of a battered world upon the small group of travelers.

It tore at their clothing, clawed at their eyes, and raised questions that no heart could bear to answer. No human heart, at any rate, though the Mah'zula warriors, the youthmistress, and the king's son hunched miserable in their saddles. Horses and churrim, warriors and vash'ai plodded along, step by step, breath by breath, enduring now with little thought to *there* or *then*.

Now is burden enough, Inna'hael had told her once, blinking his yellow eyes in a slow laugh. *Especially when one is hunting.*

Or when one is being hunted.

Though her face was well wrapped, the sand-dae kicked dust into Istaza Ani's eyes so she could not see, stuffed their wicked claws into nose and mouth and into her ears, as well. Blinded and deafened as she was, still Ani knew they were prey. For some nights now, the horses had pressed close to the fire at night, the churrim had grumbled and fussed at the lines as they chewed their cud, and the vash'ai had bristled so that warriors gave them wide berth.

The stars pressed down upon them, the sand pressed up, and the world pressed in from all sides till their small group seemed smaller still, and weak, prey to the greater predators that screamed in the dark.

If these warriors are prey, Ani wondered, glancing at the women around her, *what does that make us?* She would have spat, but water was life, and life was precious.

It is, Inna'hael whispered. *You are.*

The vash'ai's words and soft sentiment were so unexpected that Ani rose up in the saddle, causing her stallion to toss his head and snort, rolling his eyes this way and that and flaring his nostrils wide. This in turn gave the other horses an excuse to prance, dance, and generally act like idiots.

"Asshole," she muttered under her breath, as with hand and leg she reminded Talieso that he was not to come up in front and dump her upon the sand. She felt Inna'hael's laugh.

If I live to be a hundred, she thought, *I will never understand cats.*

If you live to see the end of this day, you should thank me with a fat pig. You humans are blind and helpless as cubs at the teat.

You and the other vash'ai may keep the greater predators at bay during the night, Ani retorted, *but I hardly see what help you might be against this storm.*

You are right, little one, he purred angrily. Y*ou hardly see.* And he was gone again, leaving her adrift upon a sea of sand and malice.

For nearly a two-moon they had ridden, skirting the territories of vash'ai and man alike, giving lie to the claims of the Mah'zula that all the Zeera was theirs by right. For all their big mouths, this handful of false warriors cast a very small shadow beneath the wings of Akari.

The riders chased the dragon by day, and Leviathus by night, forcing fermented mare's milk down his throat until he staggered and fell upon the sand, and then they would make other sport of him. His cries of pain and rage, the women's laughter, and Mariza's sideways sneer as she judged the youthmistress's reaction burned inside Ani's belly like venom in a wineskin. It was only a matter of time before her anger ate through and got them all killed. She kept her face stone, and her heart. Ani bode her time, playing a children's song as they rode.

It was a simple tune, played on a simple flute made from cactus-bone. She had learned it from Hafsa Azeina, back when the world was young, when there were men to chase and usca to drink and bodies to dump into the river.

The Mah'zula were young yet, still hot to pursue the boys, to ride over the next dune and chase the setting sun. Young, and beautiful, and dumb as the dung that dropped from their horses' asses.

Youth and beauty, the voice of Theotara whispered, *will always be overcome by…*

…age and treachery, Ani finished, but Theotara would never have been made captive, would never have allowed a guest under her protection to be beaten and raped. She would have cracked the world open like a dragon before she let such an age come to pass.

You lot are a strange species, Inna'hael observed, not kindly. *I had begun to think I was wrong about you… but I see now that I was mistaken.*

Ani burned with shame beneath the veiled gaze of Akari, and said nothing. She sat astride her horse, and listened to the fell wind, and played her flute…

…and played her flute…

…and the storm came, providing cover to those predators who stalked the sweet two-legged meat.

At last the song was finished, its final notes sucked dry as marrow bones by the hungry storm. Ani tucked the flute away, pressed her face into the mane of her good and faithful horse, and let the world do with her as it may. Had Akari himself come screaming through the storm to devour her for this trespass, Ani would not have been surprised, nor would she have resisted. She had broken a law that stretched back to the Sundering, a law set down into the bones of the world itself, and there would be a reckoning.

What was that Sulema always said? *"It is only trouble if you get caught."* Well, then she would simply have to avoid being caught. *A fine job I have done so far.*

You are alive, yet, Inna'hael reminded her.

Yes, she answered, *and where there is life, there is yet hope that I might fuck things up even worse than I already have.*

A strange species… he reaffirmed. Ani did not answer. She

bent her mind, as they all did, toward surviving the storm so that whatever stalked them might not have its chance at them until later.

Year after year she had told her younglings that a good dust storm might last minutes. A bad dust storm might last years. By highsun, it was apparent that this storm had no intention of being good. By latesun, Ani began to suspect that it was, at its heart, truly wicked. It howled about them, rousing the sand-dae into leaping, gyrating columns the height and breadth of a man so that it seemed, at times, as if they were surrounded by enemy warriors.

Neither could they hope to climb the higher dunes in an attempt to rise above it. This was a proper *buraq*, a storm with a heart of lightning. The hairs stood up all over Ani's body, strange dark colors crackled and danced among the sand-dae, and twice the peaks of nearby dunes lit up with fire blue as the bowels of Jehannim, and as foul-smelling.

Mariza's chestnut mare emerged from the paste-thick gloom as she fell back to ride between Ani and Leviathus. She leaned from her saddle, tugging aside the sand-caked cloth wrapped round her face. Ani leaned in, as well.

Had they not taken Ani's shamsi, she would have run it through the woman's heart right then. Had they not taken her dagger, she would have slit that tender throat. But she had neither of these things. They had left her nothing save the flute, more fools they.

"We camp here," Mariza called out.

"What?" Ani tipped her head.

"We camp here," the woman shouted again, dark eyes narrowing to slits.

"*What?*" Ani tipped her head the other way.

"Here! *Here!*" Mariza hollered, flapping her arms. "*Kharra, yeh Makhumla.* Stupid old woman."

Ani nodded and looked around. The storm had thinned just enough for her to see that they were hemmed in on three sides by steep dunes, and her thin water-sense told her there would be no fresh water for them or their animals. There was no easy route for escape, should the things that stalked them choose to attack, and neither could they hope to post watch from higher ground, as lightning still gnawed the air above them. This was perhaps the *worst* place Mariza could possibly have chosen to set up camp for the night.

Perfect. Ani nodded again, shrugged, and swung a leg over Talieso's back. Her old stallion rolled an eye at her and attempted a half-hearted bite. He was smart enough not to want to spend the night here, but he could hardly expect her to reveal all her plans to him.

She reached up to help Leviathus from his churra, but he had already slid down from the tall saddle and turned away from her, refusing to meet her eye. Her heart hurt for the young man.

It is not your fault, she wanted to tell him. *Not your shame.*

No, Inna'hael agreed, soft and quiet as a sharp blade through flesh. *It is yours.*

Far behind them, in the gold-and-blood murky heart of the storm, Ani caught the faint notes of a child's song. A plaintive note it was, high and pure, a sound that no human throat could ever mimic, and it turned her blood to water. Voices answered from south and east, discernible from the wind only because she was listening for them.

What have I done? she wondered, too late. *What have I done?*

Well, mused Inna'hael, *it will be an interesting death.*

Ani struck her tent, a raggedy old thing which had seen her through more battles and tears and lovemaking than any woman should wish. She had worked oil into the fabric twice a year, sometimes more, till the hemp-and-silk was soft as kidskin. It was a homey shelter, plain and unadorned, nearly as scarred as Askander's hide.

She led the churra Leviathus had been riding to lie in the lee of the tent, chewing her cud and muttering angrily. Her own Talieso hardly needed urging to drop to his knees and scootch ungracefully inside. Leviathus followed, and Ani was last, tying the outer flaps and lacing the inner.

Talieso pinned his ears briefly at the meager bag of churra butter and grain she offered him, and ate with many long-suffering sighs. She wished she could give him better, not least because churra butter always gave him a sour belly. Leviathus took the handful of salted pemmican and mouthful of stale water without so much comment, before turning his back to lie as far from her as he possibly could. Ani lay between them, wishing she could give the boy more room. Though he feigned sleep quickly, he did so poorly, going stiff all over at her slightest movement.

Her faithful tent shuddered as the sandstorm clawed at the fabric, trying to get at the tasty meats inside. It shook from within, as well, when Talieso lazily moved his tail aside and erupted with the first in what was to be an epic storm of flatulence. Outside the churra emitted a series of high-pitched and whistling shrieks as Inna'hael curled up beside her, subsiding only when the vash'ai snarled a warning.

Oh, leave off, she told him. *The poor beast is afraid of you.*

She is smarter than you, then, brave little huntress.

Ani thought again about the sounds she had heard, and wondered what, exactly, was singing the chill song she had begun with her cactus-bone flute. She wondered whether she would live to see another morning, or be torn apart by predators, or die in her sleep, suffocated by a horse's farts.

An inglorious death, Inna'hael agreed, yawning so hard she could feel it inside her head. *Though not without honor.*

And who will sing my bones, if I die out here? she asked, though the question had never occurred to her before. *Who will see my story through to its end?*

The great cat was silent so long that Ani thought he must be asleep. Eventually she, too, drifted off, and so never heard his reply.

Akari Sun Dragon sang the world to life, as he had every morning since finding his love asleep in her bed of rock and brimstone, and as he would every morning until she woke and returned his song, shattering this world with her delight.

Morning was a given—just as the sky, just as the sand, just as the moons and stars and a river's endless journey to the sea were given. But life… life was never a given. Every morning upon which a warrior might gaze with clear eyes, a heart beating in her chest, and lungs filled to bursting with sweet desert air was a gift, rare and precious.

So Ani reminded herself when she woke with her face next to a horse's ass, sand in her nethers, and a mouth that tasted as if she had licked the churra pens clean. She lay for a while, loath to wake either of the snoring creatures that shared her tent. Talieso was likely to wake in a panic, feet-first, knocking the whole tent to Jehannim. Never mind they had been camping like this since he was a suckling. And Leviathus…

Let him sleep, her mind urged. *Let him have these moments of peace.*

It was not to be.

Someone yanked at her tent, as if the flaps had not been properly tied against last night's storm, and yanked it again. Talieso thrashed, instantly trying to regain his feet in the small space, and whinnied so that her ears rang. Leviathus went stiff all over, as if by doing so he could separate himself from this world entirely, and sink into the next.

The tent jerked again, and Mariza's shaking voice croaked out.

"Istaza! Come look at this!"

"Shit from a pox-riddled goat's arse!" Ani yelled. "Give me a minute!"

"Hurry," the other woman said, her voice low. "And bring the prisoner." The tent shook again, and Talieso almost hit Ani in the face with his head as he tried again to stand.

"Of all the shit-brained, cheese-assed daughters of a half-brained goat rapist… *stop that!*" she snarled—at Mariza and the horse both—and of a wonder they stopped.

Ani unlaced the tent flaps, and urged Talieso to scooch out backward as he had done most of his life. Of course, the moment he was free her idiot stallion took off bucking and farting as if he had just survived a reaver apocalypse. She nodded to Leviathus as he emerged from the stinking tent, as well. He stood shaking the sand from his clothing as best he could, still not meeting any of the women's eyes.

"Come," Mariza said, reaching out and nearly touching Ani's arm. "Come on." She turned and hurried up the side of the nearest dune, which had crept closer as they slept out the storm.

She is afraid, Ani thought, and a slow smile crept across her heart. *No, she is* terrified. The youthmistress of the Zeerani prides did not let the smile touch her face, though, nor did she reach down to the flute still tucked into her waistband. She followed the false warrior up the sand mountain to see what she could see. Leviathus came after her, and Talieso as well, for he had got the foolishness out of his system, and was hoping for breakfast.

Three of the Mah'zula were waiting at the top of the dune, vash'ai by their sides, and the women's faces showed even more fear than Mariza's. Ani's heart gladdened to see it.

I will welcome whatever it is that puts such a look on their— Then she looked down, and her blood turned to river water, cold and full of serpents.

What have I done? she wondered again, far too late. *What have I called?* But she knew. Any child of a bonesinger would recognize the tall spiked figures that stood far below. Untouched by sun or wind they stood, shadowless and motionless, branches outstretched like limbs, narrow leaves longer than her arm sprouting from their tops like a warrior's headdress, ragged and broken.

What have I—

"What have you done?" Mariza snarled, but she was staring past Ani at the king's son. "What fell luck have you brought upon us, Outlander? What foul magic is this?"

Leviathus froze where he stood. Though they had been so long under the sun, he looked pale and haggard, and the yellowing bruise on one cheek smote Ani's heart. In that moment, she regretted nothing. Inna'hael padded up the dune to stand beside them, flanked by two of the smaller vash'ai queens. He stared down on the still figures, then turned his hot yellow gaze upon Ani.

So, you have chosen an especially *interesting death.*

"Tell him, Istaza," Mariza said.

It is Istaza, *still*, she thought. *They turn to me as to a teacher, and do not yet realize it.* Ani let her voice harden. These stupid girls thought they wanted a teacher, now, after all they had done? She would be the teacher they sought, and gladly. She would teach them a thing or three about what it really meant to live as a warrior. And die as a traitor.

"Those are *na'iyeh*," she explained to Leviathus, raising her voice so that all might hear. "Greater predators from the beginning times, and they are stalking us."

"Na'iyeh means… to weep?" Leviathus blinked. He shaded his eyes with one hand and squinted down at the unassuming shapes. "Those just look like some kind of cactus to me. Are you sure those things are predators? They do not move, that I can see."

"Stupid." Mariza spat, but her face was stark with fear. "Stupid male."

"Na'iyeh means 'mourners'," Ani answered, "because they look like weeping warriors standing at a pyre, and because once they are on your trail, it is only a matter of time before your family is weeping. You will never see them move." She softened her voice, drew them in with a storyteller's cadence. That, too, she had learned from Hafsa Azeina. *I am more like her than they know. More than I knew, even.*

"You could stand here all day, watching them, and never see them move. But you must sleep eventually. We all must sleep eventually, and when we do…"

One of the Mah'zula let out a long, shuddering moan.

"The na'iyeh do not flower like trees or herbs, they grow no fruits, produce no seeds. They catch you in your sleep—it is said they feed only on humans—enfold you in their thorny embrace, and dissolve your flesh. Slowly. Even as they do this, the na'iyeh coat your still-screaming corpse with a kind of slime, and this slime eventually hardens to become the flesh of a new mourner.

83

All that is left of you will be your bones, deep inside a newborn na'iyeh. You will grow branches, and leaves, and spikes, and hunt human flesh with your new brothers and sisters."

"If you cut one open," Samiyeh whispered, "you will find the bones of a man, or woman, or child. They say that its mouth is open, screaming for eternity."

"If you cut it in half," another said, "those two pieces will become two new na'iyeh. You cannot kill them by chopping them up like plants. You cannot kill them with water, or poison, or any weapon forged by man."

You cannot eat them, Inna'hael added. Around him the smaller vash'ai crouched, snarling. *You cannot end them by claw or by tooth.*

"How do we kill them, then?" Leviathus asked. All eyes turned toward Ani. The youthmistress smiled, deep in the pit of her heart, in that hidden room where the bonesinger's child yet lived.

"You cannot kill the na'iyeh, save perhaps by fire hot enough to turn human bone to ash. Nor will they turn aside from the hunt. Once the Mourners have your scent, they will chase you to the very corners of the earth, never giving up their prey, never sleeping. There is only one thing for us to do."

"And what is that?" Leviathus asked, though Ani could see the answer waiting in his eyes.

"Run."

And run they did, under a clear sky and a benevolent sun, on little water, less food, and no hope, till their horses stumbled and the churrim spat, till the Mah'zula were too weary and strained to bother making sport of Leviathus.

Aftha, their best scout, stood in her stirrups and let her ka unfold. She cast about for any hint of shade or water till she was half-fainting in the saddle. Ani, who was nearly as deaf to sa and ka as the king's son, could have told them that the search was in vain. This route to Min Yaarif was known as *Haz Qurut*—the Dry Road—for good reason.

But she did not tell them, nor did she see fit to explain to these—*Kha'Akari*—that there was no running from the na'iyeh, once a pod had your dream scent. The fleetest foot, the swiftest steed could never outrun Weeping Dreamers, as the dreamshifters called them.

"Eventually you will have to sleep," Hafsa Azeina had explained, *"and it is then they will catch you. For though they remain rooted in this world, they travel in Shehannam. The moment you enter the Dreaming Lands, they will find you by your scent. With every dream they draw closer to you in the world of flesh, until you are caught."*

"Is there no escape, then?" she had asked.

"For me, it would be possible. For one or two other dreamshifters, perhaps. For one such as you?" Hafsa Azeina had shaken her head, great golden eyes half-lidded. *"Better you should steer clear of the na'iyeh, as all greater predators."*

Here I have done exactly the opposite, Ani thought, *and drawn them to us. Truly, I am more like Sulema than either of us knew.* There were, indeed, ways in which one might escape or even kill the na'iyeh, but they were beyond her power altogether, and she would not have shared this information with Mariza and her ilk, had they thought to ask.

No, these arrogant young idiots would not think to ask a used-up youthmistress—and impure of blood, at that—what she might know.

Age and treachery. She grinned.

Exactly so, youngling, Inna'hael remarked. *Exactly so.*

They struck camp that night far from shelter or water. For the second night in a row, the horses were on grain-and-butter rations, and the churrim on none. Neither were the prisoners given more than a scant mouthful of water. It was "prisoners" now, not "the prisoner and the youthmistress."

When she and Leviathus sat shoulder-to-shoulder in her tent, however, and she was reasonably certain they would not be disturbed, Ani picked apart a bit of the tent's hem and retrieved a waxed paper packet of lionsnake pemmican. He accepted half with a silent nod of thanks, though his eyes flashed bright in the tent's dim interior. They flashed again when she took out the flute and began to play.

King's son or not, he is no fool, Ani thought. *Although he is a fool to believe that any mad plan of mine might do anything but get us killed.*

Inna'hael, for a change, said nothing.

Soon enough, one of the Mah'zula shook her tent and yelled for silence. Ani tucked the flute away and lay down, heart pounding, and waited for sleep to come.

Sleep did come, eventually, and it brought terrible dreams. Umm Nurati, first mother of the Zeeranim, lay dead, legs split open like a fresh-caught fish with the bones gone. Tammas and her other children—save Ismai—were arranged beside her on a pyre that would not light. Hannei, the young Ja'Akari warrior, stood over them all, dry-eyed and silent, hacking at her own flesh with a pair of grey steel shamsi.

Hannei turned from the sight only to find herself surrounded by—

"*Na'iyeh!*" one of the Mah'zula screamed, in a voice so shrill it was scarcely human.

"I feel nothing!" another shrieked. "Nothing! There is nothing! *Ai yeh!*"

Ani burst from her tent, Leviathus close behind her. The Mah'zula were running about like a swarm of russet ridgebacks, undisciplined as children.

Just as Hafsa Azeina had warned, the pod of na'iyeh were closer now than they had been the previous morning, so close Ani could see the daggerlike leaf-crowns swaying as if in a breeze. So close she could smell the carrion stench of them. Though she had been warned, though the dreamshifter had explained why doing so might be deadly, Ani could not help but reach out to them, unfurling her ka…

Nothing.

There was nothing, not even the faint water sense or life sense that she had always taken for granted.

"What?" Leviathus asked, frowning. "What is it?"

Of course you would not know, she thought. *You are surdus. You never had what we have lost.* For a moment, she almost envied him his deafness.

Ani cast about in a panic, every muscle in her body, every sense straining outward with the effort, but still there was nothing. No life sense, no breath sense, not a whisper of warmth from human or beast, not even the slow trickle of fire or water deep underground. It was as if a music that had been playing before her birth had stopped. As if the world had stopped, as if Sajani Earth Dragon curled tight and silent.

"Sa and ka," she whispered to him, heart pounding. "They are gone. The world has gone silent. As if we are all surdus." Her heart, her soul kept reaching out, but there was no answer. Truly, they had been forsaken.

His indrawn breath was a low whistle.

"My father—"

All around her, warriors began to cry out as one by one they realized what had been lost. What had been taken from them. Some of them wept, hands over their faces. Two of them erupted in a flurry of blows and screams. One of those drew her shamsi, and when a third tried to intervene, that blade bit deep into her flesh, nearly severing an arm. Even those screams were not enough to fill the silence that rang in all their hearts. In vain, those bonded Zeeravashani turned to their kithren—

—and as one, the vash'ai turned away from the Zeeranim, as if that bond had never been. The old queen was first, a lovely elderling with a coat so pale it was more silver than gold. Green eyes blinked lazily as the warrior with whom she had ridden and hunted and played for years—perhaps half the span of the young woman's life—threw herself upon the sand at the queen's feet. Those eyes were as flat and indifferent as those of any wild vash'ai. Ears pressed against her head, the great cat yawned a toothful yawn, stood, and walked away with an irritated twitch of her tail.

When the warrior cried out and clutched at the vash'ai's paws, the great queen whipped around, snarling. Ani had never seen such murderous eyes, such a deadly face. Not even the dreamshifter could have managed that look, for she was human. The vash'ai, they were reminded in that sudden silent moment, were not.

A paw as wide as the girl's face lashed out, cat-fast, and those black claws laid her throat open to the bone. The silence was broken—not by the young Mah'zula, who died without so much as a whisper, but by the vash'ai. The old queen roared, the other vash'ai answered her, and they turned and walked away as if waking from a dream they had no wish to revisit, leaving their hearts' companions to fend for themselves against the world—and the na'iyeh.

Inna'hael went last. Ani thought for a moment that he might speak with her, but the broken-tusked shaman could not—or would not—answer her heart's muted pleas. When the other cats had gone he, too, turned and disappeared into the yellow haze of morning.

"What have you done?" Mariza screamed. "*What have you done?*"

What have *I done?* Ani turned, but the leader of the Mah'zula was not looking at her. Instead, the woman raised a shaking hand to point at Leviathus, face twisted into a mask of hatred nearly as frightening as that of the vash'ai queen.

"You will die for this, Outsider," she spat. "You will *die.*"

TEN

"**Y**ou will *die*."

Those words wrapped round Leviathus like the coils of a sea serpent, squeezing the breath from his lungs. Blood pounded in his ears, deafening him to the rest of Mariza's words. His hands shook, bowels turned to water, and he was drenched all over in a sudden cold sweat, despite the oppressive Zeerani heat.

So that is what it feels like, an odd, quiet voice in the dark of his mind remarked. Leviathus had read about fear-sweat, of course, but he had never experienced it himself. *Now I will be able to write about it in my memoirs. If I live.*

The odds, he had to admit, were not in his favor.

It occurred to the son of Ka Atu, in that moment, that he very much wanted to live. This in itself was a surprise. For days now—days so long and bleak they had bled together into a single endless nightmare—he had *expected* to die. As the women beat and caressed him in turns, as they mocked his body's shameful responses to their cruelty, he had come to think that he would welcome death.

Better to die a king's son, he had told himself, *than live as a slave*. Surely death would be a gentler mistress than these hard-eyed women. Yet as the fear-serpent loosed its coils, as breath filled his lungs once more and the shadows drew back from his eyes, Leviathus thought that the air had never tasted sweeter. Nor had the sunlight felt so sweetly warm as in that sharp moment. The desert shone rainbow gold beneath the gaze of Akari. It sang sweet and low in the dying wind.

One of the horses snorted. How had he never before noticed the perfection of the horse, the way its neck arched with graceful power, the gentle poetry in its eyes? How had he thought the churrim, shaggy-haired and sturdy, was anything less than wonderful? Even the na'iyeh, as still as cacti in the rising light, seemed marvelous. And the Mah'zula, famed warriors of the days before the Sundering…

Well, the Mah'zula can go fuck themselves, truly, he thought. *But the rest of this world is wonderful, and I am not yet ready to leave it for the Lonely Road.*

A dark voice grated in his mind. *Ah, but what does life hold for you?* This voice had woken sometime during his first night of torment among the Mah'zula, and Leviathus had not yet been able to force it to silence. *What do* you *have that is worth living for?*

"Books," he muttered. There were books in the world he had not yet read—books that had yet to be written—books that he, himself, longed to write.

"Books?" Mariza barked a laugh. "All you can say is 'books'? Truly, King's Son, you are mad."

"Those poets who speak of the Zeeranim," Leviathus answered, words an awkward tangle, "speak thusly of your warriors…

"'…and Zula Din sent them forth as a mercy upon the world…'"

Mariza snorted. "Your books are not complete, Outlander. The rest of that verse died in Saodan, burnt to ash in the Sundering. But we remember, we daughters of Akari. 'Verily, Akari has one thousand grains of mercy. One of them is to stay the warrior's blade, and the rest are reserved for the Day of Waking.' Mercy will not stay my blade this day, Outlander. It is more merciful by far that you should die. *Ehuani*, it is justice."

She drew her sun-bright blade.

"*Ehuani*," the rest of the Mah'zula breathed with one voice. "*Shu'ah kha'ani, bas Akari ehuani.*"

"Mercy." Mariza spat. Her face was a mad mask of hatred, her eyes fever-bright. "Your father sits far away on a golden throne, knowing nothing of the world, nothing of us, yet he expects us to bow at his feet. He steals our magic, he drains the Zeera of sa and ka, he breaks the bond that holds us Zeeravashani, leaving us to the greater predators… and his son cries to us for leniency. Do you call your father's reign merciful, King's Son? Where is your father's mercy, when his magic tricks kill our people? When the slavers steal our children to fill the ever-empty belly of Atukos?"

Leviathus blinked. "My father... he... he keeps the world safe from the dragon's waking." It sounded weak, even to his own ears—a pitcher too full of holes to ever hold mead. "Only he can—"

"Lies," Mariza hissed. "Lies, lies. There is no dragon sleeping beneath Atukos, no magic in your king save that which he has stolen from us, and with our thanks. That ends now, that ends here. He has stolen his power from us and we will take it back from him."

"*Ehuani*," the Mah'zula muttered in unison. There is beauty in truth.

Leviathus opened his mouth, but no argument came forth. Too much of what was said here held the ring of truth.

"We will take our power back from him, our songs, our strength," Mariza said. She no longer looked at Leviathus. Her eyes stared blindly into a future that held no place for him. "We will return the Zeeranim to our former glory, and once more will the world tremble at the thunder of our passing. We will strip the Dragon King of his stolen power... but first we will strip him of his son."

Leviathus drew a deep and shuddering breath. "There is some truth in what you say—"

"Shut your hole, boy." Mariza's words, pure venom, were delivered with the sweetest of smiles. "The only truth you need concern yourself with now, King's Son, is this. All men die." She stabbed her sunblade straight up as if she meant to pierce the soft underbelly of the blue, blue sky.

I should run, Leviathus thought, but his feet seemed less resolute about living than did his mind. They remained firmly in place. *It is not meet that a king's son should die so, in the middle of nowhere, doing nothing. Should not my life make a difference? Even a small difference?*

The blade arced down, but it met a lesser blade, and screamed to a halt.

"*Eh-la, Mariza, lest hayam*." Ani stood still and calm, holding

91

her knife with no more effort than one might hold a writing quill. The tension that had been building in the youthmistress's body had bled away and she smiled, an easy smile that reached her eyes and lit up her face from within.

Oh, Leviathus thought stupidly. *I see now why Askander loves her.*

"A blade that seeks this boy's flesh will have to go through mine first—and I am no easy meat, *ehuani.*"

Mariza's mouth went slack with shock before spreading into a sly grin, and she lowered her shamsi.

"Will you die for him, then, Dzirani? Will the bonesinger's daughter give her life for the son of a false king? I had thought you were wise." She laughed, and the Mah'zula laughed with her.

"If I choose to do so it is my right," Ani replied. "How do you hope to restore the old ways, if you break our laws now?"

"'Our' laws, Dzirani? '*Our*' laws? Would you keep pretending to be one of us? Or do you champion this *das'anas*, this son of the enemy? It is time for you to choose sides, bonesinger scum."

Ani glanced at Leviathus and sighed dramatically, though the gleam in her eyes spoke of nothing but mirthful anticipation.

"It is a good day to die, *ehuani.*" The smile on her face never faltered. "It is a better day to live."

"Indeed it is," Mariza agreed. "It is a very good day for *you* to die."

Ani threw her head back, and laughed.

When the Ja'Akari, wild women of the desert, ride into battle, it is a glorious and fearsome sight. They shave the sides of their heads and fasten all manner of bones, beads and feathers into their tight braids.

Their faces are painted in feline snarls, and those who have managed to tame one of the giant desert cats—vash'ai, they name them—may also tattoo their limbs and torsos with lines and spots, in an attempt to make themselves appear even less human.

As they join in the fray, the barbarian females eschew all decorum, going so far as to bare their breasts as they howl and snarl for the blood of their enemies. These wanton displays, perhaps meant to encourage lust in the barbarian male, cannot help but freeze the blood of a civilized man…

——Pedantus ap Geoppus, Loremaster to the king, in the twelfth year of the reign of Azhi Dahaka

Mariza was right about one thing, Leviathus mused. *All the king's bards and all of his fools could scarce begin to describe the utter strangeness of the Zeeranim.*

He had suffered at their hands, and had he a tenth of his father's magic he would slay them all as they stood, and yet he found them fascinating in their strangeness. Much as one might find a viper fascinating, he thought, even beautiful.

A circle was prepared for the fight, laid out in fragments of stone colored red with chalk. Ani and Mariza stood facing each other. Feathers and beads of bone had been woven into Mariza's stiffened mane and Ani's graying braids, and their faces had been painted so that it seemed they were a pair of snarling vash'ai. Laid bare, Mariza's body proved to be mottled and striped as a cat's—as was Ani's, he realized with some surprise. When had the Shahaydrim youthmistress received the barbarian tattoos? For surely she had possessed none when their journey began. The patterns, though very faint, nevertheless marked her as Zeeravashani for all eyes to see.

She said that she and the wild vash'ai were not bonded, he remembered.

So much for beauty in truth.

The other Mah'zula sat in a wide ring outside the battle-circle. Two of them held small skin drums, and these they tapped with long, strong fingers, *thrum-thrum-shushhhh, thrum-throb-shushhhh*. Four of them sat so close behind Leviathus that he could feel the heat of their excitement.

Thrum-thrum-THROB-shushhhh.

The two women threw back their heads as one, and in unison they yelled their war cries, yowling shrieks that recalled the death

93

songs of hunting cats, high and growling and wild, slashing the still air like claws and sending a chill down his spine. Together they yanked the laces of their beaded vests, baring their breasts in the ancient sign of contempt for an enemy.

The drums fell silent, and two sunblades flashed beneath the hot eyes of Akari.

When his sister Sulema fought her friend, the dark-eyed Hannei, Leviathus had considered it a breathtaking display of warriors' skill. Now as the older women spun into battle, a mad storm of growls and blades and dark, flashing eyes, he quickly realized that the earlier contest had been little more than the tussling of half-grown cubs.

This, he could not help but think, *this is art. This is beauty. This is what my father's poets try—and fail—to capture in their weak dribbles of ink.*

Lithe brown bodies slashed and dodged, thrust and parried. At first the younger, shorter woman seemed to hold the advantage. Her steps were a shade faster, her leaps higher, her battle cries ringing out across the sands with the heedless vigor of youth. The older woman, graying and sinewy, favored the left knee and seemed to tire quickly, mopping a forearm across her brow even as she narrowly avoided a vicious slash to the midsection.

And yet…

…though Ani's movements seemed hesitant, tentative, though she shielded her weak leg and seemed to flinch from contact with her younger opponent, her eyes betrayed nothing but cold, hard calculation. She was a queen, stalking prey much hardier and stronger than herself, never doubting but that she would be licking blood from her whiskers as the dust settled.

Ani faltered, nearly going to one knee. Mariza leapt, screaming, feet churning the air and sunblade sweeping out and down in a vicious arc. Her fellow riders cheered her on. At the last possible moment Ani regained her feet, staggering back just out of reach as Mariza landed—

—a little too hard, having overshot her center of gravity. Her guard dropped low as she fought to regain her balance.

Her eyes, Leviathus thought. *You should have been watching Ani's eyes.*

Even as his thoughts betrayed him, even as his heart was caught up in the ferocious grace of the contest before him, the blade of Ani licked out like a tongue of flame. A spray of Mariza's life fell in drops upon the sand, a poem written in blood. The leader of the Mah'zula clamped her left arm tight to her side, and her snarl-painted face contorted in pain and fury.

"Dzirani scum," she panted, "you…"

"Oh, shut *up*," Ani replied. Her blade flashed again, and again, opening toothless red smiles across Mariza's throat and across her ribs. Red froth poured upon the sand, thick and hot as mulled wine.

Mariza's mouth dropped open in a soundless shriek.

Her blade dropped to the sand, and she dropped to her knees, eyes going wide and blank as she realized that she was dead.

Silence fell once more upon the Zeera. The singing dunes went mute, and the warriors' drums tumbled to the sand. Akari Sun Dragon seemed to stoop in mid-flight, casting a curious eye upon the tableau so far below him. The world held its breath beneath that hungry regard.

But dragons, being dragons, never pause for long to consider the matters of men and women. He flew on, the world turned, and the Zeera once more took up its low, slow song.

Or so it seemed to Leviathus.

As life rushed once more into the world, fury rushed back into the Mah'zula. They leapt to their feet, screaming at the sight of their dead leader. Mariza had toppled to lie upon her back, knees up, one arm behind her in what would have been a terribly uncomfortable position had she not been dead.

Dead, he thought, and he smiled.

It is a good day to die, he remembered the youthmistress saying, *but it is an even better day to live.* He looked with new respect upon the old warrior, who had cleaned her sword and sheathed it, and who now stood lacing her vest as if nothing else in the world could possibly concern her. She had taken wounds in the battle—blood trickled from a cut across her forehead and two cuts on her off arm, washed down her leg from one high on her right thigh—but she paid them no mind.

Askander is a lucky man.

"You killed her!" one of the youngest warriors screamed. Oufa, her name was, and Leviathus knew her to be less cruel than her sword sisters. "You *killed* her!"

"As one does," Ani agreed. She considered the deeper cut on her arm, licked the blood away, and shrugged. "What did you think swords are for, little one? Cutting your meat into pieces small enough to chew?" And she laughed.

"Dzirani scum." Ghaleta spat. "Now *you* will die."

At that Ani looked up, blood still on her mouth, and again Leviathus was reminded of a wild vash'ai queen. "*Khutlani*," she said, voice as soft as a purr. "The laws of the proxy fight are older than the bones of the Zeera, and they are clear. No hand may touch the warrior who emerges victorious."

"As you are no warrior, the laws do not apply." Ghaleta spat again, twisting her mouth into an ugly mask. The other warriors drew in close till they stood in a tight circle, just outside the battle ring where Mariza lay dead.

Leviathus stood as he realized that the warriors who had guarded him had joined their sisters. For the first time in two moons, he was unattended and ignored. The spotted churra he had been riding was but a short sprint away. *I could escape*, he thought, heart pounding. *With enough of a lead, I might escape.*

"You would break the ancient laws, then?" Ani drew her sunblade and faced them, defiant. Her face was a mask of dark disdain, and still her eyes showed no fear. "Truly, you are Kha'Akari."

Was he the kind of man who could abandon a woman, after all she had sacrificed for him? *No*, he decided. *I am not. I am more than a king's son. Though my name die here, it should have meant something.* He looked around for a weapon, that he might stand and defend the older warrior, but he saw none.

"You misunderstand me, *shara'haram*." Ghaleta smiled an ugly smile. She unslung the bow from across her shoulders, nocked an arrow and drew in a single, smooth motion. "No hand will touch you, this day." With those words, her arrow flew. Ani dodged, but not quickly enough. The arrow took her high in one thigh, and she let out a deep grunt of pain as that leg threatened to buckle.

Several warriors dropped their swords and bows upon the sand as they stared aghast at Ani, then at Ghaleta. Two or three others, laughing, took up their bows and drew.

Ani drew herself up to her full height, grimacing as she took a warrior's stance. For a moment, she locked eyes with Leviathus, and her lips quirked in a hard little smile.

Go, she mouthed. *Go. Run.*

Against the urging of his heart, the Dragon King's son did a thing that would haunt him to the end of his days. He turned and sprinted for the spotted churra. He grabbed up the churra's lead—it would serve as reins, he hoped—clambered onto its back, and kicked the squealing, protesting beast into a flat-footed sprint. Away from the warriors, away from the battle, away from his courage and pride and everything that he had thought made him a man. Away from Ani, whose final battle might buy him enough of a head start to survive this day.

Behind him, Leviathus heard the final battle cry of a brave warrior, he heard the soft twang as arrows were released. He heard the scream of an enraged stallion, ringing through the air, more powerful and pure than any ancient law, more broken than any human heart.

He did not look back.

E L E V E N

Hannei drank deep of the sweet, sweet water, and smiled at Tammas over the rim of the loving cup. She could see her forever in his eyes.

"My man," she told him. "Mine."

He looked at her, and his eyes widened with puzzlement.

"If I am yours," he asked her, "why did you kill me?" The words spilled from his lips like blood, poisoning the love she held between them.

"I never did," she protested. "It was Sareta."

"Liar." Tammas drew his lips back, baring teeth in a rictus snarl. "You lie."

And the moons drew a shadow over his face.

Someone slapped her, hard. Again. Then again.

Hannei jerked upright and would have broken the hands that struck her, but all she managed to do was jerk ineffectively against her rough bonds and blink as she was hauled into the harsh light. Rough hands grabbed her arms, dug into her ribs. Fingers twisted into her warrior's locks and dragged her from one nightmare only to toss her into another.

How long had she been in that pit, bound and left to lie in her own stinking misery?

A skin of water was smashed against her lips and Hannei opened her mouth. At first she had refused water, and food, and all that had gotten her was a missing tooth. It was not worth the effort.

After so long in the dark, the hot stare of Akari blinded her. After so long in silence, the roar of voices was deafening. Hannei swallowed the tepid water, muddied with her own blood and bile, then chewed the bread they stuffed between her teeth, and swallowed the anger of her people as they called her murderer. None of it mattered. She would be dead soon enough.

As the shadows pulled back from her eyes, Hannei could see that the day was still young. It was not yet midsun. The warriors would have tended the horses, and perhaps gone hunting. The kitchen mothers would be pounding out bread, young girls laughing in disgust as they cleaned the churra pens and pretended not to notice the boys who just happened to veer close as they fetched water for the wardens. Another day rolling by under the sun, shiny and bright with the promise of beauty.

Not for me, she thought, poking the tip of her tongue into the space where a tooth had been. *Never again.* The world rolled on as if Tammas had never been. She wanted no part of it.

They marched her past the smithy, where small children poured water into urns, there to be salted and oiled for the quenching of shamsi. Past the churra pits and the eyes of young girls who paused in their chores to watch the small, silent group. Sareta walked in front of her, sandals kicking up puffs of angry dust to coat the hem of Hannei's tattered and too-big prisoner robe.

Lirya and Isara walked to either side. These were warriors she had laughed with, trained with, warriors whose backs she had guarded— and who now turned their backs on her, when the hour was dark.

Behind her, Hannei knew, the people were setting aside their chores. They would brush wood chips from their aprons and flour from their hands, set aside fishing pole and pestle and sword, and those same hands would pick up stones as they followed her, stones with which to weigh her guilt.

Three times in her life had Hannei watched a criminal be tried. One of them, an accused thief, had survived the ordeal—though by no means intact. Never in her life could Hannei have imagined that hers would be the feet to walk this road. Never in her darkest dreams had she looked into the eyes of her people to see… this.

All because Sareta sought to destroy Tammas's entire family. What was it she had said? *"The line of Zula Din has grown soft and wicked, and so must be ended."* Thus Hannei's one great love was dead, and she had become just another victim of the First Warrior's schemes.

Her dreams were much darker now.

The path was not well worn, nor was it long. It led them a little to the east of Aish Kalumm, past the groves and the pastures where the mares Hannei had owned and loved ran with the herds, under the watchful eyes of young girls who did not know that one day they, too, might wear the robes of the accused, the yoke of the condemned.

Lirya bumped into her so that Hannei tripped. Bound and unable to save herself Hannei fell, hard, upon her knees and then her face. She struggled for a moment to right herself, with no more hope than a turtle upended on the butcher's block. Then a hand twisted into her warrior's braids and dragged her upright, panting and moaning at the pain despite her best efforts.

It was Sareta who held her. Hannei looked up into that ageless face, the face she had loved more fiercely than a mother's, and spat.

"You," she croaked, her voice as dry and dead as old bones. *"Murderer."*

Unconcerned, Sareta wiped the spittle from her cheek with the hem of her tunic. "Gag her," she told Lirya. "That tongue speaks only lies."

"Kha'Akari," Lirya growled. She tore a filthy strip from Hannei's own robe and used it to bind her mouth. "I hope they kill you."

Infuriated tears pricked at Hannei's eyes as she stared at her former sister.

I do, too, she thought.

Then they arrived.

A small tree, bent and wizened as a crone, stood atop a low and rocky hill, immune to the ravages of time and wind and the tears of innocent girls. Before the tree lay a low stone table, and around the table stood those who would judge her—those who had already judged her, she knew—elders of the prides, craftmasters and mothers, warriors and wardens...

…and Ismai, last of the line of Zula Din.

Hannei was led as a kid to slaughter through rows of people silent and grim as the Bones of Eth, and made to stand upon the stone. Tears upon her cheeks, a filthy gag in her mouth, stewing in the stench of her own sour sweat, nevertheless she raised her face to the sun, and met the fierce gaze of Akari Sun Dragon with her own fire.

I am Hannei Ja'Akari, she told him, mute though she was. *Warrior of the Zeeranim. See what they do to your daughter.*

When she looked once more upon the people, her eyes were as dry as her heart. Umm Jeila, First Mother of all the prides, stepped from beneath the tree's thin shade to stand at the foot of the stone table. She was flanked by Sareta and by Mastersmith Hadid, who acted as first warden in the absence of Askander Ja'Sajani.

Pain lanced through Hannei, but she firmed her trembling mouth. *When a warrior has already fallen*, she asked herself, *what is one more arrow to the heart?*

"People of the Zeera," Umm Jeila began, "warriors and wardens, craftmistresses and 'masters, Mothers and children. My children, all. We are brought together here in grief and in rage, and on this day we beg Akari for justice."

Justice, the crowd hissed. *Justice.*

"One among us stands accused of the most hideous of crimes. On the night of Sharib, even as we celebrated new life, we were attacked by the Kha'Akari, shadow-warriors whose tongues speak only lies. Murder was committed that night. Murder, and worse than murder. An attempt was made that night to erase the line of Zula Din by slaughtering the children of our beloved Umm Nurati…"

A sour taste filled Hannei's mouth, the taste of blood. She felt light, as if she had stepped outside the shell of her own body and might float away. She swayed, but the rough hands that held her would not allow her to fall.

"…Rudya, four years of age. Umm Neptara, nineteen years of age, who was with child. The unnamed infant of Umm

Nurati, butchered as she slept. Tammas Ja'Sajani…"

Hannei screamed around the gag, as every drop of blood in her veins cried out for absolution. The eyes of her people were upon her like hot coals, burning her with their condemnation. She would have screamed again, but something hit her hard in the back of her head. She fell to her knees, ears ringing.

"As I have said, these murders were carried out by Kha'Akari. All of these murders… save one. Tammas Ja'Sajani was murdered by one of our own, by a sister of the sword, who wooed him with words of love and a poisoned loving cup, and then thrust her sword… through his back."

The crowd moaned, a long sound like sand beneath a killing wind. The sound of Tammas's last breath. Hannei closed her eyes as Sareta stepped forth with her proofs—a cup, a sword. A flensing knife, wicked thing, with a golden spider crouched atop the hilt. Hannei closed her eyes. She had seen these things before. Would that she could close her ears, become deaf to the voices that called for her death. Would that she could close her heart, pierced again and again.

Make it stop, she begged Akari. *Under your eyes, I am innocent. Make it stop.* But Akari Sun Dragon held his silence and let his people condemn her.

They formed two long lines, a gauntlet of fury, as the scales of justice were fastened about her neck. As the clasp snicked shut it pinched the skin of her throat, and Hannei grimaced as a trickle of blood welled free to snake between her breasts.

First blood, she thought, heart pounding madly. *But not the last.* She stood upon the table, reed baskets swinging gently at her shoulders, and the people began to file by, passing their judgment.

"Guilty," the first said, dropping a stone into one basket. It was a small stone, such as a child might skip upon the river, yet Hannei bowed under its weight.

"Guilty," the second proclaimed, a man who had looked the other way as two young girls stole into the stallion's pasture to braid beads into the manes of Zeitan fleet-foot and Ruhho the brave-hearted black. He did not look away, now. His stone dropped into the second basket.

"Guilty."

"Guilty."

"Guilty."

As the baskets filled with stones, Hannei staggered and went to one knee.

"Guilty."

"Guilty."

They kept on, long after the weight of their judgment had pinned Hannei's face against the hot stone, every voice and every *clack* of stone on stone sealing her fate. Akari Sun Dragon turned his face from them all, deaf to the lies that called for her blood.

The last pair of feet, a boy's feet and too big for his sandals, stood before her long enough that Hannei rolled her eyes upward. Ismai stood above her, a dark silhouette against the yellow haze, peering at her from the veils of a new blue touar.

"Did you do it?" he asked her directly, violating all tradition. Hannei heard gasps from the people closest to them. Ismai ignored them, eyes dark and hard as flint as he stared at her. "Did you kill my family?"

Pinned as she was against the stone table, Hannei could only twitch her head *no*, could only mouth the word around the vile gag.

He closed his eyes, and his pain was one more arrow to her heart, but Ismai held his stone out to one side and let it drop. It rolled across the table and came to rest against her cheek, soft as a kiss.

"Innocent," he said. "Under the sun, I find Hannei Ja'Akari innocent of these charges."

One stone lay there, one stone weighed against all the others. One voice called her innocent. Hannei watched Ismai's feet walk away. One stone would not be enough to save her.

But it was enough to break her heart.

Hannei's tears washed the stone clean.

T W E L V E

Among the Zeeranim, the worth of a man was measured in different ways. Did he wear the touar? Did he ride a fine horse? Had the vash'ai found him worthy of a bond? If the answers were "yes," "yes," and "yes," he would be considered among his pride's finest treasures, for a man of valor was worth more than his weight in salt.

By these standards, Ismai should have felt whole in his heart. He wore the blue, and with his brothers strove to guide and protect his people. Though his Ehuani was a found horse, and her line could not be traced in the mare books, one had only to observe the depth of her chest, the arch of her neck, and the intelligence in her wide dark eyes to see that she was a daughter of the wind.

He bore a golden shamsi, the mark of his mother's pride, and a sleek vash'ai princess ran by his side of her own free will.

Still, in his mind and in his heart, Ismai believed that the measure of a man should be greater than the sum of those things. That his value might be weighed in the pure truth of his actions. Did he conduct himself with the courage of his convictions? Did he dare to speak when others were silent? Was he as true to the least of his people as to the greatest?

These thoughts growled in his mind as uneasily as the emptiness in his belly as he sat upon the rocky hill with his back pressed firmly against the bark of a knotted tree. There he waited for darkness to fall, with drawn shamsi laid across his knees, a meager fire at his feet, and Ruh'ayya bristling at his side.

The hill, the tree, and the ancient stone table were far enough from Aish Kalumm that the city was little more than a faint orange glow against the indigo sky. Surely the scents of fish and flesh and spice, of bread baking and frothy warm ale, were only the heart's yearning, just as the night which came so swiftly could not possibly be as dark and cold as it seemed.

Hannei still lay, trussed and gagged, on the low stone table. Again and again Ismai cut her bindings, peeled the gag from her mouth, held his waterskin to her parched lips. Time and again he draped his touar over her motionless, cold form. Once, he bade her take his own beloved horse and ride away, far away, to Atualon perhaps. Surely Sulema would welcome her sword sister, would keep her safe where Ismai had failed.

Yet he did these things only in his mind.

He was bound by laws older than the ancient tree, bound as surely as his friend lay tied upon the stone table, and the laws were clear. If he touched Hannei, if he made any attempt to free her before the light of judgment touched the stone table upon which she lay, both of their lives would be forfeit. She had been judged in the sight of Akari, and she would live—or die—beneath the many eyes of Illindra, the weaver of worlds.

Ismai had looked into Hannei's eyes, and his Zeerani soul had recognized *ehuani*. Truth. She had not killed his family.

Murderer, she had spat at Sareta.

Ismai ran his fingers along the side of his shamsi, the golden sunblade gifted to him by his mother. On a bright day, it reflected his face. On a cold night such as this, it reflected the darkest wishes of his heart.

"*Kishah*," he promised aloud, even as he named his sword. "Vengeance I name you, and vengeance is what I will have."

Ruh'ayya stirred against his leg. Her ears were trained hard on the darkening desert, and through their bond he could feel her tension.

What is this kishah? she asked him. *Is it something to eat?* She was still growing, and constantly hungry.

It is what eats at the heart, he explained to her. *Vengeance. When someone has done you wrong, you right the wrong by finding and punishing them.*

Ruh'ayya's ears flattened, twisted forward again, and the tip of her tail twitched in agitation.

I do not understand.

Someone murdered my family, he told her. *My brother, my sisters… my little baby sisters. I will chase them down like tarbok, and I will kill them. Would you not do the same, if someone killed your sire?*

Her tail twitched. *If I were with my sire and we were attacked, I would fight tooth and claw to the death. But after my sire's body was cold and empty, I would not hunt his killers. Such matters are for the* kahanna *to attend to, not for such as I. It is forbidden.*

It is not forbidden among my kind, he responded. *It is… expected. My family was murdered, and I will not rest until I see the torn bodies of their murderers, lying upon this stone table. Perhaps they killed my mother as well. I have wondered before whether she was poisoned.*

The Mother Queen of your people? Ruh'ayya asked, her thought voice colored with surprise. *She was killed in Shehannam, her soul stolen by a dream eater. You did not know this?*

His heart tightened. *You are sure?*

She twisted her head back to stare at him. *The soul was gone before you burned the body. How did you not know this? Her bones were black and empty. There was no song left in them.*

Humans cannot see such things, he told her. His whole body trembled, and he gripped his shamsi so tightly that his hand hurt.

I do not see how you can go through life like that, stumbling around blind and deaf. Ruh'ayya shook her head as if a fly had bitten her ear. *I think I would rather be dead.*

Somewhere in the cold, dark night, a woman screamed. Even as Ismai scrambled to his feet, sword at the ready, her cry was answered by another, a child's shriek that gained in volume and intensity. The cry was joined by another, and another—wails of fright and pain that stretched on and on, past the capacity of human lungs.

Ruh'ayya stood, hackles raised, a low singsong growl rising in her throat. *Mymyc*, she said.

Abruptly the screams stopped. Ismai walked in a half-crouch to stand by the stone table. Hannei lay still, trembling in her thin robes. Visible in the weak firelight, tears rolled down from the corners of her tightly shut eyes, leaving trails through the filth on her face.

"I cannot free you," he whispered, "but I can protect you."

The stars wavered and winked out as a figure larger than a horse, blacker than night, bled out from the darkness. Dragon-red eyes rolled back in merriment as a horse's mouth opened, revealing the yellowed fangs of a greater predator, and it laughed a man's laugh.

We will protect you, Ruh'ayya agreed as she joined him. Her mouth dropped open to reveal her tusks in a cat's grin. *Or we will die.*

There were four of them.

Ruh'ayya was on the first before the beast had fully moved into the thin firelight. In leaping she nearly knocked Ismai on his behind. Her claws were extended and she screamed in fury. Her fangs sank into the mymyc's face even as they both fell back into darkness. There was a series of terrible, coarse screams—from the cat or the mymyc, Ismai could not tell—a deep *thud-thud*, and then a series of low, bubbling grunts.

Vivid images swept over him—*hot blood, bitter, bitter, burns the throat. Strong, strong. 'Ware the hind claws! 'Ware the*—a jumbled mass of bloodlust and excitement, and then it broke off. Ismai felt a surge in his own heart as the second mymyc appeared, just across the low stone table. The predator froze, staring at him and blinking in the thin firelight.

Ismai had only ever seen mymyc from a distance, and they had just looked like largish horses, though with odd, thick, catlike tails arched up over their backs. This close, he could see that they were most decidedly *not* horses. Their eyes were set wide, but facing forward like those of a person, or a vash'ai.

The sleek black hide was not hide at all, but overlapping scales black as obsidian—so black that they drank the firelight. The creature had a stiff brush of bristles where a horse's mane would be, wicked hooked claws on its stubby four-toed feet, and at the end of its tail was a barb like a scorpion's sting, twitching and aroused, a thick stream of viscous liquid drooling from its tip.

Ismai raised his shamsi and was dismayed at how it wavered in his grip. "Show me yours, foul creature!" he yelled—and just then, his voice broke.

What is it? a voice whispered in his mind, sleek and oily as the mymyc's nightstained hide. *Is it a man? It squeaks like a mouse.*

Hardly bigger than a mouse, came a second voice, and Ismai whipped his head back and forth, seeking its source. *A nice mouthful of meat, nevertheless.*

Where is the toothed one? a third voice asked, high and nervous. *And where is Chaitan? I cannot feel her. I think—*

Chaitan will kill the worthless cat, the second voice said. It seemed to Ismai that this one had moved closer, and he edged nearer to the table.

Hannei did not move. She scarcely seemed to breathe. *If I fail*, Ismai thought, *they will kill her, and she cannot even fight back.* The thought gave him courage. False courage or no, he would use it, and he firmed his grip upon the blade.

Tucking one foot behind the other so that most of his weight was grounded in the ball of his forward foot, he twisted his hips slightly and raised both hands. He held his weapon steady and true, as if daring his foe to leap onto its blade. Moons ago, a lifetime ago, *Catching the Cat* had been a form beyond his ability. On this night, it came as easy as breathing.

As easy as dying, the second voice said. At that very moment Ismai *knew*. He pivoted, keeping his stance true and bringing his blade up even as the mymyc reared behind him, striking out with clawed forelegs, envenomed tail lashing madly from side to side as it screamed his name.

She came like black fire in the night, smoke and heat, fury and death. Ruh'ayya did not scream but sank her tusks to the hilt into the mymyc's spine, both of her forepaws raking at the armored black shoulders and her hind claws kicking and clawing at its softer underbelly, seeking to disembowel the enemy. The mymyc fell hard, thrashing and screaming in a voice not borrowed from its prey, a deep thick shriek of outraged agony.

Ismai pivoted again, expecting the smaller mymyc to be upon him, but the creature stood wide-eyed and frozen at the sight of its packmate being disemboweled by a vash'ai. Ismai charged forward on wings of excitement and fear, shamsi flashing in the firelight, and brought his blade down across its face.

The mymyc reared, squealing, and the blade was torn from his grip. One thick forepaw caught his shoulder, while the other scored his throat with a thin line as the beast thrashed blindly, spraying blood across his touar, across Hannei on the low stone table, across the cooling sand. It dug at its face with one paw, dislodging his sword, and wheeled to run bellowing into the night.

Ismai crouched and waited, but there was silence. The predators had gone, leaving only the smell of death.

He was past caring about ancient laws, be they the laws of man or vash'ai, the laws of the Zeera, or the word of Akari himself. Though his life might be forfeit at sunrise, he retrieved his sword and cut the rough ropes that bound Hannei so cruelly. He peeled the gag from her mouth and pushed back the braids plastered to the side of her head. He fetched his waterskin for her, and made a poor blanket of his touar.

Neither of them spoke. After a time he lay beside her. There were no words, and they would likely both die in the morning. Ismai curled his body around Hannei's, and Ruh'ayya curled around them both. The three of them fell fast into the boneless, heedless, absolute sleep of broken youth.

Ismai stood and faced his elders chin up, chest out, hands tucked beneath his armpits to hide their trembling. Before him, in a half circle, stood people who loomed as large in his life as statues carved into a mountain. Sareta, First Warrior of the prides, was chief among them, and she looked as if she would like to skin him neck to ankles.

I almost miss the mymyc, he confided to Ruh'ayya. *They were not half as bad as this.*

They were bad, his kithren replied. *I feel as if my sire picked me up by the scruff of the neck and shook me until my bones popped.*

Ismai rolled his torn shoulder. *They were pretty bad,* he agreed, *but at least they did not lecture us before attacking.*

"… could be forfeit by your actions, do you understand me, boy?" Sareta said. "I do not believe that you understand the severity of your trespass. What you have done is—"

"I understand." For a mercy, his voice was steady. It stung that she had called him *boy.* "I understand that my duty as a warden is to protect even the least of my people."

"He is right." Ismai stared wide-eyed as Jasin stepped through the crowd of elders. He planted his feet and scowled fiercely, but Ismai noted that his fellow Ja'Sajani, too, kept his hands tucked out of sight. "The stone table stands within our borders, and Hannei Ja'Akari is still of the people."

"Hannei Kha'Akari." Sareta spat. Her face was stone. "She has been named exile by her sword sisters, and the face of Akari has turned from her. I am of half a mind to exile you, as well, boy. Were I first warden…"

"But you are not." Hadid stood easily, face smooth, hands on his hips, and he did not flinch as Sareta rounded her furious gaze upon him. Ismai supposed that the mastersmith had faced hotter fires than even that stare. "In the… unexpected absence of Askander Ja'Sajani Akibra, I am acting first warden, Ja'Akari, and I say the boy has not broken our laws in any meaningful way. He is young and misguided, yes, but his intentions were true, *ehuani,* and by our most ancient laws allowances for such must be made."

"So he will face no punishment?"

"He will lose a friend this day, First Warrior. Is that not a harsh punishment? Have we not lost enough of our people, that you would throw this life away, as well? Would you, yourself, end the line of Zula Din? The boy has lost too much. *We* have lost too much. Let the bloodshed end now."

"His kithren," Jasin blurted, then he blushed a deep red as all eyes turned to him. "I mean… his vash'ai… she has not deserted him, when so many others have returned to the wild. Surely that means something."

"Young Jasin has a point," an older warden agreed. "We should heed the wisdom of our kithren. My own Avahha has been gone this fortnight past, and I can only hope to be worthy of her return. Let us not in our haste offend the vash'ai further than we already have."

A murmur ran through the small crowd and Sareta frowned. Ismai saw her eyes dart this way and that, weighing her options, then she shook her head in disgust.

"As you say… First Warden. Truly, it is not I who will end the line of Zula Din, or incur the wrath of the vash'ai." She turned. "Very well, young Ismai, I commute the sentence of death for your actions this night."

Commute?

"You will not be killed," she continued, "nor yet exiled. Hannei Kha'Akari will not be killed… but neither will she be fully pardoned and allowed to return to the people. Your actions, and not her own innocence, allowed her to survive her night of atonement."

Ismai opened his mouth to protest, but a rapid shake of Hadid's head stilled his tongue. *Be wary*, the mastersmith's eyes warned. *Be'ware.*

Best keep still, Ruh'ayya agreed. *That woman smells of the hunt. She is being deceitful. She will kill you, if she can.*

The people stirred and parted as a fist of warriors, led by Lirya, arrived bearing bundles of dry wood. Ignoring him completely, they began to build a fire at the base of the stone table, very near where Ismai stood. He shivered in the dry heat of morning as chill sweat ran down his spine.

"Hannei has survived atonement, and by law I cannot

put her to death for the murders of Nurati's children." Sareta leaned forward and spat into the sand. "However, I know in my heart that she is guilty. Guilty! And though I cannot put her to death for these crimes, I can—and I do—banish her from the pridelands forever. Ja'Akari no more, I name her Hannei Kha'Akari, abandoned and despised by Akari Sun Dragon and by his true people. She will be taken from the pridelands and sold into slavery in Min Yaarif, never to return, upon pain of death."

Another fist of warriors arrived, and another.

Hannei, still seated upon the stone table, curled into herself and collapsed, sobbing.

"And *you*, young warden, you will be among those who will escort the prisoner to Min Yaarif, to see this sentence carried out. You will see what manner of life your actions this night have bought your… friend."

The younger warriors built the fire high, higher. Lirya took out a long knife and laid the blade in the flames.

"This Kha'Akari wears a warrior's braids, and she used her warrior's tongue to speak lies," the First Warrior continued. "Neither of these things belong to her, now. They will be taken from her and fed to the flames. May the scent of their smoke please Akari and buy us favor in his eyes once again."

"No!" Ismai shouted. An older warrior grabbed him by the shoulders and dragged him away from the stone table, kicking and yelling. "No! You cannot do this!"

"Sareta—" Hadid stepped forward, but Sareta stopped him with a hand to his chest. The warriors made a ring around the stone table and the weeping prisoner, hands on the hilts of their swords as if they would fight their own people.

"This is Ja'Akari business," Sareta informed them. "The rest of you may leave." With that, the crowd was herded away—some protesting, most not—by a fist of older warriors.

Their faces are stone, Ismai thought, *and their hearts, as well. They follow their First Warrior more truly than they follow the way of the people.* He tried to look back, but a shove between his shoulder blades sent him stumbling forward.

"Keep going, little man," the warrior who had pushed him said roughly. "You do not want to piss us off any more than you already have."

Little man, indeed. Ruh'ayya, pressed to his side, snarled. Ismai opened his mouth to protest.

Then Hannei began to scream.

THIRTEEN

There came a *tap, tap, TAP* upon the bamboo screen.

The dammati jumped to their feet. Those who had survived their Inseeing had without exception been shattered and scarred, inside and out, and wore violence as once the pearl diver's boy from Bizhan had worn his new yellow silks. Jian looked up from his calligraphy and nodded to Perri, who stood closest to the door.

"Enter," he called out, voice breaking on the second syllable. His voice had been doing strange things since... that day. Nobody laughed. There had been many changes among the Yellow Road princes, still new to the ways of Daechen, including the loss of laughter.

Come the next Nian-da, he and his fellows would move into the Red Palace—Jian did not wish to dwell upon what fresh pain the Red Road might have in store for them. A new horde of yellow Daechen would take their place.

A troop of lashai marched in, nodding first to Jian's dammati and then to him. There had been changes among the pale servants, as well. As the ranks of Daechen had dwindled, so had the numbers of the lashai grown. Jian forced himself to meet the white-powdered, blank-eyed stare of one who bore a silver pitcher. Hakkuo had been among his dammati, and Jian had failed to protect him.

"I am sorry," he whispered as the other boy bent to fill his cup with fragrant water. He had grown... less... since leaving them, Jian thought. Thinner, certainly, and shorter, if such a thing was possible. "Hakkuo..." Their eyes met, and Jian recoiled. The thing wearing Hakkuo's face smiled with his mouth, and laughed at Jian through his eyes, but Hakkuo was no more.

"Sorry for what, Sen-Baradam?" Xienpei laughed, swaying into the room. She came on a dancer's feet, every move of her body, every turn of her head calculated far in advance and carried out like a battle plan. The yendaeshi spun round, taking in the room full of sullen young men on the brink of violence, and her grin widened, jewels flashing in the candlelight.

Jian fought the urge to jump to his feet, to apologize, to hide. Had he once thought her smile motherly? If she was a mother, then she was as the daemon mothers in the old stories, the ones who swallowed children whole and gave birth again to monsters.

The nib of his pen broke, splattering black blood upon the parchment's fine white skin. He blinked at the ruined pen for a moment, then laid it beside its fallen comrades. Jian went through a great many pens these days. Picking up a stained square of silk, he wiped ineffectively at his fingertips.

"I am sorry," he repeated, "I seem to have forgotten that you were coming today. I had thought to spend the time in contemplation of the philosophies of General Yu Fengui. The man was a brilliant strategist." Yu Fengui had, indeed, been a distinguished general. He had also been one of the worst traitors in Sindanese history, whose betrayal had ultimately led to the defeat of the Red Emperor.

Her smile hardened. "You walk a sharp road, Daechen Jian. 'Ware it does not cut your feet."

"If I walk this road, it is because you drew the map," he countered, pressing his hands hard against the table to hide their shaking. But there was no hiding in the Yellow Palace, certainly not from the eyes of the yendaeshi.

"Leave us," Xienpei said, sweeping the room with her gaze. The lashai turned as one and departed. The dammati looked first to their Sen-Baradam. Jian nodded his assent and they sauntered from the room, unhurried and arrogant. Perri went last, shooting half a dark and displeased look at Xienpei as he did so.

"Sen-Baradam…" he began.

"Go," Jian told him. "You should work on your penmanship, as well, Daechen Perri. Your calligraphy reminds one of a drunken chicken dipped in ink."

It was not a lie.

Perri nodded and turned to go, every line of his body stiff and reluctant. The screened door banged shut behind him, and Jian was alone with Xienpei. He finished wiping his fingertips with the silk cloth, and tossed it aside.

"You wished to speak with me, Yendaeshi?"

"You walk a sharp road," she reiterated, "and a dangerous one. Are you certain you wish to continue? It may not end as you expect. What lies has Mardoni been feeding you? That he and others of the Sen-Baradam will seize power from the emperor, and make the world a safer place for young Daechen?" She swayed closer and plucked a blood orange from a bowl at the edge of his table. "Mardoni has the courage to confront the emperor, perhaps, but he does not possess the strength to challenge the might of Daeshen Tiachu. Such an army does not exist in this world."

Jian lifted the ruined parchment and regarded it. Even before the spray of ink, it had not been a masterpiece of calligraphy. In truth, his hand was little better than Perri's. He crumpled the paper and tossed it aside, even though the paper and ink had cost as much as a villager's life might be worth.

"What choice have I?" he asked, voice low and soft. "If I walk this road, it is because you set me upon it. If I run to my doom, it is because you crack the whip at my back. We both know that I have less choice in this than a farmer's ox on its way to market."

"You speak a great many words, Daechen Jian, for one who knows so little." Her teeth flashed, her eyes flashed, bright and hard as knives. "This road leads, as you say, to slaughter. Your own, most certainly. One such as you does not defy the emperor and expect to live. Would you throw away your life, then? It seems such a waste." She raised her hand, and Jian could see that she had crushed the orange in her palm. As her lacquered nails tore into its flesh, a sweet fragrance filled the room, and juice ran down her forearm like blood, to stain the silks of her twilight robe. "I have worked so hard to get you here, it would be a shame to see you throw it all away. Will you not choose another path?"

"What other path?" he demanded. Pleaded. "I see no other way." Cold sweat trickled down his spine. How much did she know of his plans? *Too much. She always knows too much.*

"Then let me draw you a new map, Daechen Jian. A map of the middle way, the path of compliance." Xienpei laughed, lovely and light as a girl gathering flowers. "Life can be bitter." She brought her hand to her mouth and bit into the mangled orange, rind and all. "But it can be sweet, as well. Would you like a taste?" She moved the ruined orange toward Jian's mouth.

"You have drunk deep of the bitterness of pain, and death," she continued. "Now you might choose to bend to my will—and the will of the emperor—and discover what sweetness this life has to offer. I ask you again, Daechen Jian. Would you like a taste?" This close, the rent fruit looked like bloody meat. It smelled wonderful.

Jian closed his eyes and swallowed bile. *If I do not bend, or at least make a pretense of it,* he thought, *sooner or later I will break.*

"I would," he replied. "Very much."

"Excellent," she whispered, close to his ear. "Excellent."

Jian was bathed by the lashai, scrubbed to within an inch of his life and with his hair scraped back into a severe prince's knot at the back of his head. He wore yellow silks—not the peasant's silks his mother had sewn for him so carefully, stained with her tears and blood, nor yet the finer, if plain, yellow silks worn by a prince in training. These were the heavy layered robes of a Daechen prince, stiff with embroidery, laced tight at waist and wrist and ankle, and so thickly padded they might make a serviceable armor.

Xienpei herself assisted in dressing him. Hers were the hands that looped the strings of amber and jade around his neck, and the string of midnight pearls that whispered *never forget*. Hers were the hands that charred his lids with kohl, and pinched his cheeks with rouge, and—to his surprise—fastened the shongwei's tooth at his waist as a soldier might wear a sword. When at last Jian was prepared for the feast, his yendaeshi stood back from him, clasping her hands before her breast and beaming with delight.

The hairs on the back of his neck prickled. He would sooner try to ride a mymyc than trust that jeweled smile.

His fears were not eased as Xienpei sent the lashai about their business and slipped him from the palace grounds. Many times now they had walked or ridden the paths to the river Kaapua. It was a treat to breathe the free air, to sit beside the restless waters, listening to them sing of wishes and flowers and mountains. If Jian had especially pleased his yendaeshi—usually through some feat of violence—he might even be allowed a swim. These were the times Jian felt almost himself again, almost the boy who had walked, wide-eyed and dreaming, and whispered those dreams to the sea.

Jian had read—in a book he was forbidden to possess—that in the heartless, waterless Zeera, visions hovered over the desert sands, ghosts of mountains and water and shade, of all things the heart might desire. It had occurred to him that these trips to the river might be such visions, that these brief tastes of freedom were tricks and shadows. If he looked at them too closely they might vanish, leaving him with a scarred back, an empty life, and a mouth dry as sand.

A mirage, they called it.

A trap, his heart warned.

Such a thing, he thought, *would make her smile so. Best be 'ware.* But it was one thing to tell the heart to remain quiet, and another altogether to stop it from singing.

When they arrived at the river's edge, they were not alone. Tsalen stood there, his mouth twisted in a grimace that suggested he had been eating green guava. Before him stood a slight figure, clad in a simple yellow robe and hood. A thin silver leash ran from a wide leather collar to the yendaeshi's fist, and he kept tugging it so that the figure would stagger back with a gasp.

Another fight? Jian sighed. He often won, but had wearied of this game long ago, and this little raggedy prince was surely less than a challenge. Still, the prickles at his nape bade him be vigilant. *See how Xienpei smiles*, his gut urged. *See how the other one scowls.*

Xienpei made a motion for Jian to stop and his feet froze of their own accord. He burned, to know that she had him so well trained, but what choice had he? What choice, if he wished to live?

To live, the river sang, *to live. It is a fine day to die, Daechen. It is a better day to live.* His yendaeshi strode on, ignoring Jian and the river and the beauty of the day. She stopped just short of Tsa-len, every line of her body drawn with victorious strokes.

"As agreed?" she asked, holding out a hand. Tsa-len yanked the leash hard, and the slight figure dropped to its knees.

"As agreed," he growled, "though it be your doom, Xienpei. This is foolish, even for you." He handed his end of the leash to Xienpei, bowed stiffly, and turned to stomp away.

"To a fool, the great seem foolish," she said after him, and she laughed. "It is done." She twined the silver chain around her fingers as if it were a string of jewels, and gave a small tug. "Stand," she crooned. "Stand and face me. Ah, very good. Jian, here!"

Jian came to heel, ever her well-trained pet. *Get it over with*, he thought, *and maybe she will let me swim in the river when I have defeated this opponent. Perhaps this time I might stay beneath the water long enough for my song to reach the sea.* Maybe his sea-king father would hear his song and come for him, after all these years.

Or maybe this time I will drown, and my whole life will have been a mirage. He stopped at her side, head bowed, giving the slight figure not so much as a glance. "Yendaeshi?"

"I have a gift for you," she purred. "Greater than salt, young prince. Greater than those pearls you wear. If you had but one wish, Daechen Jian, what would that wish be?"

Freedom, his soul whispered.

'WARE! his heart screamed.

"I would wish to serve the emperor, Yendaeshi."

She snorted. "A good answer, Daechen. It is a lie, but a good answer none the less. And you will serve the emperor—in a way. Let me grant you your wish, Daechen Jian, though you were not wise enough to ask for it." She reached forth and plucked the hood from the yellow-clad figure.

"I know you," Jian blurted without thinking, and he did, though he had seen her only the one time, when both of them had just escaped death. He had dreamed of her, more than once, that pale face like a painting of grief, and those big, dark, sea-deep eyes. Those Issuq eyes blinked against the harsh light, and snapped as angrily as the sea after a storm.

Her little mouth turned down in a frown.

She hates me, he thought, and for a moment it seemed as if he might drown after all.

"Behave," Xienpei told the girl in a mild voice, and Jian ached when she flinched. The yendaeshi reached to unfasten the collar at the girl's throat, and she reached up to rub at the raw skin, never taking her eyes from Jian's.

"I am Jian," he offered lamely. "Daechen Jian."

The girl's frown deepened, and his heart quailed. In all the world she might be the only other creature like him, and already she hated his guts.

Xienpei cleared her throat, and the girl ducked her head.

"I am Tsali'gei," she whispered.

"Tsali'gei," he echoed. Her name danced on his tongue like honey, it stung his heart.

"*Daezhu* Tsali'gei," Xienpei named her thrice, sealing the bargain. "Your new wife."

And the river carried his song to the sea.

FOURTEEN

Akari Sun Dragon was gone, taking light and life and warmth with him. The Mah'zula had gone and left her alone, taking her horse and her sword. Where she was going, Ani would not need them. Inna'hael had gone away, and the world was empty, having been drained of sa and ka even as she had been drained of blood. The wind remained, ever the same, rousing the dunes to a sweet lament for a woman who loved the Zeera.

Too stubborn to run, she thought, *even if it meant saving my own life. And now too stubborn to die.* Askander had often said she would live forever, and for just that reason.

In the end, he had been wrong.

Ani lay half on her back, half on her side with her sword arm twisted uncomfortably beneath her. She was too tired and weak to move. One would think that a chest full of arrows would render such a small irritation meaningless, but the longer she lay there, the more her twisted shoulder pissed her off. Eventually, and with nearly as much effort as it had taken to kill Mariza, she was able to shift her weight enough that she could roll completely onto her back.

Oh, that hurt. That fucking hurt.

She groaned, a bubbling whisper of sound.

Her hand clenched around the hilt of her shamsi. Odd that they had left such a valuable weapon behind. Her hand clenched again as a tremor seized her, and Ani realized that she was not holding her sword, after all, but the cactus-bone flute.

She might have laughed had she the breath. *You*, she thought at the instrument of her destruction, *you did this*. But she could not lie, not even on her last day of life. Most *especially* on her last day of life.

Ehuani, she thought in apology to Akari, *I have done this myself. I made the flute, as Hafsa Azeina showed me. I called them, the na'iyeh, knowing what they were and what that meant. I did this, I alone.*

I regret nothing.

She had been successful, had she not? Mariza was dead. Her faithful arse-licking false warriors were scattered to the wind, and Leviathus had escaped. Ani wished him well. She wished Askander might have witnessed this, her final victory. She wished with all her pierced heart that she could have seen him, one last time.

Another tremor took her. It started as a tightening of her scalp and crawled down her spine like spiders. Every muscle in her body jerked tight, and her arms and legs twitched feebly on the soft bed of sand.

Still she clung to life. The sky was so blue, so beautiful. There was a little breeze, and the desert was singing. She thought there were words in that song, always had, and regretted that she would never have the time to learn them.

Her throat tickled. She coughed—*that fucking hurt*—and could feel the bubbles of foam bursting warm at the corners of her mouth. She was lung-shot, chest-shot, and there was an arrow stuck high in one thigh. Every wound but that last was a fatal shot, but none of them promised a quick death.

She groaned again as tears trickled from the corners of her eyes, blood from the corners of her mouth. She had wanted to face death more bravely, with her sword in one hand, a horn of usca in the other, astride her faithful—

A shadow fell across her face, and she flinched. That hurt, too. She blinked, to clear her eyes of sand, and would have wept if she could. Her Talieso stood above her, a lead rope dangling from his halter. His perfect little ears—how many times had she rubbed them, as he butted his head into her chest?—swiveled this way and that as he tried to figure out why his mistress was taking a nap in the middle of the day, with no tent.

Talieso lowered his head, gently brushing her face with his

122

whiskers. His whuffling breath was sour with grain and churra butter, where it should have been sweet with grass. The ribs stood out against his dull hide, there were fresh rope burns around his neck and shoulders, and he was lame in front, his pastern swollen. Her faithful old stallion had joined her in captivity, and—judging from the rope burns—had fought his way free to be with her.

He deserved so much better than this.

Oh, you silly horse, she thought as fresh tears welled in a flood down her cheeks. *Go home. Go home, and spend your last days surrounded by adoring mares. Do not die like this, here, with me.*

Talieso lipped her hair and shuffled away, favoring his bad leg. When he had gone some distance he dropped to his knees, then fell to his side, and rolled in the sand, grunting his pleasure, all four legs flailing in the air.

"Silly horse," Ani whispered. With all her pierced heart she wished him gone, but wept in gratitude for his presence. It was not a good day to die, after all, and it was a worse day to die alone.

Talieso thrashed to his feet, shook the sand from his hide, and whinnied his contentment with the world.

Another horse whinnied in reply, off to her other side. Ani rolled her head, heart pounding painfully against the arrow that had nearly pierced it. A thrill of anticipation and dread shivered through her bones. She was beyond any further harm, and nothing anybody could do to her now could possibly matter.

A road shimmered before Ani's eyes, like a heat-vision, like a mirage. A warrior sat tall and proud astride a bay war mare, a black-maned, gold-eyed vash'ai at their side. It might have been a dream, so perfect and true were they, or a painting in some ancient and precious book. The mare whinnied impatiently and danced as the rider threw her head back and laughed. The vash'ai threw his head back, too, and roared *hnga-hnga-rrrrr*. They stood upon a wide and cobbled road.

The Lonely Road, Ani thought. The breath stopped in her pierced lung, and the thought squeezed her heart clean. *It hurts, oh it hurts.* But the pain no longer mattered.

The warrior, still grinning, held her hand out toward Ani. Her mare stopped dancing, the vash'ai shook his shadowy mane and went still, watching her with his enormous eyes, tusks gleaming in the gathering darkness.

"Come, Ani, my old friend," the woman said. "It is time for us to go."

Ani squinted. The woman's face was not familiar, but that voice…

"Ani Ja'Akari," the warrior said, and she laughed, "why do you hesitate? The hunt is on, but I have come back for you. Why do you lie on the sand, when you could ride? Why do you remain old and wounded, when you could be young again, and whole?"

Shock rippled through her.

"Theo," Ani croaked. "Theotara."

"Indeed." She could see it now, Ani could see her old mentor in the flash of smile, the haughty sharp bones. "Did you think I would not come for you? That I would leave you to find your way alone? You know better. I taught you better. Sword sisters unto death…"

"And beyond," Ani whispered. It still hurt, but the pain was receding, lost to memory like the notes of a shepherd girl's flute. "And even beyond."

"Just so." Theotara smiled, a light in the gathering shadow. "It is time, Ani Ja'Akari, for you to ride once more. Will you come with me?"

"I cannot—" But Ani found that, indeed, she could. She sat up, though it was an agony, and wheezed a whistle. Talieso pricked his cute little ears forward and limped to her side. Ani took hold of his lead rope, pulled herself to her feet, shuddering and panting with the effort. "Help me," she croaked.

"I cannot help you," Theotara answered, voice soft with shared pain. "Not until you step upon the Road. But I am with you, my sister."

Ani swayed. She shuddered, but kept her feet. She took a short, painful step toward Theotara. Another. With every step, the Lonely Road grew nearer, and clearer. With every step, her pain grew less.

Nearly there, she thought, squinting. The darkness had rolled in like a sandstorm. Shadows roiled about her, whispering and grim.

Nearly—

A sickly light burst before her eyes. Talieso screamed and reared, yanking the lead rope from Ani's grasp. She fell to her knees, a thin shriek of agony forced from her tortured lungs.

Five beings stood between her and the Lonely Road, appearing to her nearly dead eyes as skeletal figures wrapped in shrouds of yellow-green. Free now from their cactus shells, stench and misery rolled from their forms so thick that Ani could see it, a miasmatic aura of grief, of wrath and despair.

No, Bonesinger, a voice grated in her mind. *The way forward is not for you. The dead travel that road, and the mercy of death is too sweet for your kind.*

Let me be, Ani pleaded. Salty froth welled up in her lung, her throat, drooled from her lips. She swayed upon her knees. *Let me die.*

No, the fell being replied. *Your kind have barred us from the Lonely Road, and so we deny you, as well. You shall not pass.* Corpse arms wreathed in diseased flame stretched out to either side, a terrible imitation of Theotara's welcome. *You will join us, instead. You will know the misery your kind have wrought.*

"Na'iyeh!" Theotara spat. Her vash'ai—Saffra'ai, Ani remembered—roared a warning. The bay mare squealed, furious. "Stand aside! Begone!"

You have no power here, wraith, the na'iyeh replied, and it laughed, a thin and horrible sound that pierced Ani's ears. *You can but watch from your Lonely Road as we devour your friend, even as her kind have defiled us. It is a fate of her own making, her own choosing.* With that, the fell beings—the pod of na'iyeh—rushed upon Ani. Fingers like claws, like thorns of bone, reached for her flesh. Mouths like hungry screams gaped wider, wider, set to devour her.

Then the air between Ani and the na'iyeh split open like cloth rent by a sword, and they came with fire like the dawn. Three beings of light so bright she could not look upon them, so great that her soul quailed in their presence—an inferno of light and love and righteous wrath that burned away the shadows. The pure, clean fire of them brought back the sun, the blue sky, it brought back light and life—and all the pain that went with it.

The na'iyeh shrieked and fled back to whatever hell from which Ani had lured them, and the way was shut. The beings of light shimmered, they roared, they resolved themselves before Ani into familiar figures, one of whom she knew well.

"Inna'hael," she breathed, and collapsed.

Little huntress, he growled, *what have you done?* The wild vash'ai padded to stand beside her, flanked by two young males. His eyes were wells of wisdom, and compassion, and fury.

The Lonely Road was so near, so clear. Theotara beckoned with a smile. Ani lay once more upon the sand, clutching the accursed flute. *I should drop it*, she thought, but there was not enough of her left to open her hand. Not enough left to blink away the sand that stung her eyes, or wipe away the blood that bubbled and crusted around her mouth, or care what Inna'hael thought of her.

My people die with me, she thought. *Last of the Dziranim.* Having met the na'iyeh, she could not but think this might be a good thing. Unbidden, unwelcome came the realization that she was dying alone.

Not entirely alone, Inna'hael chided. *There are those here who think much of you.* A shadow fell across her face, and whiskers tickled her cheek. Talieso stepped so close she was in danger of losing an ear.

Take him back to the people for me, she asked Inna'hael. *When I am gone. He does not deserve to share my fate.*

Little huntress, Inna'hael purred. *Keeper of the Song of Time, you are alone, abandoned by all you held dear, and in great pain. We could end this for you now. I would ease your way. Or do you wish to live?* He stepped close enough for Ani to see, and the two young males flanking him regarded her in a somber manner. Inna'hael curled his lips back in a cat's grin, displaying his broken tusk. *What do you have here that is worth living for?*

What, indeed? Ani had lost her home, her place in the world, her friend, the daughter of her heart. What reason could she possibly have to go on fighting?

My horse, she replied, mental voice tart. Talieso lipped at Ani's hair, urging her to rise, to ride. *My good horse.*

A horse? Is that all? This was a new voice, unfamiliar. One of the younger vash'ai males stepped forward, staring into her soul with eyes like burning rock. *He is old, and lame. Hardly a fit meal for the pride, let alone reason for you to live.*

He loves me, she whispered in her mind.

Ah, replied the cat. *You humans and your love.*

The horse will die, a third voice growled. The smallest and darkest of the vash'ai stepped forward. His eyes were green fire, and with malice he displayed his strong white tusks. *Then what will you have? Perhaps the two of you should take the Road while you still can, before the na'iyeh return.*

Askander's face appeared in her mind's eye. He was laughing and holding a child.

I have a good man, she told the being of light. *He is precious to me, more so than all treasure.*

Beyond the vash'ai, Theotara raised her shining sword and laughed. "The love of a man… the most foolish reason of all," she laughed. "And the most worthy!" Her war mare screamed and pranced, eager to go.

Unimpressed, the vash'ai bared his tusks even more. *You are past the age to bear live young*, he scoffed. *Your desire for this male does nothing to serve the pride. You should die, that he may seek a younger, fertile female with whom to mate.*

He will not, Ani retorted, and in that moment she knew the truth of things. *He is for me, and I for him. There will be no others.* A spasm seized her, little more than a slight trembling. She gasped, but could not get so much as half a breath.

Your time draws near, little huntress, Inna'hael said. The three

127

vash'ai stepped close, so close she could smell the musk of them, feel the heat rolling from their bodies. *Which would you choose? The Lonely Road, or the Road of Thorns? Is this not a good day to die? Why would you choose to live, and suffer, when I might ease your pain?*

Ani closed her eyes. She thought of the Zeera, of fishing the Dibris, of the songs of Jadi-Khai, of the way Askander's eyes squinted to half-moons as he laughed. She thought of Sulema as a child, stubborn as her mother. She thought of her friend Hafsa Azeina, how the two of them had hunted the golden ram.

"I would live," she whispered at last, opening her eyes to a world filled with pain and unrealized hope. "Where there is life, there is love. I would have love."

Is that all? Inna'hael asked. *Love? That is the most foolish of answers, little huntress.*

Love is all I have, she answered. *That is the greatest treasure any of us can hope for, after all.*

Finally, her hand fell open, and the cactus-bone flute rolled away. Ani sighed in relief… and found that she could not draw another breath.

I am finished, she thought. *My journey has ended.* Her eyes closed, slowly, stealing the last sight of her beloved Zeera. *So beautiful.*

"Not by half, Sister," Theotara whispered in her ear. "Come with me—such wonders I can show you."

Not now, Ani wished with all her heart. *Not yet.*

She is dying, Inna'hael remarked. *What say you, my sons?*

She should live, the first replied. *The horse loves her. Her heart is true.*

She should die, the other said. *She called the na'iyeh. Her heart is false.*

A great weight pressed down upon Ani's chest. She would have cried out, had she breath. Claws pierced her flesh, even as the arrows had.

Then it was over. The weight was lifted from her, and the pain. Ani opened her eyes to find herself standing beside the Lonely

Road, Talieso at her shoulder. She drew a long, shuddering breath and laughed in relief.

"Welcome, Sister!" Theotara threw her head back and greeted her with an ululation of such joy and welcome that tears flowed freely down Ani's face. "And well come! Let us ride, let us ride now!" But Saffra'ai stepped between them, eyes wide and deep with regret.

Not now, Kithren, he whispered. *Not yet.*

Hot, red agony tore through Ani, and she screamed.

She should live. It was the voice of Inna'hael, fire and thunder and sorrow. *She* will *live. Her heart is mine.*

Her world ended, as all worlds end, in fire.

Ani woke to the smell of fire, the smell of burning flesh... and the smell of coffee.

Huh, she thought, *I must not have ended up in one of the hells after all.* She wriggled her toes first, then her fingers, and sighed in relief at the lack of pain. She had not looked forward to riding down the Lonely Road, full of arrows. *I suppose I should find my horse.* She opened her eyes—and her jaw dropped open.

Askander was there. He was sitting back on his heels beside a small fire, roasting a hare, and making coffee, as if it were the most natural thing in the world. *In the afterworld*, she remembered. His Duq'aan was there too, twitching the tip of his tail and pretending to sleep. Talieso stood close to Askander's mare, both of them dozing beneath a blue sky not unlike the one she had left behind.

Despite the fact that she was dead, rendering it completely unnecessary, Ani's heart rolled over in her chest.

How did you die? she wanted to ask him, and, *How did you find me?*

"There is coffee in the afterworld?" she asked instead. "Is it any good?" Surely that would be one way to tell whether or not they had gone to a hell. Askander went still. After a long moment, he looked over his shoulder at her and smiled.

Such a smile.

"Ah, my beauty awakens. I had begun to fear you would sleep for a hundred years." His hands trembled as he took up the coffee pot and a clay mug.

She did not wish to know, but she had to ask.

"How did you die?"

"Die?" He frowned. "I did not die. Neither of us died. At least, not yet." Then he poured coffee into the mug, and handed it to her. As his fingertips brushed hers, a small shock passed between them, and Askander winced.

Ani sat up and took the cup, glancing down as she did at her body. Naked—and *healed*. She sucked air through her teeth in a sharp hiss. Not only were there no wounds, not the slightest sign that she had been pierced and slashed and beaten next to death, but the scars she had earned over a lifetime of fighting had disappeared. The scar she had worn across her ribs since she won the championship—gone. The slashes and gouges and snake-tracks of a lifetime worth of fighting—gone.

It felt like a betrayal, like an invasion.

"What is this?" Ani dropped the mug and jumped to her feet, staring wide-eyed and angry at her flawless skin. "What the goatloving fuckery is this?"

"I am not sure," Askander replied, folding his hands before him. "Your Inna'hael brought us here, all the way from Aish Kalumm, him and those two sons of his. They... pulled us along dark roads, using vash'ai magic. I found you like this. Duq'aan will tell me nothing." He pointedly refused to look to his vash'ai, who pointedly did not open his eyes. "We have been here for three days, waiting for you to wake up."

"Vash'ai magic?" Chillflesh stood out all over Ani's unfamiliar skin. Vash'ai never spoke of their kahanna magic, not even to their bond-mates.

"Perhaps a wild kahanna saved you with his wild magic." Askander shrugged, visibly setting the matter aside, and stood to face her. "Talieso has not left your side. Inna'hael tells me that he fought his way free from the false Mah'zula, just to be with you. And I…"

Askander took her hands in his. Held her arms out to the side, turned her this way and that, then enfolded her gently in an embrace.

"I have set aside my duties as first warden, to be with you. What is it, my beauty, that inspires your males to such devotion?"

Ani's heart pounded, so strong, so full of life. She pressed her hands against her lover's strong, scarred back. His smell, his voice, his body were more familiar to her than her own, now. She smiled against his shoulder.

"Doubtless it is my sweet tongue and gentle nature." Askander laughed bright as the sun, wide as the dawn.

"Ah, my girl, kahanna or no, magic or no, I do love you."

"And I you," she answered, and she kissed him.

Ehuani, that was all that had ever mattered.

FIFTEEN

*S*weet Bohica, he thought, not for the first time, *a soldier's prayer to you. Shield me with Your strong hand. Protect me with Your bright sword. Guide me with Your light…*

Leviathus had never been one for following fashion, but if praying to the divines might help, he was more than willing to bend a little.

He was lost, well and truly lost. The spotted churra, enraged at having been roused and kicked into a sprint, had not stopped running until the sun was nearly at the far horizon, and now the cursed thing refused to move at more than a teeth-grindingly slow walk. When he tried to urge it to a shamble, at least, the evil thing bit him. Hard.

A squall had picked up, nothing like the previous day's sandstorm but enough to scour the exposed skin on his face, hands, and feet, and obscure the world around him. The dunes were indistinguishable one from another, each painted a bloody gold by the dying light, each singing a disparate whining tune in the sharp wind. Had the dust not been so thoroughly kicked up by the wind, Leviathus thought he might have been able to navigate by the stars, and at least make his way to the Dibris.

As it was, once the sun disappeared over the horizon he would be utterly adrift, days' ride from water and without even the weak water-sense of the Zeeranim. The only real question was whether he would perish of thirst before the na'iyeh or some other predator caught up with him.

Still, he thought his circumstances somewhat improved. Yesterday it had seemed as if he had no chance of escape, and yet escape he had. By this time tomorrow, doubtless he would be dining in the gardens of his own fortress.

Doubtless.

Sweet Bohica, he prayed again, as fervently as a nonbeliever might. *Divine Snafu, get me through this soldier's mess and I swear I will raise shrines to you, statues of lapis and gold and alabaster. I will write poems to lay at Your feet, just please...*

The churra came to such an abrupt halt that Leviathus tumbled off its back and onto the sand, which was never as soft a landing as he might hope. For a wonder, the thing did not run away but stood bawling and nodding its ugly head so that its lead rope slapped him in the face. He grabbed it and used it to pull himself upright, then stood shaking the sand from his trousers as he stared open-mouthed at the wall that had seemingly sprung from the desert.

Well, he thought, as a shiver of trepidation rippled through him. *Perhaps I should not mock the divines so openly, after all.*

The churra tugged at its rope, impatient to get to shelter. Leviathus supposed the beast probably had senses keener than his own—he hoped so, at least—and that it would know whether the broken stone walls and cracked roofs that loomed before them held any threat.

Any living *threat*, he amended as he led the eager churra through a broken gate and into an ancient courtyard. There was a collapsed well at its very center, surrounded by a small ring of pale brick buildings, dome-shaped, with round windows and doors like nothing he had seen before. Most of the roofs had caved in, but some few looked as if they might be intact. The whole was no bigger than a good-sized stable yard, a barracks perhaps, or a trading post.

Holding tight to foolish hope—which had served him well so far—Leviathus crossed to the small well. No doubt it was dry, of course. He reached for a large round stone set into the well's edge, thinking to drop it down into the dark hole in the hope that he might hear a splash.

Only the stone was not a stone. It was a human skull, and a fresh one at that. At the sight of its accusing stare Leviathus let it drop, shaking his hand in shock. It bounced twice on the edge of the well—which was set all around with stones that were not stones—and tumbled down into the dark.

He waited, heart pounding, a sense of dread crawling up his spine. After a long moment, and another, a sound issued forth from the well. Not the kind splash of water, nor yet the dry crack of a skull breaking open on bare rock, but a chittering hiss as of something he did not want to face, waking angrily what had probably been a long slumber.

Bohica was, after all, a capricious divine, fond of irony.

He backed away, but nothing sprang from the well to eat his face, so Leviathus sighed and turned toward the little huts. One in particular looked most likely to survive another night, and he needed shelter nearly as much as he needed water. He was tired enough not to care overmuch whether he ever woke, so long as he could curl up and sleep somewhere.

The hut he chose was empty as the inside of an old skull—*bad choice for an analogy*, he thought, too late—no more than five strides across, with a pounded dirt floor and one small window. There was nothing on which he could sit, nor anything to eat, but there also seemed no place to hide anything that might wish to eat *him*. Leviathus counted that as a win.

The churra refused to enter, choosing instead to fold its legs and lie just outside the little door, chewing its cud and shooting him side-eyed glances now and again.

"Stay there, then, if you like," Leviathus groused, dropping its lead onto the ground and hoping that would be enough to keep the rotten thing from leaving. "If any predators come for me, they will have to eat you first."

The churra rolled back its upper lip, and Leviathus ducked away before it could spit at him. Theirs had never been a love match. He watched the churra settle in, chewing and swallowing in perfect comfort, and for a moment the king's son envied his beast of burden.

"I do not suppose you want to share?"

The churra looked away, lowering its long lashes so that it would not have to look at him.

"Ah, well, to the hells with you, too," he said, and he laughed.

Though the day had been long and nothing short of horrific, though he was lost and alone and likely to die—a horrible death by thirst, a horrible death by sandstorm, perhaps a horrible death down the throat of a predator from the well—still, Leviathus's spirits lifted. Horrific or no, this had been the *least* worst day he had experienced in longer than he could remember.

And all because you left a good woman to die.

"Shut up," he told the dark voice. "Shut up."

He took his tunic off, shook out the dirt as best he could, and rolled it up for a pillow. The far side of the hut served to guard his back, the hard dirt floor served as a bed, and the dark voice in his head served as well as a mother's lullaby to send him to sleep.

The next day dawned a vibrant red-gold, clear and warm and beautiful. It looked to be a perfect day to walk the halls with his Draiksguard, laughing at their tales of romance and derring-do. A perfect day for fishing, for the hunt, for a game of stones and bones, a horn of mead, a hot meal, and a lovely girl—in whichever order those might happen.

Or perhaps, he thought as he stared out the little window at the na'iyeh, which stood but a few strides distant, *a good day to be eaten by a cursed plant.*

His churra had moved during the night, and lay near the skull-ringed well, sound asleep and completely unconcerned by the presence of the predators. Ani claimed that the monsters never harmed any creature but humans. She also said that once they had a person's dream-scent, the things never gave up the hunt.

Ani, who had died that he might live.

Perhaps she is not dead, the dark voice laughed. *Perhaps even now she lies bleeding and injured, alone in the sand, wondering whether you are brave enough, man enough, to return to her aid.*

Just like the na'iyeh, once the thought had his scent, it would not let go.

What kind of a man are you, King's Son, to run and hide while a woman is killed? Better you had died defending her. Bad enough that you are deaf to magic. Are you deaf to honor, as well? For once, Leviathus did not tell the voice to go away.

Who am I, indeed?

He closed his eyes and bathed in the early morning light, tattered robes of the ne Atu stirring around his motionless limbs. The sun rose, as it always did, far away beyond the Forbidden City, glinting upon the blades of a thousand thousand vanquished enemies. If he put the sun to his back and rode hard he might reach Min Yaarif, or at least an outlying trader's post, before dying of thirst.

If instead he rode toward the sun in a foolish attempt to find the warrior Ani, he might as well ride down the throat of a dragon. He had no food, no water, nothing but the breath in his lungs, the rags on his body, and a churra that at any moment might remember its omnivorous nature.

Oh, he remembered, *and a pod of na'iyeh tracking me as I sleep.* He opened his eyes and stared hard at the damned things, daring them to move while he watched. Had he a sword, he would have hacked the fell things to bits, warning or no. Had he a blacksmith's furnace, he would burn them to ash. Let that ash stalk his dreams, if it would.

Had I food and water, a nice bit of land, and a thousand slaves, I would raise a city, he thought, and he snorted. *I would have lights, and dancing, and music, and the greatest library the world has ever seen.* Leviathus smiled as in his mind Akari spread his dragon's wings over a shining coastal city, a center of learning and light to rival ancient Saodan. *I will name it Leviathia, and dedicate it to the glory of the divines.* Praying to them was fashionable among the very young and the very old, though nobody he knew really believed.

At the thought, thunder rolled through the land, a long low note as sweet and terrible as a dragon calling to her mate. The rumbling faded slowly to the west, and was followed by three ground-shivering knocks.

Boom. Boom. Boom.

The churra lurched to its feet, bawling, and whipped its head around to stare accusingly at Leviathus as if to say, *what have you done?* Cold sweat trickled down his spine, and he shivered. Though he had never truly believed in the divines, it seemed to him that promising them a city was folly in the extreme.

"O Great Bohica," he said aloud, "O Mighty Snafu, if you wish me to build you a city, I suppose I shall have to build one for you—but I can hardly do it here. A little help getting me back to civilization would be welcome, if you do not mind. But first, there is a thing I must do."

At that, his heart became as light as a feather, even though it seemed his life as a king's son was about to come to a foolish end. He would ride—not to the river, Min Yaarif, and safety—but down the throat of the dragon in search of a woman who was likely already dead. Resolve lifted a great weight from his shoulders. Striding out of the hut, he reached for his churra's lead rope.

You will die, the dark voice hissed.

"It seems likely," he answered aloud. "But I will not turn my back on a friend."

"Very honorable of you, Outsider," a voice called from behind him. "Though turning your back to an enemy is nearly as bad. Drop the rope. Turn slowly."

Leviathus froze. Fear trickled down his spine, but it was met by a torrent of hot anger. *They will not take me again.* He dropped the rope and turned, every muscle in his body tense as he prepared to leap toward his captors and die fighting. *They will not take me again.*

But the warriors who surrounded him, laughing, were nothing like his former captors. Tall they were, and proud, heroes from the oldest tales of mankind in their golden robes and bright breastplates. Dark eyes burned him with their laughter. Foremost among them rode a woman sleek and spotted as the cat who stalked beside her, its shoulders nearly on a level with her horse's. Her stiff black mane was heavy with lionsnake plumes and beads of gold. She was one of the First Women in the flesh. She was...

"I am Ishtaset," she told him, "true daughter of the Zeera, rajjha of the Mah'zula. And you, Outlander cub—unless I am mistaken…" She winked as the other warriors laughed. "…you are Leviathus, brother to Sulema Firehair."

Leviathus gaped. "You know my sister?"

"I know your sister," the woman said, "as I know of your father. Leviathus ap Wyvernus… you are the son of an ancient enemy, ne Atu."

Just as Akari breached the ruined walls, and she was bathed in glory, the golden warrior drew her sunblade.

"And you are trespassing."

SIXTEEN

Hafsa Azeina had spent half a lifetime with Khurra'an. Theirs was a rapport deeper than friendship, deeper than that of lovers. Deeper even than the bond between a mother and the child she had nourished with her own body. They had conspired, they had quarreled, they had hunted together.

Now, as she watched him lap pale liquid from a shallow bowl, it took every remnant of her courage not to snatch the dream milk tea away from him. Would that she could pour it out onto the thirsting ground, and find some way to fix his dear and broken body. Would that she might finish the drink herself.

Perhaps, she thought, *it would give me enough strength to wrest Sulema from her father's clutches, and then Khurra'an and I could face the Lonely Road together, a fitting end to a successful hunt.* She could not heal her friend, however, but she could give him this much. Dream milk tea, a drink sacred to the Zeeranim, which would give him three days of false life and vigor, and after that—

Three days is not enough, my friend, she thought, reaching to stroke the thick, coarse fur. *Another lifetime with you would not be enough.*

Silly human, Khurra'an chided, looking up from the empty bowl and licking the last of the tea from his whiskers. *It has always been enough.* You *have always been enough.* He struggled to his feet, shaking his once glorious mane, purring as he began to feel the effects of the herbal tea.

And now we hunt.

The mountains of Atualon were unlike the green hills of her childhood, which had been good for rolling down and for picnics. Nor did they hold the harsh mein and harsher ideas of the Zeera, that golden anvil upon which the heroes of old had been forged.

These mountains, she thought, *will see the death of humankind, even as they witnessed its birth*. How, then, could she expect them to be touched by the plight of a lone woman and her dying vash'ai?

She could not. Still, Hafsa Azeina studied the ground, the rock, the trees for some message of hope. It seemed to her—and perhaps it was the fault of the sharp, thin air, reminding her of days best left forgotten—that her human heart held onto hope as if it was a tangible thing, much as a child clutched a handful of salt tablets at the market. Like a child, she thrust her heart toward the world, the sky, the cold-faced mountains, trying to buy one more sweet, one more trinket.

One more day with her beloved friend.

And this, she thought irritably, *is why I killed my own kima'a. I cannot afford the weakness of a human heart. The human heart is weakness, it is—*

The tastiest part, aside from the brain, Khurra'an finished irritably. *Your constant heart prattling and cage rattling hurt my head, human, and I tire of it. Hush you now, and find me a fat goat. Or shall I find softer prey, and rid myself of your noise?*

Hafsa Azeina surprised herself by laughing aloud. *If you are threatening to kill me, I suppose this means that we are not dead yet.*

No, he agreed, and she saw amusement flash across the half-lidded eyes. *Not yet.* Then they went back to hunting.

Hafsa Azeina crouched low, fingers splayed across the rich and rocky soil. She let her sa unfurl across the rocky land, touching a ground squirrel here and a black grouse there, still and silent, tiny heart pattering as she spread glossy wings over her precious babies.

You have nothing to fear, little Mother, Hafsa Azeina sent out upon the wind. *Not from us, at any rate. Not today.*

The grouse did not believe her.

In all fairness, she told the bird, *I would not believe me, either.*

She had come, as always, to kill.

❖

They found prey late that afternoon, four ridges down and in a very difficult position for the kill. There were three rams, two of which were relatively small, and one magnificent beast with horns longer than Hafsa Azeina was tall, straight along the length and curved at the end like fine swords. The rams were a shaggy, soft blue-gray, with barred stripes on their legs and necks, and faces black as soot. Half again as tall as the stout mare she'd left tied at camp and with a temper like a woman just past her childbearing years, they were the kings of these mountains, and well did they know it.

These three males, alas, had been browsing their way down the ridge and were nearly at the bottom. It was a long trek, a long, slow way treacherous with sliding rock and echoes, and little more than brush and fistfuls of grass behind which to hide.

Are you afraid? Khurra'an teased. He dropped to his belly behind a big, lichen-crusted rock and lay panting. Covered all in dust as he was, with his chopped-up mane sticking up in clods and clumps, he all but disappeared before her eyes. At least he would not have a difficult time blending in. The tea had done its work. His eyes were fever-bright, his mind and body strong again.

No, she said. *We are the terror of the Zeera. What have I to fear, when I am with you?* She sat crosslegged and sharply pulled in her ka so as not to alert the rams to her presence. *But I am weary, and still weak from that beating. Let me rest a bit before we go on.* Now that they had found their prey, she found herself reluctant to make an end to it.

As you humans say… ehuani. Khurra'an flattened his ears, narrowed his eyes, and thrashed his tail twice sharply to let her know that he did not believe her.

She cut her eyes at him, amused. *I did not think the vash'ai found beauty in truth.*

We do not, he admitted, flicking his ears forward. *Only a fool gives up the advantage of a good lie. Are we not lying to these rams, even now? I cover myself with dirt, and you with shadows and dreams, and we tell the world that we are not here. But I am here, and you are here, and we have come to shed blood.*

Let there be lies between hunter and prey, for so it is and has always been. But between you and me, Dreamshifter, let there be nothing but truth. I have come here to kill, or I have come here to die. Let us get on with it.

Yes, she agreed, rising to a killer's crouch and reaching for her bow. *Let us get on with it.*

They headed swiftly up and around the end of the canyon in order to take a position directly above the rams, who were by then browsing their way slowly up the other side. Hafsa Azeina had some trouble spotting them again, loath as she was to unfurl her ka, but a twitch of Khurra'an's ears and a flick of his eyes let her know that he had seen them, and where.

Finally she spotted them, bedded down below some rock outcroppings to the south and west, chewing their cud drowsily in the warmth of the ripening day.

I will go down and see what I can see, she told him. She would stalk the rams, and take a shot if she could, likely wounding one of the great beasts so that Khurra'an could go in and finish the kill. It was a thing they had done a thousand times before.

Let this be a thousand and one, she wished. *Let us not fade like mewling kits into the long shadows, quiet and without a fight. Let us go instead as Theotara went, screaming down the throat of a dragon with the blood of the people's enemies on our swords.*

Or in our mouths, Khurra'an suggested helpfully.

Or both, she smiled.

Taking up a good position behind a large rock ledge, just above the goats, she could see two of the three—the smaller ones—and thought the one on the far right to be a very good prospect.

No, Khurra'an chided. She could not see him, nor smell his cat-musk, but he was close. *We will take the big ram, or we will take none.*

She agreed, and crawled on one hand and her knees, holding her bow close. Hafsa Azeina peered around the far side of the ledge and… there he was, her prey, and he was indeed magnificent. The late sun shone on his hide, and his pale blue eyes scanned the

142

world like a true king's, watchful and boastful and possessive all at once. He flicked his ears lazily—at a fly, she thought, for she had not made a sound—and turned his head a little to look to the north and south. He never once looked up.

Rising up on her knees, Hafsa Azeina strung her bow in silence, nocked and drew an arrow. Steady was her breathing and steady her hand as she readied herself to bring death to this beautiful creature, this king who had never wronged her, and in whose heart's blood she might find salvation.

She stilled her sa and ka, her heart and breath, and let death fly.

The shot was true. It connected solidly, passing through the ram just behind his shoulder. He leapt to his feet bawling and wide-eyed as blood poured from his side. The younger rams bounded away even as their wounded elder took flight, stumbling a little in fear and shock but desperate to live.

Hafsa Azeina lowered her bow and watched, heart in her mouth, as a golden shadow detached itself from the mountain and leapt through the air, to fall upon the wounded ram like the wrath of a damned soul. Forelegs wide in a death-hug, mouth open in a gaping snarl he struck the side of the ram, scrabbling with his hind legs for purchase, and—

The blue goat fell, head twisted to one side, as Khurra'an sank his tusks into the back of its neck. The ram thrashed, striking out with sharp black hooves at the ground, the sky, at his attacker. Khurra'an held fast, jaws restricting its breathing and hind claws digging deep into the soft underbelly, disemboweling the great ram even as he fought on.

It was an ugly death and hard-fought.

It was glorious.

Hafsa Azeina dropped her bow and ran to kneel beside her friend, her love, the one true companion of her heart. She grabbed fistfuls of his mane and buried her face in it, blotting out the harsh light of a truth in which there was no beauty to be found.

Hush now, Khurra'an purred, more gently than she had ever heard him. *Dry your tears, Dreamshifter.* He released his hold on the dead goat, rolled onto his side and draped one great paw across her body, holding her like a mother as she wept. That great heart still beat, there was warmth still in his flesh, but already she could feel him pulling away from her.

Khurra'an, foremost sire of all the prides, had made his last kill.

SEVENTEEN

Akari Sun Dragon fled westward, past the salt lakes and the rice farms, past the city proper and her father's fortress, warming the dragonglass walls as he roared overhead. He raced to touch the smoking, seething pinnacle of the great black mountain Atukos, the very heart of the world.

Where Akari went, Sulema Ja'Akari followed, always chasing him, determined to claim his power for herself. The dragonglass steps, carved into Atukos ages before the fortress had been built, flashed a welcome with every step, glowing warm behind her and leaving a trail of approbation. The fortress walls did this, too, and some of the floors. It almost seemed to her she could hear the stone singing, greeting her every touch, responding to her every move.

She almost could hear Sajani Earth Dragon dreaming, dreaming a song so old and so vast that a single note of it could shatter the mind of an untrained girl. Cold iron bit into her palms and knuckles as she gripped the chains she had wound around her hands.

Focus, she reminded herself. *Focus*. Whatever her father's plans were—whether he meant to raise her up as his heir in truth, groom her powers so that he might steal them, or fatten her up for dinner—she thought it was high time she made plans of her own, and every path she might wish to take began with learning to wield atulfah.

Then, in her teacher's voice, her mind spat the dreaded word. *Again.*

The steps became slick, and narrow—so narrow she could scarce set her two feet beside one another, so steep she could reach out and touch the mountain ahead of her with her sore hands. Sulema pounded up them. As the air thinned and the smoke and mist burned her throat, she practiced her breathing. Slow, shallow breaths in through her nose, a steady trickle of acidic air when her lungs screamed at her *more, more*.

She was barefoot so that Atukos would come to know the taste of her skin. *And my blood*, she thought as she leapt over a cracked step. That one had bitten her at least a half-dozen times before. The leap jarred her legs, sending a shock up into her belly. She used that small pain as a reminder to pay attention to the disruption in her breathing, and to notice how the slight hitch changed the feel of the steps beneath her feet.

"Feel the mountain," her teacher had urged her, his voice hard and angry. Even as she ran, or slept, or ate. *Be the mountain.* Even as she danced her forms his cane had lashed out, trying to catch her unawares, leaving a trail of welts on her skin when he succeeded. *Feel the mountain.*

Well, she felt the fucking mountain now, and it burned. It burned where the soles of her feet skipped across the dragonglass, it burned her eyes when the fortress flashed a hot welcome, it burned white hot like the new-forged bars of a cage made for someone much smaller than her.

Belly soft, heart open to Akari, drawing the heat of a dragon's dreams up and into her body she breathed, she ran, and as she did so the tears rolled freely down her face. It seemed sometimes as if she was *always* running—always running, but never getting anywhere.

The scent of dragonmint, planted along the steps long, long ago, made Sulema smile. She nearly opened her mouth for a deeper taste, but her teacher's voice rang through her memory. *"Focus,"* he reminded her. A flash of white teeth. He was very patient, with a student come so late to his instruction. She was fortunate to have him.

"Focus. Feel the mountain."

She could hear Sajani Earth Dragon singing to herself in her dreams, and Sulema let that voice carry her up, up, up into the clouds and beyond the sky where Akari Sun Dragon waited with infinite patience. Eventually the path ended and she staggered to a stop. Her legs trembled, and she was nearly blinded by sweat and dust and the stuff that rolled from the crown of Atukos.

Not fog, she thought, *not smoke. Something…* A wisp of cloud, red and gold in the light of a dying sun, brought a smile to her face. It looked like a horse, leaping through the sky.

It looked like her Atem…

Atemi…

The thought would not stay. These days, any image of home slipped away from her like sand sifting between the fingers, and any thought of her mother—

The lake gleamed in front of her. It was so beautiful at sunset. Not really a lake, she knew that, just as the black shore was not really dragonglass sand. The water was not really water but pure magic, death to any surdus should they look upon it or breathe its sweet cool mists, death even to any echovete who might slip beneath the cool, silvered surface. Even so, she took a halting step toward the shining waters, so cool, so sweet, and she so hot and thirsty after the chase.

There was a polite cough, and Sulema jumped half out of her skin. It was her teacher, her father's shadowmancer Aasah, waiting so patiently upon the sand. He was dressed as always in scraps of scarlet silk, and his skin glowed with stars, beautiful as the night sky. She offered embarrassed apologies. He smiled and waved aside her words of shame.

"There is nothing to forgive, *Endada*," he assured her. "Are you ready?"

"I am, *Malimu*," she replied, using the Quarabalese word for "teacher." He was so much more patient with her than Istaz—

She frowned. What had she been thinking of?

She must learn to *focus*.

"Excellent," Aasah said. His voice rolled over her, and her thought slipped away like the others. "Let us begin again."

❖

"I am sorry, Father, you were saying…?" Sulema shook her head to clear it of cobwebs, and reached for her goblet of wine.

"You look exhausted, my dear one," Ka Atu said. "Aasah tells me you are most diligent in your studies." He gestured with his own wine toward the shadowmancer, who bowed his head in assent. Aasahsud's little apprentice, Yaela, shot her a rare look of sympathy. Sulema supposed the girl knew better than anyone what a strict taskmaster they served. "How are you feeling?"

Her feet hurt, her lungs burned, and she had grown so accustomed to having a headache that she had almost forgotten about it.

"I am well," she said.

Her father snorted and set his wine down. "One should not lie to her king," he reminded her. "It is a bad habit."

"Very well, I feel like shit," she admitted. "Like three-day-old horse shit after a hard rain."

The lower tables went silent. Master Ezio dropped his knife. Loremaster Rothfaust coughed so long that one of the serving girls stepped forward to pound his back. Yaela turned to face her, pale eyes wide, and for the first time ever Sulema heard her laugh.

Her father picked up his knife and speared a chunk of lamb. "You smell like it, too," he remarked. "From now on, think of visiting the baths after a run and before dinner, if you do not mind." He winked at her.

Sulema grinned back. "Yes, Father."

Finishing her wine in one long swallow, she wished it were usca, wished the meat had been aged properly. Wished she were back home in the Zee—

She set her glass down and stared, wondering when she had finished it, then covered an unexpected yawn with one fist. She really was tired, but how could she complain in front of her father? The man was old before his time, wrung to the bones every day with the effort it cost him to wield atulfah, the song of dragons, and keep them all safe. She had tried to assist him in raising the Sulemnium, and had been overwhelmed. It shamed her. She could only hope to be a small part of his shadow some day. She could only wish she had come to him earlier, that she might be better trained by now, and able to bear some small part of the burden he bore for all of them.

If only her mother—

Mother, she thought. For a moment her heart beat faster, and fear nibbled at the edges of the fog which held her. *Where is my mother? She should be here—*

"You look tired," Ka Atu said, as he reached out to touch her hand. His face showed such love, such concern. "You should get some sleep, in order to be well rested for the spectacle." The whole city was abuzz with anticipation. Ka Atu meant to reveal his new Sulemnium to the world, by hosting a demonstration of magic and wonder "fit for a thousand years' worth of stories."

"I should get some sleep," Sulema agreed, standing and stifling another yawn. "I will wish to be well rested for the spectacle. If you will excuse me, Father. Parens."

All stood save her father, and Yaela, whose hooded eyes reminded her of a hawk's, quiet and sharp all at once. Istaza Ani would have liked—

Sulema blinked as she stared at the entrance to her chamber. She could scarce remember the walk through Atukos.

I suppose I am lucky that my feet did not take me to the bedchamber of Mattu, she thought, then she reached up to rub at her temples. Halfmask had gone away, had he not? Surely she remembered—

But she did not remember. Perhaps after she had had some sleep, the mist would lift from her mind.

"Sleep," she muttered, and jumped at the sound of her own voice. "I need sleep, is all."

"Do you?"

She jumped again, heart hammering behind her sore ribs as she whirled around. It was only the shadowmancer's little apprentice.

"Do I what?"

"Do you need sleep?" The girl ghosted closer, hips swaying

149

in the dancer's rhythm that Sulema envied every time she saw it. "Perhaps you are not as tired as you think, Sa Atu. Perhaps you should visit your fine horse; I hear she is pining away in the stables, and that she has taken to biting the stable boys. Perhaps you should visit your mother, who even now lies between this world and the next. When is the last time you went to see her?"

Sulema staggered, caught herself against the stone wall, which flashed red in anger at her distress.

"My mother. My mother. I… my mother…?" Her voice whispered away, so unlike a warrior's that she hardly recognized it as her own. "It hurts."

"I thought as much." Yaela ducked under her shoulder—not much of a duck, as she was a full head shorter than the shortest warrior—and helped her into the bedchamber.

"You are strong," Sulema remarked, and heat flushed into her face. Her heedless words always marked her out as a barbarian.

"I am *very* strong," Yaela corrected, helping her sit. "So are you. Do not forget that. Do not let him *make* you forget that." With a gentle shove, she toppled Sulema back onto the bed.

Soft. So soft. Her eyes wanted so badly to close that they hurt, but falling asleep with a stranger in her bedchamber was—

Dangerous.

—very rude, and she was tired of being seen as a barbarian.

"Do not fall for his sweet lies," Yaela went on, tugging at Sulema's sandals as she talked. Oh, the relief of having those damned things off her feet was so true she could have wept, *ehuani*.

"*Ehuani*," she breathed.

"You Zeeranim and your 'beauty in truth,'" Yaela snorted. "There is much beauty in Atualon, child, but there is very little truth. Already you have fallen for his tempting deceptions. You think he loves you. He loves no one but himself—there is a truth for you—and he loves power even more than he loves himself."

Despite her best efforts, Sulema's eyes closed. They were playing tricks on her. For a moment, it looked as if Yaela was dancing. Dancing with the shadows.

"Who are you talking about?" Her words were slurred. "Surely not my father. My father adores me. Are you talking about Aasah…?"

"*Ehuani.*" The word rang false against the chamber walls. "Do not give him your heart, child. He will eat your heart, and wash it down with your mother's tears, and your name will be less than a memory to him. Less than a dream." ·

"I am not a child," she complained. Her tongue felt heavy, her bones gone to mush. "I am a warrior."

"Then fight back," the shadowmancer's apprentice said. "Fight them, little warrior. Fight, or die."

I will fight, she thought, and she meant to say it. But the dragon rose up from the singing mists, and carried her heart away.

EIGHTEEN

The sun was a thin yellow haze in the west by the time they reached the place where Ani had fallen. The wind had hidden much of the tale that had been written here, but there was still evidence of blood, a broken lionsnake plume, and cat tracks all around in a pattern of concentric circles that looked deliberate.

"I do not understand," Leviathus muttered, as he let a handful of sand and dried blood sift between his fingers. "Why would they have taken her with them?"

"More likely something ate her," one of the Mah'zula offered helpfully. "A wyvern, perhaps."

"It would not have been the na'iyeh," another added. "They only eat the living. There is too much blood here for your Ani to have survived."

"Sssst, Anika," Ishtaset chided. "Enough of that."

"No, it makes no sense," Leviathus insisted. "Where did the cat tracks come from? The vash'ai had abandoned the... Kha'Akari." He used the term Ishtaset had taught him, indicating that his captors had been honorless renegades, and not true Mah'zula. "Unless... vash'ai do not eat people, do they?"

One of the vash'ai, a big queen so pale she was nearly white, whipped about and snarled at him. There was a sharp pressure in his head, a pop in his ears like the time he had dove too deep underwater, and surfaced too quickly. Two other males, smaller and younger, turned to regard him balefully.

You dare much, human, the queen growled in his mind. She had a voice like a bass drum.

"Forgive me," Leviathus replied aloud, bowing low as he might to visiting royalty. "I am woefully ignorant."

The queen lashed her tail once, twice. *Very well.*

He has pretty manners, for an interloper, he heard her tell one of the younger males. *Let him live, for now.* Leviathus realized that he had been holding his breath and let it out in a long, shaking sigh. Speaking to the vash'ai so had been wonderful. And terrible. And wonderful.

The Mah'zula were staring at him. Ishtaset blinked.

"You… hear them?" she asked.

"Yes. Is that not allowed?"

Ishtaset traded sidelong glances with another warrior. "Allowed? Not allowed? You have much to learn of the vash'ai, Outlander. Sadly, you will not have time to learn it. I have granted your boon, in return for the information you have given us about those who rode with Mariza Kha'Akari—" She spat.

Several of the other Mah'zula spat, as well, leaning well out of their saddles and scowling dark promises.

"—we have sought out your Istaza Ani, and she is not here."

"We could track her…" he offered.

"*We* could," Ishtaset answered, face as smooth as a sea-stone. "You could not, even were you not my prisoner. You would not hope to survive, especially with the na'iyeh on your trail. And you are my prisoner, ne Atu. As I said, I have granted your boon, and now you ride to Min Yaarif. Teika." She turned. "Anika, you go with him, and Hayisha, as well… her Zeihat is a kahanna and will keep the na'iyeh at bay. The pod may not attack you once you arrive in Min Yaarif. They usually avoid large numbers of people."

"Usually?" Leviathus asked. "Wait… are you not coming?"

Ishtaset quirked her lips. "Are you afraid you will miss me, King's Son?"

Leviathus glanced at the women who had been named. Ishtaset had proven so far to be a woman of honor, and none of her warriors had so much as looked twice at him. When he had told them of his treatment as the hands of Mariza and her followers, they had expressed outrage and disgust. Yet…

"They will not harm you, Leviathus ap Wyvernus ne Atu," Ishtaset said, and her voice was so soft, so understanding, that tears prickled

153

at his eyes. "My warriors are true warriors, and the old laws flow through our veins. You will be taken to Min Yaarif, and there you will be ransomed back to your father. You are my prisoner, and you remain under my protection. My blood on it, Outlander."

"And mine," Hayisha agreed.

"And mine," Anika echoed.

You are under my protection, the vash'ai queen informed him, as if that was the end of it. *None may harm a whisker on your face while you are in my presence, little two-legs.*

Thank you, great queen. Leviathus bowed again. She had not eaten him the last time. *Be certain that I will return the favor, if ever I may. One never knows.*

Even so, little fa'ar. *One never knows.* The queen twitched her tip of her tail again, and those enormous yellow eyes laughed at him.

"As for myself"—Ishtaset drew her sunblade and held it before her—"I have sworn an oath to protect and serve my people. These Kha'Akari dress themselves as Mah'zula, they ride asil." Several warriors growled at this. "By that alone have they earned their deaths. I and mine will purge these pretenders from the Zeera, then I will ride to Aish Kalumm, the Outlander-style city built in the heart of the Zeera.

"It is plain that the Zeeranim, the true children of Zula Din, have lost their way," she continued, "and need to be guided back to the true path, so they may ride once more for the glory of Akari Sun Dragon, and live lives of truth under the sun. I swear to do this thing, or die in the attempt." She kissed the flat of her sword, just as the sun flared bright and dove beyond the horizon.

"*Ehuani*," her warriors echoed. "*Ehuani*."

"*Ehuani*," Leviathus whispered. It seemed to him that in the dying light the sands were bathed in blood. The king's son who had set sail to bring his sister home would have been horrified at the thought of a bloody purge, but Leviathus had been broken and forged anew. He imagined Mariza's riders mown down like so much wheat, a feast for wyverns and crows.

The thought made him smile.

NINETEEN

With her father the Dragon King, Sulema attended the Sulemnium's maiden spectacle. High above the fray they reclined on cushions of gold and white, surrounded by courtiers and guards, servants and Baidun Daiel, the warrior mages who served Ka Atu.

She had never endured such loneliness as she did on that day, watching her sword sisters play in the sand while she sipped spiced goat's milk and pretended to smile at her flatterers. The King's Gallery overlooked the spectacle grounds, and the curtains had been drawn back to let in the morning sun and the cool salt breezes. It had been built of quartz-of-gold, and roofed in golden tiles. Golden spidersilk lanterns from the Forbidden City drifted gently about the roof, waiting for night's first breath to set them aglow.

For all our fear and hatred of the Sindanese, she thought, *we do love their magics*. It was a beautiful scene, and a beautiful day, marred only by the stench of illness that clung to her like perfume.

"You do not look as if you are enjoying yourself," her father chided. "Is something wrong?" He sat in an enormous wooden chair, a scaled-down and simplified version of the Dragon Throne.

"No, your Arrogance," she answered, painfully aware that they were not alone. "I only find myself tired from my studies."

"Aasah works you far too hard," he answered, patting her hand, but then he winked. "It builds character."

"Just what I need. More character." For appearances' sake she smiled and turned back to the festivities. It was, she had to admit, truly spectacular.

The grounds of the Sulemnium had filled as fools and acrobats, fighters and beast-handlers swaggered onto the arena sands in turns and displayed their most dazzling skills with beasts and fire, with throwing-knives and high wires, with song and dance and martial cunning. Banners had been hung from doorways and balconies all around the arena, proclaiming this troupe or that tribe. A yellow serpent for the Snake Dancers, while a black mymyc on a red background advertised Matteira's fools. The unmistakable dagger-tusked form of a rampant vash'ai, gold against a blue background, announced the presence of the Ja'Akari.

When the few Ja'Akari who had remained in Atualon demonstrated a game of aklashi, the people of Atualon leapt to their feet in thunderous applause. Sulema noted, with some amusement, that no few of Atualon's noble ladies had taken to wearing elaborately beaded vests, the laces of which were left decorously and—in the eyes of the ever-disapproving parens—dangerously loose.

How she longed to join her sword sisters. She sipped the milk, which she hated, and glared over the goblet's rim at her father.

Ka Atu had surprised her by dressing as a warrior-king. Granted, he still looked fine for an old man, decked out in red silk and bright golden scale, and the sight of his strong calves still caught the serving women's eyes. Yet he was taking a risk, for the very last thing any of them needed was to witness a weakened king, wound up by the sights and sounds of combat and determined to join the fray.

Kings were no more than men, after all, fragile of will and prone to act rashly in the heat of the moment. The simpering sycophants batting their cow-eyes at him did not help. Sulema watched her father's chest swelling as he sat straighter still under the gaze of admiring females. *My father is a man*, she thought, *and women want him.*

Ewww…

Nor was this interest limited to women. No few young men cast their eyes down in his presence, apparently hoping to whet an appetite for more than wine, or bread, or sweetmeats.

One stood out from this adoring gaggle of courtiers. Half

a head taller than any other in the room, the young man had a shaven scalp oiled to a mirror finish, and had dressed himself in a scrap of yellow silk like that worn by the shadowmancer. He had darkened his skin with fragrant oils and dyes, and every inch that Sulema could see—which was most of him—had been covered in delicate tattoos in an attempt to imitate Aasah's intricate spider-webbed scarring. From what she had been told, it was typical of Atualonian fashion to emulate the dress, talk, and even beliefs of peoples from foreign lands.

Sulema wondered what the king's shadowmancer thought of this upstart boy's tattoos, and shivered. *That* man was a web in which she did not wish to become entangled.

Wyvernus caught her eye, and Sulema saw the corner of his mouth twitch.

Watch this, he said, mind-to-mind. Sulema tensed, not yet used to having someone intrude upon her thoughts. Ka Atu turned to the young courtier, who seemed to grow half a hand taller under his king's gaze. Yet the king did not return his shy smile.

"Young Claudus," he said. "You are one of Matreus Bellanca's boys, are you not?"

"Yes, your Arrogance." The young man swept a graceful bow.

"And I see by your appearance that you also follow the dark arts of Quarabala. This pleases me, for I have need of a strong young shadowmancer. I am of a mind to present the emperor in Sindan with a trained wyvern, and Aasah assures me that he is too old and much too busy to undertake such a dangerous quest. You are up to the challenge, are you not?" He smiled like a vash'ai sire, all tooth and slow cunning.

"Your Arrogance…"

"You *are* a shadowmancer, are you not?" The courtiers drew in closer, attracted to the smell of blood in the air. "You look the part of a shadowmancer, you dress the part of a shadowmancer, so you must have the powers of a shadowmancer. Do as your king commands."

"But, but… your Arrogance, forgive me, but…"

"But, your Arrogance," Wyvernus mocked, and his eyes flashed

157

bright red. "*But, your Arrogance.* I do not believe I am familiar with this protocol. Matreus?"

A large woman in robes of gray and blue, with tiny silver bells sewn along the hems and a net of flowers holding up her mass of silvering curls, stepped forward and bowed.

"Yes, Ka Atu?"

"If I asked you to slit this one's throat, would you do so?"

"Yes, Ka Atu." She bowed again.

"And would you stammer and bleat 'but your Arrogance' at me, like a sheep?"

"Certainly not, Ka Atu. Though I believe I would expect you to pay for a new dress, if I got this one all bloody."

The assemblage chuckled obediently. Sulema did not share their laughter. Her heart went out to the ridiculous young man, who was trying to blink away tears of shame and fury. However, the Dragon King was not finished.

"There, Claudus, now you see how I expect things to be done at court. If I ask you to do something unreasonable, for the love of the Dragon, simply do it and then afterward try to swindle expenses out of my Master of Coin. Claudus of Atualon, I name you *shadowmancer* and to you I give this quest. Travel to the Zeera, or to whatever distant lands you deem fit, and return to me with a menagerie fit for the emperor in Sindan. A thousand churrim white as sea-foam. A single asil mare in foal. A young wyvern trained to obey a human handler. In return, I give you life." He sighed, as put-upon as any parent of a wayward teenager. "If you cannot do this simple task for me, perhaps Matreus Bellanca can find me a more willing—shadowmancer—from among her many boys."

The young man went stiff all over. "Your will be done, Ka Atu. If I have your leave…?"

"Yes, excellent idea. Leave. Leave, all of you." He waved a languid hand to disperse the small crowd of moneyed and influential citizens. "Not you, Sulema, dear. You stay."

Sulema blinked. It had not occurred to her that she might leave. Things had turned… interesting.

"You stay, too, Davidian. And… Saskia, is it?"

The girl nodded, beet-faced and mute.

"Excellent. Lovely lass. Friends with my Sulema? Be a sweet girl and guard the steps, would you? At your ease, if you would. Here." And he tossed a cloth-of-gold pillow from the benches to the Ja'Akari. "And you. You… Thaddeus! Bring food, a great deal of it. Red meat on the bone. Fruit, cheese, wine, whatever you can find that cannot outrun you. Make sure that girl is fed, too." He pointed to Saskia. "She is too skinny." The Ja'Akari clutched the pillow to her midsection and fled to her post. He managed to keep a stern mein until they were alone, then he grinned broadly.

"A tamed wyvern?" Sulema shook her head. "An asil mare in foal? You will find a thousand tamed wyverns before you find one warrior willing to sell you her horse. And a thousand white churrim? In all my life, I have only ever seen one white churra. Where do you expect him to find a thousand of them?"

"In the same merchant's stall as the trained wyvern, no doubt," he replied. "Oh, come now, you have to admit the little cockstrut begged to be humbled."

"Perhaps he wishes to emulate his king. Ka Atu, the man who, I hear, plans to challenge the Daemon Emperor in his own city." She sighed. "Father—"

"What, my daughter?" he said. "Are you going to tell me that I should not ride to Sindan at the head of my army?"

"I had thought to, yes." Sulema nodded, then nodded again to the servant who came at a half-run bearing food. It remained where it was set, untouched. "Are you certain, ah, your health—"

"How about you, General?" Ka Atu turned toward Davidian, who stood stiffly nearby. "Do you think I am too old, too feeble, to wage a war? What would you have your king do?"

"What ever is your will, Arrogance."

"And if my will is that you should burn a village? Murder your own family?"

The man swallowed hard.

"Even so, Arrogance."

159

"You see what a ruler has to put up with, Sulema?" he said, turning back. "Oh, do not look at me like that, either of you. I have no intention of making the journey to the Forbidden City." He picked up a skin and filled a glass of wine, then held it up so that the light shone through, draping a bloody mask across his face.

"Davidian, leave us. Take that young woman Saskia out there to watch the performers warm up for tonight's festivities. And do feed her." The Imperator General bowed, clutching fist to mailed chest, and left in a swirl of golden cloak and injured male pride.

"There, you see? I send them on glorious quests, and they sulk. I try to take care of them, and *still* they sulk. More and more I feel like Father of Time in the old stories, him with a thousand children all crying to be first." He shot her a look. "You eat, too, Sulema. You are so thin you hardly cast a shadow. Oh, and stop fussing at this old man. I will not be riding out to wage war upon the Forbidden City. Not today, at any rate. It suffices that the Daemon Emperor hides in his palace, behind a wall of victories long forgotten."

She frowned at him, and picked up a piece of flat bread. "You will not be riding to Khanbul? Then why let the people think it is your intention?"

"Why not?" he replied. "They need a new bone to chew on, and even this wonder of a spectacle will lose its savor before long."

"So the rumors are…"

"A diversion." He nodded. "Yes, the spectacle, the Forbidden City, nothing more than diversions for the citizens of Atualon… pretty boys and girls dressed in finery and playing with new toys, as the house burns to the ground and their father lies dying."

Her frown turned to a scowl. "You are not dying today, Father." Indeed, but for the bald head, he looked much as she remembered him from the night she fled Atualon.

He stood. "Daughter… look at me." An expression of impatience spread across his face. "No, *look* at me. With your *dreaming* eyes, as I know you have been taught." Wyvernus spread his arms wide, opening his ka wide as well. Sulema concentrated, and with some effort was able to open her Dreaming eyes. What she saw through them made her gasp.

Wyvernus had told her his sa had always been weak, even for a man. His *intisallah*, the heart's fire, gave off a thin and ruddy light that glowed a little ragged about the edges. But his ka, his soul's fire, burned so low she could hardly tell it was there at all, save for the occasional hiss and flare of a dying fire the color of burnt blood. Even a dead man, she knew, should show some spark, some sign that the man had once lived and loved, but Wyvernus's *intikallah* lay dead and cold as rocks.

And now you know. I am not simply ill, dear girl, nor even old. I am dying.

Sulema gasped, and tears sprang to her eyes. She had known all along, and yet… *I've just met you*, her heart cried out. *I thought we had more time. Who will teach me to wield atulfah, if not you? Who will be my father, if not you?*

I am sorry, my sweet girl.

Aloud he said, "I will not be making the trip to Khanbul because I will not be alive long enough to see them off. You—my heir— will have to send a delegation in my place, as the jackals of the world snarl at one another over what power might be left in my bones. You are all I have left, the legacy I leave to this world, and you are more than enough." He held his arms wide even now, but his eyes, his smile, were tinted with sorrow. Sulema went to him, and let him enfold her in those still-strong arms.

"You cannot die," she told her father, clutching at his robes as a child might. "Atualon needs you. The world needs you."

I need you.

He was the most powerful man in all the world, and he terrified her, but Wyvernus was the only father she would ever have.

"I will die," he said in a voice both stern and kind, "but you will live on. You are my daughter—the Dragon's Legacy—and as long as you abide by your duties Atualon will not fall, nor the world fail."

"I am not ready."

"No. But you will be." He kissed her forehead, and pushed her away gently. Gently.

Sulema bowed her head. "Yes, Father."

"Now," he told her, wiping the tears from her cheeks, "let us watch this spectacle, shall we? It is in your honor, after all." He smiled as wide and bright as the sun, even as the crowd exploded into screams and thunderous applause.

TWENTY

Sulema looked down upon the arena, and this time gasped in wonder. Aasah strode onto the bright field like an eclipse, and the crowd hushed even as the shadows stretched forth to welcome him. He wore a long robe of red spidersilk that fastened at one shoulder, a scrap of red around his waist, and little else. Unconsciously she whistled her admiration. The man was magnificent.

"Shadowmancer!" a young woman screamed somewhere back in the crowd. "Shadowmancer! Shadowmancer Aasah!" The crowd took up the chant, though he scarce seemed to notice. Stopping near the middle of the arena he took on an air of stillness, his red cloak billowing about him like a dancer.

Wyvernus turned to Sulema, and his smile was again full of mischief.

"The ne Atu, of course, should not place bets on the outcomes of these competitions. It would be unseemly. Were I a betting man, however, I would weigh the salt scales in Aasah's favor."

The crowd stilled again as Matteira came into view, carrying a pair of bronze-tipped fighting sticks and walking with an insolent swagger. She was dressed in a tunic of black, with an overskirt of black leather strips studded with bronze, and a short black cape with a blazing sun embroidered on the back. On her face she wore a lapis half-mask in the form of Sajani Earth Dragon, and Sulema frowned. Was the woman's mask supposed to remind them of her missing brother, Mattu?

Surely, she played a dangerous game.

Matteira stopped beside a small brazier and a skinny child dashed across the arena to light it. Red flames leapt upward with a *pfwoof* and the crowd cheered, having forgiven her any indiscretion.

However, Wyvernus's face went to stone. As it did, a single cloud obscured the face of the sun. Thunder rolled in the distance. He had not liked Mattu Halfmask since Sulema had taken him as her lover, and that dislike seemed to extend to the innocent Matteira.

Sulema patted the Dragon King's knee. "Tell me you are not going to be one of *those* fathers," she teased.

"Is there any other kind?" But he loosed his scowl, and the cloud passed.

Aasah raised his arms in a graceful gesture and began to sing. His voice was low and powerful, like the brass bells in Aish Kalumm. The shadows at the edges of the arena leaned in toward him, eager as children, and moved to gather above his head as Shadowmancer Aasah sang of the night.

Matteira flowed into motion, dipping either end of her fighting sticks into the brazier of red flame, then twirling the weapons around her waist, under her arms, above her head, leaving a trail of bright sparks and black smoke in their wake. The crowd gasped. This was much more exciting than a singing magician.

"I should have bet on Matteira. She would make a fine warrior." Sulema planned to corner the other woman as soon as this was over, and demand to learn the flaming staff trick.

"I would not be so hasty." Wyvernus looked toward the combatants, and not at her, but she imagined his smile. "Watch."

As Matteira stepped toward the shadowmancer, staffs spitting a promise of red death, Aasah brought his hands down in front of him with a surprisingly delicate twist of the wrists, and the shadows that had gathered above his head flowed down around them, becoming a writhing ball of starless night. For a moment he stood, still singing, and then the writhing mass exploded with a scream.

"Wyvern!" Sulema leapt to her feet, groping at the side where her sword should hang. The crowd lurched back from the spectacle in a hysterical wave.

Wyvernus laughed.

Aasah, red cloak billowing behind him, had summoned a wyvern made of shadows... and yet, he had not. A true wyvern, even a male of one of the smaller species, would stand twice again the height of a man, and many times over his weight.

This wyvern was scarcely a man's height—even counting its proud crest of spikes—and black as deepest night. This marked it as a female, whereas males were known for their garish colors. Neither was it wholly substantial—when it moved, faint outlines were visible of the far side of the arena, as if the creature were made of glass filled with smoke. The little wyvern tipped its broad head from side to side, birdlike, following the movement of Matteira's flaming staffs. Then it opened its broad and toothy maw, and squeaked.

Sulema's mouth fell open. "Is it real? I want one!"

Wyvernus chuckled. "Illusion," he assured her, "though real enough for this. Aasah is one of a handful of magicians skilled enough to create a shadowshift solid enough to touch, and he can only sustain it for the length of a single song. Watch!"

Seemingly unfazed, Matteira stood poised on the balls of her feet, waving her flaming torches back and forth, back and forth in a pattern that might have been meant to confound the shadow beast. It followed the movement for a few passes, and then paused as Aasah's voice changed in pitch, shaking its head as if waking from a dream. Then it gave a whistling little hiss, flapped its wings, and pounced, though it did not fly.

Matteira twirled one way, while her sticks twirled a counterpoint, and she ducked and rolled as the creature squawked its disappointment. There was applause, then laughter as the thing stomped its clawed feet and began to scratch at the ground as if searching for lost prey. Sulema watched Aasah. His hands moved as he sang, making graceful little bobbing and weaving motions.

Like a puppetmaster, she thought. *Interesting.*

Matteira leapt from her roll, snapping her spine around in a way that made Sulema wince, and brought both sticks together with a crack in a move meant to crush the beast's head from behind— but her blow met only air. The wyvern snapped its head back and whipped around in a shadowy blur that had the crowd moaning *oooohhhhh*. It struck like a snake at Matteira's feet, sending her into a quick backward dance, and again, snatching one of the flaming sticks from her grasp and sending it in a high blazing arc to be snuffed out on the far side of the arena.

The creature—or perhaps it was Aasah—misjudged the third strike, however, and received a burning poke in the eye. The shadow-thing let out a high, angry *kai-yii-yii*, rearing back and clawing at its face. The crowd moaned again, unhappy that the beast should be harmed, illusion or no.

Matteira took a defensive stance as the thing reared back. A dull shadow covered her face as the sunlight filtered through its leathery wings. Its spiked tail waved gracefully from side to side and it bobbed its head, hissing malevolent threats from between those sharp little teeth, and then it charged. This time when Matteira rolled the wyvern leapt after her, back arched and talons extended for the kill. It landed with its full weight upon the young woman's back…

…and Aasah brought his arms up, sharply. The timbre of his voice took on a low, commanding note. The wyvern flapped its wings, clumsily, and stumbled to stand beside its opponent instead, one clawed foot holding her firmly to the ground. It craned its neck and regarded Aasah for a long moment, then drew back its thin reptilian lips and hissed.

Very interesting, Sulema's mother would have said.

The wyvern ceased its protest, stretched its long neck out, and nudged the prone form beneath its feet. Matteira struggled under its claws for a moment before tossing the second staff away and slapping the ground three times.

"Yield!" she cried. "I yield!"

The sound of a gong shivered brassily across the spectacle grounds, and again, and thrice, throbbing away into silence. The wyvern's spiked head rose to consider the crowd, and one might have heard a rabbit's last breath for all the sound there was. Then it bellowed.

"*Aasah!*"

And again.

"*Aasah!*"

Thrice it called out, and suddenly the shadows spiraled back toward the shadowmancer, dancing, playing, then back to their proper places far from the bright eyes of the sun. The still-singing sorcerer brought his hands slowly in and to his chest, pressing them together, and his voice slowed, softened, caressed the last notes of his song in a way that had every woman in the crowd— and doubtless half the men—entranced.

Aasah strode to the prone and panting form of his opponent, helped Matteira to her feet, and then turned to face the crowd, arms upraised. The gems in his skin glittered in the sunlight, and sweat sheened his face.

The crowd was silent.

The crowd went wild, and he acknowledged their adulation with a tired wave of one hand as he turned and walked away from the arena. Two of the Draiksguard came to help Matteira, though she waved them away and saluted the crowd before gathering her smoking sticks and departing.

Sulema leapt to her feet, ululating and shouting, face flushed and split in a wide grin. The Dragon King stood beside her. Gone for the moment were her fears for the future.

"Did you see that?"

Wyvernus smiled indulgently. "This is why I never bet against Aasah. If you think that was something, just wait till you see his apprentice. The girl is… surprising."

Sulema raised her eyebrows in mock surprise. "I thought you said we ne Atu do not bet?"

"I said *should* not." Wyvernus took his seat again, and below them the crowd followed suit. "Even a king does not always follow his own best advice."

A new hush fell over the crowd, and when Sulema looked down, Yaela stood in the center of the arena, still as a summer day. In truth, she was one of the prettiest women Sulema had ever seen. Nurati had been possessed of a beauty that would one day be legend, and her daughters were all known to be lovely from infancy, but something about this girl drew the eye and invited speculation.

Yaela showed far less flesh than the desert-born, even less than the Atualonian women. She was wrapped and draped neck-to-ankle in spidersilk of palest green that matched her eyes, contrasted beautifully with her ebon skin, and hinted at lush curves while revealing nothing.

Unlike her master the shadowmancer, Yaela neither inspired nor sought illumination. She seemed quiet, devoted to her mentor and seldom seen far from his side, though doubtless many a man would have liked to lure her away from her studies. Sulema's servants had whispered that Yaela had been little more than a child, stick-thin and feral, when Aasah had fetched her from their homeland in the Seared Lands, and though she had grown into a cultured young woman, she still wore an air of wild mystery wrapped as close to the skin as her silks.

At first, they said, it had been rumored that she was an exotic plaything Aasah had bought from the slavers in Min Yaarif, but the shadowmancer quickly cut those whispers to the bone. He made it clear that he would brook no threat nor unkind word toward his strange young charge, and none dared risk the wrath of Shadowmancer Aasah.

Isara Ja'Akari and her vash'ai entered the arena, and the crowd sighed like a wind through the river reeds. Sulema leaned back in her chair with a grunt of satisfaction.

Now we shall see.

Isara claimed the arena as her own, moving with a catlike air of possession equaling that of sleek Sinharai at her side. She was the very image of a warrior, from the golden cat's-mane headdress that marked her as Zeeravashani to the gold-and-soot dappling of her skin. The laces of her vest were loosely tied, and the golden bands on her arms matched those set high on Sinharai's tusks. Sulema could not help but smile at the sight.

"I wish we *could* bet on the fights." She leaned forward in her seat, and Wyvernus patted her hand indulgently. "Now you outlanders will learn what it means to face the Ja'Akari."

Wyvernus grinned. "I would take that wager, were we not ne Atu."

Yaela raised her arms above her head in a fluid gesture, pointed one bare foot before her, and held this graceful pose for a long moment. She closed her extraordinary eyes and took a deep breath, as if seeking courage.

Isara drew her shamsi, threw her head back, and ululated a challenge. Sinharai accompanied it with a bone-rattling roar, the golden cuffs on her tusks seeming to catch fire in the sunlight. The Zeeravashani rushed toward the magician's apprentice. It looked to be a short match.

Then Yaela began to dance.

Her foot snaked forward, up and around in a graceful curve, and she twisted her wrists and undulated her hips as she began to spin. Slowly, at first, then faster, hands describing strange symbols in the air and bare feet patter-pattering against the ground. Faster and faster. Her green silks billowed about her lithe form, and the air seemed to thicken, time to slow, and shadows were sucked into her dance as debris into a whirlpool.

Sand kicked up and spat forth from beneath her feet, and specks of black like sparks from a dark fire danced in the air as the shadows congealed and obscured the dancer's whirling, twirling, writhing form.

Isara Ja'Akari threw up an arm and turned her face away, and Sinharai crouched, snarling. Tongues of dark flame licked up from the ground, consuming the dancing girl. They pulled inward like the bud of a dark, dark rose and then blossomed above her head, exploding into a screaming darkness that had the front rows of spectators shrieking and scrambling over one another to get away.

Bintshi!

In the center of the arena stood a sleek, almost birdlike form with glossy black feathers rising into a crest atop its narrow head, neck long and scales so black that it drank the sun and let no light escape. Half again as tall as Aasah's wyvern had been and more solid, the thing unfurled its batlike wings and brought them down to the ground with a sound like thunder and a smell of burnt sulfur. Long, beaklike jaws gaped, and its black eyes narrowed, glittering with malice. The thing shook its head from side to side and hissed, a rattling whisper of pure malevolence that raised every hair on Sulema's body.

The onlookers were consumed by a wave of panic, but Isara shook herself and laughed in the shadow's face. That sound, pure and light and mocking, drew every eye in the arena, and the crowd held its collective breath at the sight of the warrior twirling her shamsi above her head, *flash-flash-flash* in the bright midsun, as likewise Sinharai yowled a cat's song of death and contempt. When the warrior paused in her posing to laugh again and raise both hands in a very rude gesture, the throng erupted in a pandemonium of shouts and whistles and stamping feet. Isara yanked the laces of her vest open, pointed her sword toward the seething creature, and her mouth moved. Sulema could hear nothing over the roar of the crowd, but she knew what the warrior shouted.

"Show me yours!"

…and the crowd went mad.

Yaela swiveled her hips, arms extended, wrists poised with almost exquisite grace, feet skimming along the ground in a quick and complex pattern. As she danced, the bintshi ducked its head back along its neck, an odd graceful movement, and bobbed twice, swaying like a venomous snake considering its prey. Then it opened its mouth and began to sing.

To Sulema's ears, newly attuned to dreamshifting and to atulfah, its voice was sweet and light as that of a finger-bone flute, dancing and sparkling through the heated air. To the others, who knows? Every woman received the song of the bintshi in her own way, or so it was said. As for the men… it was well known what effect the song had upon men, even a false bintshi crafted of shadow and night and the dark whispers of a young girl's heart. The crowd's murmur grew, and grew ugly, giving voice to the beast's fell hungers.

Then Yaela slipped. It was the slightest misstep, quickly corrected, but it was enough. The bintshi paused in its singing and whipped around to face the dancing girl, shadowy form writhing and billowing as if something inside it was trying to escape. It crouched, tail lashing side to side as it prepared as if to leap upon the shadowmancer's apprentice.

It all happened so fast. The warrior and her vash'ai charged the crouching bintshi, roaring at the tops of their lungs. Sinharai leapt toward the beast, mouth open, claws extended, even as the warrior's blade flashed down. Nothing could withstand the Zeeravashani—not the false bintshi, not the city, not even Death herself. Even as the sun-blade struck, the form of the great black beast shuddered and writhed, consumed in black flame and emitting a terrible darkness that was seen rather than felt.

Sulema held her breath and gripped her father's hand until his knuckles cracked. Even so, he sat silently. The bintshi squealed, a high, thin sound that shattered the air, and a blast of dark energy sent warrior and vash'ai alike tumbling through the air with such force that they hit the arena wall and fell boneless to the ground. Many among the crowd screamed.

As the beast turned and advanced upon the unmoving forms, wings half-furled, head low to the ground and hissing, the red-cloaked form of Aasah stepped from the shadows. He stood between the bintshi and its intended prey and lifted one hand, fingers extended. His face showed not the slightest trace of fear—indeed, he smiled at the shadow-thing, and his voice rolled like thunder before the rains.

"Enough."

The bintshi paused and rattled its wings, feathered crest rising high and long black tongue flicking out in agitation. It took another step, more cautiously, and another, and its jaws gaped wide.

"*Enough*." Aasah held up his other hand, and then spread them wide apart, more in benediction than in warning, and then he began to sing. Sulema did not know the words—indeed, she did not recognize the language—but she knew a lullaby when she heard one. The tension was drawn from her body, and she heard a long, low sigh sweep across the gathered audience. Where there had been fear, there was none. Even the sky seemed to brighten as shadows were sucked into the shadowmancer's song, and the creature's head snaked side to side, side to side, black-flame eyes blinking in the sunlight, growing heavy, heavy.

Finally those wicked eyes shut and the great night-feathered head drooped to the ground, and with a sound like the end of a sandstorm all the shadows were sucked from its scaly hide and the beast dissipated, leaving the arena empty but for the shadowmancer, the warrior, her vash'ai, and the curled and senseless form of the druid's apprentice.

Aasah scooped the girl from the ground as tenderly as if she were his own daughter and walked slowly away, still singing to her, ignoring the audience's shocked silence as he had disregarded their panicked screams, moments before.

The crowd erupted with a deafening roar.

"*Za fik*," Sulema breathed. "*Za fik!* Is it over, then? Is your shadowmancer to be named champion?"

"No, child, the spectacle is not over." Wyvernus laughed, and even he sounded a touch breathless as he patted his daughter's knee. "There are still the fools' plays, the beastmasters, and so many smaller fights and skirmishes that even you will have your fill before the day—" He stopped short, eyes flashing dangerously, and stared down into the arena. Sulema followed his line of sight and wondered what had so drawn the king's ire.

Salarian troops, white-robed and resplendent astride their slender mounts, flowed onto the grounds of the Sulemnium like a wave of salt and steel, like the heroes of ages past springing full-fleshed from the pages of a book. Sulema nodded in approval at their horses, which were long-limbed and sleek, with delicate ears curled back toward the rider. They were close cousins to the desert asil, and fine to look upon.

The thundering cavalry split into two groups. One group wore red belts under their white cloaks, the other blue. They circled the outer edge of the arena, shouting insults to one another in a rhythm that was almost a song, flowing now together and now apart, bright-tipped spears and salt-steel daggers flashing bright. Sulema smiled.

"They are very good."

"They are," Wyvernus answered, but he did not smile. His face was unreadable as he leaned back into his enormous wooden throne. "The Salarians have a powerful army—and they mean to remind me of it."

"Oh," she said, deflated, and she slumped into her own, much smaller chair. "Does everything here have to have a hidden meaning? You outlanders need to learn to relax and just have fun."

"Hm." Wyvernus nodded, stroking his beard. The Salarian foot soldiers entered the Sulemnium and began to run concentric circles within the ring of riders, blue and red banners streaming, pikes bristling. "You have a point… but, my dear, you do need to learn to refrain from calling your own people outlanders."

Sulema shrugged, face heating.

Red and blue faced off across the arena. Horses charged the pikemen and fell, riders tumbling to the ground to lie still, their well-trained mounts kneeling, heads bowed. Swordsmen danced across the sand, twirling, whirling, flashing, robes streaming behind them like clouds, only to fall like white petals to the riders' spears and swords. Back and forth they went, back and forth, fewer and fewer each time, until only a lone horseman remained. This rider—a woman, Sulema thought—snagged the enemy's blue banner and rode a victory lap round the arena on her fine-boned gray, standing in the stirrups, voice raised in an ululation of victory as spectators threw bundles of braided herbs and flowers.

Sulema would have applauded. The Salarian horses were very well trained, and she doubted even her own Atemi would lie still like that. She stopped short, however, at the look on the Dragon King's face.

"Father?" she asked.

"Watch." He pointed as the great double doors at each end of the Sulemnium drew back.

A wind began to blow from one side of the battlefield to the other, catching the white cloaks of the salt-soldiers, stirring them to life. One after another of the defeated combatants rose, though they kept their faces down, and fluttered out through the far end of the arena like ghosts scattered by the wind. Horses rose with their riders and exited in a stately march, until eventually all that remained as a reminder of the mock battle was the shining detritus of abandoned weapons, and the victor, still cantering about the periphery, oblivious to the coming storm.

The wind grew stronger, stronger, and an eerie low moan rose from the ground. The crowd remained utterly silent, gaping. Finally the lone rider seemed to take notice. She rode to the center of the arena and wheeled her mount so that it faced whatever was to come. The horse reared, mane and tail streaming, and together they screamed their defiance.

Long streamers of red and gold silk burst into the arena like flames carried upon the wind. These were borne by yet more soldiers, all in red and gold and yellow, with golden dragon's helms like those worn by the Draiksguard and Divasguard, and wyverns were wrought upon their backs in thread-of-gold. They were driven, moaning, before the source of the storm, and Sulema gasped to see it—an enormous wooden dragon, gold-scaled, golden-eyed, mouth gaping wide and red, swayed this way and that as it coiled its way onto the arena sands.

It was a great, dancing puppet. Sulema had never seen anything like it, and clapped her hands to her mouth in wonder even as her father stood, his face a mask of cold rage.

"They dare," he said, voice sharp as a dragonglass knife. "They *dare*."

The victorious rider quailed at the last before the dragon's silken flames and fled before them. The wide wood-and-iron doors shut with a resounding crash that shook the stadium, and silence fell as the dragon coiled in upon itself, flames falling still all about him, wide head nodding in satisfaction as he lay in a bed of fire and swords.

Sulema turned to her father and was startled anew to find herself alone but for Saskia, who had returned to guard the door. The other warrior was wide-eyed and scowling.

"Fuck this place," she muttered. "We should go home, Sulema."

Sulema could not disagree, but neither was she free to leave, and so she turned back to the tableau beneath her. The crowd gasped in awe, falling back as the mouth of the dragon opened wide, wider, and a woman dressed in the brilliant blues and greens of Sajani Earth Dragon stepped forth just as the Dragon King himself took to the sands, golden robes blazing, the mask of the Sun Dragon catching the sunlight and throwing it back so that Sulema winced and shielded her eyes.

A second woman, dressed all in purest dazzling white, emerged from the mouth of the dragon to join the lady in blue.

The Dragon King stopped some distance from them both.

The lady in blue knelt, bowing her head. The lady in white, most pointedly, did not. Wyvernus stared at them, and his fury was such that the sands shimmered, and faint wisps of smoke rose from the dragon puppet.

"Ninianne," he said to the lady in white. Then, to the other, eliciting gasps from the crowd:

"Bashaba."

TWENTY-ONE

"This is treason," Master Ezio shouted. "Treason!" He had not been the first to utter the word, but he was the first to dare it before the Dragon King.

Wyvernus raised his hand, and the mutters fell silent. "It is I who will decide what is treason and what is not. Ninianne, what have you to say for this… this travesty?"

They had gathered in the Sunset Chamber. Matreons and patreons, mistresses and masters of craft, and a few who had not been invited but had seen fit to sneak in under the shadows of their betters. Food and drink had been laid out by terrified servants, and went untouched.

Untouched except by Sulema, that is. *"If you are going to die anyway,"* Ani had said, and often, *"try not to die with an empty belly."* She bit into a rind of fine white cheese as Ninianne, the Salt Queen of Salar Merraj, tipped back her head in a manner of arrogance nearly as great as that of the Dragon King, and mocked the assemblage with a bold eye.

"Treason has been committed," she agreed, and the silent room fell to dread. "Treason, I say, but not by me, and not by this one." She gestured to the blue-robed, blue-masked woman who stood a pace behind her, face bowed and eyes downcast. "The one you would call Queen Consort has committed murder and foul magic in the very heart of this great city. While Bashaba—"

Wyvernus rose from his seat and every person in the room shrank back—including Sulema, this time, though she held stubbornly to her cheese and a small loaf of bread.

"To speak that name here is to die," he said, in a voice of soft thunder. "Do not do so again."

Ninianne bowed her head. "As you will, your… your Arrogance."

She swallowed hard before continuing. "But I have a grievance, and we have a treaty. I do not come here to banter, or for pageantry. I come here for vengeance."

"Vengeance." Wyvernus resumed his seat, and the room resumed breathing. "Pray, what matter of vengeance?" He waved a languid hand at the courtiers, who began to sip and nibble obediently at their food.

"One close to you has committed murder. The murder of my great-niece Eleni, a girl who was dear to me. She and other members of my family were slaughtered by blade and fire in our holding at Bayyid Eidtein, not a two-moon past." She paused and glared a challenge at him. "Do you deny this?"

Wyvernus brought his goblet of wine up to his lips, beneath the golden mask, and sipped. He did not answer, but his eyes shone with such anger that Sulema pushed her food aside.

"I see," the lady in white said at last, and drew herself up to her full height. "Wyvernus, first of his house, Ka Atu, Dragon King of Atualon, I call upon you under the terms of our treaty to—"

"You shall not have her."

The woman stopped, mouth gaping in a furious "o."

Ka Atu continued in a voice as hot and smooth as burning silk. "I have seen the demands your ministers have drawn up, I have listened to your whispers and lies for moons now. Do you think me deaf? Do you think me blind?" The eyes in the golden mask glowed red, and the Dragon King's voice was an inferno. "The deaths at your inn were nothing but an excuse for you to bring that woman here. Remove her from my sight, or I shall have all of your heads removed and served to my faithful parens for supper."

Master Ezio fainted. A fist of Draiksguard surrounded the woman in blue and led her, weeping, from the chamber. The dragon mask fell cold and silent.

Finally Wyvernus said, "Now then, my dear Ninianne. What reasonable demand would you make of me?" His eyes, blue once more, flashed with a cold and cruel amusement.

This man is my father, Sulema thought as the bread and cheese she had forced down tried to fight its way back up. *He will not harm* me.

She did not believe it for a moment.

"My King." Ninianne took a long and shuddering breath, and at last bowed in obeisance. To her benefit, the lovely voice did not falter. "I beg you for the return of my son."

"Your son Soutan Mer is to be put to death," Wyvernus noted. "He and his men attacked my Queen Consort for no reason, and stand accused of arson and murder, as well."

The salt queen flinched at his words. "Your Arrogance, please—"

"However," he went on, ignoring her, "I understand full well the passions of a misguided youth, having been such a one myself, a hundred years ago or more." The parens chuckled dutifully—if nervously—and he nodded. "I am also reminded by Loremaster Rothfaust of our treaties, and long friendship. In light of such, I am willing to make a trade with you, Ninianne il Mer."

"Yes, your Arrogance?"

"I will release your son Soutan Mer to you, alive." He held up one finger, silencing the room. "In exchange you will return my ward, Mattu Halfmask, whom you have been holding as a... guest, for some time now."

"I will send to Salar Merraj for—"

The walls of Atukos trembled and flashed red with the Dragon King's ire.

"Do not try my patience any further, woman. I have none." Ka Atu set his wine goblet down with great care. "I know the young man is with you. Return him to me immediately—with no further harm to his person, mind—and I will give your son to you in one piece, which is better than either of you deserve."

Ninianne il Mer swayed where she stood, and Sulema could see that her face was wet with tears.

"Immediately, your Arrogance."

"Oh, and Ninianne?" Wyvernus picked up a small loaf of bread from the plate in front of him.

"Yes, your Arrogance?"

"If you ever come to me in such a fashion again—or if I hear so much as a breath of that woman's existence ever again—" He closed his fist, and smoke rose from between his fingers. When he opened his hand, a scattering of smoking black ash was all that was left. "*That* for you, and your soldiers, and your whole dae-ridden city. Do you understand me?"

"I understand, your Arrogance," she replied, in a subdued and unsteady voice.

I understand, too, Sulema thought. *At last.*

> *Her magic woke, and her magic broke*
> *The night the Dragon King sang*
> ——Bard Davrasha, *Song of the Dragon King, vol. II*

If Sulema had thought the shadowmancer's song powerful, if she had thought Yaela's dance beautiful, those notions were blown away like sand in the wind that night, in the gentle moonslight, by the might of the Dragon King's song.

He looked out across his city, his people, his world, and the light of the loving moons, the distant stars, and the many-colored lanterns of Atualon chased one another across the golden scales of the dragon mask in a scintillating display. Sulema watched from a quiet corner as Ka Atu cradled the Sundered Orb in his hands, much as he might have held her as a newborn, with all the tenderness in the world.

And well he might. The skull-sized Orb, as she had come to understand, was the world. He drew a breath into the deep furnace of his belly, and Sulema breathed with him. She relaxed her shoulder with his, held her head like his, closed her eyes.

When the Dragon King sang, his daughter was struck silent with awe.

Never in ever, she thought, *has there been such a voice. Never will there be again.*

The voice of Ka Atu was soft as lambswool, sweet as flowers. It was strong as the river Dibris. It rolled like night across the waking lands, soothing them to sleep, to sleep. The bright houses and homes of Atualon dimmed, darkened, as the residents within found themselves called to bed. Noises of merriment fell to nothing as late-night partygoers, loath to end the day's festivities, yawned mid-sentence and turned to stumble home. Sheep in their pens, horses in their pastures, stopped their grazing and dozed.

The very clouds, pale against a velvet night sky, seemed to settle against the mountain peaks. The Dragon King's song filled with love the dark and empty places between stars, and the darkness did not comprehend it. The shadows fled, the dragon's doom lifted, and in that moment Sajani Earth Dragon slipped deeper, deeper into the everlasting dreams of life. She slipped—

—and the Dragon King fell.

Sulema watched as in a fever dream as Wyvernus stumbled and went to one knee. The dragon mask slipped from his face, and his skin went ashen gray. Her mind screamed at her to move, *move* but her body was slow to respond. Her shoulder where the golden spider had bitten her had gone cold and numb, and her skin was stiff all over. She could only watch in horror as her father toppled slowly to one side and lay on the floor, motionless, still clutching the Orb.

After a moment he moaned, one arm moved a little, and that seemed to break the spell.

"Father!" Sulema shouted, and she ran—though slowly, as if through muddied water—and fell to her knees beside him. "Are you—?"

"I am all right," he said, his voice thin and watery. "Or I will be, at least. Help me, help me up." Sulema helped him to stand. He held the Orb close to his face, turning it this way and that, finally breathing a sigh of relief to find it undamaged.

"What would happen…?" Sulema did not finish the question, afraid of the answer.

"I am not sure. Perhaps nothing… but I rather doubt that." Wyvernus's hands trembled, and he tucked the object deep into a fold of his cloak. "I am tired, Sulema. So tired. This spectacle, the healing of your mother, even your training—they have sapped reserves that I do not have to give. If only there were two of me. If only you had come to me earlier, so that you might have been trained to assist me…" His voice trailed off in a deep sigh.

"Nothing to be done for it, I suppose," he added. "We do what we must with the tools we have at hand." Wyvernus smiled at her, a smile so deeply sorrowful Sulema's breath caught in her throat. "Would that I could leave you my kingdom only, and not my burdens. Would that you might not have to bear it alone, as I have."

"I will try, Father. I will try to learn faster, to bear this burden with you." Aasah had told her, however, that her body and vocal cords were not yet sufficiently mature to withstand the strain of wielding more than a thin trickle of atulfah. The thought was like a sour taste in her mouth.

"I know you will. You are a good daughter, the best I could have asked for." He smiled at her and stifled a yawn. "Let me walk you to your rooms, Daughter. I can manage that much, at least." He did yawn then, and laughed. "Then it is to bed for both of us, I fear."

By the time Sulema bid her father good night, she was as drained as he appeared, barely managing to stumble upright through the door and past the dragon's-head hearth to her bedchamber. She paused to pinch out the few candles that had been lit for her, much preferring to rest in true darkness. As she did so, a pair of eyes appeared, pale green lanterns hanging in the air before her.

Sulema squeaked and stumbled backward so that she fell into her bed.

A single candle hissed to life, cupped gracefully in the palm of the shadowmancer's apprentice. She frowned at the thrashings as Sulema tried to fight free of her bedding.

"I have come to give you your medicines," Yaela informed her, "and none too soon, it seems. You look like three-day-cold shit."

Sulema gaped at the girl—*woman*, she corrected herself, *of an age with me, at the least*—and extricated herself from the cursed linens. "I was singing with the king," she said haughtily. "It is hard work."

"You were singing." The lush lips quirked a little. "I thought you Ja'Akari spoke only truth. *Ehuani, ta? No ka iko.*"

"My father was singing," she replied, stiffly. "I was assisting."

"Of course." All manner of laughter faded from Yaela's voice as the girl drew nearer. She looked closely at Sulema's face, tilted her chin down—she was a full head shorter than Sulema—peered into her mouth, pulled Sulema's lower lid down and looked at her eyes. "In truth—*ehuani, do*—you were helping the king more than you know. You are feeling drained, are you not?"

She could hardly deny that. It was nearly impossible to keep her eyes from closing.

"The Dragon King's song soothes us to sleep."

"Rat shit," Yaela scoffed. "This is more than sleepiness, *he pa no'e.* You have been sucked nearly dry of power, as a bloodsnake drains a rat. You did not know? Permission was not given?"

Sulema blinked.

"*Ffffft.*" The shadowmancer's apprentice wrinkled her nose, and she held out a vial filled with a clear liquid. "Drink this. It will help. No good, *ta*, to mix the king's meddlings with that *Araid oe no a'u.*" She spat. "And you not knowing it. *Fffft.* You are like a small child, falling asleep by the fire while the elders make plans for your future. It is time for you to wake up."

She shouted that last as Sulema drained the vial. Aasah and his apprentice would bring her the loremaster's concoctions whenever Rothfaust himself was too busy, and she swore they added something that made the stuff even more vile. Sulema jumped, choking on the draft and more than a little pissed off.

"I *am* awake," she said, and she scowled.

"You are *nah* awake," Yaela scolded. "*Nah wey ta*, and if you do not wake up, *now*"—she snapped her fingers in front of Sulema's nose—"you will die-o. These men feed you sweetmeats and honey lies, and you eat their words up like Chuyuni eating the sun."

"Chuyuni?"

"Raven god of my people. He will eat the sun so that we may leave the Seared Lands, some day. At least, that is what the bards tell us." She shook her head. "Me, I do not hold my breath. I make my own way out of Quarabala, I make my own life. As should you, *ta*. These men, these patreons and masters, this king, they tell you *dey* and *tey* and you go where they point, never looking to see whether the path they put you on leads over a cliff."

"Do not step into a pit of vipers with your eyes closed," Sulema said, slowly. She shook her head. "You sound like my youthmistress, and I am sure it is sound advice. Thank you. But my father would never—"

"Would he not?" Yaela asked, softly, softly. "My father sold me into the Edge to save his own skin, and yours does much the same. He has told you that he is teaching you to wield his magic, his atulfah, *ta*?"

"*Ta*," she answered. "Yes."

"*Ffffft*. Has he told you yet that you cannot wear the mask of Akari? Have any of these men told you so?"

"He—I—what?"

"Have these men told you that although you are, indeed, the last daughter of the Dragon King, you are not the first?"

Sulema sat down, hard. Her head was spinning.

There are vipers in this pit, and I jumped in with both feet.

"A warrior should know better," Sulema said.

"A warrior should know better. Are you awake now, *nau'ilio*?"

Sulema shrugged her bad shoulder. The pain and numbness had subsided, somewhat. "I—"

"Yes, or no?"

"Yes." She smiled, reluctantly. "You would make a great youthmistress."

"No thank you." Yaela snorted. "I hate children. They taste *terrible*."

Sulema gaped for a moment. When she saw that lush mouth tremble with a suppressed grin, she burst into laughter.

"Ah," she said at last, wiping her eyes, "we should go drinking some time. There is this inn—"

"No time for drinking. No time for inns, or lovers, or dreams, *nau'ilio*. A woman cannot wear the mask of Akari, but she can be drained of her life force to feed the one who does, and as he—"

"My father would never do that. He loves me." Sulema forced herself to unclench her fists, and lowered her voice. "If you—"

"Did he love his other daughter? The one he made Baidun Daiel, a warrior mage? The one he drained until she was nothing more than an empty vessel to fill as he would? The one he killed on the day you were found?"

Sulema clutched the front of her vest, and said nothing.

"You are a fly," Yaela continued, though not without a hint of pity, "walking along a spider's web, thinking that you are a spider. You should fly away before you find the sticky strand, *nau'ilio*."

"If I go," Sulema said, "Ka Atu dies without an heir… and the dragon will wake. Yet you tell me that I cannot wear the mask of Akari in order to wield atulfah, and sing the dragon to sleep. What is there for me, then? I cannot simply ride back to the Zeera and be a—a warrior." Her voice faltered as she realized, fully, that such was indeed her fondest wish—and that it would never come true. "If I stay, you tell me I will be, what? Drained like a fly in the spider's web? And eventually the king will die anyway, and the Dragon will wake."

"Yes," Yaela nodded. "You understand."

"This is a steaming pile of horse shit."

"*Ta.*"

"Fuck that." Sulema let her vest hang open once more. "There must be another way."

"There is," Yaela agreed. "You will not like it."

"I do not like any of this," Sulema said. "What could possibly be worse than either of these impossible choices?"

"You could travel to my homeland, to Quarabala," Yaela told her, eyes shining with mirth, "brave the old paths to the ancient cities, find the mask of Sajani—"

"The what??"

"—find the mask of Sajani, learn to wear it, teach yourself how to use atulfah, and then return to Atualon, challenge and defeat your father, and become Sa Atu in truth."

Sulema stared at her for a long moment. Yaela smiled.

"You find this amusing?"

"I find many things amusing," Yaela told her. "My master often tells me that I have an inappropriate sense of humor."

"Your master." Sulema frowned, thinking. "Your master works for my father—"

"*With* your father," the apprentice corrected.

"Your master works *with* my father because he has been promised land, am I right? A homeland for your people?"

"Yes, that is correct, *ta*. If we can ever figure out a way to get them all out of Quarabala and across the burning sands at once. That is his dream."

"So why are you telling me all this? Is this not working against your own master? I cannot offer you a homeland. I have nothing to offer you, at all."

"Aasah owns me *not*," Yaela snapped, "and his dream is not my dream. I care nothing for the people who—I care nothing for those people." Her pale jade eyes seemed to glow with poorly suppressed fury. Sulema felt her way as carefully as if she were stepping into a dark pit, feeling for vipers.

"So. You would, what? Take me to your homeland, help me find this mask, and why? What do you want from me?"

"I would not take you," Yaela said. "I cannot. I am… *khutlani*? Your Zeerani word? I am forbidden to go."

"Exiled."

"Yes, exiled, but I can give you the name of a woman who could help you find your way to Saodan, deep in the dark heart of the Seared Lands—*if* you could break free of your father, which is impossible, and *if* you could manage to cross the Jehannim, survive the Edge, and find your way into Quarabala, which is beyond impossible."

"I am to make an impossible escape in order to undertake an impossible quest." Sulema sat heavily on her bed, feeling so tired again that she could weep. "This really is a steaming pile of horse shit."

"Horse shit can be dried to make fuel," Yaela reminded her. "I killed my husband, taught myself to shadowshift, and escaped from the Edge. All of these things were impossible." She shrugged. "Are your tits smaller than mine?"

They were, in fact, but Sulema ignored the taunt. "What is it you want from me? As I said, I have nothing to offer."

"You go to Quarabala, you find the mask, you return—and you bring to me my sister's daughter, my little niece."

"You have a sister? Is she as much of a pain in the arse as you?"

"My sister is dead," Yaela said in a flat voice. "Her daughter is all I have left in this world. She is all I care for in this world. You do this, Ja'Akari—bring me my Maika—"

The shadows in the room grew darker, darker, they grew thick and heavy and aware.

"—and I will give you the Dragon Throne."

TWENTY-TWO

To the shores and sandy beaches lead the sparkling Ka'apua
Lead the roads of man, the hunting-paths
Lead the coruscating stars.
That this young man's feet should take him down
this path should be forgiven
Though it end in tears and sorrow
'Neath the faces of the moons...
— Nenren Zhang Hengli, *Book of Two Moons*

Tsun-ju Jian, the pearl diver's son, returned to his home village of Bizhan in the four hundred and ninety-ninth year of Illumination, during the final moons of the reign of Daeshen Tiachu.

The new emperor's historians maintain that Jian Sen-Baradam rode before an army of one hundred Yellow Daechen and thirty Black Daechen, each of them sworn by sword and by blood to place his life before their own, and that his wife Tsali'gei Sea-Born rode at his side, silent and beautiful as the moons. It is widely accepted that when introduced the two of them, soul-bonded at birth, fell instantly into a love so deep it was a kind of madness.

A second school of thought, less heeded but still respectable, maintains that although the young Sen-Baradam was smitten, his bride was more reluctant, and violently spurned his early advances.
— Bilbil Chagha'an, *The War of Pearls and Twilight*

"W here is she going?"

Tsali'gei—his *wife*—stood on tiptoe beside her brown spotted horse, shading her eyes against the midsun glare and watching the puffs of red dust fade away as Xienpei and her entourage rode hard for the city.

"To Khanbul. She has been summoned to the emperor's side." A messenger had caught up with their group just that morning, and Xienpei had shocked Jian by sharing details of the man's message. Even as the messenger lay thrashing in his death throes, mouth foaming green and blue and red from the poison capsule he had bitten, Xienpei had shared the good news.

Emperor Daeshen Tiachu's spies had uncovered a plot against him. Karkash Dhwani had plotted to murder the Tiachu and name as heir the emperor's youngest, a girl infant still at her mother's breast. Thus Karkash and a group of powerful sen-baradam might… influence… the child's upbringing.

Jian did not ask what part Xienpei's network of spies might have played in hastening the emperor's discovery. Her eyes shone as his yendaeshi gazed upon her future.

"Even as the dawn rises beneath the Sun Dragon's wings, Daechen Jian," she had said to him as the lashai readied her horse, "so does your fortune rise with mine. It is a beautiful morning, is it not?"

"Beautiful, Yendaeshi," he agreed, ever dutiful, ever careful, and he did not share with her his mother's wisdom regarding red skies in the morning. *To bind yourself to the dragon*, as the villagers said, *is to court tragedy*. Surely his fortunes had risen with those of his yendaeshi—but what would happen to him when the wheel of fortune ground them down again? What would happen to his dammati, and to his mother?

Now he glanced at Tsali-gei—*my wife*, he reminded himself for the millionth time that day. She was flushed with anger and the crisp mountain air. With one hand she clutched a necklace of sea-bear claws, and with the other she held her horse's reins

188

with a touch so delicate it broke his heart again.

What will become of her?

"To Khanbul," she repeated, and a storm gathered behind her dark eyes. "To the emperor's side. What dangerous waters have you dragged me into, *Husband*?"

Jian had learned better than to remind Tsali'gei that their marriage was no more his choice than it had been hers. He wished neither to anger nor to hurt her—and, truth be told, in his heart of hearts he would have chosen her over any other girl in the world, as surely as the moons chase the sun.

"I will not let anything happen to you," he said with far more confidence than truth.

"Oh?" She arched a brow at him and grabbed her horse's black mane. "Xienpei holds your leash, Jian Sen-Baradam, as surely as you hold mine. Your fortunes rise with hers, they will fall with hers, and I have no choice but to follow you like—"

"The moons follow the sun," he finished, heart pounding in his chest as her words echoed his thoughts. "I would not leash you, Tsali'gei. I would set you free, if I could." They both knew that he meant the words, he was certain, and they both knew that it meant nothing. Tsali'gei bit her lip and stared hard at him, eyes bright.

"Well," she said finally, "that is something, I suppose."

She pulled herself into the saddle, graceful and strong as the sea, and rode on ahead without looking back. Jian mounted his own horse, a fine high-stockinged bay with a white blaze and fire in his step, and followed at a safe distance. Perri urged his mount to catch up with that of his Sen-Baradam.

"How is married life?" Perri asked, as if asking what it might be like to catch a wyvern by the tail.

"If I live to be as old as the emperor," Jian muttered, "I will never understand the first thing about women."

"Ah, Sen-Baradam." Perri grinned and winked his remaining eye, "Finally you speak wisdom."

"As you say, *bai dan*," Jian agreed, and he laughed as Perri responded with a rude gesture. They rode on a red sky morning to

Bizhan, at the head of a respectable army, the triumphant return of princes to a land which had once driven them to Khanbul as slaves.

Jian was reminded of the magician Hafou in one of his mother's stories, who could neither sleep nor die until he had unburdened his pockets of gold and his heart of regret. As the magician shed his wealth and his sins, his heart grew lighter and lighter until at last he flew up into the sky and away to the land of peaceful dreamings.

"See that eddy, with the three white birches?" he told Garid Far-Eye as they crossed a small cold stream. "That is where I caught my first redfish. Dao-dao's father taught us to make little canoes out of birch bark, but ours were not very good, and we all got wet.

"Here," he told Tsali'gei, "I would come with my mother to collect wool from the blue goat. See how it clumps in the blackthorn? I was the only boy in my village with a cloak of blue goat's wool."

"In the Twilight Lands," she told him, "we collect the golden fleece, and our old men weave it into tunics for our honored hunters, as the old women sing songs of glory and luck for the hunt." Her smile was beautiful, but faded quickly. "*They* collect the golden fleece, I should say. I will never do so again."

Jian had heard stories of the golden flock, and the great ram who guarded it, but Tsali'gei's eyes were far away and full of sorrow, so he did not press her for more. Still, it was more than she had said to him since their meeting, and he decided to take this as a good sign.

I would hunt the blue goat for you, he wanted to say, *and the golden ram, too, if it would make you smile at me like that.*

Here, he thought as they passed the old rice mill, *is where I tried to convince Faizhui the miller's daughter to kiss me.* He had not been successful in his quest, but since that time he had learned enough about women to keep that memory to himself.

The land had not changed much—an old apple tree that Jian had loved had been felled, a new vineyard planted, but these were ordinary things—but the people of Bizhan were not at all as Jian remembered them. They melted away at the sight of the emperor's troops, driven before the Daechen princes like schools of silverfish before hunting serpents, blown away like chaff separated from the wheat. The pig farmers, the miller's family, even the fishmonger's boys so full of vinegar and swagger fled at the sight of banners, and armor, and horses.

Bizhan had seemed the world to Jian, in the long-ago days of his childhood and up until this very spring. Looking at it now through the eyes of a Daechen prince, he saw it for what it was—a poor and unimportant province of Sindan, filled with poor and unimportant slaves of the empire, small people with even less power than he could claim.

Jian found, to his secret shame, that this suited him very well. *You reviled me not a year past*, he thought at their retreating backs, *you spat and cursed my name. "Daemon spawn," you called me, you spat upon my shadow and drove me from your midst. Now I am returned to you as Sen-Baradam, you and your lands are to be given over to my control, and you flee from the sight of me. Am I so different from the child you cursed, from the youth you cast aside?*

Jian knew he was, and it pleased him. As he rode at the front of his army, and his retainers, and their retainers, he thought it a very fine thing to find the village guard posts abandoned, its gates thrown wide as Bizhan reluctantly awaited his embrace. The cobbled streets were abandoned, houses and shops shut tight against the storm that was Jian Sen-Baradam.

Ah, but there was one who had not fled, who stood in the middle of the village square straight-backed and bold, eyes flashing.

"Jian!" Tiungpei cried, "my son!" and she flung her arms wide, welcoming the storm.

Welcoming him home.

The village had changed, and Jian had changed, but the house of Tiungpei was as enduring as the sea. Fish stew simmered as always over the warm hearth-fire, and the sunlight through sea-glass sent colored lights to dance upon the walls. Jian served soup and bread and spiced wine to his mother and to his wife, and with every move, every mouthful of soup, every woman's smile, his heart grew lighter and lighter till it seemed he might fly.

They did not speak of winnowing, or Inseeings, or the rumors of Sen-Baradam uprisings. Neither did they speak of sundered lands, or stolen girls, or the lords and ladies of twilight. Rather they spoke of important things—of fish nets and found treasures, of pearls and goats and weddings.

Tsali'gei took to his mother as she had not yet taken to Jian and the two women sat close, so close their knees and foreheads were nearly touching, as they discussed the medicinal properties of seaweed. Tsali'gei clutched a pearl his mother had gifted her, a bride-gift worthy of a young empress: a rose-colored pearl bigger than Jian's fist, which she had kept hidden away for half a lifetime. Such a pearl might have bought Tiungpei her freedom and a life of ease. She had saved it, instead, for the wife of her son.

"For my daughter," she said as she pressed it into Tsali'gei's palm, and they had both cried.

This, Jian thought, as he settled by the fire to eat his soup, *this is worth any pain, any sacrifice*. In that moment he realized that he would do anything, pay any price, if only time would march on and leave in peace this little house and those he loved.

Later that night Tsali'gei came to him, his twilight princess, his Daezhu love, and she led him down the path to the sea. These things he would remember till the end of his days, her skin smooth as a pearl, gleaming beneath the moonslight as she ran before him, shedding her clothes and laughing. The cries of the night-birds, and of the sea, and of his Tsali'gei as he caught her up from behind and spun her round in a dance as old as life. The warm waters that welcomed him home, as her warm embrace welcomed him home, for such as she and he had no need of feather beds or firelight when they had the sand, and the stars, and the wide, wise sea.

Their necklaces—his of pearls and hers of sea-bear claws—tangled together at one point, and broke, and the sight of his treasure spilled upon Tsali'gei's breasts drove Jian mad with desire. Long they lay together, and long they loved one another, and long would he hold her memory as a candle against the cold, cold night.

The moons rolled by, and the stars wheeled overhead, and Jian's heart soared among them light as a feather—but the storm came, a roiling mass of bright shadows and dark lightning, shredding the fragile web of this illusory peace.

He startled awake when the storm rolled over him, a shockwave of music and intent like the tide pulling back, back, back, then crashing upon the world once more in a blinding cacophony. Jian clung to the beach, fingers digging into the wet warm sand as wave upon wave of mist and magic and music laved the world, stealing him away, tossing him into the abyss like a fish tossed into the bottom of a boat. For a moment his hand met that of his wife, and she held him fast.

"Tsali'gei!" he called, and coughed as his lungs filled with cold wet mist.

"Jian!" Her voice was muffled, as if she were far away and under the sea. "Jian!" In the end the storm was too strong for him, too strong for them, and her fingers slid away from his, away and away, a handful of pearls scattered upon the wind.

He struggled blind against the gale, the sand, the sea, fought through the blanket of fog to find her. His bare foot found something cold, and round, and he bent to retrieve it:

A pearl.

Three steps more, and he found a sea-bear's claw, dropped from the necklace Tsali'gei always wore. Another pearl, another claw, and his heart twisted with hope. She was leaving a trail for him, so that he might find his way home in the storm. A pearl, a claw, a claw, a pearl… Jian picked them up one by one and clutched them to his breast.

The storm waned, as storms do—even magical storms roused to anger by wicked kings in far-off lands. The fog lifted and Jian walked faster, following the trail of claws and pearls, till his hands overflowed with them and his heart overflowed with relief and joy to see, at the end of this path, a small and perfect footprint. He lifted his eyes to find a strange and pale light, peered into the waning mist and he beheld a shadowy figure.

"Tsali'gei!" he called out, and began to run along the beach, pearls and claws threatening to spill from his grasp. "Tsali, wait—"

The figure turned, and through the mist Jian saw that it was not her, not at all. Shoulders as wide as a bear's he saw, as the light grew, hair wild and tangled as seaweed, eyes wide and round as...

...as his own.

Jian stopped running. He stopped breathing, and stood on the cold sand with his pearls and her claws and his heart all tangled together in his hands. The man smiled at him, a wide smile full of welcome and sharp white teeth, and he growled in a voice like the sea.

"At last, at last, welcome home at last. My son."

That first night they fought, tooth and fist and claw.

The twilight drums sounded, *tha-rum tha-rum tha-rumble-rumble* like the beating of the heart of the dragon, asleep at the center of the world. Red flames leapt, and dancers leapt over them, and the horns blew like the wind. It was an ancient song, a memory like bones and dust, calling Jian to live and die and live again.

His body was slick with fat and oil, blood and sweat, and he bared his teeth in a snarl. His opponent snarled back, laughing, slapping at the red dirt with his clawed forepaw, a challenge.

Jian roared and charged, and in the sweat-thick mists of twilight they met in the middle, claws grasping, teeth snapping, vital and true and alive.

❖

The second night they feasted on meat and bread, salt and water.

He sat with his father, dining on fish and meat. No singed flesh, this, charred beyond recognition and spiced till not even the spirits of the animals themselves might have guessed which was flesh or fish or fowl. Raw meat, fresh and good, still quivering with sacrificed life. They drank spiced wine and fermented milk, thick and sour, cream and berries and honey-comb.

Twilight lords and twilight ladies came to stare at him, to honor him with song and dance and battle, to meet this child who had returned from the lands of Men, as no child ever had. Never had Jian beheld such people. Furred and clawed, antlered and winged they came to stare at him with hands outstretched in welcome. They plied him with salt and water and bread, making him one of them, making it true.

They were not Daechen, half-human princes honored and reviled in the same breath. These were the Dae, first-born, true-born, to whom magic was as natural as breath.

"My son," the lord would say, and clap him on the shoulder. "My boy." Jian's father was a sho'en, a high warlord, first among his peers. He was whole, gentle and good, and he was strong, besting Jian as easily in battle as a young girl catching butterflies. He plied Jian with endless questions about Tiungpei, about her health and wellbeing, her life, her loves. He made a fist and growled when Jian described his stepfather, and laughed at the story of the goats.

"Traded him for goats," he chuckled. "And got the better part of that bargain, I wager. Tiungpei, my girl, my pretty girl. And do you have a pretty girl of your own, my son?"

"I do," Jian answered, chest swelling with pride. "I have a wife. Her name is Tsali'gei…"

"Tsali'gei!" A woman who had been seated halfway down the long table shouted and leapt to her feet, eyes flashing, teeth snapping, a dagger of jade in either hand. "Tsali'gei! My Tsali— she *lives*!" The woman threw her head back and howled, a hair-raising, bone-shattering sound, and the host howled with her.

"Tsali'gei was born among us, Jian," his father explained in a soft and sorrowing voice. "Such children are rare, and almost never survive. They do not easily bend to the emperor's will, and so they... They break. We are bound by ancient treaty to cast them into your world in their sixteenth year." His large and liquid eyes were filled with a thousand years' worth of grief.

"Why send them away, at all?" Jian asked. "The emperor can hardly march into your land and wage war, can he?"

"We must send them into the world of men because their blood, and our tears," his father answered, "are all that bind our worlds together. It is a thin bond and weak, but we are lost without them. Without the world of men we have no sun, as you can see," he gestured out the window to the twilit skies, "and without us, the land of men has no magic. Were the Sundering to be completed..." He slapped his hands hard onto the table, palms-down, knocking his goblet over so that the wine ran red as blood between his fingers. "Both worlds would die."

Tsali'gei's mother howled and wept.

Meat and bread, salt and water.

On the third day Jian was given three gifts—sea-stones, dragon-bones, and a blade of bitter tears.

There were two stones, polished rounds of sea-gray and gold half the size of the palm of Jian's hand. Tsali'gei's mother gave them to him, and explained that these were symbols of sea and sunlight, female and male, and were a traditional gift to new-married couples. Jian bowed low to his second-mother and gifted her, in return, with his mother's pearls that he had plucked from the beach.

"For the day may come," he told her, "when our two worlds are made whole again, and you are always welcome in my house."

"You are a good boy," she told him. "I may not kill you, after all."

Jian smiled weakly and decided to believe she spoke in jest.

The bones—there were three of these, given to him by a goat-horned man—were the smooth polished disks known to Jian's people as blood pennies. Found very rarely inside the skulls of the most ancient shongwei, blood pennies were thought to have magical power, the power to grant one's deepest and darkest desires. Just one would be worth enough to buy half a village— land, cattle, people and all. Jian stared at the three he now held in his hand, and sang softly.

"Heart of Illindra, Soul of Eth,
Blood of the innocent condemned to death.
Under the moons, combine the three,
Coin enough to set you free."

"Even you," the goat-horned man agreed. "Even me." He was blood brother to Jian's father, rather like the dammati, Jian thought, and he favored him with an avuncular smile, bowing low. He gifted the man with the bear claws that Tsali'gei had worn. He ached to let them go, but what else could he do? He had arrived in this land with a fistful of pearls, a fistful of bear claws, and his own skin, something he was even more reluctant to relinquish.

"You are a good lad," the uncle said. He smiled with his wide white teeth. "I may not eat you, after all."

I am beginning to understand, Jian thought, *where some of my mother's dark cradle tales come from.*

The sword of bitter tears was a gift from his father, and it took his breath away. The blade was blue as the sea, with fine waves that ran the length of its blade and rippled like water before his eyes.

Jian's father held it to him hilt-first, as was proper, and wrapped in silk the color of a dangerous sky. Jian accepted the gift in silence and drew the sword from its plain red scabbard. The blade whispered as it slid free. Calling his name, it sang a dream of blood and glory.

"Magic," Jian breathed.

"No more magic than is in my bones, or yours," his father admonished, "nor in our blood or breath. The power of this sword is no less and no greater than the magic in your soul, son. Heed them both wisely."

"We gifted blades like these to the emperors of Sindan in the long ago," his uncle added, eyes snapping yellow-sharp, "but they did not listen to the songs in their hearts and the magic became tainted. Corrupted."

"It is our wish," Tsali'gei's mother continued, as if the three of them had rehearsed this song, "that the son of our sho'en be strong enough to resist this taint, and that he may return us to the lands of Akari, that the gentle beauty of our magic might once more shine bright." Her smile was beautiful, indeed, but it was most certainly not gentle.

"The gentle beauty of our magic—and of our armies. This is the wish of all our hearts," the uncle agreed. "The *darkest* wish."

"How am I supposed to do this?" Jian asked, for his heart knew now where his loyalties lay. The lords and ladies of twilight laughed at this.

"With sea-stones," one of them called, as the world around Jian began to fade away. It was the morning of his third day in the Twilight Lands, the longest any mortal is allowed to remain in a dream.

"And dragon-bones," a woman called. She wore red feathers in her hair and had yellow claws for hands. The land grew thin and pale as watered paint on linen.

"And a blade of bitter tears," his father finished. A hand squeezed Jian's shoulder, lingered, melted away with the dawn.

"Father!" Jian called out. He struggled against the mist, against the growing light, but the magic of his own land drew him back. "Father!"

"Allyr," his father said, smiling even as he disappeared before Jian's too-human eyes. "My name is Allyr."

"*Allyr*," the wind chided. "*Allyr*," the waves scolded.

"Allyr," the dutiful son agreed. Bowing his head to his new-forged blade, he waded back to the shores of man, weeping a song of bitter tears.

TWENTY-THREE

The air in Shehannam reeked of ash and murder.

The empty eyes of dead children, a dagger that reeked of evil, the bones of a slaughtered vash'ai... Hafsa Azeina had one hand full of questions, and no answers in the other. Were those responsible for the deaths of the ne Atu, the royal family of Atualon, also responsible for the attack which had left her sorely wounded, and Khurra'an dying? The Quarabalese, the Daemon Emperor, even the Zeeranim might wish themselves free of Ka Atu, but wishing for the bright rose and grasping the blackthorn branch were two different matters entirely.

If the King of Atualon died before Sulema learned to wield atulfah, the backlash of magic would be powerful enough to unleash a second Sundering. It was unlikely that the world would survive this one.

If you wake the Dragon, she asked her unknown enemy, *who will sing her back to sleep? Do you hate us enough to destroy yourself?*

A soft tap at the door interrupted her trance, bringing her back from the place of dreams.

"Some outlander man wishes to see you, Dreamshifter," Kailee called. The doe-eyed Ja'Akari had taken Saskia's place as her personal guard. "He is not naked. Shall I tell him to bugger off?"

Hafsa Azeina could not help it. She laughed, even as she opened her waking eyes.

"Send him in." She kept her Dreaming eyes half-lidded, wondering who might come to call at this hour, what threat he might pose, and where best to dispose of a body in the Tower of Issa Atu.

The door opened and her visitor stepped into the room. He

was a slight, stooped figure cloaked in the rags and the smell of a root-peddler. His face was concealed in a deep hood, and skinny, begrimed hands clutched a bag that reeked of onions. Hafsa Azeina came slowly to her feet, shaking the last of the dreamwebs from her fingertips.

"Who are you?" she asked, rocking forward so that she stood on the balls of her feet.

"I am every man," he said in a low growl. "I am no man. I am death." Throwing his hood back, he revealed the leathery face of an old man, topped by a shock of red and white hair.

"Mattu Halfmask." She scowled. "Cut the crap." She was not displeased that the young man had survived the Salarians' hospitality, but neither had she wished to see him.

He sighed theatrically, and dropped his bag of onions—at least, she hoped it was onions—with a thump.

"What gave it away?"

"I watched you and your sister put that play on when you were ass-high to a churra," she reminded him, without relaxing her stance. "What are you doing, coming to my rooms dressed like this?"

"Would you rather I had come naked?" He laughed at her from behind the snarling mask, and took a seat, without her leave. "Lovely as you are, Issa Atu, and I mean that most sincerely, I have no desire to rouse the wrath of the Dragon King. No man in Atualon has balls that heavy, I'd wager."

He had a point. "What do you want?"

"A kiss or two, but not from you. A thousand white churrim. A pet wyvern. World peace, but I will settle for a horn of usca, if you have it. In my travels I seem to have acquired a taste for the stuff."

Hafsa Azeina smoothed the scowl from her face, though it took some effort, and poured them each a measure of usca. Then she sank into her favorite chair, feet planted firmly on the floor.

"What do you want?" she asked again. The man was stubborn as a churra, but she had been giving stubborn lessons to churrim before he was born. Mattu lifted the mask from his face and tossed the strong drink back, ending with a grimace. Hafsa Azeina was mute with shock. She had not seen his true face since he was a boy of six or so. Younger than Daru.

And I had thought the mask was just an affectation.

"World peace, as I said, but I will settle for Atualon coming through this war in one piece."

"War?"

"There is no time for a game of spiders-and-shadows, 'Zeina—do not pretend there is." He leaned back with a tired sigh, the empty cup dangling from his fingertips. "You know as well as I that this spectacle of Wyvernus's was nothing more than foolery, meant to divert people's minds from the growing threat. Ka Atu is dying, and the Daemon Emperor would rise to take his place. Shadows and spiders and knives in the dark, Issa Atu.

"It was intended that Wyvernus should lead the delegation to Khanbul, and never return," he continued. "Not alive, at any rate. The Great Salt Road is a treacherous place, and our king is not as strong as the people think. Then you return from the dead, dragging this echovete brat home by the ear... you were supposed to stay dead, you know. Some people, I would imagine, are very irritated with you." He paused and frowned. "I need more usca." Rising gracefully, he poured himself another shot, knocking this one back as quickly as the first.

Hafsa Azeina set aside her own glass, and her knuckles whitened as she grasped the wooden arms of her chair. The usca burned in her gut.

"Whose plan is this?"

"Who do you think?" he mocked. "Who loves Ka Atu best? Whom does he trust the most? The trusted hand wields the cruelest blade, you know this as well as I do. Better, I should think."

"Aasah," she whispered. "Or..." *Leviathus?* But she could not say it. *Damn the boy, where is he?*

"As I said, your guess is as good as mine. Does it even matter?"

"Yes. No. I suppose not." She let go of the chair, if not her anger. "Why have you not come to me sooner?"

"Now *there* is a question I can answer," he responded. "I did not trust you, beautiful lady."

She blinked at his sudden honesty.

"The ne Atu have been dying for so many years, and under such suspicious circumstances... nearly all of them while you were still in residence, I might add. Now you return, on the very eve of the king's death, most conveniently with his only possible heir in tow. You will forgive me if I found your story somewhat less than convincing."

"So what changed your mind?"

"I have not changed my mind, but time is running out, and I find myself with no other ally. No real option other than to trust you and hope for the best. I have to think that if you were planning to kill my king you would have done it by now, and placed your daughter on the Dragon Throne before she was well enough and prepared enough to fight your influence." He spread his hands wide. "Ka Atu would have simply forgotten to wake one morning... the use of atulfah has worn his soul thin, he has admitted as much, and no one would suspect a thing. Not in your presence, in any case. As your barbarians say, 'ehuani.' There is beauty in truth."

Hafsa Azeina said nothing as the taste of heart's blood flooded her mouth. *That is exactly how it would have happened.*

Might still happen.

Ehuani.

"Life is pain," she whispered. "Only death comes easy." In that bleak moment, she wanted nothing more than to return to the Zeera, where the predators were huge and venomous and honest in their intentions. Where she and Khurra'an would once again be just another terror in the night.

"Please do not leave us just yet," Mattu said. "Dragon wakes, woman, you wear your every thought on the skin of your face. I have to wonder how you have survived this long. Yet you are the only one Ka Atu listens to."

She snorted. *Listen to me? He is a stubborn old goat.*

"The only one he listens to," Mattu insisted, "and certainly the only one of us he can trust. I have seen him with you, Dreamshifter… and more tellingly, I have seen you look at him. Truly, you wear your heart on your face." He pulled the mask down over his own features, and the cowl up to conceal the mask, then he strode across the room to reclaim his bag of onions and the shuffling walk of an ancient seller of roots. Shaking his head at her, he slipped from the room.

"Try not to let your heart get eaten," he said over his shoulder, "before we figure out a way to save the world."

TWENTY-FOUR

Twice before in her life, Hannei had journeyed to Min Yaarif, the city between two worlds. Each time, she had gained a name.

The first time, she had been a babe-in-arms. Her mother, Horsemistress Tisara, had carried her across the Dibris to meet and be named by her father. His name had been Daoud, and he had been one of the ul-Khalma'a, a river pirate. Hannei had never seen him again.

The second time to the city of slavers, she had been a young warrior-in-waiting, traveling with the Ja'Akari as they escorted a herd of churrim to market in hopes of trading the second-choice animals for a few healthy children. Late one night, while a fellow guard was distracted by the sight of a pretty slave boy, Hannei had caught a thief trying to steal a spotted buck. She had stabbed the man with the pointy end of a borrowed shamsi, and watched trembling as he bled out upon the sand.

First Warden had gifted that blade to Hannei, had named her Ja'Akari for the first time, in front of her pride-mates.

On this third and final visit, Min Yaarif was in another world entirely. On this day, Hannei Ja'Akari—now and forever Hannei Kha'Akari—was to be named *slave*.

The day was as right and alive as any along the river Dibris. A golden haze hung like a veil over the lands to the east, from which she had been cast. Red stained the sky to the west, a warning to those who would brave the peaks of the Jehannim mountains, or the Seared Lands beyond. The river herself, sharp and silver as an unblooded sword, sliced the two apart as neatly as flesh from bone.

Hannei let the sights and smells and stench of Min Yaarif blow past her like wind across the Zeera, though it raised no song in her heart. She was as dead inside as Eid Kalmut, the Valley of Death, as empty as a loving cup spilled upon the sand. Ismai rode before her, splendid upon his bright asil. He led her to market like a goat, all the while thinking he had saved her life.

A life in chains, she thought again, *is worth less than a handful of sand in the desert.* Better she had died upon the low stone table, that she might seek Tammas upon the Lonely Road.

Swallowing the bitter thought, she stifled a whimper at the pain it caused her.

Lirya, riding to one side, glanced down at the prisoner. Her mouth twisted in disgust. "Do you miss your tongue, liar? Does your mouth hurt, murderer?" She spat upon Hannei's bald head in disgust. "Akari willing, you will feel the loss every moment of your miserable life. If it were up to me, you would be dead already. If it were up to me, you would be walking, not riding so much as a broken-down churra."

Unbidden, the voice of her sword sister whispered in Hannei's ear. *How can you walk, if you are dead?* Sulema would have laughed. *Who ever heard of the walking dead? Stupid as a cup of churra piss, that one.*

Hannei grunted a laugh, but that hurt, too. *Getting me in trouble even when you are long gone*, she retorted. *Typical.*

"You laugh at me?" Lirya drew the lips back from her teeth, and reached for her shamsi. "I will teach you a—"

"Enough, Lirya."

The voice of Sareta, First Warden of the Zeeranim, hacked through the stinking air like a flensing knife. "One does not waste words on the Kha'Akari." She rode into view astride Hannei's own mare. "After all… she cannot answer." And she smiled.

Hannei pressed the aching stump of her tongue hard against the roof of her mouth, hard enough that she could taste—or remember the taste of—blood. Her heart, still beating, urged her to vengeance. In that moment, Hannei learned that she could still feel, after all. She felt hatred.

In that moment Hannei chose a name for herself.

I am Kishah, she thought, stealing the ancient word for her own. *I am vengeance, and these are my people now, for the rest of my life.*

However long that might be.

The stench and noise deepened to a fine stew as they drew nearer the slave houses. Hannei's vision narrowed so that all she could see was the tall wooden stage upon which she might soon stand, bound and naked, to be sold for a pig, a couple of goats, a handful of beans. So had she watched slaves dispatched in the past, but she had never *seen* them.

Now, as a man with a hooked pole shepherded a naked old man up the steps and onto the next leg of his wretched journey, Hannei watched her own fate unfolding before her eyes, and this time she saw clearly. She saw the whip marks and bruises upon the old man's begrimed skin, saw how one ankle turned under his slight weight, likely due to an old, untreated injury. His hair, shorn close so as to discourage lice, was bald in patches as if it had been torn from his head, and his eyes...

Those eyes. Hannei wondered what those eyes had seen, to make them go dead like that. Though Hannei had thought herself past all fear she shivered, and her hands broke out in a clammy sweat. *Will my eyes come to look like that?*

"Afraid, liar?" Lirya tossed her warrior's braids, mocking Hannei's loss. "You should be. I hear there is a demand for your kind, in the whore pits. Perhaps you will get lucky, and someone will buy your skinny ass for fish food. Perhaps..."

"*Enough*, Ja'Akari. It is done."

Ismai turned in his saddle so suddenly that his lovely mare Ehuani did an agitated dance. Lirya's teeth snapped shut and her eyes widened in fury at having been addressed so, especially before outlanders, but she desisted. Ismai had, after all, lost his entire family.

As I have lost mine, Hannei thought, even as Ismai's eyes slid past hers. *My family, and more.* Though he had declared her innocent and had spared her life—such as it was—he obviously was not convinced of her innocence. That hurt as much as the loss of her tongue. *"It is done,"* Ismai had said, but for Hannei, the nightmare had only begun.

You never said much, anyway, the ghost of Sulema teased. *Now, if I had lost my tongue, that would be a tragedy.*

Hannei almost smiled behind her gag, trying to imagine Sulema Ja'Akari without a voice. Somehow, she was sure, her sword sister would have talked her way out of this storm of shit. Sulema would never allow herself to be so helpless.

But I am not Sulema.

Akari Sun Dragon gazed down impassively as the old man was sold for less than a handful of beans, and the slave handler stepped down from the platform to approach their little group. He favored them with a wide smile, and spoke in halting Zeerani.

"Ah, children of the other half of the world that is not our half! What are you doing this evening, showing your asses at mealtime?"

Hannei blinked. Lirya sniggered. Sareta rode to the head of the group, face impassive.

"Khutlani," she chided, then in tradespeak, "Do not speak our words. Your tongue is too dull to cut such fine cloth. We are here to sell *this*"—she gestured to Hannei, even as Lirya stepped aside to reveal their captor—"as well as the churra it sits upon. We have no further use for either of them."

It was the man's turn to blink. He was short, and wide, and round, and his confusion made him look like a turtle basking on a log.

"You are selling a warr—"

"*Hsst!*" Lirya and Isara hissed, as one.

"Khutlani," Sareta repeated, her face as smooth and expressionless as river-stones. "This one is Kha'Akari, nothing more. Akari Sun Dragon has turned his face from her, and now we do the same. What will you offer us?"

As the lies fell from Sareta's lips, Akari Sun Dragon looked down upon his chosen warrior, his champion, the girl who had loved him with all her heart for as long as she could remember… and once more, he did nothing.

Akari has turned his face from me, Hannei thought, poking at the idea even as she poked the stump of a tongue against her teeth, testing the pain, tasting it. *First Warrior of the Zeeranim speaks falsehoods in his name… and he does nothing. She sells me before my sisters, my brothers, and they do nothing.* She poked at the pain, prodded it, finally embraced it with her whole heart.

And she felt…

Nothing.

She did not watch as the man poured a fistful of salt tablets into Sareta's waiting palm, did not react as the people for whom she had vowed to die turned their backs on her and left without so much as a backward glance. Nor did she spare them a tear. As Ismai himself had said, *it is done.*

The man snapped his fat fingers and a pair of scrawny dust-skinned lads darted from a low stone stable. They dragged her down from the back of her churra, letting her fall to the ground— badly, since her arms were still bound. Pain lanced through her jaw as she struck it. They led the bawling animal away, likely to be sold at a better price than she had fetched. Hannei winced as the fat man hauled her upright. Her still-swollen face throbbed and her tongue was a ball of wet fire. He scowled, grabbing her jaw in both hands and wrenching her mouth open.

Hannei blinked back tears of pain as he yanked the gag down and thrust his dirty fingers between her teeth. At the last, even her body betrayed her. She shivered from her shorn scalp to her torn feet, and it was all she could do not to piss herself in terror.

"Cut-tongue," he growled in trade. "Filthy savages cheated me. She's pretty enough, I suppose, once you get her washed. Are you intact, I wonder, little desert slut? Let us see…" The fat little man let go of her jaw and, quick as a snake, grabbed her by the pussy.

The world went red.

Hannei slammed the crown of her head into the man's face and was rewarded with a wet crunch as bones gave way. As he staggered back she brought her knees up into his crotch, one-two, channeling rage and heartbreak and betrayal into the need to hurt, to kill. Even as the man fell Hannei spun and leapt, pummeling him with both feet. He flopped backward like a speared fish, shrieking and spraying blood. Hannei leapt and drove her heel down, screaming wordless profanities as she aimed for the man's exposed throat, intending to end his life.

That blow never landed.

Something hit Hannei hard on one side and sent her flying. She ducked her chin, hit the ground with one shoulder and rolled as she had been taught, once to take the shock of landing, twice to gain momentum, three times and she gained her feet to stand in a low crouch, panting and growling as onlookers gaped at the sight of a barbarian warrior standing over the fallen slaver.

Grab me by the pussy, will you, fat outlander? She spat dirt—or drooled dirt, rather, as lack of a tongue made even such a simple thing impossible—and waited for them to kill her. She was a warrior. He should have expected she would hit like a girl.

It is not so hard to die, she thought. The dreamshifter had been right. *Life is pain. Only death comes easy.*

A curious noise to her left drew Hannei's attention. She cut her eyes to the side, not wanting to divert her focus from the small group of men who struggled to raise the spluttering, bawling slaver to his feet.

The breath caught in her throat.

The thing that had sent her sprawling stood not an arm's reach from her side. Scaled lips drew back from row upon row of yellowed teeth as long as her fingers. A crest of brilliant gold and blue feathers rose along the top of its head and ran down its spine… but it was no bird. Iridescent scales in greens and golds and blues shone in the sunlight and whispered as it swayed this way and that, but it was no snake, not even a lionsnake.

It was nearly as tall as she, lean and muscled like a cat, and Hannei had no doubt that it could kill her as easily as she had beaten the outland slaver.

What is it? she thought, for one moment forgetting the misery her life had become. *It is beautiful.*

It wanted to eat her.

Hannei shrugged. It was a good day to die, after all. She took a step toward the beast. It blinked at her and hissed, rattling a fine set of claws held before its scaled breast, and the tight crest rose higher. Another step and it crouched low, preparing to leap.

A hand closed over Hannei's shoulder, holding her back. Warm breath hissed into her ear.

"Girl." A woman's voice, and it spoke Zeerani. "You really fucked up."

TWENTY-FIVE

For as long as he could remember, Ismai had held a dream of his life, like a painting in one of his mother's books. A vision of riding across the desert on a fine horse, with a vash'ai by his side, surrounded by warriors. Had there been a painter among them on this fine day, she might have captured just such a scene with her brushes and pigments, to hang on the walls of Aish Kalumm, the city of the Zeeranim.

The image he had held in his heart was so at odds with the truth that the images bled together until all that was left was an ugly mess the color of dried blood, leached of all beauty.

They rode north with the waters of the Dibris to one side and the wicked peaks of the Jehannim too close for comfort on the other. Not so long ago, Ismai might have slipped away from the group and explored the foothills, seeking wights and spider druids and adventure. He might have ridden hard to the north, to Bayyid Eidtein and the Great Salt Road, and from there to Atualon. Surely Sulema had had her fill of brazen bare-legged men by now. She would see him in the touar, with his fine horse and his Ruh'ayya, and she would...

She would do nothing, he thought, sinking lower in the saddle. *Even if I could find her among all those people, she is the daughter of the Dragon King, and will be queen one day. I was nothing to her when she rode among the Ja'Akari, and I would be nothing to her now. Less than nothing.*

You are something to me, Ruh'ayya whispered in his mind. He thought she sounded hurt.

And you are everything to me, my beauty, he told her. *You are the fire in my sky.*

I am, she thought. *You are a good human.*

211

He almost smiled at that.

"I am pleased to see you in better spirits, Ja'Sajani." Isara rode up on his left. Her fine flaxen stallion, Nahhar, whickered at Ehuani. "The heart should not linger on what is past. Live in the day, as does your Ruh'ayya."

Ismai shot the warrior a sideways glance. Her braids were freshly oiled, and her skin as well. She glowed with health, the very picture of *saghaani*. Her vest was beaded in blues and greens—the colors of fertility—and her dark eyes flashed interest as she stared directly at him.

He closed his mouth with a snap.

Isara? Pretty, sweet Isara, interested in him?

'Ware the hunt, human male. Ruh'ayya dropped her mouth open and huffed a cat's laugh. *This young queen has your scent.*

The memory of the warrior's treatment of Hannei hit him like cold water on a new fire. Ismai firmed his mouth and looked away from her.

"On this day, in this moment, we betray one of our own."

"Do not waste your pity on that one, Ja'Sajani." Isara pushed closer. Too close, so that Ehuani pinned her ears and snapped at the chestnut flirt. "She is Kha'Akari and none of ours." Her tone softened. "It is good, however, that you have a soft heart. A soft heart and a hard body. These are fine qualities in a man." With a grin and a wink of her huge dark eyes, Isara was gone.

Mastersmith Hadid rode up on his right, laughing softly. "I am surprised that you are surprised, young Ja'Sajani."

"But—" Hadid held up a hand and extended his fingers, one by one.

"You wear the touar. You ride a fine mare. You have been chosen by the vash'ai, just as so many abandon the people." His face darkened at this, for his own Orujho had been gone for a moon now. "You are the last of the line of Zula Din, and of late I have heard the warriors comparing you favorably to your elder brother. It would not surprise me if young Isara soon approaches our First Mother for breeding-rights, if she has not already. Nor might she be the first."

"They might as well braid stud beads into my hair." Ismai's face grew hot, even as his brows drew down in a scowl.

"That is exactly what they are after, my boy, or did you think a warden's duties were limited to taking census and settling border disputes?" His smile faded. "The duty of a Ja'Sajani is to his people, young Ismai. You are young, and strong, and not entirely ugly. Your brother was not much older than you are, now, when he first gave the gift of life to a young Mother." He grinned. "Not such an onerous duty, when you think about it."

"I do not like the idea of women discussing me as if I were some… stallion. I will choose for myself."

Hadid laughed so hard at this that he bent over in the saddle, slapping at his thighs.

"I wish you the best of luck with that! If you figure out how to manage such a thing…" He straightened, wiping tears from his cheeks. "…please let the rest of us know. Truly, you would be a hero among men." Still chuckling, he trotted off on his dun mare.

Isara rode not far ahead, and Ismai was sure she had overheard the whole conversation. She glanced over her shoulder at him and smiled, the smile of a vash'ai queen eyeing a fat young tarbok. He sank even lower into his saddle.

I do not understand females.

You are not meant to understand females, Ruh'ayya chided. *You are meant to obey us.*

An image of Char's face, swathed in rags and veils, swam unbidden into Ismai's mind. He suddenly longed to be with his friend, to sit by a fire in the shadow of Eid Kalmut, sharing roast hare and companionable silence.

I will ask her advice, he thought, and he straightened in his saddle. She was the one friend he could count on for unbiased advice. *She always knows just what to say.*

Kithren, Ruh'ayya warned, as she always did when he thought of Char, *you should be more wary of that one. She is not what you—*

"First Warrior!" one of the Ja'Akari, farther ahead, shouted.

"Riders. 'Ware, *riders*, and they… they are…" Her voice rose into a thin, high shriek of purest terror.

"Arachnist!" another bellowed.

All around Ismai, the warriors exploded into action. Swords and bows were drawn, horses screamed as they caught the enemy's scent, and the few vash'ai who still rode with their human kithren leapt into action. A moving, living ring formed around the Ja'Sajani in their midst. Isara rode past, face a mask of fury as she screamed a war cry. One hand held her bow and her stallion's reins, high on his neck, giving him his head as she yanked the laces of her vest.

"Show me yours, filthy bastards!" she screamed. "*Show me yours!*"

Ismai stood tall in the stirrups, craning his neck to look up ahead, trying to see…

…and then he saw, and wished he had not.

At first glance his eyes told him that a man sat on a horse, ahead on a low hill, raising his arms as if he would welcome them in a friendly embrace. A handful of other men stood in a loose ring around him—an escort of sorts, perhaps. When Ismai's mind finally heard what his eyes were screaming, however, his head jerked back as if he had been struck.

The man on the horse was no man at all, but a nightmare riding a nightmare steed. He had too many arms—arms that twitched and flapped like dying things as they reached toward the Zeeranim, and his horse's head flopped from side to side as if its neck had been broken in several places. The pale man-things that swayed about those fell hooves, insectoid eyes glittering, chitinous pale not-skin seeming to glow red in the dying light, could only be—

"Reavers," Hadid whispered hoarsely. The mastersmith pressed his dun close to Ehuani, and Ismai's silver mare was so upset she did not even protest. "Akari help us, those are reavers."

The arachnist waved his dead and twitching arms, and Ismai's stomach clenched as the reavers, insect-like tools of the arachnids, sprang toward them. Ismai drew his sword, kissed the blade, and raised it high, letting it reflect the last light of Akari upon his upturned face. He threw his head back and yelled, a war cry that trailed off into a fit of laughter.

What is so funny? Ruh'ayya asked. She half-stood, half-crouched, hackles stiff and tail lashing from side to side. *We are about to die, you and I.*

Exactly, he replied, laughing again. *We are about to die.*

He kicked his mare, and they sprang forward to meet their doom. To dream of battle and glory was one thing. To watch blood shed under the sun was quite another.

The Ja'Akari hit the reavers in wedge formation, rolling over them like a sandstorm. Blades flashing, eyes flashing, ululating war cries, they danced a dance, and played a game upon the sands, a game with rules as ancient and venerated as the Zeera herself.

The reavers did not dance, and they did not play by the rules. Two of them crouched, skittered sideways, and leapt upon a single rider. It was Hudada on her lovely bay mare, a woman nearly as old as Ismai's mother and with a smile and wink ready for any boy who might sneak down to the kitchens in search of an extra meal. She went down horse and all, shrieking beneath the weight of her attackers, their flashing limbs and wide black mouths. A gout of blood and gore rose into the air like a dark blessing.

Isara screamed and charged, shamsi raised to the sun, terrible and glorious. Sareta, snarling like a vash'ai, knocked a reaver from the back of another warrior's horse and crushed it beneath her mare's hooves.

Reyhanna was pulled from her horse. She rolled, leapt to her feet, and charged her attacker bare-chested, bare-handed, fierce as the midday sun. The reaver sprang toward her—

Mastersmith Hadid rode past Ismai, blacksmith's hammer held high, smith's robes thrown back from his face.

These scenes flashed before Ismai's eyes. Then he crashed headlong into battle, and the world about him exploded into chaos. Smashed between two Ja'Akari, his Ehuani jostled so that she staggered and nearly went down, he hauled hard on the reins and then dropped them altogether, of necessity trusting his mare to keep them both safe as a reaver clawed its way over a riderless horse and leapt upon him. A smell of sulfur and burnt cloves engulfed Ismai, stinging his eyes and making him cough. He beat the thing in its face with the pommel of his sword and his off hand.

It hissed and chittered, striking at him with arms hard as staves and serrated like knives down the sides so that they cut him. Its mouth opened wide, wide. He struck it between its burnt-black eyes, screaming—

Ruh'ayya leapt through the dust and gore, mouth gaping in a gorgeous snarl, claws extended. Her tusks sank into the reaver's back. The thing squealed, let go of Ismai, and they fell away, lost to him.

He swung at the face of another reaver, missed, and nearly lost his sword. The shamsi's grip was slick with ichor and blood. *Grip lightly*, he reminded himself. *Move slowly and with grace. To move too quickly is to lose the way. Keep your gaze broad and strong.* He took a deep breath, but let it out again in a long, shuddering moan when the confusion before him parted and he saw, too clearly, the nightmare that was an arachnist.

Istaz never taught us about this, his mind gibbered. *He never.*

The many-armed figure sat on his freakish mount and watched the battle with an air of detached amusement. He wore black robes, Ismai saw, tattered and worn as corpse rags. They fluttered about him like cobwebs in a foul wind. As the Ja'Akari overcame his reavers one by one, smashing and hacking the foul things and turning their attention toward their fell master, half his face twitched upward in a terrible grin.

The spider-priest raised his upper arms high, over his head, and the dead arms twitched and flapped excitedly as the sand all about them began to roll and boil. Ehuani screamed as the ground beneath her hooves burst open and wave upon wave of spiders vomited forth.

Ismai had seen russet ridgebacks before, of course. The ground-dwelling spiders were as much a part of the Zeera as wind or sand, their eggs considered a delicacy among the prides. But he had never seen them like this. A mad, hissing mass of grasping legs and snapping mandibles swarmed over man and woman, horse and vash'ai.

Ehuani squealed and then screamed, a sound that pierced Ismai's ears and his heart. His good, true mare, lost to terror, threw herself into the air. Ismai pushed himself away from the saddle as the mare went up, and he was nearly crushed as she fell back and over, legs flailing, to land full upon her back. She thrashed to her feet, screamed again, and took off at a full gallop, bucking and kicking at anything in her path.

'Ware, Kithren! Ruh'ayya screamed in his mind. *'Ware!*—

Her voice cut off.

Ismai pivoted, crouching and raising his sword defensively, and in the end was betrayed by shamsi and sun and sand. His heel slipped so that he staggered back a step, the precious golden blade twisted just so and reflected the hot gaze of the Sun Dragon full into his eyes, blinding him. The moment passed, but in that instant a reaver had closed the distance between them. Hands as strong and hard as tree roots gripped Ismai's shoulders so tightly his arms went numb and he dropped his sword into the sand.

The thing's small black eyes, shiny as obsidian, twisted in their burned sockets and it opened its mouth grotesquely wide, wormlike tongue writhing as if it would lick his fear from the air between them. The thing leaned in to bite his face off. Ismai stared into the eyes of death…

…and laughed.

He laughed even as he twisted, Snake in the Blackthorn coming as easily to him as if he had worn the blue his entire life. He laughed as ichor sprayed across his face, stinging skin and eyes, he laughed even as beneath his heel he crushed a spider bigger than his head. Three smaller spiders raced up his legs, too fast for him to shake off, and a giant red-spiked arachnid the size of a small tarbok waved its forelegs as it advanced, mandibles tucking and chewing in anticipation of the taste of his flesh.

"Show me yours!" he screamed at the fell thing, as if he had become a warrior after all. He laughed as its cluster of beady little eyes twitched in confusion. Ismai threw back his head—

His laughter was cut off as a strong arm wrapped around his throat from behind, lifting him up and out of the battle. Golden scales blinded his eyes, golden wings enfolded him in a silken caress as Akari Sun Dragon swept down from the heavens to take him home.

"Burn the bodies. No, the spiders only. The *gha'alim* must be burned with dragonfire, pile them here, and the *shakkat*," she spat, indicating the body of the arachnist, now lying some distance from what remained of his head. "Dismembered and burned. Also with dragonfire."

"Dragonfire?" Ismai flung another dead russet onto the growing mound of corpses. The reavers, as Ishtaset had ordered, were being dragged and put in a separate pile. Nobody had, as yet, volunteered to collect the remains of the spider-priest.

Their own dead had been carefully wrapped and laid together. They would, Ishtaset had declared, be making the long ride home.

"Dragonfire," she agreed. The warrior regarded Ismai with some amusement. "You will see."

When she turned her head like that, and the sun caught in her bleached mane, Ishtaset was the fiercest and, Ismai thought, the most beautiful thing he had ever seen. In her gilded wyvern's-scale armor and glittering robes—which had made him think he had been stolen away by Akari—she seemed hardly less magnificent than the Sun Dragon himself.

Sareta walked up to the golden warrior, frowning, though she tried to hide it. She had been frowning, Ismai thought, since these warriors of legend had ridden out of the sun and saved them all. "Mah'zula" they named themselves, after those first warriors who had ridden with Zula Din.

"I hardly think such measures are necessary," Sareta said, straightening. She was half a hand shorter than Ishtaset, and too obviously found that irritating, as well. "We need to get our wounded back to Aish Kalumm, that our healers may see to their needs."

"Ah, yes, Aish Kalumm, the City of Mothers." Ishtaset folded strong arms across her chest. "Houses of stone in which you… Ja'Akari… crouch like feeble old men, hiding from the very mother who gave birth to you. No wonder the vash'ai have all but deserted you." At this, the warrior's own sleek cat, nearly as big as Khurra'an, padded to stand beside her. "It also is no wonder you allow your men to ride so far from the prides, so that they may protect you."

"Khutlani," one of the golden warriors hissed.

Sareta's face was hard as rock. She opened her mouth to speak, but Ishtaset walked past her without so much as a glance.

"Ah, Anarra! *Je halan shukri*, thank you for responding so quickly."

"*Je halan el'aish*," a woman responded. She wore brilliant hooded robes of green and blue, red and black, and pushed the hood back, revealing her face. "It is an honor and a duty to serve."

Ismai stared. The woman's face was heavily tattooed in reptilian patterns, also of blue and green and gold. Bright plumes had been fastened into her braids so that she looked more than half lionsnake. In place of a warrior's vest she wore a harness fashioned of straps of lionsnake skin, from which depended a myriad of snakes' teeth, plumes, and small glass bottles of blue and green.

"Aulani!" one of the Mah'zula yelled in a voice high with tension. "They are stirring!" Ismai did not like the sound of that, at all. He turned slowly toward the voice, even as he heard Mastersmith Hadid gasp.

"One of the reavers is alive!"

Ishtaset rolled her eyes. She and the lionsnake woman strolled casually to the place where they had thrown the dead reavers. Ismai could see that the body of the arachnist had indeed been dismembered and thrown onto the pile.

For the first time since he could remember, Ismai did not feel hungry at all.

"The reaver is not dead," the snake woman said to nobody in

219

particular. She stopped at the heap of corpses, where serrated arms were waving feebly, fingers twitching like the legs of a squashed spider.

Kithren, Ruh'ayya warned, limping over to join him. She had been sorely wounded by the reaver, and stitched up again by the Mah'zula—who, as she pointed out in her silent, catlike way, were stepping warily back from the corpses and especially the snake woman. Ismai stepped back, as well.

"Neither issss it alive," the snake woman continued. "It is a reaver." As if that explained everything. Unfastening a long green bottle from one of the straps, she held it up to the sunlight. Dark, iridescent liquid swirled within, and Ismai caught a faint scent of musk.

Lionsnake venom, he thought, surprised. *What...*

One of the Mah'zula lit a torch and handed it to the snake woman. Ismai backed away even further, so quickly he almost tripped over his own feet. Lionsnake venom and fire did not mix. Or rather, they mixed entirely too well.

"What!" First Warrior snapped, striding toward Ishtaset and the snake woman. "What are you—"

"Sssssssssssss!" the snake woman hissed. "You will ssssee." She brought the bottle of venom to her lips as if it were a skin of usca. Cheeks puffed gently, the pink tip of her tongue sticking slightly out. She held the torch up in front of her mouth.

Pursed her lips...

...and *blew*.

A gout of flame, bilious green streaked with red and gold, shot from the woman's mouth as if she were dragonkin. It engulfed the near side of the corpse pile, and every nightmare Ismai had ever had came to life at once.

Not dead, he thought. Ruh'ayya pressed into his legs, half-hissing, half-snarling, and they backed away from the seething, screaming conflagration, backpedaling at a near run. Neither were they alone. *Not dead, not dead.*

Neither were they alive.

Flaming reavers rose and leapt and dragged themselves from

the tangled pile, shrieking and chittering like mad things even as their chitinous skin crisped and crumbled in the vermilion flames. One of them ran hissing at the snake woman, who took another swig of venom and spat flames into the thing's face till it was nothing but a pile of stinking ash. The arachnist's severed arms flapped and flopped like live fish thrown into a hot pan, and a smell unlike anything Ismai could have imagined rose in a thick, black cloud, burning his eyes and lungs, staining the sky.

Before his eyes, the arachnist and his reavers were reduced to a stinking, twitching, oily mass of slime. The snake woman finally ran out of fire and leaned forward, hands on her knees, panting hoarsely. Ishtaset patted her on the back, murmuring soothing words as the woman regained her breath.

"*Yeh Atu*," Mastersmith Hadid breathed at Ismai's shoulder. "*Yeh Atu*." Ishtaset straightened and turned to face them. Her eyes met those of Sareta in a steady, challenging gaze. The First Warrior was the first to look away.

"You have… our thanks," she muttered finally, and bowed low. The other Ja'Akari followed her lead, most of them eagerly, eyes shining. Ishtaset smiled, and the hairs all along the backs of Ismai's arms raised up in alarm as she looked straight at him.

"You are most welcome, cousin," she purred. "Now… first we will see you children safely home. Then we will set things to rights."

TWENTY-SIX

He came to her in that hour before dawn, when all of the world lies sleeping save soldiers, poets…
…and lovers.

"I am sorry to wake you," he said, though he was not.

"I should kick your ass," Sulema muttered sleepily, though she knew she would not. She heard the *shush-shush* of his clothes being shed, and moved aside to make a place for him.

"You must like me, to give up your warm spot." His voice was smiling. "Oh, now, hush… no need to cry, sweet warrior. I am here. Hush now."

"I was *worried* about you," she said indignantly. "I really *should* kick your ass." Her mouth found his in the dark and she kissed him. Repeatedly.

"That might be difficult to do," he said, pulling back a little. His voice was ragged, and warm, and full of laughter. "With you clinging to me like… oh, hey now. Oh. Ah, *Sulema…*"

She shut him up.

Later—much later—as the sky began to blush and the stars turned their faces from the Sun Dragon's glory, Sulema lay listening to the music in her lover's heart. He was well, he was home, he was returned to her. She twitched in half-sleep, laughed, and kissed his warm skin.

"Home," she murmured.

Mattu, who had been playing with her braids, froze in midfondle. "What was that?"

"Oh, I think I was dreaming, but I am happy to have you home." She stretched, winced, and grinned the most delicious grin. "We should have a second breakfast."

"So Atualon is home to you now?" he said curiously. "I thought you would have ridden free of this place by now." He sounded… wistful.

"I had thought to—after I rescued your saucy ass." She turned her face a little so she could bite his shoulder. "Mmm, but it seems that you do not need saving now, so—" She rolled toward him, the better to take advantage of his proximity.

"Sulema, wait. I—oh, hey now, that—I need to—ow—*Sulema*!" He laughed. "I am trying to tell you something important. I… *uhhhh*…"

"You were saying?" she asked after a time.

Mattu grabbed her shoulders and rolled them both over so that he had her pinned beneath his weight.

"It can wait," he growled.

Much later, as they sat together upon the balcony dining on pears, tart cheese, and a fluffy round bread which was Sulema's new favorite thing—

Second favorite, she thought with a grin as she eyed her lover's battle-scarred shoulders.

—Mattu told her what he had come to say.

"Atualon cannot be your home, Sulema," he said. "You must leave. You must go, and now."

"*Whuffut?*" She swallowed. "What is this? You wish me to leave?" Her eyes flashed, and the bread stuck in her throat.

"Of course I do not want you to go," he replied. "Ridiculous girl, but I cannot bear to see you harmed, and if you stay here in Atualon…" Juice dribbled from between his fingers. Mattu grimaced, unclenched his fist, and dropped half a mangled pear over the balcony rail. "Sulema, there are things happening here, and things that are about to happen of which you know nothing. These things are dangerous to you. Very dangerous."

He does not wish me to leave. Sulema picked up her mug of

coffee and made a face. *Cold, ugh.* "The world is dangerous, Mattu. I cannot simply leave it. I must learn—"

"You cannot learn to wield atulfah, Sulema. It is impossible for you to wear the dragon mask."

Not the Sun Dragon's mask, she thought. Aloud she said, "Did everyone know this but me?"

"In a city of lies and shadows, my dear, nothing remains secret for long. You knew this already? So why are you still here?"

"I just found out," she said irritably. "Nobody had seen fit to tell me earlier..." She peered at him over the rim of her mug. "One moment. Why did *you* never tell me?"

"I only found out recently, myself. I was going to tell you last night, but..." His voice trailed off.

"Are you *blushing*, Mattu Halfmask?" Sulema laughed with delight. "And where *is* your mask, this morning?"

"I do not need it. Not when I am with you."

For once, Sulema had nothing to say.

Mattu cleared his throat. "In any case, you must go. Return to the desert, if you would, and if you can remain hidden among your people... or find some other place, where you can keep yourself hidden. Keep yourself safe."

"There is no safe place in this world, Mattu," she said. "Not for me, or for anyone. I would remain with you. Or..." She sat up straighter. "We could leave together."

"I cannot leave, not now," he said, and he frowned. "Not for a long while, most likely. I will be watched very closely, since I am newly returned from Taz Merraj... since she let me go."

"She?" Sulema tore a loaf of bread in half. "Oh... you mean the salt queen. Ninianne."

"No," Mattu said. He took the mangled bread from her, set it aside, and gripped both her hands in his. "I mean, yes, the salt queen, who eyes the Dragon Throne with as much avarice as any, but there is one other, Sulema, who would use me to get at your father. Someone who sees the Dragon King's daughter as a threat which must be destroyed. I speak of Bashaba. She wishes to return to Atualon and resume her place as Queen Consort. Your mother had gone to meet her—"

"Bashaba?" The name was familiar. "Wait… was she not concubine to the last Dragon King?"

"She was Sa Atu, the Heart of Atualon—Queen Consort, as your mother is now. Later, Wyvernus accepted her as his own concubine, but then he met your mother, and…" He spread his hands wide and shrugged. "The lovely lady disappeared. Most thought her dead—the usual fate of displaced concubines, I fear—but Hafsa Azeina and Bashaba had been friends from youth, and your mother would not hear of it. So Bashaba was sent to live in hiding, in exile, in Taz Merraj, away from everything she had known. Her children remained behind in Atualon, held hostage to her good behavior, and raised as the Dragon King's wards—"

"Wait. Wait." Sulema's heart was pounding. "Bashaba is your—"

"My mother. Yes."

"Bashaba is your mother. She now seeks to supplant *my* mother—"

"With your mother's blessing."

"—with my mother's blessing, and *what*? Bear more children by my father? So you and I would be as brother and sister?" She wanted to throw up. "That is disgusting."

"Bashaba is past childbearing. Birthing my sister and me nearly killed her, but she *does* intend to see her son on the Dragon Throne."

"You? But you are—you cannot—"

"I am nearly surdus," he agreed. "Like Leviathus. No, not I, Sulema. Her other son, her eldest son, her echovete son. *Pythos*." He spat the name as if speaking it had filled his mouth with venom.

"But… but… he is dead." She remembered that much. When her father had seized the Dragon Throne, the crown prince of Atualon had been thrown down the side of Atukos, to fall to his death.

"Rumors of his demise have been proven sadly premature."

"Guts and goatfuckery." Sulema leaned back, shaking her head. "But Ka Atu will never allow it. He—"

"Needs an heir," Mattu said softly, "who can wear the mask

of Akari, and learn to wield atulfah as he does. As you, being a woman, cannot."

"My father would never agree to this," she said, and she clenched her jaw, blinking back tears of anger. "He would *never*—"

"Sulema," Mattu said softly. Gently. "He already has."

TWENTY-SEVEN

Hafsa Azeina sat crosslegged in front of the dragon-face fireplace, twisting her hair absentmindedly between her fingers and humming a nonsensical song. Though it was a warm day, the kind that might make a chamberman wish to run off with his bold-eyed soldier and make babies, she had built the fire up and huddled beneath a shawl, a pale shadow of a once mighty queen.

Not far from her lay a giant saber-tusked beast, one of the greater predators of the Zeera, now gone to dull hide draped over a rack of bone, eyes half-slitted and gleaming dully in the firelight as he dreamed of greater days. An aging woman, a dying vash'ai, terrors of the night who had outlived their prime.

Unless, that is, one knew how to *look*. One with the eyes to see would behold a much different picture, painted in darker colors edged all around in shadows and blood.

She stared into the face of a dragon carved from living stone, and the dragon stared back. Her waking eyes half closed, dreaming eyes half open, she reclined in one world twisting herself a fine new set of wizard-locks, while in Shehannam she hunted.

Khurra'an had made his kill, and now it was her turn.

In both worlds she sang, she hummed, for in both worlds her Khurra'an was dying. He sang the death song of his kind, a low, slow dirge of mourning that was devoid of sorrow and regret.

Khurra'an should be home, she knew, surrounded by his pride, swept along his journey to the Lonely Road by the voices of his people. As it was, she gave him what comfort she might. It was not the death he deserved, but it was all she had to offer.

Even as she said goodbye to her beloved friend, there were matters to which she needed to attend. Even as she sang her last farewells to Khurra'an, Hafsa Azeina walked the Dreaming Lands, seeking to free her daughter and defeat their enemies.

In Shehannam, the dreamshifter prowled about the edges of the clearing where her daughter lay dreaming. Here the girl appeared at times as a tiny fennec, then as the warrior-queen she might become, the dreamshifter she might become, the monster she might become. All of these and none of these at once. A pale light like fungus blossomed and pulsed upon one shoulder, sending tendrils of ill intent down her arm and toward her chest. Those tendrils stretched, reached, clawed at her flesh and found little purchase, frustrated as they were by the loremaster's potions and the shadowmancer's magics, but ever they pulsed and reached, and bit-by-bit crept closer to that precious heart.

Though the dreamshifter had been successful in severing many of the bonds that kept Sulema from waking fully, from claiming her own power, none of her magics and none of her weapons had seemed to affect the taint.

As they had ridden to Atualon she had been able to free Jinchua, the girl's kima'a, and that had helped, but now she was blocked from entering into the clearing. It was ringed all around with a golden haze, thin and insubstantial-seeming as a dancer's veils. This magic was new to her, and Hafsa Azeina was reluctant to assault it directly with blade or bow or any of her instruments of death, for fear she might harm her daughter.

Hafsa Azeina, in her dreaming state, could walk through walls of bone or stone or wood, but this ridiculous, diaphanous barrier kept her from reaching her daughter as surely as the Lonely Road separated the living from the dead.

Guts and goatfuckery, she thought as Ani might have. *And a steaming pile of horse shit to boot.* Perhaps the youthmistress's coarse humor would serve where her own magics had failed. Though the vulgarity did not lift the veil, or her mood, neither did it seem to do any harm. A flash of movement at the very edges of her vision stilled her, filled her with the usual thrill of excitement and dread. She turned her head slowly, slowly... in both worlds.

To one who observed her waking body, seated in her rooms in Atukos, it might seem as if she had glanced into the corner of her room, eyes darting back and forth, watching nothing at all.

There she saw them.

Na'iyeh. Hafsa Azeina grimaced. Foul things, fouler wrought. They hunted the Dreaming Lands even as she did, and she wondered at their intended prey. Did they dare to stalk her daughter? Fury rose in her heart.

Fire roared on the hearth. The dragon's face glowed ruby-hot.

No, the na'iyeh turned aside from the golden veil. Sniffing, sniffing, wailing, waiting for their prey to fall asleep in the waking world, that it might appear in this one. The na'iyeh were deeply rooted in both. No matter how hard, how fast their prey might run away, no matter how cleverly they might hide, eventually they would sleep and the na'iyeh would find them. The na'iyeh hunted in both lands, and so the na'iyeh always won.

Unless a greater hunter stopped them.

The foul things were not hunting her daughter, but their proximity to her suggested that they had singled out prey close to Sulema's life, to her heart. That would be the na'iyeh's first mistake, and their last.

Hafsa Azeina allowed herself a wide, cold smile. She could not help her daughter, and she could not save Khurra'an, but Shehannam was her world, her magic, and in this she was particularly, splendidly gifted.

She could *kill*.

The na'iyeh left trails for those who had the eyes to see. Wide trails like blood-streaked mucus, foul with rot and shining sticky in the odd light of Shehannam. Sharing tangled roots and a communal mind, hunting as a single entity. Their regenerative abilities made them desperately difficult to kill. Cut one na'iyeh scion into three pieces, and within a half-moon's time you would have three na'iyeh on your tail. Fire—regular fire, from a hearth or campfire—would do nothing more than scorch the fell things and make them angry. They could be melted down with lionsnake venom, as if obtaining such an amount of snake spit would not get you killed. They could be desiccated in the dead waters of Taz Merraj and *then* burned.

Or they could be killed by a dream eater with a demon blade.

This drowse of na'iyeh dreamers had five scions. It was an ancient growth, a couple of hundred years old at least, and wily. Hafsa Azeina could see among its succulent members a new bud, fresh and green, waiting to consume the human body that would bring it to half-life. Dreamers budded rarely, and a bud that was not properly wedded to a living human would soon die and begin to rot, endangering the entire drowse.

The drowse had to catch a sleeping human unawares, and press her into the bud's hungry maw, where she would be digested over a matter of moons. Digested, but not killed. To slash a na'iyeh open was to expose the screaming, live, and too-aware skeleton of its maiden prey.

Hafsa Azeina hid in plain sight, wreathed in shadows of her own making, and sang a long song, a slow song, a song of death and twilight. Intent on their prey, waiting, waiting, the dreamers began to sway as if their thick and thorny branches were caught up in a gentle breeze, but they did not hear the storm coming.

She raised her voice, just a touch, and drew Belzaleel from his soft sheath. The demonblade said nothing, for the dream eater had come to kill, and it was not in his nature to dissuade her. She raised her voice, and tightened the noose, the net. Let the jaw of her dreaming snare slip just a little, just a little bit closer.

The na'iyeh twisted, they danced, they writhed to her song, but still they did not hear the storm coming.

Hafsa Azeina dropped the glamour that kept her secrets. She raised her voice to a crescendo, she raised her demon blade, and the jaws of her trap snapped shut upon the startled na'iyeh. They screamed, they writhed, and beat against the power of her song which held them in thrall, but they could not break free. They were dreamers, but she was the Eater of Dreams, the destroyer, the storm.

She was upon them.

Belzaleel bit through the leathery outer skin as teeth through an overripe peach, exposing that scion's stinking, gelatinous, and foul innards. Hafsa Azeina held the knife carefully, lest that foulness come into contact with her flesh. She was not certain whether a dreamer's juices would digest her dreaming flesh as it would her waking flesh, and she had no desire to find out. Belzaleel shrieked with glee as he sliced through the thing's thin and watery soul, absorbing it, until that scion stiffened, jerked, and fell over dead. Gelatinous putrescence oozed from the slit in its side and a human skeleton slid free from its long prison, hands held before its chest as if to ward off a nightmare, mouth open in a long and disconsolate wail.

The na'iyeh tried to fade from the Shehannam, but Hafsa Azeina's song held it—them—without letting go. They lashed out, trying to rake claw-tipped arms across her flesh, but she whirled away, insubstantial as smoke. The pod gaped at her, vulgar pink and hungry, lusting after her flesh and soul, but the blade rose and fell, rose and fell, and one by one the na'iyeh fell, too.

I am the storm, she thought, face hard, heart hard as one-by-one the skeletons of the dreamers' victims fell free. One of them wore a necklace of stones and bones unlike anything she had ever seen. Another was tiny, the half-formed remains of a toddling babe. The dream eater looked upon them all with eyes hard as stone as the demon blade Belzaleel glutted himself on their souls. She did not tell herself that it was necessary, or that it was good. It was neither.

In the end, however, it was done.

She watched without passion as the grasses and mosses and fungi of Shehannam crept in over the foul leavings. The Dreaming Lands let nothing go to waste, and let no trace of death belie its mask of serenity.

And now—growled Belzaleel, voice thick, drunk on a feast of old souls—*now, Dream Eater, it is your turn to…*

Oh, stuff it, she told him with a weary sigh, and shoved him back into his sheath. *You are not going to dine on my soul, not now. Not ever.*

231

It was worth a try.

Hafsa Azeina let the green light of Shehannam grow sharp and thin, let the edges be edges and shadows become shadows, and slowly she breathed herself fully back into her own lungs and took up the onerous task of living as an old woman might take up her weaving.

Khurra'an still lay at the outer edges of the fire's dying light, fading from her waking and dreaming eyes. Hafsa Azeina was startled to find Sulema seated beside him, stroking his great head and staring into the flames.

"He is dying," Sulema said.

Hafsa Azeina grunted, flattening her lips together, and grunted again as she stood. How long had she been sitting in one place? Years, it seemed. *Perhaps it is time for me to take up weaving*, she thought irritably.

"*Ehuani.*" She bit the word off, and in so doing she meant *all truth is beautiful, but not all truths should be spoken.*

"Not Khurra'an," Sulema protested, hands clutching at the sooty mane, a look of shock on her face. "That's not who I mean."

She did not know, Hafsa Azeina thought, and her heart clenched like Sulema's fists. *For a wise woman, I am a very great fool.*

"Who, then?" she asked softly, and in doing so she meant *I have failed you again and I am sorry.*

"The Dragon King. My father."

"You knew this already," she reminded her daughter, gently. "Before we ever came to this land." As her eyes fell on Khurra'an, it occurred to Hafsa Azeina that knowing, and *knowing*, were two different things.

"He is dying," Sulema went on, "and his power is like a great whirlpool in the Dibris, sucking me down to a watery hell, like in one of Nurati's old nurse-tales. I cannot swim away from him, I have nothing to hold onto, and I will drown." She looked to Hafsa Azeina. "Help me, Mother."

Hafsa Azeina touched the fingers of one hand against her heart as the room swam around her. *"Help me,"* Tadeah had pleaded, on the night Hafsa Azeina fled with her daughter, her true daughter, her own flesh and blood and no one else's. *He will destroy me…*

And he had. Now, it seemed, he would consume Sulema as well.

Not while I live, she vowed. *Not if I have to destroy the world to stop him.*

"How long have you felt… drained like this?" she asked.

"Since I saw the skulls? Maybe? Since I saw his mask for the first time? I am not certain," Sulema answered, passing one hand over her eyes as if they pained her. Hafsa Azeina saw that her daughter's eyes were shadowed, her face thinner than it had been, and that she moved as if her shoulder hurt. "It was strongest when he raised the Sulemnium, but I can feel him dragging at me even now. Even now," she repeated, as if to herself, "when I am here with you I can feel him pulling at me. Mattu says—"

"Mattu Halfmask," Hafsa Azeina interrupted, "is not to be trusted."

"Mattu says," Sulema went on, setting her chin in the stubborn slant that her mother knew only too well, "that Father does not intend to teach me how to wield atulfah. He says that instead, he—"

Her voice broke. Hafsa Azeina's heart, cold and dead as it was, broke with it.

The girl loves her father, she realized. *Just as Tadeah did. Just as we all did.* The dragon-faced hearth roared to life as she was seized with a sudden fury. *We all loved him. And he has betrayed us, every one.*

"He killed her, did he not?" Sulema asked, and Hafsa Azeina watched as her daughter's face tightened into a warrior's mask. "His other daughter. Talia."

"Tadeah," Hafsa Azeina corrected. "Yes, he did."

"Why did you bring me here? Why did you let me come?"

"For the same reason I stole you away, all those years ago," she answered, and this time the beauty of truth rang through her words clear and pure as a new-forged sword. "To save your life. Ka Atu is the only one with the power to heal reaver's venom.

233

Had it not been for that, I never would have—"

Too late, she saw that it had been the perfect trap.

"Can you help me?" Sulema asked. "*Will* you help me?"

"Yes," Hafsa Azeina answered. She strode to where the girl still sat, held out her hands, lifted her daughter to her feet, then did a thing which surprised them both. She embraced her daughter, kissed her forehead. She had to pull the girl's face down to hers, and tugged at her fiery warrior's braids. In doing so she meant *I love you*.

"I can help you, and I will. I am your mother," she finished, as if that explained everything. Or, perhaps, as if it excused anything.

"You are my mother," Sulema agreed with a smile, and some of the tension melted away from her body. "And my mother is fierce. What have I to fear, in all the world?"

"Nothing," Hafsa Azeina agreed, though the lie pained her. A little. "Go now, get some rest. Mama has work to do."

TWENTY-EIGHT

Were Daru here, her small apprentice would have done his best to dissuade her. Were Khurra'an not dying, her kithren would have grabbed her by the scruff and shaken some sense into her. But she was alone, truly alone, with no one to act as her conscience.

She smiled. *At last I am free to pursue my destiny. Death comes easy, indeed, when carried upon the breath of a dream eater.*

One by one, Hafsa Azeina prepared together the instruments of her dark magic. The shofar akibra, an instrument fashioned from a horn of the golden ram. Basta's Lyre, strung with the guts of a man who had sought to slay her daughter. The flute made from the leg of a woman who thought to betray her, and, finally, the dragonglass dagger infused with the soul of Belzaleel, a wicked and powerful Annu.

She hesitated for a moment, startled by a strange feeling, but then shrugged and retrieved the leather-wrapped bundle that contained the wicked flensing knife Ani had brought from the Bones of Eth. She had no idea what use the fell thing might have, but the instincts of a dreamshifter were nothing to dismiss, and in any case it was better to have too many weapons than too few. Finally she drew Belzaleel from his sheath and used a soft cloth to clean away the last traces of their battle with the na'iyeh.

When I am gone, she wondered idly, *will some sorcerer recall me from whatever hell I am sent to, and stuff me into a knife such as this?* The thought made her laugh. *The wicked and powerful dagger Annubasta, used to chop vegetables for a stew.*

At last she was ready.

Though she had journeyed as a dreamshifter's shade, the dragonstone walls of Atukos had been bespelled to block her physical form from Shehannam. She had grown stronger, however, she had learned much more than even Ka Atu might imagine, and so he could not prepare against her. She drew Belzaleel sharply across the palm of each hand, ignoring the knife's sharp hiss of pleasure. Flaring her nostrils at the sharp scent of her own blood, she pressed her bloodied hands upon the walls of Atukos.

Help me, she implored the dragonstone, cold and living heart of Sajani Earth Dragon. *Help me again. Help me help my daughter*.

The walls of Atukos began to change beneath her touch, growing warm and oddly translucent as dreaming Sajani answered her plea. A long, low, round hallway appeared before her eyes. It shimmered as if through a wall of glass, of water, of light made flesh, and at its far end glowed the false light of Shehannam.

"Thank you," Hafsa Azeina murmured to Atukos, though this passage was more likely to lead to her death than to salvation. She pressed harder with her hands and stepped forward toward the light, shuddering at the feel of her flesh sliding through the world of the living and into the world of dreams.

The hallway was colder by far and more silent than the surety of death. The dreamshifter tightly furled sa and ka, lest her living essence draw unwholesome attention. Her actions were forbidden by laws as ancient as life itself. To enter Shehannam in the flesh was beyond folly. Twice before had she done such a thing. The first time was an accident. New to dreamshifting, acting on instinct and half mad with terror, Hafsa Azeina had dragged herself, her small daughter, and a small Dzirani caravan from world to world. She and Sulema had survived, only just. The Dzirani were not so fortunate.

That was one of the few regrets she had ever allowed herself to feel, as they had perhaps been the last of their kind.

She had never told Ani.

The second time was intentional, though she acted out of ignorance. She had thought she might learn to use the Dreaming Lands as a path between worlds, as the na'iyeh did, that she might come upon her enemies in the flesh and deliver vengeance as they slept. Thus she hoped to breach the walls of Atukos and slay Wyvernus as he slept. It had to be her physical form, for his kima'a—a great golden wyvern—was too powerful for her own small Basta to overcome.

When she set foot upon that forbidden soil the second time, however, she had stepped into the Huntress's snare. The Huntress had been stalking her for a score or more of years, furious that she had slain the golden ram and stolen one of his horns. It had taken everything Hafsa Azeina possessed, and more, to survive. As it was impossible for a mere human to fight the Huntress, or escape her hounds, she had been forced to kill and eat her own kima'a, her human heart, and in doing so become Annubasta. Demon.

Dream eater.

That she could not regret, for regret was a human emotion. Though Basta had eventually returned to her, and though watching her daughter grow from childhood into a fine young warrior had healed some measure of the wound she had inflicted upon herself, she would never again be fully human.

Just as well, she thought, reaching down to touch the gut-string lyre and the leg-bone flute. Regret was an emotion she could ill afford, if she was to save Sulema. This would be the third time she set foot in Shehannam in the flesh. Deep in the very marrow of her bones, where the secrets of her heart lay, Hafsa Azeina knew that this would be the last.

When she reached the end of the hallway, the forbidden doorway and the verdant lands beyond, Hafsa Azeina stepped through without hesitation. She would not creep into death as prey, cringing at the thought of claw and fang. She would roar into its face like a true queen, she would go down fighting.

Ah, little one, Khurra'an whispered into her heart, *you would have made a fine vash'ai*. As she felt the vash'ai slip away from her and into true sleep, Hafsa Azeina knew she would hold those words to her heart like a talisman for the rest of her days, few though they might be.

The moment her bare foot touched the strange, soft grass, a shudder ran through the Dreaming Lands, like the tolling of a great bell, the tintinnabulation of a swordsmith's forge, the cry of a golden shofar. Shehannam itself had marked her for death, and there would be no hiding for her now, not in this world or any other. Hafsa Azeina smiled and took a deep breath as a lifetime of fear lifted from her soul.

When all roads lead to death, she realized, *there is no wrong path.*

Finding a place in the Dreaming Lands would be all but impossible, even for the most experienced of dreamshifters, but finding her way back to a known place was as simple as breathing. She set off at a run, in a land where running could be as dangerous as breathing, and never once bothered to look over her shoulder. In the distance she could hear the first notes of a shofar, and the baying of hounds.

Let them hunt me, she thought, *let them come. They will find that I am no easy meat, after all.*

She arrived at the clearing where Sulema lay bound, now in her kima'a form. The first bindings gave way before her physical presence as they never would have beneath the touch of her dreaming shade. She played Basta's Lyre, and the golden veil shattered at the first notes, dispersing like fog under the wrath of Akari.

The fennec—

Jinchua, she thought. *Her name is Jinchua.*

—lay on one side, panting, her pale form wrapped in layer upon layer of bonds. The Shroud of Eth, foul webs of darkness woven by an arachnist, had grown strong since last she had cut them. Hafsa Azeina knelt and drew Belzaleel in the same movement. Snick-snick went the wicked blade, chortling with glee as he absorbed the fell magics, and those bindings once more fell away with a scream.

Very good, Belzaleel purred, *and now we are finished.*

Hold your forked tongue, Annu, she told him. *I am done with your lies. Did you ever think me so foolish as to believe them? You told me before that I should leave these bonds be. I think... not.*

Snick-snick went the blade in her hand as, unwilling though it was, she used it to free her daughter. Belzaleel howled with outrage, but Hafsa Azeina paid him no mind. She had eaten souls more powerful than his, after all.

She cut the golden bonds that Wyvernus had fashioned from honeyed lies and false adoration, and she cut the bonds that Sulema herself had woven in her hunger to be loved. She cut the Web of Illindra which, indeed, stretched in either direction farther than she could see, in so doing freeing her daughter from the wheel of time and destiny.

Finally, the blade in her hand trembled over the blackthorn bindings, which throbbed and pulsed with the unlight of all the worlds, binding Sulema to the fate of another.

What of this? she asked Belzaleel in a tone that forbade deception. *Answer me true, or I will destroy you here and now. What is this binding?*

It is the fate of this world, for good or for ill, the angry demon hissed. *Sever it or leave it be. I care not.* He would say no more. She hesitated, and in that moment the decision was made for her.

The fennec opened her eyes, and as she woke the blackthorn vine began to fade. The tiny fox sprang to her feet. With a yawn, a wink, and a flash of her bushy tail, she began to dash from the clearing, trailing the smoke-thin vine.

A great shadow fell upon them, and the fox yipped with fear.

"*Kii-yii,*" she cried, and tried to run, but the blackthorn slowed her, the land forbade her, and the being that chased her was too powerful to be denied.

Scaled hide flashed painfully bright in the thin gleam of Shehannam, as gleaming claws reached forth, and wicked teeth gaped wide in a victorious snarl as an immense golden wyvern, the kima'a of Ka Atu, stooped and snatched the fennec up. Those immense wings beat once, twice, three times and he rose into the sky, as untouchable as Akari himself. With a flash and a laugh the wyvern disappeared. The Dragon King was gone from this world.

He had taken her daughter's soul with him.

You should never have left, beloved. His voice rolled across her soul like a hot desert wind. *And you most assuredly should never have come back.*

Hafsa Azeina screamed. She roared her fury as her own magic—no match for the wyvern's—slipped from her grasp like a handful of shadows. She faded as her song faded, but even so, she was not so easily bested.

She was Annubasta, Eater of Dreams, and her work was not yet finished. Even as she was flung from the Dreaming Lands, even as the way back pulled at her feet, Hafsa Azeina clung deep to the bonds of her stubborn heart. The passage back dragged at her, but to return the way she had come, now that she had been marked out for the Huntress, was folly. Neither did it put her in a position any stronger than she had held before this venture.

It seemed to her that for all of her efforts, there should be some gain.

Hafsa Azeina had never been one for games of chance. She held tight to control and left the gambling to her friend Ani. But when hunted, the path most taken was the path best left be. Once more she reached into the void, touched the dream best left dreaming, and one final time she begged for help.

Help me, she pleaded. *Help me help my daughter.*

This time, the Dreamer heard. This time, She answered. Hafsa Azeina felt a wrench as if some great hand had stretched forth, diverting her from her path.

The walls glowed and gave way before her. She stepped forth, not into the false light of Shehannam, not into the red light of some blasted hell as she had feared, but into the welcome light of a fireplace much like the one in her own room. She strode forward one step, two, three, and *pop!* into an overly warm chamber.

The overly warm bedchamber of Aasah, shadowmancer to the Dragon King, to be precise. The man was seated crosslegged on a low, round bed piled high with pillows and silks of crimson and gold and bright, hot yellow. He blinked at her twice with those big, pale blue eyes, but that was all the surprise he showed. His large hands cradled a small red book, which he closed carefully and set aside. Then he stood.

Yeh Atu, get a hold of yourself, woman, Hafsa Azeina snapped at her own distracted mind. *You have seen naked men before.*

Yes, whispered some sly, hidden part of herself, *but you have never seen such a—*

"Queen Consort," Aasah intoned in a voice she could feel through the dragonstone, "this is a… pleasant surprise. How might I serve you?"

She bit back the first answer that occurred to her, and said instead, "I need your help." She had not planned to ask him. Then again, she had not planned to come here, at all.

"Of course." Aasah nodded, solemn blue eyes seeking to peer through the glamours and lies she wore. "But what makes you think I can help you against the might of Ka Atu, Meissati?"

He knows.

"What makes you think I might betray your king?" he continued. "It is not as if we share a bloodline… or a common enemy."

"Your king," not *"my king,"* she thought. Why would she ask this man, of all men, for aid? And what could she possibly say to entice him toward her cause? Unless…

Of course.

She brought forth the flensing knife in its leather wrapping, and held it between them.

"Oh," she told him, "but we do share a common enemy."

He stared for a long moment at her—at her, not at the bundle she held—and the room deepened, darkened. His eyes deepened, darkened. A shiver ran through the shadows of Atukos as deep away, far away, the Nightmare Man laughed.

"Let me call my apprentice," he told her finally, "let me have the servants bring up food and drink. If we are to speak of treason, and war, and dark magics, we are going to need sustenance."

"Yes," she agreed, and cleared her throat. *What would Ani say?* Hafsa Azeina allowed herself a small smile. "Sustenance… and clothes."

TWENTY-NINE

The mantid Pakka had fallen asleep, curled tight in the crook of Daru's bad arm. Daru worked his way carefully down the endless tunnel he had found, groping ahead and to the side in absolute blackness, using his good arm like a blind and very lost old man.

It was a winding, twisty little passageway, and again he was reminded uncomfortably of what it must be like to be on the inside of a lionsnake, trying to find his way out. Though the ceiling did not touch his head, it was close enough to ruffle his hair once or twice, and the walls to either side were close enough that a good stumble would result in a bruised shoulder. There were no side passages, or at least he thought not. It was hardly possible to touch both walls at a time, what with his arm being broken and all. The *throb, throb, throb* of it was as good as a war drum and he marched ever onward, ever downward.

Down the lionsnake's gullet.

So vivid was this image that when the passageway swooped open all at once, falling away on either side, under his feet, and above his head, Daru gasped and stepped back.

I have reached the snake's belly, he thought, and though he knew that was silly, still it was everything he could do to slide his bare foot forward. His toes found a sharp edge, and nothing beyond. *It might be a staircase*, he thought, and he was heartened at the thought that somebody had built these tunnels, after all, and likely they had not all died down here.

Then again, maybe it *was* the belly of a giant stone snake, filled with acid and the bones of foolish young boys.

"Pakka," he whispered, jogging his bad arm a tiny bit. *Ow.* "Pakka, wake up. I need your light."

"*Pip-pip*," she chirruped sleepily. Standing on his arm, she did her best. There was a slight *tik* as her light appeared, and the barest hint of heat. It was faint and sickly, and Daru feared what the effort might cost her. Nevertheless, it was enough.

A wide stairway stretched down ahead of him, and to either side farther than Pakka's little bug-light could reach. The steps were as sharp and new as if they had just that day been cut into the living rock, and little gold motes swam in the depths of the dragonstone so that as he took a hesitant step, then another, it seemed to Daru as if he trod upon a star-filled sky.

The steps were wide and shallow, as if they, like the tunnel, had been built with children in mind. It was not, somehow, a comforting thought. When had the plain gray stone become dragonstone? He did not know. It seemed that they had journeyed far beneath the fortress, perhaps to the very heart of the world.

I am not in the belly of a snake after all, he thought. *I am in the belly of the dragon.* That was not a comforting thought, either.

Just as his legs began to shake the stairs came to an end. He sat down on the last one to gather his thoughts, and to comfort Pakka, whose light had begun to flicker and dim in an alarming way. He was tired, sore tired, and he hurt everywhere. And he was hungry, and…

"I am stronger than they think," he told the shadows as he pushed himself to stand on legs as wobbly as a newborn foal's. The shadows very much wanted him to lie down, and to sleep, to sleeeeeep, and so he knew that it would be the death of him, no matter how his body begged for rest. Rest, and something to eat— even lionsnake pemmican, *yuck*, something to drink, and a warm fire. A kind voice, a hand pushing the hair back from his forehead.

I miss Dreamshifter, he thought, and his eyes went so big and round with the revelation that by all rights he should have been able to see in the dark. Looking back, he could remember times when he was ill, or when his apprentice's training had drained him past the point of exhaustion. Dreamshifter would tuck him into bed, bring him bone broth and bread with honey, and sometimes she would be humming a little song, just like—

Like a mother, he thought. *If stone can be said to be a mother, then I am not such an orphan after all.* It made him smile, and it made him pause. *What would Dreamshifter do?*

She would tear a hole between worlds, walk through Shehannam, and emerge again wherever she wanted, lips red with the heartsblood of her enemies and a mouth full of new stories for him. He sighed and his shoulders slumped again.

All right, what would the dreamshifter's apprentice do? He took a deep breath and closed his eyes, though it was not strictly speaking necessary, and gathered his thoughts up. Besides his knives, and his Pakka, and sheer tenacity, thoughts were his only asset at the moment. But he was a smart boy, and stronger than they knew.

First things first.

What was his most pressing problem?

I am hungry, his stomach growled.

We are blind, his eyes wept.

It hurts, his everything whined. *It all hurts.*

Sleep, the shadows sang.

"Shut up!" Daru yelled, jumping as his voice echoed back. He was in a chamber, then, or a cave of some sort.

My main problem, the one from which all others are spawned, he realized, *is that I do not know where I am. I know where I wish to be—safe in my bed in Dreamshifter's rooms—but I do not know where I am. If I figure out where I am, I can figure out how to get to where I need to be, and then I will be safe.*

You will never be safe, the shadows hissed. *Never be—*

"Fuck off," he snapped, then giggled in shock to hear such a word come out of his own mouth. "Goatfuckers!"

The shadows had nothing to say to that.

So. First figure out where I am. He squinted into the gloom, and shuffled sideways along the bottom step. It seemed to Daru that if he was in a room, or a cavern of sorts, finding the walls and scooting along them would be a wiser choice than running headlong into the middle. For all he knew there could be a pit of snakes, waiting for him to tumble in headfirst, or a hole without end, or a lake filled with slimy blind things, slimy blind *hungry* things, or—

He tripped over his own feet and found the wall he had been seeking, smashing nose-first into the merciless rock. His teeth snapped together on the tip of his tongue, and his busted arm was jolted so hard that stars danced in the darkness before his eyes. Not the stars for which he had wished. Pakka tumbled from the crook of his arm with a tiny *skreeee* and her light pulsed like a weak heartbeat as she fluttered to the ground.

"Fuck," Daru said again, then decided that it would be better not to fall into the habit of cursing. It would not do, he supposed, to survive the belly of the dragon only to face Dreamshifter's wrath. He groped along the wall with his good hand, wiggling his nose a little in case it might be broken—he thought not—holding his injured arm as close as he could, and trying not to whimper under his breath.

I am stronger than they know, his mind whispered, *but I am still just a boy.*

Daru could see Pakka's light bobbing higher and higher as she skittered up the wall and then stopped, screeching and doing a funny little wiggle-dance of excitement. Heart in his mouth, he reached out to touch… a branch? Some sort of tree branch? When it did not bite him, Daru wrapped his fingers most of the way around the length of wood and drew closer, peering against the gloom.

Not a branch, he decided, it was too smooth for that. *Something handmade. A club, perhaps, or…* He ran his hand up the length and encountered a bundle of rags, tightly wrapped and sticky with foul-smelling pitch. *Oh!* He thought, and was so overcome with elation his head swam. He lifted the object from its metal bracket and hugged it as if it were his best friend in all the world.

"A torch!" he shouted. "A torch! I have a torch! Good girl, Pakka!" Daru swayed on his feet, pain and all, nearly dancing in his excitement. "Now all I have to do is light… oh." And his heart sank, down from the blue sky to join him in the belly of the dragon, and further still. All he had was his knives, his clothes, his bird-skull flute, and his Pakka. He could not light a fire with those.

Still, it was more than he had possessed a moment before, and he straightened a bit with a sigh. Pakka chirruped again, questioning as she crawled onto his shoulder.

"You are a good girl," he reassured her, stroking her cheek with his. "I just wish I had something to light it with. Maybe if I find another one, we could rub them together and make fire?" It was a doubtful proposition, but still, it was something.

"*Pip-pip-peeeee-oh!*" Pakka skreeked, bobbing up and down. "*Peeee-oh!*" Chittering to herself she all but ran back down his arm, and he couldn't feel her any more. "*Peee-eee-oh!*" Her light reappeared, bobbed this way and that, this way and that, this way and—

There was another *tik*, a spark, and Daru jumped so that he almost dropped the torch.

Another spark, and another. Then it dawned upon him.

"Fire!" he yelled, as a tiny green flame licked at the pitch and found it to its liking. "Fire!" he said again, as Pakka ran back up his arm to crouch upon his shoulder, *pipp*ing and *peeee-oh*ing with delight at his reaction. "Pakka, you made fire! Oh, clever, beautiful girl."

Fire raced up the head of the torch, bathing them in a warm, welcome glow and a bitter tang of bitumen and burnt metal. Daru stopped his dancing, half holding his breath for fear he might put it out again. It was a strong light, though, pure and good as if Akari Sun Dragon himself had reached down from the heavens to give one small boy a morsel of hope. Daru looked away from the fire at last, blinking the shadows from his eyes, and gasped at what he saw.

There was no endless hole, no pit of snakes. There was no dark lake full of slimy things waiting to gobble his bones. Nor had he come to a cave, as he had feared, an end to all things with no way out but death.

Daru stood in a chamber so large that even his torch did not light all the way to the ceiling, or the far end of the room. There were tables and chairs of dark stone, wearing layers of dust and cobwebs. Carved into the walls from floor to ceiling were shelves, and more shelves, and more, row upon row of them, and each groaning under the weight of hundreds and hundreds of…

"Books," he gasped, and he took a deep breath filled with the musky, dusky, wonderful scent. Daru had never seen so many books in one place in all his life. Had never heard of such a collection, outside the tales of…

"Pakka," he squeaked, and she squeaked back. "Pakka, do you know where we are? Do you know what this *is*?"

"*Pip-pip-pipipip-peee?*"

"We found it," he breathed. "We found it! Pakka, this is the Library of Kal ne Mur."

"*Pip-pip-peeee-oh*," Pakka whistled, impressed.

There were a score more torches. Daru lit every one he could find, and then stood upon a low sturdy table in the middle of the vast room. He turned in a slow circle. His eyes were as large as he could make them, the better to drink in his surroundings.

The Library of Kal ne Mur was a myth, a fable, the one place he would have given his heart to see, and here it was. A long drink of sweet water for someone with a thirst for knowledge.

I am thirsty, he realized, and with that thought his tongue clove to the roof of his mouth. Daru unhooked the water skin from his belt, allowed himself a miserly three mouthfuls, then grimaced at the stale taste. *Just my luck*, he thought, *to find the place of my dreams and die of thirst or hunger*. This place was long lost—or it never would have been called the Lost Library, he supposed— and that boded ill for a boy who hoped to find his way back to civilization, food, and a soft bed.

"Pakka," he said, "I have fire, and I have books, and I have you. If only I had food and water, and somewhere to sleep, I could probably live here forever."

"*Pip-pip-tatta-tatta-treeeeeee*," his sweet little mantid agreed, and she launched herself into the air.

"Wait!" he called, but she was already gone, a faint luminescent trail floating behind her. Daru sighed, stepped down from the table, and headed toward the nearest shelf full of books. *If all roads lead to death*, he supposed, *I might as well die reading.*

He propped his torch carefully against the back of a chair and stood for a long moment, nose a hand's width from the shelf, breathing it all in. There were scrolls stacked carefully on the highest shelves, some in cases of leather or wood or stiffened cloth, others tied off and left to fend for themselves. On the lower shelves he could see neat stacks of paper and vellum and papyrus, tablets of wood, bone, and ivory, and on the bottommost shelves, standing shoulder-to-shoulder like warriors prepared to do war, there were books. Codices penned and bound by hand in the long ago, stories and histories and the very thoughts of people who had walked the earth in the days of lore and legend when men were warriors, women ran the Hunt, and Sajani Earth Dragon was safely, soundly asleep.

He sighed deep as a heart's prayer and reached out to touch the spine of one such book, half expecting it to collapse into dust and dreams. It was as real and solid as he was. Magic, he thought. He had never imagined that a magic might exist that would allow books to remain undamaged for a thousand years or more, but what other explanation could there be? This place looked to him as if the bookkeeper had tucked her charges into place on their shelves, and wandered off to bed.

A thousand years from now, he wondered, *will they find my dry bones at one of these tables, face down in a book?* It was a strangely comforting thought.

It would take a thousand years to read all these. A thousand thousand. A thousand thousand thousand… Daru selected a book at random, a heavy woodbound codex that smelled of ink and spice. Tucking it under his good arm, he returned to the table and blew away some of the dust. *I may as well get started.*

It turned out to be an accounting of crops and livestock yields. It was written in a small, neat hand, by someone named Barad ni

Hameesh, in Low Suqqa, the merchants' tongue, which was known to be less prone to change than, say, Common or Atualonian. Though it was interesting to see how the letters and language had changed through the years, it was not likely to help him in his current predicament.

What Daru needed was a map. A map of Atukos would be a wonderful thing to find—a map of Atukos that showed where in Yosh he had gotten to, and how he might return to the surface, would be even better.

Unless Khurra'an is still waiting to eat me. He pushed the worry away. *If I get any hungrier,* he thought as his stomach growled ominously, *I might eat* him. Among all these piles and stacks and rows of writing, surely such a map existed. And if such a map existed, Daru vowed, he would find it.

The next three books he selected were similar works, one in the same hand, so he moved further down the row and stood on the tips of his toes to reach a higher shelf, reasoning that a map was likelier recorded in a scroll than a book. It was tricky maintaining his balance, especially with his throbbing, injured arm, but he was determined. His fingertips brushed the soft leather cover of a thin journal and he tugged it to the edge of the shelf, sticking his tongue out in concentration.

"*Pip-pip-peeeeeeeee!*" Pakka shrieked in his ear. Daru fell back with a yelp, pinwheeling his good arm and smacking his broken arm *bam* into the books. The slim volume he had dislodged fell *thwap* onto his head and then rustled onto the floor, scattering pages as it went. Daru turned, scowling, with angry words in his mouth for his little friend. She hovered just out of reach, tilting her head back and forth at him and looking entirely too pleased with herself. She had blood on her mandibles, he saw, and her little bug-light pulsed merrily, stronger than it had been in some time.

In her forelegs she clutched a very large, very dead rat.

Daru gasped as the rat's hind legs paddled weakly at the air. It was not very dead, after all.

❖

They dined on roasted rat cooked by torchlight. Daru ate the meat, and Pakka dined neatly on the entrails. The two of them shared a handful of stale water and Daru was surprised to find himself humming contentedly under his breath. After all, he had a friend, food in his belly, and a world full of books.

What more could he possibly want?

A bath would be nice, he thought wistfully. *A bed.* He pulled the soft leather book close, laid it open, and began to read.

Of all the books, on all the shelves, in the greatest library in the world, this *book falls into my hands.* The irony and suspicious nature of it did not escape Daru. He had been stalked by shadows, apprenticed to a dreamshifter, and he had fallen down into the belly of a dragon. Such experiences did not leave a mind unmarked.

The book was not a record of bumper crops and poor yields. Neither was it a book of love poems, or a bestiary concerning the mating habits of wyverns. It was, Daru learned within the first few pages, the diary of a young boy, written in a very old form of Atualonian.

His name was—had been—Somnus. He hated the taste of fish, and a girl named Onassa, who was beautiful and smart and did not know he existed. It seemed to Daru, as he leaned his chin into his good hand and read past hunger and pain and exhaustion, that Somnus existed mostly in his own writing. He was unable to speak, if Daru's translation was correct, or perhaps it was that he could not speak well, and those around Somnus thought him stupid.

Stupid and weak.

He could be me. Daru turned another heavy page. In another lifetime, these could be my words. Somnus had been chased into the belly of the dragon not by a vash'ai, but by his own feelings of shame and fear. Deep in the Downbelow—he called it the Underside Down, which Daru found charming—he discovered cages and rooms filled with peculiar children. "Exceptional Children," Somnus named them, and even his penned voice seemed to whisper. These were children who shouted too much or spoke too little, rocked silently in dark corners or ran wildly about, striking one another. Children who showed great promise in the realms of music, poetry—or magic.

Children like me, weak in some ways, gifted in others. Dreamshifter warned me. The Loremaster warned me, too, and if they know about these children... Chillflesh raised painfully along the backs of Daru's arms. *If they know about these children, it means that those children who are taken are not given a good life, as the king has said, but kept down here in the Downbelow for...*

For what purpose, exactly, Daru did not know, but he knew it was not good. He had uncovered the dark secret of Atukos, or at least one of the dark secrets, and it occurred to him that a boy who was known to have discovered such a thing might very well disappear forever.

He read on, though his eyes ached and everything else ached worse and his torch was spluttering low. There were plenty of torches on the library walls, so that was not a real worry. The fate of the exceptional children, however, and his fate should he be caught in that net, was—

Daru sat up straight so quickly that the pain in his broken arm brought tears to his eyes. He blinked, brought the book even closer to his face, blinked again. Somnus had found more than the library, and he had found more than the exceptional children, here in the Downbelow. There, in a very precise hand, Somnus had drawn a perfect, detailed, beautiful map.

"Pakka," Daru whispered, as though the ghosts of the past might hear and swoop down to catch him. "Pakka, look. Look!"

"*Pip-peee-rrup?*" Pakka skittered closer, tipped her head this way and that at the open book.

"It is," he answered, tracing the lines and words with a trembling finger. "Pakka, this is a map, he drew a map of the Downbelow! Look here, see, this is the library," he showed her, voice rising with

251

his excitement. "Here are the chambers and the teaching rooms and the sleeping rooms for the children. Here is the sewer where you caught that rat, and—"

He all but yelled the last.

"This is the way out!"

THIRTY

They were waiting for him when he walked from the sea and into the world of men. Bright in lacquered armor from the four corners of Sindan—yellow and black, red and white, the colors of the four roads to enlightenment, the four blooms of everthorn. They were armed and dangerous, but Jian felt more dangerous still.

Xienpei stood at the head of a hunting party. The soldiers behind her stood with their feet shoulder-width apart, hands to the hilts of their swords, to their bows, clenched at their sides. These last, Jian thought, were men he might wish to speak with later, in private. He noted those soldiers who had drawn their weapons and those who had not, for the road to Khanbul was a deadly game. He needed to know which pieces on the board belonged to his allies, which belonged to his enemies—and which of those he might steal.

Xienpei strode toward Jian and met him upon the beach. She eyed the clothing he wore—a tunic and leggings of sea-blue and sea-gray, woven of thistledown so light and fine it shed water even as he stood with the sea kissing his ankles. She stared at his sword, the blue steel seeming to ripple like storm-tossed waves in the high sunlight. Last she looked at his eyes. Long and hard she looked, and her mouth pursed in a hard little pucker.

Jian looked past his yendaeshi, through her. He had eyes only for Tsali'gei. She stood some distance up the beach, clad in bright robes of yellow and white and peacock-teal, with pearls in her hair.

"You were gone so long, Daechen Jian," Xienpei said, "that some believed you had been lost to us."

"I have returned." Jian looked into her eyes. *I am taller than her by a head and a half,* he thought. *Why have I never noticed this?*

"You have returned," Xienpei agreed, and her smile was wide

and wicked as a blood-sky dawn. "Fortunately so. Your Tsali'gei was so worried, I feared she might die of it, and your mother…" She shook her head, mouth downturned in a mockery of sorrow, her eyes never leaving Jian's face. "I am afraid this was all a bit much for her poor old heart. She is quite ill, and has taken to bed."

Jian felt his chest tighten, his mouth harden, and knew—too late—that he had let it show. Xienpei nodded, victorious.

"Word of your disappearance has reached the emperor's own court," she continued. "He was so concerned for your wellbeing that he sent me to ensure your safety. Now that the wicked Karkash Dhwani no longer has his ear, his Brilliance has shown a great deal of interest in the sea-born." She took a step closer and reached out, as if to help Jian onto land.

He reached for her without hesitation. They clasped arms, and she pulled him close into an embrace.

"Your fortunes have risen with mine, Daechen Jian," she whispered into his ear. Her breath was warm and wet, and smelled of dragonmint tea. "Do not think they will continue to rise without me, or that you have flown so high I cannot shoot you down."

"I do not understand, Yendaeshi." Jian squeezed Xienpei's forearm in a companionable manner. "I should think you would be happy that I have returned safely to your side, that I might continue to serve."

"Yet whom do you serve?" Her lacquered nails bit into his flesh like wicked little teeth.

"I serve the emperor, of course," he replied easily. "As I serve you. As my dammati serve the emperor through me." At that moment he noticed Xienpei's avoidance of the honorific "Sen-Baradam." It was no oversight, of that he was certain, but the title was not hers to give, nor to take from him. The presence of the emperor's troops, and the fact that they had not yet killed him, told Jian that his position was still secure.

"Good," Xienpei responded. "That is good." She released her hold but her wink gave him to know that she did not believe his lies. "The emperor will be pleased to hear of your safe return.

As I said, he holds a growing interest in the sea-born, and has specifically asked to meet one of you. As your mother is not well, you must of course remain by her side while work is completed on your estate."

Akari Sun Dragon soared high into midmorning, and the rays of his brilliance caught in Xienpei's jeweled smile.

"Tsali'gei will accompany me as I return to Khanbul," she continued. "Such a pretty thing, and the sea-born are so rare as to be a novelty yet. The emperor will be delighted to have her at court."

Jian looked up toward Tsali'gei, and knew that Xienpei had him. *If I do not bend to her will*, he thought, *it is not only I who will be broken.* He could feel his dreams failing, much as the sun's warmth fades into twilight.

"You should kiss your bride goodbye, Sen-Baradam," Xienpei told him. "We leave for Khanbul immediately."

Jian swallowed his fury with every bite of broth-soaked bread he coaxed his mother to eat. Her face, her sweet face was a mess of dark bruises, her eyes swollen shut, and she was missing two teeth. Jian would not insult Tiungpei by asking her what had happened, and she would not insult him by insisting that she was just a clumsy old woman. Neither would fish for a lie.

"Enough," she said finally, waving the spoon away with a trembling hand. "Enough. I am full." Jian wiped her sunken mouth with a soft cloth. He pulled the thin blanket up to her chin and leaned close to kiss her forehead gently, gently.

"You are a good boy," she whispered, then grimaced and worked her mouth, poking with her tongue at the empty space where teeth had been. "A good son."

"I will kill them for what they have done to you," he said, wishing that he could take back the words even as he spat them out. Tiungpei did not need to worry about her son's treasonous plans, on top of everything else.

"I know," she said, and the ghost of a smile played across her lips as his mother closed her eyes. "Is that not what I just said? You are your father's son, you know it now. But first you were *mine*."

Allyr, he wanted to tell her, *my father's name is Allyr*. How much did she know of him, he wondered. Did she ever think of her sea-lord lover, met on a moonstide night? Certainly Allyr remembered *her*, but before Jian could catch the questions that swam round his head like so many little fish, her breathing deepened, her face fallen slack as Tiungpei waded away into the sea of dreams.

A sea-queen diving for pearls.

That night, as Jian drowsed by the bedside and watched his mother not dying, a knock sounded at the door. *Rat-tat-tat tap-tap*, it sounded, *tap-tap*. Perri, then.

"Come in," he said, keeping his voice soft and low. The door opened a crack, wider, showing a glittering sliver of starlit night. Perri poked his head into the room. He was blushing.

"Sen-Baradam?"

"Yes, Dammati?" Despite his weariness, and bitter worry, Jian felt his curiosity stir.

"Uh, there is a girl here to see—*ow*!" Perri's head jerked backward and his blush, if possible, grew even deeper. "A *woman* here to see you, Sen-Baradam. She says, she says you know her?" Perri's eye was so wide that Jian might have laughed on any other day.

Perri squeaked in unmanly surprise as the door swung wide, and a young woman swayed into the room. She was, she was…

She is, Jian thought, *terrifying in her perfection*.

Her skin was white as fine parchment, and her hair a fluff of snow, of sea fog and moonlight. Her almond-shaped eyes were the deepest black of a starless night, and her lips painted the same deep scarlet as her shimmering, silken robes.

She was a comfort girl, Jian realized, even as he realized that he had half-jumped, half-fallen to his feet. He had heard of the emperor's comfort houses, of course, and the girls and boys who worked there, but he had never met such a person, outside of his most embarrassing dreams. He bowed in a clumsy attempt to cover his confusion and growing alarm.

"My dear, ah, my... I am afraid I do not—"

Tsali'gei would tear my throat out, he realized, *if she could see me now*. With that thought he cleared his throat and stood straight, though he feared his face was as red as Perri's. "If we have met before, I am ashamed to say that I cannot recall." There, that was better. He glanced at the bed where his mother lay sleeping. "And it is a little late for... my mother is..." He grimaced.

The girl laughed, a sound like smoke and water over cold stones.

"I am Giella," she told him, keeping her voice low. "The White Nightingale, they call me. Neither do you know me, but you may have met my mother during your... recent travels." She turned her head, and Jian saw that she had a small spray of red feathers behind one ear.

"Ah," he said, remembering the red-crested woman among the Twilight Court. "Yes, I believe I have. My apologies, ah, *Daezhu* Giella?" When she nodded, he went on. "As you can see, my mother is... she is ill, and she is sleeping."

"She is not ill, Jian Sen-Baradam," Giella scolded with a small and angry laugh. "She was beaten half to death by that horrid she-beast Xienpei and her *sao-re dan* followers." Smiling at his shocked expression, she swayed deeper into the room and took a seat by the fire. She brought forth a small harp and busied herself with the strings. "I will make sure that your mother does not wake—and that we are not disturbed. We have much to discuss tonight, de Allyr."

De Allyr. Heart pounding, Jian sat by his mother's side again, and nodded to Perri, who backed out with obvious relief and shut the door softly behind him.

"So you know my father."

"Jian Sen-Baradam." She laughed and began to play. "*Everyone* in the Twilight Lands knows your father."

❖

They spoke long into the night, though Giella's voice was such that her words came forth in song, and Jian found his own voice rising and falling in a cadence to match hers. Before long this seemed easy, natural, more right than the human way of speaking. Giella played her harp, and his mother never woke, nor were they interrupted.

Her music was magic, then. Dae magic unsanctioned by the emperor and therefore illegal. Their actions spoke of treason, highest treason, and the words they sang back and forth, had those words been put to script, would write their names in blood on the executioner's book.

"Jian," she sang to him that night, "by the salt and water that flows deep in your heart, by the wind in your lungs and the earth in your bones, we call upon you now to take up the sword wielded by your father and his father before him, that the song which was shattered be sung once more, and the lands that were sundered made whole." Her fingers danced like pale shadows over her harp-strings, tugging at his soul.

"Join with us, those of the Daezhu and Daechen, the dammati and Sen-Baradam who have sworn loyalty to the lands of our fathers and mothers. There our loyalties lie, not with this"—Her fingers struck an ugly discord, and her voice was gorgeously harsh—"this walking lie, this soulless usurper who has stolen us and has stolen *from* us our families, our lives, our bodies and souls."

There it was, then, a white nightingale bright in the full light of day. The twilight lords would have their kin overthrow the emperor of Sindan, and put one of their own in his place.

My father, most likely, Jian thought. His heart roared like a bear in a cage, desperate to break free. But—

"I cannot," he told her. "I cannot. My mother…"

"She is an elder," Giella told him, voice soft and implacable as the river in spring, "and she is beloved of a twilight lord. She will not be alone, Jian Sen-Baradam, that much I can promise you."

He shook his head. "They have Tsali'gei, hostage to my continued good behavior. They would kill her—"

"Jian," she interrupted him, and her harp fell silent. "My sweet

Issuq brother, I am grieved for you, but they will kill her either way. Surely you know that. A spoonful of honeyed poison is still poison, de Allyr, and telling yourself different will not make it hurt any less."

Jian closed his eyes tight against the pity in the bard-girl's dark eyes, and against the truth in her sung words.

"That may be," he said, "but I wish to think on this before throwing in my lot. I will consider your words." He opened his eyes and stared into hers. "Your honeyed words, before deciding whether I should swallow them." The corners of Giella's mouth twitched at that.

"Oh, de Allyr, you tease," she crooned. "It is always better to *swallow*." Jian blushed and she laughed again, light and lovely as a killing frost.

"I will consider your words," he said again, and rose. "Thank you for your visit, cousin. Perri will show you the way back to your, ah, your house."

"Oh, no need for that, *brother*," she assured him. "A nightingale sings best in the dark… and I know my way home."

Jian stood for a long time after she had gone, staring at the closed door, thinking of the wide world beyond it, and the treacherous roads—yellow and red, black and white—that all seemed to lead to Khanbul.

I know my way home, too, he thought, *but I can neither take my family to the Twilight Lands, nor leave them here to die. For me, and for them, the only possibility of freedom lies in throwing in my lot with those who would overthrow the emperor—and in doing so, I most certainly condemn myself and those I love to death.*

Well is Khanbul named the Forbidden City… all roads lead there, but whichever I choose leads to a fate I cannot accept.

Out in the darkness, a nightingale began to sing.

THIRTY-ONE

The silence was long and dark, as if the entire Valley of Death lay between them. It was a comfortable silence nevertheless, the kind of peace that can be found only when killers take the measure of one another.

Hafsa Azeina bit into a plum and it burst upon her tongue, sticky-sweet juices dripping down her chin like the heart's blood of an enemy.

If the merit of a sorcerer could be measured in blood spilled, she thought, *this man would cast as long a shadow as my own. Nor less his little apprentice.* The girl had never made much of an impression upon the dreamshifter, one way or the other, quiet as still as a hare might be beneath the shadow of hawks, she had thought.

Looking across the narrow table, she saw that those wide jade eyes held nothing of a prey's fear, and all of a predator's patient cunning.

Interesting.

The Quarabalese, like the Zeeranim, obeyed the ancient laws of hospitality. Bread and salt were shared, the niceties observed, and then three of the most dangerous people in the kingdom reclined at their ease. Hafsa Azeina drank sweet water made tart with the juice of a whole lemon. Aasah drank one of the brandies Leviathus had described to her with such excitement. The girl Yaela drank ale that was black and thick, a great deal of it, and when she set her horn down it left an amber moustache above her full mouth. She licked her lips, and was the first to break their silence.

"Queen Consort," she began formally, casting her eyes down as if impressed by the title, "you have come to beg our aid. What is it you seek?" *And what is it you offer?* her eyes added, deliberately avoiding the bundle of leather that lay to one side.

Beg, indeed. The dreamshifter snorted into her water. She had been playing such games before this girl's mother first set eyes on her father, and would not be so easily baited.

"Say rather that I come to make a bargain," Hafsa Azeina corrected, "and neither do I come to your... master... empty-handed." The girl's lush mouth flattened in irritation. It occurred to her that perhaps Aasah was not, in truth, the girl's master, nor she his apprentice. *That is* very *interesting.* The girl's eyes flicked to hers, and she smoothed her face into a perfect, lovely mask. The dreamshifter reminded herself not to underestimate the enemy.

You are so sure she is your enemy, Khurra'an noted. He sounded regretful.

Everyone is my enemy, she responded. *Save you, save my daughter.*

You are not as alone in this world as you believe, Kithren, he chided, but in his weariness the words held no salt. *Not by half.* Hafsa Azeina shrugged mentally and returned her full attention to the here, the now, and to the enemies who sat before her. Aasah wet his lips with the brandy and gave her an odd, deep smile.

"With what do you think to cross my palms, Dreamshifter? By now you know that I dream neither of salt nor of lovely women, however salty they may be."

She inclined her head. "You dream of a new homeland for your people."

"Indeed. The Dragon King has offered land—land enough for the few remaining Quarabalese to settle upon, can we but get them here from the Seared Lands. Land, crops, livestock. He has offered us life, Dreamshifter. What can you possibly have to offer us that is greater than life?"

Belzaleel chuckled. Yaela's eyes flicked toward the sheath at Hafsa Azeina's hip. But Hafsa Azeina had no more time for hunting mysteries. She retrieved the raggedy bundle, pushed aside wine and water and salt, and began to unroll her package before the shadowmancer's eyes.

"I can offer you the greatest gift of all," she assured him. "I offer you—"

The leather fell away, revealing the wicked flensing knife.

261

"—death."

"*Zassa Arachni o.*" Yaela bared her teeth, which stood out white against her midnight skin, and hissed like a nest full of angry snakes. "Where did you get this?" she demanded.

"Death," Aasah whispered. His hands twitched, but he did not reach for the knife.

"Death," Hafsa Azeina agreed. "This was found in the Zeera, deep within the Bones of Eth. It was left there by one who attacked my daughter and left her... damaged. By a man who has made himself my enemy."

"Then we do share an enemy." Aasah tore his eyes from the gleaming knife and met hers. "This does not mean we share a bed."

"I should hope not," she agreed. "The last man who shared my bed ended up being something of a... disappointment."

To her great surprise, Yaela laughed at that. It was a big laugh, from the belly, and Hafsa Azeina found her own lips tugged into a reluctant grin.

"A disappointment," the girl howled. "A... *disappointment...* ah." She wiped tears from her cheeks with the back of one hand. "Ah. I do hope this lover of yours met an untimely end?"

"I ate his heart," she admitted.

This sent the girl into another fit of laughter. The dreamshifter and the shadowmancer shared a bemused smile over the murderous blade. Finally the shadowmancer's apprentice—or whatever she was—regained her composure. Her laughter faded away, to be replaced by a grin fit for a vash'ai queen, all gleaming eyes and the promise of sharp teeth.

"We may not share her bed, Master," Yaela said, "but to share such an enemy—that is no small matter."

"No small matter," he agreed, "and no small gift you offer us, Dreamshifter. I could use this knife to find the one who wielded it."

"I am well aware."

"Of course, and what price would you ask for such a thing?" His eyes hooded, and the girl at his side stopped grinning. "I will not agree to bring harm to his Arrogance. The Dragon King and I have a pact… and I will not go back on my word."

"I would not dream of asking you to break your word." It was her turn to smile, and to watch the Quarabalese sorcerers squirm at the sight of it. "I ask you for no more than I offer—the chance to find my enemy. As I have taught my own apprentice, if you want someone dead…"

"Kill them yourself," Yaela purred. She looked at Aasah, and there was nothing of an apprentice's deference in her eyes. "We must do this," she said.

The shadowmancer sighed and dipped his chin to his chest.

"As you wish," he agreed.

Servants were called in to clear the food away. When they had gone, Yaela shut and barred the door behind them and doused all but a single candle.

Darkness for a dark purpose, Hafsa Azeina thought. It seemed fitting. The shadowmancer and his apprentice took a loom from its place by the front door and set it in the middle of the table. This loom was nearly as tall as Hafsa Azeina herself. *And if it is meant for the weaving of rugs and tapestries*, she thought, *Basta's Lyre was made to play children's songs.*

A web was stretched between the wooden loom's beams, a simple spiral, and in the middle of this symmetrical beauty sat a spider as big across as Hafsa Azeina's two hands splayed wide.

"What a beauty," she murmured, and Yaela favored her with a smile.

"She belonged to my master," Aasah said in a hushed voice, "and to his before him. She is a Mother of Mothers."

It is an honor to meet you, Grandmother, she thought, but if the spider heard her, she did not deign to answer. Her cluster of eyes, the largest of them like dark pearls set in a face of silvery fuzz, tilted this way and that as she considered the humans before her.

Yaela gathered several wooden bowls, a trio of glass pipes, thin wooden sticks polished to a rich luster, and other oddments of their peculiar magic. Hafsa Azeina looked on, curious. She had witnessed the shadowmancers' tricks before—everyone had—but the secrets of their true magic were as jealously guarded as her own.

"You will tell no one of this, of course," Aasah remarked as Yaela set a wooden mug before her.

"Of course," she answered, and she had to smile. Who would be fool enough to beg magical knowledge from her?

Daru, she realized with a guilty start. *Daru would wish to see this.* The boy would have pestered the shadowmancers with questions till their heads ached, and likely they would have answered him, too. The boy had a way with people. She knew he was alive, and not in distress, and she had been busy... but this was no excuse. He was her responsibility.

I wish you were strong enough to go find the boy.

As do I, Khurra'an replied, *though I doubt much he would be glad to see me.*

Yaela poured something into a cup, and Hafsa Azeina returned her attention to the here, the now, and the enemies in front of her. She picked up the cup and sniffed carefully, flaring her nostrils like a cat.

"Winterweed," she said, "and wyvern-mint. And... lamb's blood?"

"Yes." Aasah nodded. "It is called so, here in the mountains. We know this as Ruh-jah, or 'heart's blood.' In Sindan they call it 'blood of the innocent.'"

Hafsa Azeina blinked away her irritation. "There are other herbs in here with which I am not familiar." She swirled the liquid around in her cup. "Dreaming herbs, I think. Calming herbs. And dried mushrooms?"

"There is nothing in that brew that will harm you in the least, Dreamshifter, on that you have my word. I would offer to trade cups with you, but the potion Yaela made for me is a bit—stronger— than what she gave you. I am used to the effects of *jinnamagi*, and you are not." Even as he said so, the shadowmancer emptied his cup in one long pull, and took a glass pipe that Yaela had prepared.

Hafsa Azeina shrugged and drank the unappealing swill, which tasted as foul as it looked. *"That is how you know it will work,"* her own master might have said, long ago when the world was green and good, and she was a princess of the Seven Isles. She accepted the pipe as well and took a long pull, holding in the smoke as she had seen the shadowmancer and his apprentice do.

The top of her head floated away.

"Well," she said, and stared as speaking the word created rippling waves of orange and purple that flowed from her mouth. "That *is* interesting."

Yaela giggled.

"Pay attention, the both of you," Aasah snapped.

Hafsa Azeina brought all her years of discipline to the fore, and it worked well enough that she was able to sit up straight and watch, fascinated, as Aasah blew colored smoke into the swirling web, causing the spider to dance in the semidarkness.

Round and round she went, up and down, up and down, weaving a web, every once in a while stopping to consider her own handiwork, nip a bit of thread here, then add a bit. As she worked, curls of the colored smoke from the shadowmancer's pipe clung to the web, weaving in and out among the sticky silken strands, creating a dazzling display of shadows and light as beautiful as any sunrise. Tiny globes formed from this magic, perfect and shining as a jeweler's beads, and the spider wove these in, as well.

Eventually the spider stopped, trembling in the shadows at the far edge of the loom, shuddering with exertion so that the web shimmered in the thin candlelight.

"It is done," the shadowmancer announced. He held out one hand, finger extended so that it brushed the web near the spider's resting place.

Fast as thought, as light, the spider struck. She scuttled along the web and pounced on his hand. Hafsa Azeina watched as two fangs as long as the tip of her little fingers sank into Aasah's exposed flesh. The spider leapt free then and scuttled back to the center of her web. She looked, if a spider can be said to have a look, exceedingly self-satisfied.

Aasah slumped and fell to one side. His eyes rolled back in his head until only the whites showed. His body went stiff all over, arching so that only his shoulders and heels touched the ground, and he began to drum at the floor with fists and heels.

"What?" Hafsa Azeina cried out, though her voice was muffled, the words slow and sounding fuzzy. "Aasah—"

She would have risen, but the apprentice's fierce jade eyes held her back.

"Hssssst! Be silent and listen!"

"Impertinent little—" Hafsa Azeina broke off as the shadowmancer began to sing. His voice wrapped about her soul as strong and light and silken as the spider's web, as beautiful as the river on a bright spring day. Like a hunting hawk it rose, hunting truth in the sunlight that it might carry it back down to its master in dark places. It seemed to the dreamshifter for a moment, all too brief, that her soul rose with it.

After a time he stopped singing, and lay staring white-eyed and blind at the ceiling. When at long last his muscles relaxed, the length of his body sagging down onto the cold stone, his eyes rolled back to show a bloodshot blue before they fluttered and closed in sleep. The spider gave her web a little shake and started to groom herself.

The top of Hafsa Azeina's head seemed to settle into place once more, though she resisted the urge to reach up and touch it.

"Is it done?" she whispered, the echo of a shadow of sound, not wanting to disturb the sorcerer's sleep. She knew what that exhaustion felt like, she knew what it meant, and she knew the dangers of waking such a one.

"Ssst." Yaela closed her eyes, as if to remember better, and began to speak in a voice near song. "You may be the spider, you may be the fly; you cannot be both.

"If you are to find that which you hunt, you must first find that which hunts you. The Huntress has what you need, and you have what she wants. Bring her the horn of the golden ram, and she will give you the weapon you need.

"Or she will kill you."

She opened her eyes to fix that jade gaze firmly upon Hafsa Azeina's face.

"It does not matter, either way. For the dreamshifter, all roads lead to death."

Hafsa Azeina drew a deep, free breath, closing her own eyes, the better to see the path that had been laid before her.

"So be it," she said. "So be it.

"So be it," she said a third time, making it true.

THIRTY-TWO

Leviathus had visited the traders' port of Min Yaarif in the past. He had often traveled as his father's emissary, and took pride in the number of deals he had been able to negotiate. Always the city had seemed a charming place—a bit rough, to be sure, but that was part of its charm. Though it was rumored to be a den of criminals and pirates of the worst sort, the king's son had thought those tales to be exaggerations and the imaginings of untraveled folk.

This time he had a somewhat different view of the city.

For one thing, his window was barred. The cell in which he was kept was not horrible, as it had been built for the express purpose of holding important people hostage while ransom prices were negotiated. It was a cell, nevertheless, and just a short walk past the hangman's block.

Negotiations, he had learned, did not always play out in the captive's favor.

So Leviathus sat, and he waited. Sometimes he walked and waited, or slept and waited. He wished for someone with whom to talk. When the slaves came in to bring him food and a fresh chamber pot thrice a day, they spoke no more than mice might have.

Or books to read. He had asked once, and the woman who held the keys laughed till tears rolled down her face. Apparently, prisoners were not meant to enjoy their time in the cells.

Then again, he thought, *three days ago I wished for nothing more than water and food. Here I have water, and food, and I wish for books. If I had books, what might I wish for then?*

His head itched.

I might wish for a bath, a long sleep in my own bed, and the company of a pretty girl afterward.

Unbidden came the image of Yaela, the shadowmancer's little apprentice, with her wide jade eyes and lush curves just hinted at beneath the layers of clothing she always wore. She was sharp-tongued, that one, but sharper-minded, and Leviathus had seen wit and kindness on those rare occasions when her mask slipped.

Perhaps I shall wish for a kiss from the shadowmancer's apprentice, then.

As well wish to taste the stars, a voice laughed in his mind. *As well wish to drink the moons, as wish for love from the shadow-souled.*

Leviathus startled at the voice. It was not the dark and angry whispering of his own soul, a cry for vengeance from those who had wronged him. Nor yet was it the dry, low growly voice of the vash'ai queen who had guarded his sleep along the road to Min Yaarif. This was different—a sibilant sound, a whisper of song, the susurrus of iridescent scales across the white sand beaches of home.

Who are you? he asked.

Who am I? The voice laughed, and that sound lifted Leviathus's heart from a dark place. *Who are* you? *Before you know who I am, you must learn who you are.*

Frowning, Leviathus walked to the window and pressed his face against the bars, but all he could see was a patch of hot blue sky and a bright sun above the gathering crowd as the auctioneer made ready to sell a fresh batch of slaves. Though the slave markets had always left a sick feeling in his stomach, today he spared those poor wretches scarcely a thought. A captive himself, he had concerns of his own to attend to.

I am Leviathus ap Wyvernus ne Atu. Last son of the Dragon King...

I did not ask who your father was, the voice responded. *I asked who* you *are.* That laughter again, like a great bell ringing deep below the ocean's surface. *When you figure that out, perhaps we shall speak again, you and I.*

The voice was gone.

It left a tintinnabulation in Leviathus's ears and a taste like brine in his mouth.

Well, I did wish for someone to talk to, he thought. *That might not have been the smartest...*

Screaming erupted from the auction block as some poor soul objected to being sold as trade goods. Leviathus heard the *thud, thud thud* of heavy blows against flesh, followed by the unmistakable wet crunch of breaking bone—the slave was a fighter, then, or had been—and afterward more screaming, shrill and wounded. He thought that came from the auctioneer, and allowed himself a small smile. The man was odious, and if he lost his life at the hands of an outraged slave, the world likely would be a better place.

He peered out curiously. The crowd rolled toward the auction block as crowds always do, drawn by misfortune, then pulled back again in response to something frightening. Perhaps one of the chinmong used by the security guards. Those raptors were enough to cool the ardor of the most blood-lusting crowd.

As the crowd moved, a face stood out from that seething, screaming humanity. A small, brown face, wide-eyed and staring not at the bloody tableau, but at him. That face, a stranger in a sea of strangers, was hauntingly and impossibly familiar.

"Who are you?" he called, knowing as he did that he risked a beating from his captors. The screaming crowd swallowed his words, so he tried again. "*Who are you?*"

Who are you? the voice laughed in his head.

The boy blinked, then smiled wide as the rising sun. He held up one hand in greeting. With his other he saluted Leviathus, fist to chest, in precisely the manner of his Draiksguard. Then the crowd swallowed the boy, and once more the king's son was alone.

THIRTY-THREE

Hannei grunted as the fat man's lash licked across her back, biting deep into her skin and tearing away chunks of flesh. Blood flowed freely down her back to be sucked up by greedy flies. Tears rolled freely down her face, to be sucked up by the greedy heat. Her shoulders burned, pulled nearly out of their sockets as she jerked against the rough bonds.

For the second time in less than a moon she had been bound and beaten, and for the second time she opened sa and ka wide to death, begging to be allowed to set foot upon the Lonely Road.

For the second time in less than a moon, death spurned her.

At last the fat man got what he wanted. A flap of skin came loose, falling aside as if she had yanked her warrior's vest open. Hannei felt it, every bit of it, the blood and the flies and the flap of warm skin hanging down against her butt. She could smell it—blood and piss and fear sweat—and taste the sour vomit in her mouth. She could even hear the effects of her torture in the gasps and hushed applause it invoked in a growing throng of outlanders, and in her own strangled cries, caught deep in her throat with no hope of escape.

Her body twitched and shuddered, struggling at the rough bonds even as she realized the blows had stopped falling, and the fat man's shadow fell across her face. She could no more lift her eyes to meet his than she could sprout wings from her ruined back and fly away, or quiet the shuddering moans that wracked her body as it hung like meat left to ripen in the sun.

The man gripped her jaw, hard, with the hand that still held the whip, and wrenched her head so that Hannei was forced to look at him through her swollen eyes. His nose was broken, his face smeared with blood—probably most of it hers—but he was assuredly a prettier sight to look upon than she.

"Think you are a tough one now, you little shit?" He hawked and spat, the warm phlegm mixing with blood and worse on Hannei's face. "Think you are beautiful, now? My dogs would not fuck you, looking like this. Think you are special, little barbarian warrior? I paid good salt for you, and you are worth less than the shit 'neath my foot. Fucking barbarians. At least I had a little fun before you died, hey?"

He fumbled at his belt and drew a long dagger, no bigger around than one of Hannei's broken fingers. "I will enjoy this, I will. Say goodbye to your Akari, little warrior." He pressed the point into the soft flesh beneath Hannei's jaw. She closed her eyes and shuddered in relief.

It is over, she thought.

"Hold!" a voice shouted.

No! Hannei screamed silently.

It was a voice no human throat could produce. It was the woman whose lizard-thing had stopped Hannei from killing the fat man. The man turned and frowned, dragging his knife across Hannei's skin as he did so, but not deeply enough.

No! Hannei screamed silently. *Finish it!*

"What? What do you want, Sharmutai? This little *puqqa* is mine to do with as I wish, and I wish to kill it."

"Why kill what you can sell?" The woman swam into Hannei's dim sight.

"Who is going to buy *this*?" The man jabbed with his knife, and blood ran freely. A fly left Hannei's back to walk across her face as it searched for tears. "You?"

"Well, since you ask…" The woman upended a small bag into the palm of one hand, and the crowd gasped. She held the hand low enough that Hannei could see.

Red salt, she thought, and her gorge rose. *She offers life for life.*

The man gaped at the fistful of red salt tablets, then at the woman who held them.

"But… why?"

"Because it amuses me. Because I am wealthy, and foolish with my money. Because I want to... which is the only reason I do anything, as you well know. Does it matter?" She jiggled her hand up and down, making the salt tablets clack and chatter against one another.

"Not a bit," the fat man replied with a laugh. He dropped the knife, and the whip, and snatched up the money with both hands. "But do not come crying to me when it dies! No guarantees! It will be dead by sundown, most like."

"Most like," the woman agreed softly. She touched the top of Hannei's shorn scalp, the only part of her that did not yet hurt. "We shall see." She picked up the man's discarded knife. *Snick-snick*, fast as a lionsnake's strike she cut the ropes, ducking her shoulder and catching Hannei upon her back as Hannei fell down...

...down...

...down into the shadows.

The first thing Hannei noticed was the smells. Wine and honey and fresh linen, and some sort of burning herb or spice.

The smoke made her nose wrinkle involuntarily and she sneezed—and then she noticed the pain. Pain *everywhere*, every bit of her a brilliant inferno of agony. She hurt on the outside, she hurt on the inside, she hurt in places she had not known she had. Worse, she *itched* as if a thousand thousand sand ants swarmed across her corpse, taking mouthfuls as they passed.

"She is awake!" a voice cried out nearby, startling Hannei so that she jerked away from the sound, and *that* hurt. "Mistress, she wakes!"

"*Nnnh*," she protested, only then remembering that they had taken her tongue. "*Ngkok*."

"You awake to the gift of sweet life, and the first thing you say to me is '*fuck*'?" a gentle voice remonstrated. "I must say, it seems rather ungrateful of you." Hannei tried to lift her face from the soft bedding, but a light touch upon her back held her still. "Ah-ah, none of that, my prize. Let us get you healed up first, then you can jump about my house breaking things like the barbarian you are."

"*Nnh.*" It hurt.

"None of that, now, either. There will be time enough for you to learn to speak properly, once the healers can guarantee to me that you will live. Until then, please do not trouble my ears with your noise."

The bedding beside Hannei sagged as the woman's weight pressed it down. Something cool was pressed against her back, and Hannei wept with relief as the inferno of pain receded to a dull heat.

"There you are," the voice crooned. "There, my prize. Rest now. Rest."

Hannei slipped away.

Later—days later, moons later, she would never know for sure—Hannei perched on a padded wooden stool, sipping dragonmint tea from a salt-clay mug and watching colorful little fishes swim in a fountain. A heavy iron collar was clasped about her throat, loose enough that she could swallow but not so loose she might hope to slip out of it, and it was fastened to a silvery chain that kept her from leaving, or even standing upright.

The fountain was colored red, and it sparkled in the late sunlight. It had been glazed with red salt, one of the girls had told her in awed tones, the same as the cup from which she drank sweet water at every meal. The robes they wore had been dyed red with salt, and tablets of red clay fell *clack-clack-clack* through the mistresses' fingers, more precious than rain.

How many lives is this all worth? Hannei wondered, turning the cup round in her hand. A small child ran shrieking through the gardens, chased by two young women in fluttering red veils, all of them laughing as they passed her by. *How many babes might the Mothers bear, if only we had this much salt?*

They, she reminded herself harshly. *Not we. They.*

"Sometimes I wonder what you are thinking, my prize." A hand touched her shoulder, the nape of her neck, and rubbed the soft strip of hair that was growing in—curly, much to Hannei's disgust. "I wonder what thoughts chase each other round and round in that pretty head of yours, day in and out as you sit here and watch us all."

Hannei *was* pretty. The surgeons had seen to that, and the girls with their brushes and paint, and golden dust for her eyelids. Hannei's ears had been pierced and hung with red gemstones, and her nose, as well. She longed to pick it.

"*Nnnnh*," she grunted, and scowled as she set the tea aside.

"Oh, stop." Sharmutai laughed and sat on the edge of the fountain, trailing her fingers in the water. Every movement she made was as graceful as an oulo dancer's, and as calculated. For all her gentle voice and warm words, the softness never reached her eyes, not one bit of it. When she smiled, Hannei's ridiculous hair wanted to stand on end. "I do not care to know that badly. I was just bored."

Sharmutai, she had learned, owned a comfort house—a whorehouse for those too wealthy to utter the word *whore*. Or she owned ten of them, or a hundred, depending on which whispers you might choose to believe. Certainly she owned this house, the one to which she had brought Hannei… and it was not a nice place. Slaves would prefer to be sold as serpent bait rather than be dragged through those front doors. It was known that none who entered that way ever left again, alive or dead. Slaves had swallowed their own tongues, it was said, rather than be sold to Sharmutai.

Hannei grunted again, softly, eyes never leaving those of the woman who owned her. *Swallow their tongues, ha*, she thought, and washed the bitter thought down with hot sweet tea. *Not like I had the choice.*

The toddler ran laughing into the garden again, saw Sharmutai sitting there, and all laughter stopped. Her big brown eyes widened, they filled with tears, and she ran away sobbing, her attendants following with quick and silent footsteps. Sharmutai stared after them. Although the smile never slipped from her face, her eyes could only be described as thunderous.

"In truth, I know what thoughts spin around in your head," she murmured. "In *all* your pretty little heads. Day in and day out, you all think of one thing. Freedom." She cut her eyes at Hannei. "Am I not right, my prize?"

Hannei shrugged. *Freedom to go where?* The question did not interest her all that much.

"I say I know what you are all thinking, and I do not care. I care about one thing, and one thing only, and that is wealth." Sharmutai ran her hand along the rim of the glittering red fountain, and her eyes shone as if she were fevered. "Wealth enough to buy what I want. What *I* want. And do you know what that is?"

Hannei blinked—at the lemon trees and the fish in the fountain, at the sight of enough red salt to buy anything at all, anywhere in the world. What would she wish to buy, if she owned so much? What could any woman want so badly?

Tammas, she thought. *I want Tammas. I want my life back.* But there was not enough red salt in the world to buy what she wanted. The closest she might ever come would be vengeance against those who had taken these things from her.

Oh, she thought. *Oh.*

Still holding her gaze, Sharmutai nodded slowly. "You understand," she whispered. "I knew you would." She took Hannei's tea, drank the rest down, and then threw the precious cup against the ground, where it shattered into a thousand sharp pieces.

"Now," she continued, dabbing her mouth gracefully on her sleeve, "it is time we have a talk. I know you have heard the whispers about me. Some of them are true. This is, indeed, a brothel, and it is one of the worst. People—mostly men, you know, but not all—come to sate their coarsest desires here, their absolute worst. My poor little whores are lucky if they survive one night, which is how my physicians came to be so good at stitching girls up. When that happens, I do not care. There is nothing you can do that will make me care. Understand this, believe it, and you may just survive this place."

Ehuani, she thought, *the woman speaks truth.* Hannei nodded, slowly, as the chillflesh raised up along both arms.

"Good. Now, I paid good money for you, wrecked though you were, and the whole of Min Yaarif is laughing in their sleeves about Ovreh finally getting the better of me in a deal. A cut-tongue slave, a barbarian no less, beat all to shit and likely dead by now. There is nothing this town loves so much as gossip, and right now you, my prize, are at the heart of it."

"*Nnnhgh,*" Hannei snorted. She only wished she had killed the fat bastard. Grab *her* by the pussy, would he?

"Still angry with him, are you, pet? There are men I know who would do so much worse to you." Sharmutai flicked her fingertips against the fountain's surface, and the little fish scattered in terror. "Men who would love to get hold of an exotic Zeerani warrior-girl, broken or not. How many times could we stitch you back together, I wonder? My physicians are *very* good. I expect I could sell you over and over again until I had made a tidy profit, enough to make that odious Ovreh eat his words."

Hannei growled low in her throat, would have stood but for the silvery chain, the collar that marked her as a slave.

"Ah. Good girl, good." Sharmutai nodded. "*This* is the girl I saw in the market. This is the prize I bought, from a fool who did not know what he had.

"I said I could sell you to these men, but I have not yet decided that I will. What would that get me? A throne of red salt? A house made of red salt bricks? Not even that much, my pet, and those things I own already. No, I want more than *things*, I want more… and you might just help me get it." She leaned close. "Do you wish to know what it is that I want?"

The collar tugged tight against Hannei's throat. Only then did she realize that she had leaned in, too, that she hung on the other woman's every word. She nodded.

When the blow came it was so fast, so unexpected, that Hannei cried out even though it did not hurt all that much. Sharmutai laughed, a merry sound.

"I am not going to tell you!" she sang. "But you are going to help me get it, all the same. There is something in it for you, too!" She leaned in again, as if they were girls, conspiring to steal spiders' eggs from the kitchen. Hannei leaned away, rubbing her face and scowling.

"Oh, stop sulking. I will not reveal to you the deepest wish of my heart, as if we were equals, you and I, as if we were milk-sisters sharing a teat! I will tell you, however, what *you* want. I might even help you get it, because I *like* you."

Hannei could only stare. *The woman is mad.*

"I know what you want," Sharmutai breezed on, unconcerned. "You want—what is your word for it? Ah, yes. You want *kishah*. You want vengeance."

Hannei froze.

"Do you know what else I own? Besides the comfort houses, I mean? I own a fighter's pit. It is very small, and only the elite are allowed to attend the fights *I* put on…"

A strange sensation grew in Hannei's heart, a warm pain, as if a tiny dragon stirred in her sleep.

"I could let men buy you, and women, all manner of wealthy filth, and they would use you up, *pffft*." Sharmutai pinched her fingers together between their faces, "Like putting out a candle, but I can think of a better use for that strong young body of yours, that fire I see in your eyes. I can afford to send you to the finest school for pit fighters this side of the Seared Lands. You could fight for me. Fight hard enough, and you might win me the thing I *really* want. Do that, my prize, and I will set you free. Free to avenge yourself upon the people who cut out your tongue…" She stuck her own out, and laughed. "…and sold you to a monster like me.

"The choice is yours," she told Hannei. "You can fuck, and you can die, or you can fight, and *probably* die, but maybe not. Uh, well, *that* sounded better in my head." She smiled, and this time the smile reached her eyes as she reached out and gripped Hannei's hands so hard that her nails bit into flesh. "What say you, slave?"

"*Ngkok ech*," Hannei agreed. She squeezed back and blood welled from her palm to spatter on the ground between them, sealing the deal.

THIRTY-FOUR

Ani woke to the sound of the Zeera singing, the taste of her lover's sweat, and the pain of having died. She lay for a moment without moving, savoring the beating of her heart. The gentle whuffling of the horses as they slept, and the not-so-gentle snoring of Askander as he lay beside her, one strong arm flung across her hips and a scowl on his face. He always slept like that, when they were together, as if he could protect her from all the dangers of this world.

Dawn came, and with it the realization that nothing was as it had been before the Dragon King stretched his hand across the Zeera. Sa and ka, always a shallow well from which she might draw, had run dry. Duq'aan was nowhere to be seen. Askander's vash'ai had refused to speak with him since Inna'hael had dragged them here. As she was the warden's lover, his vash'ai would sometimes grace her with conversation, but now when she tried to touch his mind…

"Nothing," Askander said, his voice low and ragged. Ani had not heard him wake. "Nothing. He is gone."

"He will be back," she assured her lover, turning to face him. Ani winced, then grinned, as the ache low in her belly reminded her of the night's loving. "As long as we are alone…"

"No." Askander reached out and enfolded her in his arms, to let her know the word was not meant for her. His heart beat a sad tempo against her cheek, its song as familiar to her as her own. More familiar to her now than her own.

Everything has changed. Everything.

"Everything has changed," he said, echoing her thoughts. "Duq'aan is gone. He is gone from my mind, from my heart." His voice cracked. "He has gone on and left me behind."

Ani frowned. She could still feel Inna'hael. The kahanna was somewhere far away, but their connection held.

A strong wind picked up outside, slapping at the sides of Askander's tent. *Everything has changed*, it told her. The desert sang a dirge, low and urgent. *Everything will change*, it said, and it wept.

Ani closed her eyes again, breathed deep, and listened to the bones of the world. She had not done this since she was a small child, young and bright. Then she was a hummingbird, flitting among the people's wagons. The song was there, as it had been long before her birth, as it would continue on long after her death, and the song agreed.

Everything is changing.

With her eyes closed she could see the color of her lover's bones, the gold and black and blood red of the Zeera. He belonged here. Their horses' colors would be the green-blue of a grassy oasis under the desert sky. Talieso's bonesong was streaked with earthen clay and iron and copper, soiled as it was after having been claimed by her all those years ago.

As was Askander's.

I am sorry, she thought, and she bit her lip hard against tears. *I should never have tamed you.*

"Come, pretty girl," Askander said at last, kissing the top of her head. "This morning grows old, and the road is long."

Ani hugged her lover one more time, and rolled away from his warmth.

They worked in silence, a dance of bodies that had long lived and loved and ridden together. There was an efficiency in everything Askander did, that Ani had always found attractive. Nothing superfluous, no movement wasted, because he knew what had to be done. Just as she did.

She sang under her breath as they broke camp, as the horses were fed and watered, even as she chewed her ration of lionsnake pemmican. Askander shot her a puzzled glance but said nothing, trusting that she knew what she was doing, that her intentions were good. In those dark and silent glances, Ani learned that she was not too old to suffer a broken heart.

I am sorry, she told him silently, and she was, but that did not stop her from singing, from working the Dzirani magic which was forbidden in every land.

Askander swung up into his saddle and turned Akkim's nose to the south and west. "We should stop first at Nisfi," he said, "then straight on to Aish Kalumm. Wardens and warriors need to know of these false Mah'zula…" His voice trailed off, and he did not meet her eyes, even as he spoke of their journey together.

He knows.

Ani paused in her singing, though the tune still whispered through her breath, through her blood and bones. The song would go on unless she chose to end it, or until the magic had enabled her to achieve her bloody goal.

"I cannot return with you."

"The Dragon King has done something to sap the land of sa and ka," Askander continued, as if she had not spoken. "Hafsa Azeina is gone, Umm Nurati is dead, Sareta is acting more like First Mother than is the new First Mother, and the people need guidance and wisdom from their elders. The world is changing, bringing with it a new day, and they are afraid there will be no Zeeranim left to meet it. I am afraid, as well."

You are afraid? Ani shuddered. *I am terrified*. But she said only, "I cannot return. I have to go to Atualon, to help Hafsa Azeina, and to help Sulema." As she said it, what had been a thought became real. Askander frowned at his horse's ears.

"They are no longer of the people."

"If they are not, neither am I, nor ever was. The Zeera is more than a place, and the Zeeranim are more than brown hair and brown eyes, more than horses and blades and bows. The Zeera is in my heart, as it is in theirs. I will remind them of this, and persuade them to use the power of Atualon to help the people."

"The last time you dragged me to Atualon, we were turned

281

away. How do you think now to whisper into the ear of the Dragon Queen, or her daughter?"

Ani smiled even as her eyes brimmed with unwelcome tears. "I will use my sharp wits and sweet tongue."

Askander faced her straight then and looked into her eyes, holding back nothing of his pain, his worry.

"And…?"

The words were slow and bitter. "If needs be, I will use bonesinger magic." She said it as if she had not begun to do so already. *So quickly I stray from the path of truth.*

"Such magic is unclean. Khutlani."

"It may be forbidden, but is not unclean. Magic is neither clean nor unclean—magic simply *is*. It is the users of magic who determine whether it is used for fair ends or fell." She smiled a little. "My mother was a bonesinger, and she was the kindest, most gentle lady you might hope to meet. When I was younger, I would vow to the stars every night that I would find her again some day."

Askander pressed his point. "If you do this, you will lose your place among the people. You will have to give up Talieso, you will have to give up teaching your youngsters. You will have to give up the love of a Ja'Sajani."

"If I must give up my people in order to save them, so be it. As for my horse…" Her hand stole up to stroke her stallion's neck. The big head swung toward her and Talieso nickered, hoping for a treat. "You do not have the authority to take him from me, Ja'Sajani. We are beyond the pridelands, and your sword stops at our borders."

"Our borders, but not yours," the warden corrected her. His voice was so low, so rough, it scraped her heart raw. "Not yours, pretty girl, not if you take this foolish path."

"I must," she told him. "You know that. My duty to the people does not end at the borders, and it does not end with their acceptance of me. *Ehuani*, my duty to the people is the only truth I have ever known." She grabbed mane and swung up into the saddle as easily as if she were, indeed, the girl who had hunted and caught the elusive Askander Ja'Sajani, long years ago.

"As you say." Askander bowed low in his saddle. "Safe roads, Dzirani."

"May the road be ever at your back, Ja'Sajani," she replied, "and may your enemies be worthy."

With those words, she turned and rode away from him.

Her tears dried quickly in the merciless heat.

That did not stop more from coming.

She rode north and east, allowing Talieso to choose the pace, dismounting now and again to walk beside him when he stumbled. The swelling and heat in his leg had gone down. There would be no permanent damage, or so she hoped. It would be better if she did not ride him at all, but the need was such that they both had to make sacrifices.

Well past midsun the stallion's pace quickened, his ears perked forward and he grunted in anticipation. They had reached a midsized oasis, a place they both knew well, where she and Askander had more than once…

No, she thought. *None of that.*

The moment their feet touched thin grass, Ani stripped off Talieso's tack and let him have his way. He took off like a colt, kicking and farting, and she laughed to see his dilemma. The old stallion wished to eat, he wished to drink, and he wished to roll in the soft sand, all at once.

Ani waded ankle-deep into the shallow water and filled her waterbags before taking a long drink. The water was more sour than she remembered, the grass brittle and dry.

Then again, she thought, *I am having a shit day. It is no wonder if I see the world through bitter eyes.*

All through the day a song had been building within her, growing and becoming until the air around her fairly shimmered with dark colors for which there were no names. Not in Zeeranim, anyway. *Khalzash*, she named them, *archat. Nach-aat, gharram, fakhash.* Fell colors born of a song with a foul purpose. Ani had

283

never attempted such magic. Until this day, she would have said that she would rather die than unleash such thing upon the world.

Everything has changed.

Everything is changing…

To the deep west, another voice joined the song. It was a low voice, low and unsavory, and it crackled with the heat of the wicked mountains whence it came.

Everything will change, it said mockingly.

Everything will end.

Ani knew the name of the demon to which this voice belonged. Such names had been taught to her at her mother's breast, before ever she learned to say "*imma*" or "*ah-ba*," before she knew that "Ani" meant her. Names, to those with the dark gift, were everything.

Khoroush-Il-mannech, she thought, and that morning's pemmican churned in her gut. The voice of Jehannim himself. She raised her eyes to the western horizon, and though she could not see the dark peaks that had birthed the demon, she knew he was there. Ani could feel him through the song, searching blindly for the one bold enough, foolish enough, to rouse him from the darkness to whence he had long been banished. She could feel him groping, seeking.

Ah, there *you are, little one.*

The words hit and Ani arched her back, ice and fire bursting in her skull like red and black flowers of pain. She fell to her knees, to her side, clenching her teeth so hard it seemed as if they would shatter. Bony fingers clawed at her essence, shredding her from within like so much dried meat.

Remember who you are, her mother's voice whispered, low and urgent. *If ever you meet a bonelord, he will try to steal your name. Remember who you are.*

"Ani," she growled, drawing her lips back as if she were vash'ai. "I am Ani, and you shall not have me." A third time. "I am *Ani*."

Ani. The pain receded, slowly, but the foul presence did not. Its laughter wound all through her song, wicked and dark and gorgeous. *Ani*, it crooned as she lay panting in the sand, bleeding from the mouth where she had bitten her tongue. *Last daughter of the lost tribes. I so look forward to meeting you.*

She pushed herself upright, refusing to weep at this. Ani had endured pain before, and heartbreak, and despair. Those had not killed her then, and they would not kill her now.

"Show me *yours*, demon," she said aloud, spitting blood upon the sand. "I am Ani of the Zeera, youthmistress of the Shahaydrim. Second Mother to Sulema Firehair, daughter of the Dragon King. I am Ani Dzirana, last of the bonesingers.

"And I am ready for you."

THIRTY-FIVE

Akari cast his baleful eye upon the happenings at the Madraj. Torches had been lit about the perimeter of the arena, red fire reaching up to a darkening sky. Even Akari Sun Dragon was abandoning his people to the tender mercies of Ishtaset.

She and her Mah'zula prowled among the grunting, sweating, crying Ja'Akari, striking hard with hand or foot if any dared falter or fail. Had Ismai thought the warriors had trained before? Had he thought they had fought, before? That had been as nothing. Compared to the Mah'zula, the Ja'Akari seemed soft and untrained as toddlers. Beneath the iron palm of Ishtaset, however, they began to transform into something harsher, harder.

It seemed to Ismai that the friends and playmates of his youth were slowly being replaced as their hearts and minds were turned away from the people with whom they had laughed and loved, and toward their enchanting new leader.

Ishtaset was their leader now, in truth if not in name. Even as Ismai watched, veiled in shadow and the invisibility of his own unimportance, she walked loose-limbed and arrogant as a vash'ai across the arena and ascended the steps to the high dais. Every girl and woman of the Ja'Akari gave way before her, eyes cast down or to the side. None dared challenge her—indeed, they seemed to yearn after her like cubs after the pride queen, doubling and tripling their efforts as she passed.

He shook his head. *I am glad, now*, he thought, *that the First Warrior ignored my request to become Ja'Akari.*

It was a silly request, anyway, Ruh'ayya chided. She sneezed, a cat's laugh. *Might as well wish to become an eagle, or a fish.*

It would be nice to fly, he thought wistfully.

A wise vash'ai once observed that no human is ever content in its own skin.

Who said that?

I did, she answered. *I am wise beyond my years.*

Ismai sneezed, then grinned as she swatted him with her tail. His grin faded, though, as First Warrior Sareta entered the Madraj and strode purposefully toward Ishtaset.

Trouble, he thought, stepping deeper into the shadow. *It is a good time to be invisible.*

Trouble, Ruh'ayya agreed. She did not move from her patch of sunlight. The vash'ai was only invisible when she intended to kill something.

Sareta attempted to mount the steps behind Ishtaset, but was blocked by one of the Mah'zula, an older woman so heavily mottled and painted that she looked more feline than some of the vash'ai. Ismai could all but smell the hot iron fury of the First Warrior as she stood at the foot of the dais.

Ishtaset took to the middle of the stage, and held up both hands, and silence fell upon the Madraj even as the last golden scales of Akari Sun Dragon slid below the horizon.

"My people," she said. Though she did not shout, her voice carried to the edges of the arena as if the wind itself strove to please her. "People of Akari. People of the Zeera. People of Zula Din… *my people*." The warriors froze mid-strike, wardens froze mid-move in their games of Stones and Bones, babies froze mid-wail as all strained to hear what the golden warrior had to say.

"This cannot be good," a voice hissed in Ismai's ear. Ismai leapt half out of his skin, clapping a hand over his own mouth to stifle his own un-wardenlike squeak. Heart still trying to gallop free, he spun to face his assailant.

"Jasin!" he hissed. "You limp *gewad*! I might have killed you!"

"With a half-eaten fish?" Jasin whispered, chuckling, and pointed with his chin at the remains of Ismai's stolen meal. "Not much has changed, I see—still stealing food from the kitchens."

"Luck favors the prepared," Ismai replied, just as quietly. "I figured I should eat before the Mah'zula forbid that, too."

Ruh'ayya licked her chops. She had prepared herself by eating a small pig.

"We knew you would be here," a third voice whispered, and the tall, blue-clad figure of Amil stepped clear of the shadows. Amil, Daoud, Jasin, Ghabril, all had taken the blue at once, though none had been bonded by the vash'ai. Now here they were, looking at Ismai with eyes wide as boys, as if they expected him to do something about this mess.

"Fish?" he offered, handing the clay platter to Daoud. Each young warden took a share of the flesh, and ate in solemn silence.

So, I am not the only one who senses that things are... not right. Chillflesh ran down Ismai's spine, and raised the hair on both his arms. It was not a comforting thought.

Even a human can see the truth in front of his face once in a while, Ruh'ayya agreed. *Sometimes before it bites him.*

Sometimes, Ismai acknowledged as he turned back toward Ishtaset. *Only sometimes.*

"...have strayed so far from the paths of your ancestors, *our* ancestors, that I am not sure they would recognize you as people at all," Ishtaset continued. She shook her head, eyes downcast and heavy with sorrow. "So far from the tenets of the Muammin, laid out by the First Women in the long ago. *Mua'immaish...* protection of our lands. *Mua'immjal...* protection of our men, the breath and future of the Zeeranim. *Mua'immasil...* protection of our herds from outlanders. *Mua'immalad...* protection of our precious children."

"We protect our children!" a man's voice protested.

"Do you?" Ishtaset shook her head again, slowly. "How many of your children have been stolen by slavers, this past year alone? How many lost to the river, to predators? How many have not been conceived at all, because you allow your men to wander heedlessly into foreign territories, spreading their seed outland instead of remaining home with the mothers and children, where they are most needed?"

Ismai's chest tightened. *Something is not right*, he repeated to Ruh'ayya.

It smells like a trap, she agreed. *'Ware, Kithren.*

"Ismai, look," Jasin whispered. "The Mah'zula. What are they doing?"

Mah'zula warriors poured into the Madraj like mead poured from a pitcher of gold, honey-sweet and dangerous. They filled the outer rows of stone seats, the stairs, and walked across the arena to stand beside their leader, stiff-maned and arrogant, dressed and armed as if for war. More than half of them were flanked by vash'ai, their tusks free of golden cuffs as if they were wild, and half again as big as the cats Ismai was used to seeing.

"They are magnificent," Daoud murmured.

"So many of them," Jasin replied, voice low and tense. "Where did they all come from? There were not so many with Ishtaset. Not nearly so many."

That is a very good question, Ismai thought. "I do not like this," he said aloud. "Ishtaset talks as if she would—"

"Sssssst!" Ghabril hissed. His eyes were round and white in the near dark. "Did you hear that? Ja'Shamsin! She has declared Ja'Shamsin!"

Under the sword. Ismai's very blood ran cold as the river. *So it begins.*

"Can she even do that?" Jasin asked, too loud to Ismai's ears. Before he could answer, their attention was drawn to a commotion at the foot of the high dais. The First Warrior Sareta and a short fist of Ja'Akari were shouting and trying to fight their way up the stairs. It was a brief struggle. Sareta and her warriors were forcibly disarmed, stripped of their warriors' vests, and escorted out of the Madraj. Among the hundreds of warriors in the arena—any of whom would have placed their lives before Sareta's, just a short moon ago—most refused to meet her eyes as she was marched past. Of those who did, a handful nodded in satisfaction before turning their faces back to Ishtaset.

"Ja'Shamsin! Would you hold a sword to our throats, then?"

a woman shouted, and a ripple of nervous agreement washed through the crowd.

"You mistake me," Ishtaset replied. "A warrior under Ja'Shamsin does not hold a blade to the throat of her brother." In a single smooth motion, Ishtaset drew her shamsi and brought the golden blade up and across her own throat. Blood welled from the shallow cut and ran down her dark skin. "A warrior under Ja'Shamsin has pledged to pour every drop of her blood upon the sands before allowing one drop of her brother's to be spilled."

"Ja'Shamsin." The woman whispered, and her voice was picked up by the people. It rolled through the empty eyes of the Madraj and carried across the Zeera, birthing a sharp new wind. "Ja'Shamsin!"

Ishtaset kissed her bloody shamsi and held it aloft. As one, the Mah'zula drew their blades, as well, drawing the sharp steel across their throats and stabbing the bloodied blades upward into the night's soft underbelly.

"Ja'Shamsin!" one of the Ja'Akari cried, teeth flashing in the torchlight as her face was split by a grin. She drew her own sword and repeated the gesture. Her blood splattered upon the arena floor.

"Ja'Shamsin!"

"Ja'Shamsin!"

A gentle red rain began to fall in the Zeera as, one by one, the Ja'Akari pledged themselves to the law of the sword. Their faces danced in and out of the torchlight, feral and beautiful and terrifying.

"They are magnificent," Daoud breathed.

"I do not know whether to throw myself at their feet or run away," Ghabril confessed. "Maybe both."

"I do not think this is a good thing," Jasin said. His forehead creased as he looked to Ismai. "Your mother was Umm Akibra. What do you know of the laws of Ja'Shamsin?" There was an uncomfortable silence at that. Umm Nurati had been dead for less than a year. To speak of her this soon was *khutlani*.

"Not much," Ismai admitted at last. He had never been a scholar. "Nothing good. Mostly I remember that there are rules for how men dress, who they can talk to, where they can go, that sort of thing, and that they are supposed to obey the Ja'Akari." He wished that Daru had not gone to Atualon. That boy had read every book in the Zeera, it seemed, and remembered them all.

"Obey the Ja'Akari?" Ghabril snorted. "I wish them luck with that."

"They might not need luck," Jasin pointed out. The crease in his forehead deepened. "They have swords, and vash'ai."

"We have swords, too."

"Would you raise yours against your sisters?" Jasin shook his head.

Ismai stroked the hilt of his sunblade, gifted to him by his mother. Surely she had not meant it to spill Zeerani blood.

"My… mother used to say that the Zeeranim are like reeds. One reed may be broken, or two, or three, but if you gather us all together, we are unbreakable. I do not think she would have wanted to see brother fighting sister. Or sister fighting sister. I think… she would have wanted us to work with the Mah'zula." It almost sounded like a question.

"I am not so sure." Jasin frowned as he looked out at the cheering Ja'Akari. "Did you hear what Ishtaset said about our people living in stone cities like outlanders? I do not think those two would have gotten along very well. I think that… Umm Nurati…" He coughed uncomfortably. "I think she would have sent the Mah'zula on their way, if she could."

It is interesting to note, Ruh'ayya said gently, *that your Queen Mother was killed before this strange pride invaded her territory. Do you suppose they have a dream eater among them?*

Ismai's head snapped back as if he had been slapped.

"Ismai?" Jasin touched his shoulder.

"Ruh'ayya says… she says… that my mother was killed by a dream eater. Are there any dreamshifters among these Mah'zula?"

"Only warriors, as far as I know. Besides, the only dreamshifter I have ever heard of who might be that powerful would be—"

"Hafsa Azeina." Ghabril shuddered. "That woman scares my balls right up my arse."

Hafsa Azeina. Ismai reeled at the thought. Sulema's mother.

"Hafsa Azeina was gone long before my mother…" He shook his head, unable to finish the thought.

"A dream eater can kill anyone, anywhere," Daoud said. "There is no distance in the Dreaming Lands… so I have heard."

Ismai gripped the pommel of his shamsi so hard his hand hurt. "It cannot—"

"Ah, there you are, young Ismai!"

The young wardens jumped like boys caught stealing honeycakes, and turned toward the voice. One of the Mah'zula, an older woman with a grandmother's round cheeks, rocked back on her heels and regarded them. She was flanked by two younger Mah'zula and, Ismai saw, two Ja'Akari, as well. Blood still seeped from wounds at all their throats, shining a warning in the dim torchlight.

Ruh'ayya growled low in her throat.

"Come," she said in a tone that brooked no argument. "Ishtaset has had us looking for you all evening."

"What?" A tremor ran down Ismai's spine. "Why? What would she want with me?"

The Mah'zula stepped closer, and Ismai felt the heat of his companions as they pressed close. *Like sheep*, he thought.

"To protect you, of course." The woman smiled at them, a grandmother's smile, but it did not reach her eyes. Blood welled from the cut at her throat as she talked. It ran down her skin and disappeared beneath the wyvern-scale breastplate. "You are last of the line of Zula Din, and precious to us."

Three more women joined them, two Mah'zula and a Ja'Akari Ismai knew only by sight. That one had unbraided her hair and chopped it short, so that it bristled like the manes of the Mah'zula.

"Come," the grandmother-warrior urged, smile deepening even as her hand tightened on her shamsi. "Ishtaset is waiting."

"Would you raise your hand against your sisters?" The words hung in the tunnels like cobwebs, like shadows.

I am with you, Kithren. Ruh'ayya pressed close. *If we die, we die.*

Ismai forced his hand away from his sword, and heard his companions' sighs of relief.

Not tonight, he told her.

The Mah'zula nodded in satisfaction and turned, confident that Ismai would follow. He stared hard at the women's backs as they led him from the tunnels. Fear, resentment, and anger simmered in his blood with every step, but he could not, *would* not raise a hand against his sisters.

Not yet, anyway.

THIRTY-SIX

"Again." Hannei picked herself up and shook like a wet vash'ai, sending a rain of blood and sweat and sand in all directions.

Sand always seems so soft, she thought ruefully, *until you land on it head-first.* She turned to face the *Rehaza*, who stood in the center of the training arena, arms folded across her chest and smiling.

Of all the instructors at the fight school, Rehaza Entanye was Hannei's absolute least favorite. On a good day, she reminded Hannei of Istaza Ani, if Ani's heart had been torn out and replaced with a lump of bloody coal. On a bad day, she made Hafsa Azeina seem like a woman you might curl up next to for comfort.

Well, she admitted to herself, *not the dreamshifter. Maybe a lionsnake.* Even a kick to the head did not make Hafsa Azeina seem cuddly.

"I thought you were a great warrior, Dungball." Rehaza Entanye shook her head. Her bare torso was as dry and dusty as her tone. Not so much as a trickle of sweat indicated that she had been kicking Hannei's arse about the arena all morning. "Dungball, over there"—she pointed with her chin, indicating the other Zeerani girl, a Nisfi who had been stolen by slavers—"says you are some kind of champion. Your mistress thinks highly enough of you that she is paying good salt for your schooling.

"Personally, I think you would be more useful as serpent bait, but hey, if they want to pay me to beat your ass dawn to dusk, that is no water from my skin." Even as she said the words, Rehaza Entanye raised a waterskin to her mouth and took a long swig, allowing some of it to spill down her front, wetting the red dust so that it looked like blood.

Hannei swallowed, and her stump of a tongue twitched

reflexively as if to lick her dry lips. *One swallow*, she wished. *Just one*. But the dungballs—so their instructors named them all—were allowed to drink only when they had won a fight against an instructor. So far three girls had collapsed of thirst and been dragged from the arena in as many days. Only one of them had been returned to the barracks.

Rehaza Entanye smiled slowly at Hannei over the lip of the waterskin, held it out at arm's length, and dropped it in the dirt at her feet. Hannei could not take her eyes from the skin. She imagined she could hear the water sloshing around inside.

"Tell you what, Dungball," the drill instructor said in a bored voice, even as she unfastened the dagger at her belt and let it drop beside the waterskin. "If you can get past me and take the water, it is yours."

Unable to spit properly, Hannei hissed blood from between her teeth, lowered her head, and charged.

"Not bad, for a first lesson."

Hannei groaned and rolled over, groaning again as the movement sent splinters of white-hot pain pretty much everywhere. Strong hands helped her sit upright, and held her there as a waterskin was pressed to her mouth.

She drank greedily, for once not caring that much of the water dribbled and drooled from her mouth. She shuddered in relief as her body soaked up the water fast as dry linen, and rubbed both hands across her face, wiping away enough of the crusted dirt and blood that she could open her eyes a crack.

Both moons rose full and sassy, painting the empty arena with a silvery light.

"*Nnngah*," she growled.

"Nnngah," the stranger's voice answered. "Does that mean 'Shit, it is late?' Or 'Fuck, that hurts?' Or do you simply mean 'I would give much at this moment for a bowl of spiders' eggs washed down with usca'?"

Hannei shrugged and nodded. *All of those and more, she thought.*

"Well, I have neither spiders' eggs nor usca, but I saved you half a loaf and some dried fish, and a full skin of water." The girl from Nisfi pressed these into Hannei's hands, as she helped her to her feet. "It is finally paying off, all those years learning to sneak food from the kitchen-mothers. The hospitality of these outlanders leaves much to be desired."

Hannei clutched the food and drink to her breast, wealth unlike she had known for a two-moon, averting her eyes from the other girl. She did not remember this warrior, but a warrior she was, obviously, with her braids and scars, whole and unruined.

"Eat," the warrior urged her, "and do not be ashamed. I have watched you before. Did these... *khafik*... cut you?"

Hannei shook her head, and the Nisfi hissed air between her teeth.

"The *people* did this to you?"

Hannei nodded.

"In Nisfi, we only cut the tongue when a warrior has spoken a lie. Did you lie? Are you Kha'Akari?" Dark eyes bored into her own, demanding truth.

Hannei squeezed her eyes shut. The face of Sareta swam before her, smiling as she opened her mouth to condemn Hannei to a life of exile, a life worse than death. She shook her head so hard her neck cracked.

I did not lie, she thought, burning to scream the words. *Under Akari, I did not.*

"I believe you." A mouth pressed against her forehead, gentle as a Mother's, and tears unbidden prickled behind Hannei's eyelids. She opened her eyes, blinked the tears away, and met the warrior's gaze.

"We must stick together, you and I," the other girl continued. "Sword sisters in a strange land. I am Noura—though you know me by another name, eh, *Dungball*?" She ruffled Hannei's hair, which had grown to a finger's length of curls and tended to mat.

Hannei grunted around a mouthful of bread.

"You are Hannei. I know who you are, I was there when they

made you champion. That was some fight." The warrior smiled. "These outlanders think they can fight, but they are dirty, *ehuani*. We fight with the heart of Akari, the light of truth in a dark land. We will show them the way. You will be my sword, and I your shield, and we will fight our way free."

Hannei chewed a mouthful of salted fish, given to her by her new sword sister. It tasted true, and clean, as nothing had since the night Tammas died, and she washed it down with sweet water.

It was good.

Akari Sun Dragon had just leaned in to kiss the sky, making it blush, when Rehaza Entanye came for her.

Hannei—*Kishah*, she reminded herself, *I am Kishah*—was not asleep. She sat, as she often did, perched in the low stone window with one leg dangling free, staring out over Min Yaarif and the jagged peaks of the Jehannim, without seeing much of either. She was tired, she was so tired, but sleep was shadows and silence and stolen blankets. To sleep was to dream of Tammas, and Hannei rejected it utterly.

As the pitmistress crossed the room, the keys at her waist rattled and sang, and the breath of more than one fighter hitched, stilled, quieted as women and girls woke only to feign sleep. Hannei ignored them all. Entanye would come for her, or she would not. She would drag her off for training, or for a beating, or to throw her to the serpents whose voices rose in homage to the blushing sky. In the end, it made no difference.

The pitmistress stopped, stooped, and unlocked the heavy chain that kept Hannei from leaping to her death. "Come," she said in a low voice, then turned and left without waiting to see whether Hannei might follow. She shrugged and padded after the pitmistress, obedient as a good horse.

When all roads lead to death, one might as well step quickly.

She followed the pitmistress down stairs, stairs, and more stairs, across the trampled flat where the pit slaves would sit in neat rows to eat the morning meal, past the squat dark building where the pitmistresses and masters slept, and at last to one of the training arenas. Hannei stopped so quickly she almost tripped over her own feet. In the very middle of the arena, someone had drawn a perfect hoti in red chalk.

Entanye paid her no mind. She strode to the chalk circle, shedding knives and choke-wires and a myriad of other hidden weapons as she went, as if leaving a trail for Hannei to follow. She gave a slight bow to the warriors who had gone before, as was proper, before stepping over the edge and to the very center of the hoti. There, she turned and waited for Hannei, with all the impassive patience of the rising dawn.

Hannei stood in the dirt with her mouth hanging open. *What?* she wanted to ask. *What?* Entanye was not Ja'Akari—she had not the look of the Zeera about her, at all, and even if she had been a bought child, the sides of her scalp would have long since been shaven and oiled.

The pitmistress laughed to see her expression. "You do not need a tongue to speak, do you, Dungball? You are hardly the first warrior to enjoy my company in lovely Min Yaarif." The pitmistress spread her arms wide and grinned. "I have learned much from your people. Come now, this time *you* can be *my* teacher. Test me and see how much I have yet to learn, Rehaza Dungball." Then she turned her back to Hannei, crossed her arms over her chest, and whistled a tuneless little song, as if the challenge of a fighting circle was no more than a child's prank.

Hannei found herself moving, anger growing in her breast with every step. How dare this… *outsider* pretend to the hoti? How dare she touch what was not hers to take? The ring was ancient, it was sacred and true. The sacred fight did not belong here in this stinking pit, *ehuani*. She stalked past the detritus of abandoned weapons to stand just outside of the circle. She drew a deep breath, stooped to erase a hand's-width of chalk. Then she stepped into the circle and stamped her foot three times.

"*Heh heh heh,*" she demanded, for once not trying to mask the hideous sounds that came from her mouth. Anyone—even an outsider—who stepped into the hoti became a warrior, and no warrior could refuse a challenge.

Hannei breathed deep, ignoring the stink and noise of the waking city. She might be a ruined and wretched shadow of the warrior she was meant to be, but the wind that ruffled her hair was the same as it had always been, and the sun still poured down like warm mead, and the heart that beat in her chest was still the heart of a warrior, try as her enemies had to silence it.

I am not beaten yet, she thought for the first time. *Not dead yet. I am a warrior, still. I am Ja'Akari, under the…*

Entanye whirled, driving her hand as a wedge toward Hannei's throat quick as a serpent's strike. Hawk Takes Mouse. Hannei countered with Snake in the Rocks, coiling back, so that Entanye dropped her weight down and kicked up…

Again and again the two women met, exchanged flurries of blows, parted, and met again, inevitable and true as the ebb and flow of sand. Blue Goat Charges. For an outsider, Entanye was good—very good.

Hannei was better.

Moment by moment more blows connected than were deflected, leaving a cut here, a welt there. Hannei tasted blood, but so did her opponent. Step-by-step and Hannei forced the pitmistress back toward the edge of the hoti. At last, she landed a kick that sent the pitmistress down to one knee, fingers touching the red chalk.

She had won.

Akari Sun Dragon glowed with hot pride as Hannei Ja'Akari strode to her opponent, hand outstretched to help her up—

Rehaza Entanye lunged up, teeth bared in a feral grin. One arm snaked about Hannei's throat. The other held a knife, and its blade sang a shallow cut across Hannei's throat.

"You lose, Dungball," the pitmistress hissed in her hear. "You are *dead*."

And she threw Hannei to the ground.

299

The worst thing about not having a tongue, Hannei reflected, was not the pain, or the humiliation, or even the inability to speak. The worst part was not being able to spit properly, when she was so often forced to eat dirt. As it was, she sprayed sand and blood as well as she could, then took the pitmistress's proffered hand and allowed herself to be hauled to her feet.

"You fought well," the pitmistress said. "Well, and honorably. Do you know why you lost this fight?"

I did not lose, Hannei thought. She shrugged, wiping blood from her mouth with the back of her hand. Blood trickled down her chest from the shallow cut across her throat. *I fought with honor.*

"You *lost*," Entanye emphasized, "because you fought with honor. Oh, I know the words you live by. You are not the first Ja'Akari to fall into my hands. 'A warrior who fights with honor may die, but she will never lose' or some such shit. Are these the words they fed you from the time you cut your first teeth? Oh, close your mouth, you look like an idiot."

Hannei closed her gaping mouth.

"You have been fed lies, sweetened with honey to make them taste like truth," Entanye went on. "To live is to win. To die is to lose. That is all—do you understand me? That is all."

No. No. Hannei shook her head and took a step back.

"Yes," the pitmistress insisted, "yes. Who fed you these lies? Your sword sisters? Your First Warrior? And where are they, Dungball? Who sold you into slavery? Who turned their backs and walked away when the slavemaster hauled you up onto the stage? *That* for their precious truth." She spat. "Your whole world has been a lie, little one, but I will not lie to you now.

"Fighting with honor, as a Ja'Akari does, will not work down here in the pit," Entanye continued. "If you are going to win, you have to give up 'fighting under the sun and with honor' and all that shit. The pit is not pretty, the pit is not fair, the pit does not care if you are so fucking honorable that the Sun Dragon himself shines out of your ass. The pit is bloody, and shitty, and gorgeous. The pit is guts in the sand and a knife in the back. The pit is *life*."

She held out her hand, smeared with Hannei's own blood. "You have been taught ehuani," she said, "you have been taught that the only beauty lies in truth, but that was a lie, every word of it. Let me teach you a new way, the true way. Let me teach you *khaani*, and you may just survive this shit-pit."

Khaani. Beauty in treachery.

Hannei took the hand of Rehaza Entanye, though she felt as if she might throw up. Akari Sun Dragon beat down upon her head.

But he is beating down on everyone else's head just the same, she realized. *Swordman, sorcerer, lover, liar, he shines down upon us all, and he sees nothing. Akari Sun Dragon does not care whether I live or die, whether I am honorable or dishonorable.*

Akari Sun Dragon did not care about her murdered lover, her shattered dreams, her broken heart. She met the pitmistress eye-to-eye, and clasped her forearm.

"Do we have an accord, Dungball?" Rehaza Entanye smiled, beautiful and treacherous as the rising sun. "Will you fight for me?"

Hannei nodded…

…and nothing happened. Akari Sun Dragon flew on, Sajani Earth Dragon slept on, and Tammas Ja'Sajani was still as dead as her warrior's heart.

THIRTY-SEVEN

The door to his cell banged open and Leviathus flinched from the window, where he had been watching a spider build her web.

The woman who held the keys stared at him with wide eyes, and stepped back when he turned, as if he might carry a plague. More alarming yet was the sight of the warden, a small fellow who rather reminded Leviathus of Master Bernardus, wringing his hands and sweating through his yellow caftan. He was accompanied by a pair of guards.

"Bind his hands," the warden instructed his mistress of keys. Then he turned to Leviathus. "You are to come with me. Make no move unless I tell you. Say nothing unless you are spoken to, or I will have you gagged."

Leviathus might have protested, but the little man was so nervous that his guards were getting twitchy, and he did not want to die before his spidery friend had finished her web. So he held his wrists together in front of him and tried to look as nonthreatening as he could, though his heart pounded and his hands shook a little.

They are not going to kill me, he reminded himself with some force. *I am much more valuable as a hostage to my father's good will than I would be as a head on a spike.* His recent experiences among the Mah'zula, however—and the Kha'Akari before them— had sapped his confidence, and the thought lacked conviction.

Hemmed in by the guards, he followed the warden down a long hallway. His prisoner's sandals scuffed against the uneven stone floor, and the rough linen shift they had given him to wear scarcely covered his manly bits. He eyed the guards' studded kilts with envy.

"See sommat you want?" one of them sneered.

"Your uniform, if you do not mind," he replied affably. "Between this shift, and the wind that always blows down this hallway, I am concerned that one of you might mistake my loinsnake for a lionsnake and try to chop its head off."

Both guards laughed uproariously, and the mistress of keys burst into a fit of giggles so hard she choked, but the warden turned on them with a ferocity that belied his size.

"If you wish to keep your jobs," he hissed at the guards, then at their prisoner, "and if *you* wish to keep your damned head, for Snafu's sake shut the fuck up. I will not have you offending my guest. Do you understand?"

"Sir!" the guards said as one. Their faces went soldier-stone, eyes straight ahead. The mistress of keys fell behind as they again started down the hallway at a brisk pace, now and again making a strangled noise as mirth and panic fought for supremacy.

"Where there is life," Ani had said to him, more than once, *"there is hope. Where there is hope, there is room for foolishness."* Leviathus had, once again, shown himself to be a fool. Perhaps some day that would serve him well. On this day, he decided to keep his mouth shut, and live.

There was a room at the end of the hallway. Leviathus had spent a bit of time in it when Ishtaset had brought him there. It was a small room, square and with a low ceiling, without ornamentation or windows. There was but one entrance or exit, a heavy wooden door bound in black iron, with pegs that could be set into the stone. The table and chairs were as solidly built as the door. It was a secure place meant for negotiating the price and return of hostages. The warden led Leviathus into this room, the mistress of keys locked that door behind him, and he could not help but feel like a bull taken to slaughter.

Though the walls were crowded with sconces, on this day the candles at the far end had been snuffed out, leaving everything there in deep twilight. In the heart of this shadow a figure stood and waited for them, a man unlike any Leviathus had seen in all his long travels.

Had he been standing, the top of his wide conical hat might have brushed the ceiling. As it was, his bulk dominated the space entirely. He wore loose trousers tucked into tall wyvern-hide boots of a blue so deep that it almost appeared to be black, a flowing linen shirt, and layers of veil beneath that hat which concealed all but a pair of wide bright eyes, slitted like half-moons.

Aside from his sheer size, the man's most remarkable feature was his short cape. Woven of linen as white as sand beaches, it was embroidered all over in geometric shapes featuring beasts and monsters in black and yellow and red. Their eyes had been fashioned of abalone shell beads and glittered in the thin light. Leviathus was reminded of nothing so much as Hafsa Azeina's tent, and shivered beneath those fell stares.

There were two guards to either side of the giant, lesser men dressed in a similar if lesser fashion. All four held hooked spears. Though menace rolled from them like a heavy fog, it was nearly an afterthought in the presence of their master.

The woman took a seat at the table. The warden bowed low, and he swallowed three times before he was able to squeak out a greeting.

"Mahmouta," he managed at last, "Ransom House is honored by your presence."

"Indeed." The giant did not stir, did not so much as blink. It was a woman's voice, low and rough but quite beautiful. Leviathus would have stared, but one of his guards hissed a command, grabbed the back of his neck, and threw him down onto his knees on the rough stone floor.

"There is no need for that," the enormous woman chided. "I will not thank you to damage my goods before I have had a chance to inspect them. Rise, son of Wyvernus, and let me look at you."

Leviathus had been born and raised in Atukos, the heart of power. He needed no urging to stand before this woman, or to bow as he might to any foreign queen. The winds of power had shifted, so that in this place, at this time, they would blow in whichever direction this woman bade them.

"An honor," he said at last, "though I regret to admit I do not know your full name."

Laughter bubbled from the shadows. "Oh, but you shall know me hereafter," she told him. She inclined her head toward the warden, and a hundred tiny bells along the brim of her hat laughed a merry tune. "Now that I have seen the little dragon prince, I am most certain," she declared, "I must have him."

"Mahmouta…" The warden coughed.

One of her guards leaned forward, frowning, and tapped the butt of his spear on the floor. "You will address my mistress as 'your Audacity.'"

"Your Audacity," the warden continued, "I, ah, I cannot, that is… I am forbidden by my agreement with the Mah'zula from, ah, ransoming the prince to any but the Dragon King. My sincerest and most abject apologies. If it were anyone else…" Leviathus could smell the man's fear sweat. *I should be afraid, too*, he thought. As it was, he could hardly refrain from laughing out loud. *I must be the greatest fool this world has ever known.*

"Your agreement with the Mah'zula." The great woman frowned, and the chair upon which she was seated groaned a protest as she leaned back. "What about your agreement with me, eh, Jainan? Your *many* agreements with me? You would abandon our long— acquaintance—in order to do business with pretenders who cling to the past?"

"'What is past is gone. Do not be with it,'" one of her guards quoted.

"Badi?" Leviathus could not help but ask.

"Shaumi el Sha'eir." The guard winked. "Earlier work."

The big woman glared at them both. "If you two are finished debating poetry? Yes? Warden Jainan, let me introduce to you my twentieth husband, Husni el Bulbul of the golden voice. Fancies himself a bard." Behind her veils, Mahmouta's eyes all but disappeared as she smiled. "We all have our weaknesses. Even I."

The warden bowed. "A thousand congratulations, Your Audacity. I wish you much prosperity in your union."

Mahmouta shook her head, and the tiny bells sang again.

"Nineteen husbands are for prosperity, everyone knows this. The twentieth is for pleasure." All four of her guards laughed at this, none harder than Husni. "Come to think of it, Jainan, I did not see you among the guests at our little party? It was not very... friendly... of you to decline our invitation."

The warden swallowed. "A thousand apologies. I was..." swallowed again.

Mahmouta held up a gloved hand. "Ah-ah, let there be no lies between us, old friend. I do not need your apologies any more than I need your congratulations, truly. What I need from you is this." She indicated Leviathus, "Nothing more, nothing less. Consider it a belated wedding gift, if you will. Adnan? Rahi? If you would, please show our host what it is we offer in return for the little prince."

The guards to Mahmouta's left bent to lift a wooden chest the size of a small child. This they set upon the table with a solid thump and a grunt of effort. The guard closest to Mahmouta unlatched the lid and opened it with a flourish.

"One thousand tablets of white salt," Mahmouta purred. "One thousand of rose. One thousand tablets of red salt. A ransom fit for a king, never mind a king's son."

Leviathus heard a low hiss as the warden sucked air through his teeth. The box was filled with salt tablets—red, rose, and white—enough to make a man wealthy for life.

Certainly enough to buy a man's life.

For the first time, he felt a pang of real fear. What man would be strong enough to withstand such temptation? Not this man, apparently. The warden took a small step toward the large fortune, sealing all their fates.

"What will I tell the Mah'zula?" he asked, but he was not listening for a reply. His head was already filled with the song of salt.

"Tell them that you thought I was an agent of Ka Atu—that is not a lie. Not a complete lie, at any rate. Tell them that you were tricked. Tell them that I made you an offer you could not refuse." All four guards went stone-faced and still, knuckles whitening as they gripped their spears. "That is not a lie, either. Or tell them nothing. With wealth such as this, you could start running today and keep running until you die of old age, happy and surrounded by your children and your children's children. I care not what you tell the Mah'zula. I care only what you tell Mahmouta." Those crescent eyes were hard as dragonglass as they stared at the warden. "Do we have an accord?"

The warden's voice was a thin whisper as he made one final, feeble, attempt at decency.

"What will become of the Atualonian prince?"

So hard, those eyes. So cold.

"I deal in exotic wares, Jainan. Perhaps I will sell him to the Sindanese emperor, for use in one of his comfort houses. Perhaps I will keep him for myself, or trade him to the shadowmancers for passage across the Seared Lands. Once the little prince is my property, he is my business—and you do not wish to pry into my business, do you?"

"No," Jainan whispered. "No, Your Audacity, I do not."

"You do not," Mahmouta affirmed. "Do we have an accord? Say it."

"We have an accord," the warden said. His voice broke a little on the last word, but he never took his eyes off the chest of salt tablets. Mahmouta clapped her gloved hands together in delight, and laughed.

"I love this city," she said. Her guards shared a grin.

Leviathus stared at the chest as they replaced its lid. *I would have hoped it might take a larger box*, he mused, *to hold the worth of my life.*

The sun felt good on his upturned face. Almost too good. Leviathus had been fed—a real meal, complete with good cheese and very good wine—allowed to bathe, and given new clothes. They were plain, such as a workman might wear—nondescript trousers and a tunic—but at least they covered his arse, and for that the king's son was so grateful he might have wept.

How low the mighty has fallen, he thought, but there was laughter in it for him, as well. Even clad in his soldier's kilt and the robes of the ne Atu, he had never been more than the king's surdus son, the deaf disappointment who could never sit on his father's throne.

What might become of him now? Most likely this woman, Mahmouta, would sell him back to his father for a nice profit. As for the life of a brothel slave, Leviathus had decided before the trunk of salt tablets had been carried away that he would not accept such a fate.

I will run first, he promised himself. *Or I will die first. I will not be touched like that again.* He bared his teeth at the thought of Mariza and her riders. *Never again.* So lost was he in thoughts, and in the memory of Mariza's death, that he ran into one of his guards.

They had stopped, and he had not. Just as well they had stopped, too. The group had come to the docks at the river's edge, and had he kept walking, Leviathus would have received an unpleasant dunking at best, or have been eaten by a river serpent.

A gull cried out, mocking him.

"We are here, little prince," the man said. "Welcome home." *His name is Husni*, Leviathus remembered. *He is the twentieth husband of the woman who bought me, and he knows poetry.* It had never occurred to him that a man who loved poetry might be a wicked person.

That disappointing thought was interrupted by the sight and sound of a young boy, scarcely older than Hafsa Azeina's apprentice, hurtling through the dockside crowd toward their group.

"Mammana!" he bellowed in a voice that would make a blue ram proud. "Mammana! You did it! You got him!" He all but flew into the laughing embrace of Mahmouta.

"Of course I did, little man." The giant of a woman squeezed until Leviathus thought the lad would break in half. "Do you doubt your mammana? Do you *dare*?"

"Never." The boy grinned.

A crowd formed around their little group, men and women dressed in the same loose clothing and short capes as his captors.

Most were armed with hooked spears like those the guards carried. Some were veiled, many were not. Those who were not sported an astonishing number of facial tattoos and piercings, and a few of them rivaled Mahmouta for size.

"We did it, we did it!" The boy squirmed from his mother's embrace and ran to Leviathus, shouting. "You are free!"

Wait, he thought. *What?*

I am… free. The words made no sense, not when strung together into a sentence and strung across the context of his life. *I am free?*

Quick as thought, the boy whipped out a small knife such as all small boys carry. With a skinny brown hand he grabbed one of Leviathus's forearms, and with the other he cut the ropes that bound Leviathus's wrists.

"What…?" Leviathus gaped in open astonishment at his freed hands, then at the giggling boy.

The crowd burst into laughter.

"Do you not remember my son?" Mahmouta stood behind the lad, and placed her enormous hands on his skinny little shoulders. "Do you not remember saving him from the Mah'zula? And now he has saved you. A life for a life."

"A life for a life," Husni echoed, hands held out before him like the pans of a merchant's scale. "Balance."

"Balance," the boy agreed, staring up into his face. "Do you not remember me? You saved my life."

"I am sorry—" he began, but then it hit him. It had been a dark night, and he had had to pee. He had caught Hafsa Azeina's little apprentice in the act of freeing… "The slaver?"

"We are not slavers, we are merchants," the boy huffed, offended. "Sometimes we are pirates."

"Sometimes," Mahmouta agreed. "Only sometimes." She took one great stride forward, so that she stood so close Leviathus could see the veils sway as she talked. This close, the merriment in her eyes was more apparent—but so, he thought, was the danger.

A deadly woman, he thought.

"You released my son from slavery, and spared him a terrible fate," she said in a voice so low it tickled his bones. "I have done the same for you. We are square, Dragon Prince, you and I. Balanced."

"I am… most deeply grateful." Leviathus bowed low, and it took everything he had left to keep his voice steady. Every fiber of his being trembled in the wind like a ship's sails. "What now? Am I free to go, just like that?"

"If you wish," Mahmouta agreed. He thought there was some sympathy in her gaze. "Though nothing is as simple as that, as we both well know. I will carry you to Atualon, if you wish it." She turned and swept her arm toward the Dibris, and a great fleet of merchant's ships outfitted for travel and war. "In my little boats." The crowd erupted, once more, in laughter.

"Or I can offer you a different path, Son of the Dragon King."

Leviathus blinked. "Another path?"

"In Atualon, you are a great man. You dress in fine robes, you eat fine food and drink fine wine. You have guards. Your guards have guards. Most likely every woman in Atualon desires to take you as a husband."

"A first husband, even," one of the guards agreed. More laughter.

"Out here, you would be another grunt, another body on the boat. You would wear the plain clothes of a merchant's man, perhaps one day become a merchant yourself. Or a scholar. Or a poet."

"Or a twentieth husband, meant for pleasure!" Husni suggested.

"You would live your life as one drop of water in the river, one grain of sand in the desert, no more than one man among men—but you would live that life under the sun, far away from Atualon, from the shadow cast by your father. You would be free, if you so choose."

"Free," he echoed, and the crowd leaned in to hear the word. It tasted, to Leviathus, sweeter than the finest of wines. A vintage he had never thought to sample.

"What do you say, Leviathus ap Wyvernus ne Atu? Have you ever dreamed of being a pirate?" Mahmouta held out one enormous gloved hand. Leviathus grasped that hand and held it fast as a grin spread across his face.

"All my life," he said.

THIRTY-EIGHT

"Your estate is coming along quite nicely, Sen-Baradam."

Jian jumped half out of his skin and whirled around, heart pounding, hand on the hilt of his sword. Giella walked slowly up the stairs toward him, grinning.

She had very sharp teeth.

Jian grinned back, shaking his head. He liked this girl. Like his Tsali'gei, she had been born in the Twilight Lands and given over to the land of men in her sixteenth Nian-da, as the ancient law decreed. There was a wildness to these girls that spoke to his own, and gave him comfort. It was not a safe kind of comfort, like a small fire well contained by a stone hearth. Theirs was a dangerous comfort necessary for the soul's survival, like a wildfire on a cold night.

Or maybe, that part of him said, *I just like the company of pretty girls.*

"The main house should be done within the two-moon," he agreed. "Look here, see what the engineers have done." He lifted a foot from the top step, where he had been standing, and stepped onto the wide boards of the front porch. The wood sang under the slight weight, a soft chirruping noise like the voice of a cricket.

Or the song of a nightingale.

"It will warn of assassins," he told her, and he stepped again. *Squeak-squeak-squeak*. Giella's face lit with delight.

"Oooooh," she breathed, "let me try!" She ran the rest of the way up, beaming as she stepped onto the first board and it sang beneath her weight. "Ooooh," she said again, clapping her hands like a small girl at festival. She picked up the skirts of her robe and ran down the length of the porch—*chirrup-chirrup-squeak-squeak*—her red robes fluttering behind her like wings, and pivoted at the end with her arms held high above her like an oulo

311

dancer commanding her audience's attention. The red sleeves fell loosely and her skin glowed white like porcelain in the sunlight.

"But what if," she asked him, "the assassin can fly?" Still smiling like a naughty child, she danced her way back to him, golden slippers flashing from beneath the hems of her robe. Giella swayed with her hips, she wound her arms and wrists and hands this way and that, dancing to an ancient song that Jian could almost—*almost*—hear.

It was not until she reached him that Jian realized the boards beneath her feet had remained silent.

"Your face!" she exclaimed, doubling over with laughter. "Ah, brother, your face!" She straightened, giggling and dabbing tears from the corners of her eyes with her long red sleeves. "Not to worry, Jian Sen-Baradam. Very few assassins are as good as I."

"You are an assassin?" he asked. "I thought you were a—ah, that is..."

"You thought I was a whore." Her teeth were very sharp, indeed. "Ah, a comfort girl, yes."

"Oh, I offer men comfort, surely." She swayed closer, so much closer Jian could smell her spiced breath. Her lips were plump and red as ripe cherries, and he could not bring himself to look away. "Though perhaps not the comfort they are hoping for." She did that thing with her arm again, and Jian gasped to find two dagger-points pressed to his throat. "I offer the comfort of death."

He held very, very still. He *thought* she was joking, but his heart dropped down into his stomach just in case.

"Now I know where the term 'cold comfort' comes from," he told her. "How do you keep your blades so chill?"

Giella laughed again, and twirled, and the blades disappeared. "Twilight magic, of course. My mother gifted them to me, just as your father gifted your sword to you. Your blade is still sleeping, unblooded. My children..." There was a flash of blue steel, there and gone before Jian could blink. "...are very much alive."

Jian gripped the hilt of his sword and frowned. It seemed to him unlikely that his blade would remain unblooded much longer.

"As delighted as I am to see you, Sister," he allowed, "surely you have not come here to discuss buildings, or blades."

"No, I have not, but the words I have for you are for you only, and where there are songs, there are ears." Giella took a step toward Jian, and this time the boards wailed beneath her weight. "The sun is so hot, and my skin so delicate. I would bathe my feet in the sea. If you would be so kind…?"

"Delicate, yes, that is *exactly* the word I would use to describe you." He laughed and offered his arm, she laughed and took it, and together they walked down the step, continuing out and through the village, down the path to the wide, wide sea.

Jian stood with one foot in the sea, and one foot on land.

"You are like a poem contained in a single character of script," Giella said. "Very clever."

Jian nodded, pleased that she had seen and understood. He had felt thus since his return from the Twilight Lands, and indeed for most of his life. Half his soul was in the sea, and the other half had been dragged onto shore in some wicked net from which he could never escape. He said none of this, of course, knowing how much worse it must be for her, for Tsali'gei, for the other Daechen and Daezhu born and raised among the Dae, only to be abandoned to the world of men.

A mist rose from the bubbling little waves at their feet. Giella stretched her arms out to either side and tipped her head back, eyes closed, mouth parted in a small and ecstatic smile as the sea wove a safe space about her children. There were voices in the mist—silver as bells, golden as a ram's horn—and they were calling, calling, calling the children home. Jian shuddered as the mist closed over his head and he was seized with a sudden desire to charge into the water and swim for the Twilight Lands, to Yosh with the world of men and all its trouble.

"You cannot," Giella murmured, never opening her eyes. "We cannot. Our people gave us into this world for a reason, Jian Sen-

Baradam, and we may not stray from that path until we have wrought our doom upon the lands of men."

Jian dug his bare toes into the sand, grounding himself, and willed the urge to pass.

"What did you bring me here to discuss?" he asked. "Surely not the futility of our hearts' desires."

She tipped her head up and looked at him then. Her dark eyes were full of reproach.

"That was unkind."

"I am sorry." And he was.

"Now it is my turn to be cruel." She tugged at her short poof of white hair and gave an exasperated sigh. "I do not usually like people, so I am not sure how to tell you this without pain, so I will just—"

"Tsali'gei." Jian knew. He knew, and sudden dread sucked the air from his lungs in a sour whoosh. He grabbed Giella by the shoulders and almost shook her. "She is dead. She is dead. Tell me she is not dead." His voice broke into a roar. "Tell me!"

"I am trying to tell you," Giella snapped, wriggling free so that Jian was holding thin air and cold fog. "No, she is not dead, Jian. At least—"

"By the sea," Jian breathed, almost staggering as his knees went weak with relief. "By the sea, thank the dragon."

"At least not yet, Brother, but I have terrible news for you." This time, she grasped his arms, and her grip was surprisingly strong. "Your wife has been secluded within the innermost circles of the emperor's wives and concubines, but wherever women gather, women talk. It is well known by now that Tsali'gei has not had her moons-blood since arriving in the Forbidden City."

Jian sat down hard. Together they crouched, suspended between earth and sea, wrapped in an opaline shroud of twilight magic, orphans clinging to each other on a foreign shore.

"She is with child," Jian told the sea, wondering whether his father could hear. "My Tsali'gei is with child. I am to be a father." The waves clutched at his trousers and robes.

"Jian Sen-Baradam," the Daezhu told him sternly, gripping him even harder, "your woman is with child, but you will never be a father. Not if that turtle-hearted Xienpei has her way. By now, she and the emperor both know."

"Wait," Jian said, struggling to his knees. "Wait. Xienpei wanted this child to be born, else why—"

"She wanted this child to be *born*," Giella interrupted again, her voice as soft and implacable as a river's song. "Because the blood of such a child holds much power. Enough power to grant the darkest wishes of her heart."

"Or the emperor's heart," Jian guessed, thinking of the blood pennies with which he had been gifted.

"Heart of Illindra, Soul of Eth,

"Blood of the innocent condemned to death."

Jian could not breathe. Fear for his child—a child about which he had only just heard, a child who had not yet been born—seized him in its jaws.

"Long has the emperor wished to destroy the false king in Atualon," the Nightingale sang, wrapping him in wings of sister-love. "He will most certainly reason that the blood of your child—and of Tsali'gei, your wife—might give him and his luminists the power they need to wage the war he so lusts after. And Xienpei wishes nothing so much as to replace the vile Karkash Dhwani at his side. Their lives will be the coin she offers up to him for that privilege."

Cold waves slapped at Jian's hand, with which he was gripping his sword. Cold fog twisted its fist in his hair, dragging him to his feet. Cold were his heart and voice as he stood and made a vow that would see him dead—or the Forbidden City in flames.

"Daeshen Tiachu will not have them," Jian growled. "He will not have them." Three times, making it true, "*He will not have them.*" Far away, across the waves, a horn sounded once, twice, three times.

Make it so.

The White Nightingale stood and faced him, dark eyes bright and predatory. She held out her hand, palm up. A twist of her wrist, a quick slice, and her palm welled with crimson.

"Are you with us, Jian Sen-Baradam? Will you join your brothers and sisters in our fight against Daeshen Tiachu?"

This time, Jian did not hesitate. He drew the sword his father had given him and ran his left hand down the sharp blade.

"By my blood," Jian vowed, "I will." He clasped her bloody hand with his own, and the bitter salt of their lost innocence dripped into the ocean. Swirling, swirling, swirling, making it true.

Blood and water and salt, Jian thought, staring into the water. It seemed to him that he had never seen anything so tragic, or so beautiful.

THIRTY - NINE

Sulema sat on the Heir's Throne, a smaller and simpler version of her father's great chair, and looked down upon the matreons and patreons, mistresses and masters and other elevated citizens of Atualon. It seemed to her that she was spending too much time looking down at people these days, and that she missed the days when she was but a single warrior among many.

She missed the tents and cushions of the Zeeranim. These damn wood-and-gold chairs were ridiculous. She wriggled her butt deeper into the embroidered cushions and grumbled. Behind her, above her, she heard her father chuckle.

"You will get used to it," he promised, "with time. If it is any consolation, this chair is much worse."

Sulema sighed and resigned herself to having a sore backside—at least, until she could figure out a way to escape this blasted place.

The heralds rattled their little hand drums, announcing the arrival of the assemblage's most anticipated guest, and Sulema sat up straighter as her heart turned over. Cassandre entered, robes of red and orange and palest yellow flowing behind her like streamers of silken fire, moonstones glittering in her hair and at her brow, the little belled slippers upon her feet, felted and turned up at the toes like the boots worn by Sindanese soldiers, chiming a merry little tintinnabulation as she strode down the wide aisle.

Behind the master painter came a veritable palette of apprentices, each veiled head-to-slipper in a single color so they seemed a living rainbow flowing behind their mistress. They bore between them a narrow wooden stage, and upon this stood the much-anticipated portrait of Sulema Sa Atu, taller than the girl herself and covered in a drape of demure white. A corner of the painting's frame peeked out, a sly wink of gold, and Sulema grinned despite her misgivings. She rather dreaded her father's reaction to the painting—he had wanted her to be made in his image, not her own—but still she felt the thrill of anticipation.

Cassandre came to an abrupt halt before the thrones so that her robes swirled about her feet in a puddle of color. The apprentices stopped more gradually, lowered the painting with a great deal of care, and two of them took hold of the white cloth.

"Master Painter," Wyvernus intoned, "we have given you this task, to create for us a likeness of our precious daughter."

Cassandre dropped to one knee, head bowed, but not before catching Sulema's eye with a saucy wink.

"Yes, your Arrogance."

"And have you completed this task to our satisfaction?"

"Only you may be the judge of that, your Arrogance," she replied. "It is my deep honor to present to you"—here she paused for yet more dramatic effect—"Sa Atu, the Heart of Atualon, the Dragon's Legacy..." She gestured, and her apprentices whipped the white cloth away with the grace of long practice, "Sulema ne Atu, first of her name."

Sulema gasped and sprang halfway from her chair, both hands covering her mouth. The portrait was stunning, it was—

"*Ahhhh*," Wyvernus breathed.

—it was all *wrong*. Cassandre had painted her like one of Atualon's high ladies, in silk robes of gold and white which gleamed pearlescent in the faux dawn. The golden rays of Akari Sun Dragon kissed her hair, unbraided and flowing down her back. Her cheeks were flushed, lips slightly parted, and in her hand she held the Orb as a child might hold a favorite toy.

I have been betrayed. Sulema settled back into her chair, aghast. *I thought she was my friend. I thought—*

Cassandre caught her gaze and raised a saucy brow. *Trust me*, her eyes said.

"Perfect," Wyvernus enthused. "Well done, Master Painter. We are well pleased, indeed. What do you say, Daughter?" His hand fell heavy and warm on her shoulder and gave a squeeze.

Sulema blinked as the portrait swam before her eyes, as if it were a reflection in the river. Another image lay behind the first, bright and true, of herself as a warrior, standing straight and proud—and free—beside her Atemi. Her eyes were harsh as gold coins, mouth set in a hard line, and her shamsi was half-drawn as if she would challenge her viewer to a fight.

She blinked again, and the glamour settled itself. Once more a ne Atu of Atualon gazed out at her, placid and sweet.

Magic, she thought. Powerful magic indeed, to fool the Dragon King. *If he were to suspect…*

"It is beautiful," she agreed, reaching up to place her hand over his warm grip. The Dragon King gave her shoulder another squeeze, and a small tug to one of her braids.

"Perhaps you should wear your hair like that," he suggested. "And you should smile more. It is a shame to hide such a beautiful smile."

"Yes, Father," she agreed, smiling in truth as she saw the true Sulema Ja'Akari swim to the surface once again, grim and gorgeous. "You are right, of course."

He sees only what he expects to see, she realized. *He has never seen* me, *at all.*

In the king's blindness lay her chance at escape.

She stood in front of her portrait in the Hall of Dragons, long after her father and his courtiers had parted. Let them think her vain, as much as they thought beyond their own illusions. This portrait was her way out. She could feel it.

Saskia cleared her throat to warn of Cassandre's approach, but Sulema had heard the master painter's belled slippers chiming three hallways down. She leaned forward, so close her nose almost touched the portrait. Though it was masked by the smell of oils and pigment Sulema caught a faint whiff of… sweat and horse. A small thrill ran through her.

"Well?" Cassandre's voice was low and amused. "Is it perfect, your Radiance?"

"You are horrible," Sulema replied. She laughed, and turned to hug the other woman. "I love you. I would ask how you did it, but I can hardly draw stick people in the sand. Only…" she bit her lip.

"Yes?" Cassandre's smile faltered, and a quick scowl flashed across her face. "Is there something wrong with the painting?" *"There had better not be,"* her voice warned.

"No-oooo," Sulema said, "but there may be something wrong with me. I do not feel any different. I see myself as I would be— free, and proud, and whole, but I do not feel any different," she repeated. "I am still wounded, and ill. I—I cannot help myself, much less my people. How do I go from *this*"—she tugged at her gold and white robes— "to *that*?" She pointed with her chin at her warrior's portrait.

"Ah, my dear," Cassandre took Sulema by the shoulders and kissed her on both cheeks. "I have done what I can, but I am only the artist. The painting is complete. I have put my magic into it, as well as your blood, sweat, and tears. Your task is to put your heart into it, and then you will realize its full potential. This painting holds no power, nor will it, until you believe in the dream yourself."

"So it is all up to me, now."

"Exactly."

Sulema sighed.

"Well, fuck."

Sulema remained long into the night, even as the moons chased each other from window to window down the length of the great hall, even as Saskia, muttering her discontent, leaned her back against a wall and drifted into the not-sleep of a warrior on guard.

She stood before the painting until her legs ached, and then she sat crosslegged on the dragonstone floor until her ass was numb and her spine a column of fire. She could see her true form revealed, could feel that this was her portal to freedom, but she could not see her way in. Even if she *could* enter the painting, would she be able to take anyone with her? Mattu and Matteira, she knew, would be in terrible danger, the moment Pythos returned to Atukos. She would take Saskia, as well, and her mother—

"What are you doing?"

Sulema jumped at the sound of Hafsa Azeina's voice. She had not heard her approach.

"I—" She turned, but there was nobody there.

"Open your dreaming eyes, child."

"Oh." Sulema tried, tried harder, and her mother's image, pale and wan, stood beside her. "I am..." She stopped, unsure how much she should reveal, even to her mother.

"Ahhhh, now, *this* is magic." Hafsa Azeina's form flickered, and she stood just in front of the portrait. "Very interesting. I have heard of—" She stopped and turned to face Sulema. "So you would use this magic to escape?"

"Yes," Sulema admitted. "I know you would teach me dreamshifting, but—"

"This is a very good idea, Sulema. I do not have time to teach you to dreamshift to the point that you might escape Atualon." Her dreaming form wavered again and stood close to Saskia. "And the price is too high to pay."

Sulema glanced toward Saskia. A sword sister was as trusted as one's own self, but this...

She need not have worried. Saskia stood slumped against the wall, eyes closed, mouth open, caught in a dreamshifter's web. She turned once again to her mother.

"What price?" She stared at her mother's flickering form. "Hold still, you are making me dizzy." Sudden realization dawned. "Do you speak of... whatever you did, when you stole me away all those years ago?"

"Yes." Her mother hovered, disconcertingly, a hand's width above the floor. "We were betrayed. The people who had promised to deliver us to freedom planned, instead, to take us to Min Yaarif and there ransom us to the highest bidder. I could not allow that to happen, and I was no warrior. I did a terrible thing, paid a terrible price, to get you away from them."

"What?" Sulema whispered. "What did you do?"

"Are you certain you wish to know?"

"Yes."

No.

"I…" Hafsa Azeina's dreaming body winked out for a long moment before reappearing. "I killed my Basta, my kima'a, and ate her heart. I became—"

"*Annu*," Sulema whispered, horrified. "Dream eater." The stuff of nightmares.

"Yes," her mother answered in a calm voice. "The demon Annubasta, eater of dreams, able to travel the Dreaming Lands in the flesh."

Dream eater. Sulema tried very hard not to cringe away from her mother.

"You can see how this is a better way," Hafsa Azeina continued as if she did not notice. "You do not become a demon, and your father—and his shadowmancers—are far less likely to suspect that you might try this. Atukos is warded against your dreamshifting, you know."

"I did not know."

"There is much you do not know." Her mother's voice was warm. "But there is much you do know, Sulema, and much you can discern on your own. You have cunning, and skill, and tenacity, and these are powerful weapons."

"Tenacity." She snorted. "You mean I am a churra-headed brat."

"Even so." The dreaming form flickered. "Much like your mother, I fear."

"If I am not to follow your path, and if I cannot find my way to open this one," she said, indicating the portrait, "what way is left to me?"

"Follow your heart, Sulema." Her mother's dreaming form began to fade.

"I am not sure I trust my heart."

"Oh, but I do." Her mother was a mist, a shadow. "I always have."

When she was certain her mother was gone, Sulema regained

her feet and stood for a long moment before walking over to the painting. When she reached out she could feel the oil paints beneath her fingers, cool and thick and solid. Almost it seemed that if she closed her eyes she could push her way into the portrait and wish herself free. For a moment she stood poised between worlds, and it seemed as if a hot wind teased at her braids.

Sulema, it whispered in the voice of Mattu. *Sulema*.

She pulled back. Once more she stood in the darkened hallways of Atukos, staring at the portrait of a princess.

"I will escape," she promised the princess, "I will be free, but I will do it on my own terms."

She turned and strode away, back straight, face proud, the very portrait of a warrior.

FORTY

This prey is beyond you, Kithren.

Hafsa Azeina smiled to herself. So many words of wisdom were meant to keep people from doing just what she was doing. Casting her fishing net at a dragon. Biting off more than she could chew. Letting her head grow too big for her braids.

Hunting the Huntress.

Abruptly Hafsa Azeina realized that she had crushed the goose's quill in her fist, and with a grimace she released the broken thing. Fletching while angry was never a good idea. On the other hand, if she waited until she was *not* angry, these arrows would never be finished.

Well I know it, sweetling, she answered. *Do you think to dissuade me?* She shook her head, half wishing Khurra'an would urge her to cease this folly, half wishing she were wise enough to heed his warning. *I do what must be done, nothing more.*

Well I know it, he replied, his mind's voice dry and rough with affection. *None so wise as I am would seek to dissuade you from leaping to your death, Kithren. It was merely an observation.* He closed his eyes and stretched out full length upon her hearth. She had lit the fire for him, though sweat beaded on her brow in the early summer heat, and tickled down between her shoulder blades.

She would do more for him if she could, but Khurra'an had refused the small pig she had requested, and goat's milk, and even the bits of cheese that used to make him pounce and purr like a ridiculous kitten. He would drink a little water, reluctantly, but nothing more since his fateful hunt.

Yet here she was, preparing for a fateful hunt of her own. At least he had stood half a chance against the blue goat, which was more than she could say about this madness.

There is no fool like two old fools, he agreed, and she could hear his thoughts grow languid as he drifted into a state of half-sleep.

Is this what we have come to, then? she wondered, quietly so as not to disturb his rest. *Two old fools stretched out before the fire, dreaming of the days when we could bring down our own kills?*

Khurra'an cracked one eye half open. *You still have a bit of blood around your mouth, sweetling. From that last kill you dreamt up.*

She laughed a little at that, and surreptitiously wiped her mouth on the hem of her tunic. The move to Atualon had slowed, but not stopped, the assassination attempts against her daughter. The Dragon King's heir was an inconvenience that much of the world would prefer to see removed. Just this morning she had caught the dreaming soul of a foreign wizard who had thought to stalk her daughter through the Shehannam.

You should have known better, Hafsa Azeina had told her at the end, *than to cast your fishing net at a dragon.* Now the woman's fingers lay nestled in a box full of beetles, and would make a fine rattle once they were defleshed. The sinew from the wizard's feet was soaking in a shallow wooden bowl and would be used to bind this fletching to Hafsa Azeina's arrows—arrows that would sing through the air toward the dreamshifter's quarry.

Will it be enough, then? Khurra'an flicked one ear.

Enough? She frowned. *Will what be enough?*

When you have fashioned this rattle, will it be enough? Or will you not rest until you have fashioned enough instruments to play the world a merry tune, and send every soul dancing down the Lonely Road?

I did not know these kills bothered you. Why have you said nothing before now?

I have said nothing because it does not bother me. Khurra'an rolled onto his back with a grunt and let his legs fall open, exposing more of himself than anyone would ever wish to see. *We vash'ai do not drag our dead along with us, save those bits we choose to eat. You will need to be fast, Kithren, quicker than you have ever been, if you wish to survive the coming hunt. These things you have made will serve only to slow you down.* He twitched his tail, twice, and fell more deeply into sleep.

Hafsa Azeina watched his rib cage rise and fall, rise and fall. Khurra'an was right. Khurra'an was always right. What had she ever done to deserve such a wise friend?

Nothing. It was the whisper of a laughing thought. *I am saving you for a snack, later.*

With a sigh, Hafsa Azeina released another crushed quill from her fist, and set the work aside. *I know better than to perform a delicate task with a hand full of anger,* she reminded herself. *I should know better, as well, than to face my greatest fear with a heart full of death.* She closed her eyes, the better to meditate upon the question.

What have I ever done to deserve such a wise friend? Khurra'an mocked, gently. Gently.

Nothing, she replied. *I am saving you for a rug, later.*

It is a fine day, she thought, *on which to shed my soul of its burdens.*

The weather was not particularly lovely. A cold fog obscured the best parts of her view, lapped at her ankles, and made the dragonglass steps slippery. Neither was it the most spectacular time of year, as the early blossoms of spring had fallen away, and the later blossoms of summer had not yet begun to bud. It was an ordinary morning, and somehow more special because of it. How many times had she risen on a morning such as this, unspectacular, unremarked, heartsick and soul-sick after a night of blood and hunting?

Too many to count, she thought. She took a deep breath, cool mist laced with dragonmint and sweet thyme. Khurra'an shadowed her footsteps as he had for the greater part of her life, though his steps dragged now so that she could hear his claws scraping against the stone, and his breathing was ragged and labored. When was the last time they had done something like this, together, that was... good? When had they last gone fishing, or hunting for the simple joy of the chase? When had they last stopped to take in a beautiful morning, foggy or no?

She could not remember. Too long to remember, she thought. She promised them both, wordlessly, that when this ordeal was behind them—if they survived it—she would do better. Was there more to life than death and pain? She owed them both the chance to find out.

This is a step… along the right path, Khurra'an said. The thought was slow, and sleepy, and warm. *Too long have you turned your face toward the sun… only to curse Akari. We used to have fun together, you and I.*

We will again, she promised him. *When this is over.*

He nudged her gently in reply, and she nearly fell to her death.

They reached the peak of Atukos just past midsun, after Akari's jealous gaze had burned away the last tatters of mist. The lake was beautiful. Hafsa Azeina had grown up running wild on the beaches of the Seven Isles, had outrun a red sandstorm on a good war mare, had risen alive and victorious after a hopeless battle, and still the silvery still not-waters of the dragon's lake were the most beautiful thing she had ever seen.

Standing for a moment poised on the balls of her feet at the edge of the waking world, she then followed the path down to the deadly mere. There on the black sand beach she unrolled the burden she had carried so far. It had dragged at her, had made her steps leaden and filled her mind with darkness.

Basta's Lyre, hideous and beautiful, strung with the gut of a golden-tongued assassin. A flute made from the slender leg bone of beautiful, treacherous Nurati. A hand-drum fashioned from the hide of… what had her name been? She had pretended to be a merchant.

Ah, yes, Ullah, that bitch. Flutes, drums, rattles of every size, half a shattered skull, and finally the finger-bones and sinew newly harvested and not yet fashioned into anything. *So many*, she thought sadly, *and so many more lost somewhere in the sands of time. It is no wonder I cannot sleep at night.*

It is no wonder it takes you so long to pack, Khurra'an offered. He let his mouth hang open in a cat's grin. *You should have simply taken their ears, like your heroes of old.*

Hush, you, she responded, giving his ear a scratch when he half-fell, half-lay upon the ground at her feet. *Thank you for coming all this way with me.*

Thank you, he replied, eyes hooded and full of mystery, *for coming so far with me, Kithren, It has been… very interesting.*

Hafsa Azeina picked up an old rain-rattle made from a hollowed-out femur and filled with teeth. It was the first instrument she had made in the Dreaming Lands, back when she was young and tenderhearted and still wept after every kill. She remembered the man from whom she had harvested the materials, remembered how he had gloated over the fine price she and her daughter would fetch him. She remembered how he had died, choking to death on his own severed tongue. The rattle, as she turned it over and over in her hands, made an ugly noise.

Noisy in death as in life, Khurra'an snorted. *Be rid of it, Kithren, Free yourself at last.*

Yes, she thought. *Yes, at last.* She turned and, with a movement fluid and sure, threw the rattle as far as she could. It clattered through the air, end over end, chattering a final goodbye, and sank without so much as a ripple beneath the silvery waters of the dragon's lake.

"Goodbye," she said aloud, "I am sorry." She found, to her great surprise, that it was true.

One by one the instruments followed, rattling and howling and whistling through the air to fall in a macabre rain into the not-water waters of the not-lake lake. Her instruments of death slid one by one from the world of men. Where they went after, she did not know.

Nor did she care.

As each fell without splash or ripple into the placid mere, each reminder of her true nature was as a burden lifted from her bloodstained soul, her long-shadowed heart. Finally, when she had lifted and thrown so many of the fell things that both arms ached, Hafsa Azeina was left with two instruments, nearest and dearest and most painful of all. She held the leg-bone flute, running her fingers up and down its length, and thought about the woman from whom she had taken this bone. With a spattering of unexpected tears she recalled the woman's ready laugh and sharp wit, her delight in books and children, and her love of her son Ismai, who loved Hafsa Azeina's own daughter.

What will become of the boy? she wondered, surprising herself. She had never allowed herself to think much about the lives her prey had left behind. To Hafsa Azeina they were enemies to be killed, but to others they were mothers and fathers, friends and lovers.

Considering this for a long moment, she poked at the thought as one might poke at a sore tooth, to see whether it still hurt. And found, much to her surprise and vast relief, that it did.

This is all well and good, Khurra'an noted, *but she was our enemy. You did what needed to be done, and no more. It is time to let go, Kithren.*

Hafsa Azeina closed her eyes in gratitude sharp as pain, and when she opened them again it seemed to her that Khurra'an lay bathed in a puddle of light, so brightly did he glow to her eyes.

You are right, she agreed, cocking her arm back as far as she could.

I am always right, he purred, even as the leg bone flew up, up, up, paused midair and let out a long shriek. Then down, down it plunged, until it disappeared silently beneath the lake's bright surface.

Without allowing herself to pause, Hafsa Azeina seized Basta's Lyre in both hands. She refused to weep over this one, refused to let his golden voice caress her to guilty tears, refused to let the memories of a golden summer torment her with guilt.

Time for you to leave me at last, you lying bastard, she thought, and she let him fly. Basta's Lyre sailed gracefully though the air, crying a long farewell, and at last it, too, was swallowed whole into the dragon's dreaming.

It is done, she thought. *It is good.*

Then she collapsed upon the beach, buried her face in Khurra'an's raggedy mane, and wept like a child.

❖

Hafsa Azeina woke to a sky as dark and deep and inky-soft as a newly dyed touar. The boldest stars were already out, and the new moons hung round and ripe as white plums, daring her to pluck them.

"You should not have let me sleep so long," she chided, pushing herself away from the wall of fur, spitting out Khurra'an's mane as she sat up. "Wyvernus will have the whole of Atualon in an uproar, trying to find us." Stealing away from her chambers undetected had been easy enough—she had been ducking guards all her life—but slipping back in undetected was likely to be a problem, after so many hours.

You needed this, he replied quietly. *As did I. It has been a good road, Kithren.* He sounded... odd.

It has indeed been a good road, she agreed with a smile. She shook herself free of sleep-shadows, pushed her short new wizard-locks away from her face, and reached out to touch Khurra'an's shoulder. *We should—*

He was cold.

No, her heart cried, as she grabbed handfuls of mane and dragged herself over to him. The flesh beneath her hands had cooled, and the scent of death mingled with his cat-musk. *No*, she cried again, and *No*, trying to make it real. But Khurra'an was gone. Her heart's companion had begun the journey down the Lonely Road without her. He had gone away and left her all alone.

Hafsa Azeina wailed. It was a heartsick, hopeless sound. She pulled the great, shaggy head into her lap, hugging his beloved face, stroking back his whiskers. By the light of the moons she washed his face with her tears, over and over again, howling her grief until she was sick with it.

Until she was mad with it.

FORTY-ONE

I smai woke from fitful dreams to the smell of smoke, to people screaming, and to the feel of Ruh'ayya's panic tearing through his mind like a trapped thing.

Fire! Fire! Kithren, wake!

He fought his way free of sleep and confusion, kicked out of the blankets that had wound round him like serpents, and half stumbled from his tent, holding his shamsi in one hand and rubbing sand from his eyes with the other. He slept with his tent flap facing the Dibris—they all did, as the slavers' raids came closer to Aish Kalumm every night. The night lay soft and dark over the river, and stars winked lazily as they floated across the night sky.

Not stars, he realized. Heart heavy with dread, he turned toward the City of Mothers, and froze as if he had been turned to salt.

Aish Kalumm was on fire.

Flames pressed into the sky like a thousand thousand hands raised in mourning, and sparks rose to float upon the gentle breeze. A wall of screams and wails rolled over Ismai, a wave of despair.

'Ware, Kithren! 'Ware!

Ruh'ayya burst from the dark, eyes wide, ears flat against her head. She would fight a lionsnake for him, his brave one, and had faced the wrath of her dreadful sire to run by Ismai's side, but she was ever terrified of fire.

There was a roar like a dragon as a building collapsed.

"Beit Usqut!" Ismai cried, voice thick with horror. Thoughts chased one another through his mind. *Run to Aish Kalumm? No, too far.* There would be nothing but ash and bone by the time he got there. *Run to the pastures, get Ehuani, ride to Aish Kalumm? A better plan*, he thought reluctantly. *Clothes? No time, no time.*

He hiked his nightrobe up about his waist, turned to run, and tripped over Ruh'ayya.

"Za fik!" he shouted, arms pinwheeling, nearly stabbing himself in the foot as he tried to right himself. "Get out of the way! We need to help. We need to get help! Maybe the Mah'zula will—"

Kithren. The panic in Ruh'ayya's voice had changed into something soft, low, and deadly. *Kithren, no. Look you to the stone caves of your people. Look.*

Ismai turned again, he looked again, and this time his heart burned to ashes.

People had emerged from the flames and were walking toward him—every person in Aish Kalumm, it seemed to him then— toward him, toward the river. Backlit as they were by the flames, they looked like daemons being driven forth from the pits of Jehannim. Even from such a distance Ismai could hear the wails of women, of children.

What of the elderly? he wondered, and felt like sicking up. *What of the ill?* Were the warriors able to save them, any of them? Perhaps the Mah'zula…

Look, Ruh'ayya urged. Her eyes were huge and filled with flame. *Stupid human—look! See!*

Ismai opened his mind to what his eyes had been trying to tell him. Behind his people rode a line of horsewomen, hair stiffened into manes, swords ready at their sides. The song of their war cries reached his ears, the drums of hoofbeats. A thousand warriors from the old stories, a thousand again, rank upon rank of them driving the people toward the river, toward safety.

Toward him.

"The Mah'zula!" he shouted, excitement rising. "They are saving our people! Praise Atu, they—"

Kithren, hissed Ruh'ayya. *No.*

Even as Ismai watched, one tiny figure broke away from the crowd and ran for the cover of darkness. Ismai was too far away to see whether the fleeing figure was a man or a woman, young or old. Even as he watched, mouth hanging open, a shout frozen halfway up his throat, three of the Mah'zula broke formation and rode the person down. There was a brief struggle, a flash of swords tiny in the firelight, and the three riders returned alone.

"No," Ismai whispered. "No, no."

We must leave. Kithren, we must run now. They are killing your kind, your warriors who will not join them. I can hear them dying, I can feel—they are killing my kin as well, those few who are bonded. They will kill me. More softly she added, *They will kill you.*

Ismai watched his people being herded like goats to slaughter, away from the inferno that had been Aish Kalumm. What of the old, the sick? What had become of the new mothers, bedridden and unable to run? His fist tightened on the hilt of his shamsi, and his heart tightened on the hilt of truth.

Ehuani, he thought. *There is beauty in truth, just as there is beauty in the sword.*

Beauty can be deadly, Ruh'ayya agreed. *We must go.*

You must go, my beauty. I must stay and help my people.

Are you sure, Kithren? It seems a foolish thing to do. Are you not afraid they will kill you?

It does seem foolish. And I am afraid. Ismai drew a deep breath. *That is how I know it is the right thing to do.*

Those great eyes regarded him, starslight and moonslight and fire all at once. *I was right to choose you*, Ruh'ayya said at last. She butted Ismai with her head so hard he staggered and nearly fell. By the time he regained his balance, she was gone.

Ismai let his sword fall to the sand and waited for the Mah'zula. He filled his lungs with the sharp, clear air of a desert night. His last as a free man, he suspected. It tasted as sweet as wine, as bitter as blood.

FORTY-TWO

Daru stared long at the small map, drawn carefully so many ages past. He was tempted to push his finger along the faded line that showed him the way to the surface, to sun and stars, to food and safety, but he kept following the dotted line instead, the one leading to the chambers where the exceptional children were kept locked away from all these good things.

"Where they *were* kept," he insisted, in a petulant voice that would have earned a growl from Dreamshifter. "A long time ago. It is doubtful that they are still there, right, Pakka? I mean, the library was lost for so long that hardly anybody even believes it ever existed. Right, Pakka?"

"*Pip-pip-prrrr-mmmf*," Pakka crooned. She was nibbling on the head of her latest kill. She liked the ears best. Daru thought of Khurra'an nibbling on *his* ears, and winced.

"Even if they are there, who knows if I can still find them? These passages are so old; surely some of them have collapsed or been filled in by now, right?"

"*Pip-pip*," she replied. Daru thought she sounded disapproving.

"And even if I can get to them, what am I supposed to do? Surely there are guards..." His voice trailed off as Daru stared at the sketches. The lines were strong and sure, and the hand that had drawn them had been steady, but here and there were splotches as if the young artist had wept to record such a thing.

"Fuck," he said, despite his earlier vow. It made him feel better, somehow—strong and certain, like Istaza Ani. What would the youthmistress do, if she thought there were children being stolen from their families and imprisoned underground for some fell purpose? Would she sneak out the side door, hoping to remain undetected and safe, while others suffered?

She would not, he knew, *and neither will I.*

With that settled in his mind, Daru tore a thin scrap from the hem of his tunic and used it to mark his place in the journal. The cloth was filthy and he made a face, but what was he supposed to do? Fold the page down?

"I may be a barbarian," he explained to Pakka as he stood, "but I am not a savage."

"*Pip-pip-trrrr*," she agreed, and swallowed the mouse's head whole.

Daru shared most of his remaining water with Pakka, tucked two spare torches into his belt, checked his knives, and made his way toward the wide stairway. Not without a glance back over his shoulder, not without a sigh or three of longing. He had found the Library of Kal ne Mur, and was walking away with just a single book. All the knowledge of ages past, his for the taking... if only he could carry more. If only he were not so weak.

"If only you were a churra," he told Pakka.

"*Pip-pip!*" she scolded. Daru grinned and gave the stacks and scrolls, codices, and rolled maps one last, lingering stare.

"I will be back!" he cried to them. "I promise!"

Promise, promisssse, the shadows chuckled. They shunned the library and whatever magic it held, preferring to lay in wait for him in the tunnels ahead. *Promisssse.*

"Shut up," Daru snapped. He pulled the bird-skull flute from his pocket. The shadows would be hungry, and he would rather they fed on music than on boy. Turning his back on his heart's desire, he began to play.

The way was long, his legs short, and the shadows in the Downbelow, having fed for so long upon nothing but their own malice, were famished. Daru played his bird-skull flute for strength, he played to give the shadows something to gnaw on besides his bones, and he played in the hopes that dreamshifter might hear echoes of his music in the Dreaming Lands and remember her small apprentice.

It was wrong that she had not come for him, that she had not sought out his kima'a in the green lands and used it to find him. He was her apprentice, and she the closest thing Daru had to a mother. She was supposed to care for him. Long had he lain where he had fallen, wishing for rescue, before binding his own arm and making his own way, and in some ways that abandonment hurt worse than the broken bones.

It occurred to him, at last, to wonder whether something bad had happened to Dreamshifter, and so she was not able to come to him. That thought was more terrifying than the notion of wandering the Downbelow, lost and blind and eaten by shadows, so he pushed it away with his music.

"*Pip-pip-peeeeeeeee,*" Pakka trilled, bobbing back and forth in time to his music. "*Pip-peeee-peeee-oh!*" She rubbed her hind legs together, adding her scritchy, scratchy little bug-music to his. *Crick-rick-rick! Rick-rick!* Daru and Pakka danced down the belly of the dragon, playing a dark little, merry little tune, and the shadows danced in their wake. *We are almost good enough to play in the Spectacle*, Daru thought, and he laughed through his music.

The shadows laughed, too, in voices like sorrow and ground bones, and Daru wove that into his magic, as well. *"If you cannot dance with a friend,"* Hannei had said to him, once when he was little and too weak to go to Hajra-Khai, *"dance with an enemy. All roads lead to the Lonely Road, and in the end we will dance together."* She had kissed his forehead and sat with him through the night, and once again he had disappointed half his people by not dying.

Daru blew his heart into the music, and sent the shadows into a mad spin.

Someday, Ja'Akari, he vowed again, *I will dance with you.*

The flames of his torch flickered to one side, and then the other. They had come to a crossroads of sorts. Tunnels gaped like hungry mouths to the north—so he thought—and to the… southeast? Maybe? Daru pulled the journal from his belt and opened it, juggling the book and torch awkwardly with one good hand and one bad.

Yes, he thought, *just here. The tunnel on this hand*—he glanced up—*leads to the Chambers of the Exceptional Children.* He did not bother to repress the shudder that took him, though it made the bones in his arm grind painfully. *And the one on this other hand leads to...* he traced the path with his little finger, wishing with all his heart he might follow it to safety.

To freedom, the shadows whispered, dancing around him and laughing. One of the shadows, bolder than most, braved the light of Daru's torch to tug at his tunic. *Freedom, freedom. This way, this...*

"Ahhh." Daru sighed out loud, though it was dangerous to address them so. His heart leapt halfway into his own throat, and Pakka clung to his hair as the shadow pressed close. "You think I should go that way? To the surface?"

Yes yes yesysssssss, they responded. *This way, thisthissssss—*

"You do not think I should go this way?" He gestured with his torch. "And try to rescue the children?" The tunnels fell silent as the shadows went still.

"Well then," he told them, with a smile that did not reach his heart, "this is the way we are going. I am going to the Chambers of the Exceptional Children, and if they are still there I am going to—"

The shadows began to wail, a noise that itched deep in his skull. The pain of it was blinding. He dropped the journal, scattering pages everywhere, and nearly dropped his torch. Pakka screamed into his ear, which did not help at all. The shadows swirled around them once, twice, three times like a dark storm, like sand-dae full of teeth and hatred, and then they were gone.

Daru stood for a long moment. His torch fluttered, his heart fluttered, and Pakka buried her little face in his hair. Finally Daru sighed, gathered up the pages and put them carefully back in the journal. He took a last, long look at the map, committing it to memory, just in case.

Just in case of *what*, he did not ask himself. Nor did he linger on the realization that he, a dreamshifter's apprentice, a mere boy and weak besides, was choosing to face something so bad that it scared the shadows away.

All roads lead to the Lonely Road, he reminded himself, and, *It is a good day to die*, and, *Life is pain... only death comes easy*. It helped, a little.

"*Pip-peeee?*" Pakka asked, clutching his ear with one dainty serrated claw and peeking over the top of his head. "*Peee-oh?*"

"Well," he told her, and firmed his grip on the torch, "I always wanted to be a hero."

Down they went.

Daru found himself in a maze of twisty little passages, all alike. Darkness pressed down upon him like a blanket meant to smother a weakling child. He was hungry, and he hurt all over. These things were all awful, and painted a bleak picture of his future, but he had a friend, and a torch, and his mother's knives—not to mention a map.

These things, taken together, shone brightly enough to banish those shadows in his heart that urged him to lay down and die. So on he trotted, mostly down as far as he could tell, nipping past the passageways that yawned to either side of him and promised a very short lifetime of adventure.

Eventually he came to a room with seven walls. *A temple*, he thought, a meeting place of sorts, perhaps, with walls of dragonglass polished smooth and engraved with all manner of symbols and scenes. He counted left one, two, three, walls and ran his fingers reverently along a very fine carving of Zula Din rousing her hounds to the hunt.

This is it, he thought. *This is the way.* He reached into his pocket and touched the bird-skull flute for confidence. *I have faced worse*, he reminded himself. *All by myself in the Dreaming Lands, I faced worse than this and survived.*

He was very young.

"*Pip*," Pakka whispered, close to his ear. "*Pip-pip.*"

"It will be fine," he whispered back as he took that final passage. "They are just children, after all. Like me. Just children." Far behind him, Daru could hear the shadows laughing.

Jusssst children, they giggled. *Jusssst children.*

"Hssst," he shushed, impatient with them and with his own fear. "They are children, and I am going to find them."

The chamber lay not far beyond that seven-walled room. He smelled it before he saw it. Daru found himself breathing through his mouth long before he came to the arched doorway overlooking the chamber. The light seemed to spring from his torch into the high-ceilinged room, and when he saw—

Daru choked on a breath that was half a sob.

They are children. His heart wept, echoing his careless words. *Children!* Row upon row of them, they lay, swaddled and draped in red, stacked foot-to-face like fish in the bottom of a boat. At first Daru thought they were dead, they held so still. One boy—he thought it was a boy, at least—hung from the wrists on one wall. His head lolled to one side as if he no longer had the strength to support it, and row upon row of inked script scarred the inflamed skin of his back.

I have made a mistake. Daru made a strangled noise deep in his throat, and Pakka clung to him in terror. *A terrible mistake. I should not have come here. I should have sent—*

Who, exactly, might he have sent? Hafsa Azeina had not come looking for him, and Daru knew deep in his heart that she was probably dead. For all he knew, the Dragon King himself had put these children here. Who could he send? Who would come? Who in all the world cared for the fate of children who were weak, or slow, or… different?

Only me, Daru thought. *If I do not save them, nobody will.* Trembling from the soles of his feet to the roots of his hair, he stepped into the chamber.

The children were not dead, after all.

As one, they turned their heads as he entered the room. There was no other movement, just that, and it sent the hairs on the back of his neck to prickling. Eyes wide and unblinking as an old blind man's, they stared and breathed, stared and breathed as a low breeze rustled through the hallway.

No, not a breeze, he realized. The children were whispering.

"Sleep," they crooned. *Sleep*, they commanded. *Sleep*, they begged. "Sleep, sleep, sleeeeeeep…"

The voices were raised from a whisper to a howl, and though the children did not move at all, not one of them, Daru felt a cry of fright rising in his own throat. Pakka screeched and launched herself from his shoulder and darted off, her pale little light fast disappearing back the way they had come. Unable to tear his eyes from the sight of the children staring up at him, mouths dark O's as they howled at him to *sleep*, to *sleep*, he backed away—

A hand closed over his shoulder from behind. Daru yelled and spun, forgetting all about the exceptional children, forgetting about Pakka and tunnels and hunger as he stared up, up, up. A black cloak billowed about the form of a man who drank darkness.

He is a shadow, Daru screamed, deep in the Downbelow of his own soul. *He is all the shadows*. Indeed shadow rippled across that perfect, ruined mask, and the eyes behind it creased in a smile.

Those eyes, Daru thought, mindless with panic. *Those eyes*. This was worse, much worse than anything he had ever faced in the Dreaming Lands. And yet, and yet…

You will live, Daru. Hannei's voice, a hand brushing hair from his fevered forehead, a kiss. *You are stronger than they know.*

Daru gathered his strength. "I know you," he whispered, clutching the journal. "Somnus."

"And I know *you*," the man said, in the voice of someone who had screamed himself awake for a thousand years. "Nightmare boy." His free hand darted to his waist, then flicked toward Daru's eyes.

"Aaaah," Daru cried. His eyes stung. They burned so that he dropped the torch and rubbed at his face with his good hand.

"Aaa—" He wobbled, sank to his knees. The man released his grip and Daru slid gracelessly, bonelessly, to the dragonglass floor.

"Sleep," the man whispered.

"Sleeeeep," the children whispered. Daru thought that they were weeping. Or was he weeping? It was hard to…

His eyes dragged shut.

He slept.

FORTY-THREE

Jian dined on squid in ginger sauce, and drank pepper tea, and marveled at the strange dream his life had become. *More of a nightmare than a dream, really*, he mused, *but the food is very good.*

Accompanied by two dozen of his most trusted dammati, he had arrived at the comfort house as Akari Sun Dragon dove behind the Mutai Gonyu. He sat at his ease, dining, drinking, and playing cards with others like himself, Sen-Baradam who had sworn to wage war upon the Forbidden City and break the emperor's hold on their lives for all time. It was most likely, he knew—they all knew—that this rebellion would end as others before it had ended, with their heads and guts staining the floors of the Palace of Flowers.

"Either way, we are most likely fucked," Mardoni had said into his ear earlier that same evening, laughing as he did so. "Us, our dammati, our families, and the towns we grew up in, as well."

"We are already fucked," Jian had observed. He had drunk a bit too much of the rice wine, and it had loosened his tongue.

"Exactly!" Mardoni had cuffed the side of his head, laughing, as a favorite uncle might have done. "So we might as well fuck the emperor, too, on our way to the Lonely Road!" They had all laughed at that, stuffing food into their faces and gambling away what monies they had, as rice wine and pepper tea flowed like tears.

Jian himself had some two hundred and thirteen dammati, at last count, and their ranks swelled by the day as Yellow and Red Daechen—even a few Blacks, to his surprise, Daeborn princes who had already walked three years down the road to Khanbul— came to Jian to drink from the blooding cup. They wore lacquered armor like his own, blue and silver and black, with his silver issuq rampant on chest and shield. They had chosen to swear their lives to him, to throw in their lot with a traitorous Sen-Baradam.

Like as not, they had chosen the quickest road to death.

Jian's visor had been fashioned to look like the snarling black face of a sea-bear with silver tusks and blue-rimmed eyes. It sat now on the low table before him and to his right, keeping company with the silver-and-white stag helm of Mardoni Sen-Baradam, the black-and-gold mymyc's head helm of Kouto Sen-Baradam, and the red-and-copper mountain eagle of Latukhan Sen-Baradam. Their dammati stood guard, straight-backed, hard-faced and proud.

Pretty young men and women in the red robes of *saiku*—comfort boys and girls—served noodles and spiced meats and tea, rice wine and dumplings and steamed vegetables. They played the loutan and flirted with the Sen-Baradam as if the men had come for pleasure and not to speak of treason.

"Jian, here, try the peach wine!" Mardoni pushed the bottle closer to him, and laughed as Jian shook his head. "Why so serious, boy?"

"I have drunk enough already," Jian said. He was not lying. The room spun dangerously.

"He acts as if he had never conspired to overthrow the emperor before," Latukhan grinned.

"Welcome to the ranks of Sen-Baradam," Kouto declared, "where our plans to rid the Forbidden City of Daeshen Tiachu are exceeded only by His Illumination's plans to rid the world of us!" Everybody laughed but Jian, who reached for the peach wine.

Perhaps I am not quite drunk enough yet after all.

"You men," Giella chided as she swayed into the room. "Stop teasing Jian. And *you* have had enough of *that*," she continued, snatching the peach wine from the table. "You landborn are likely enough to get yourselves killed without drink urging you on to ever greater feats of idiocy."

The men, as one, hung their heads and looked like boys who

343

had been caught shirking their chores. She clucked her tongue, shook her head, and with her fan shooed the saiku from the room. When the last painted youth had wiggled his way out, she shut and locked the wide door behind him and turned to face the suddenly serious, and very sober, Sen-Baradam.

"My Lords of Lesser Twilight," she intoned, and her eyes were pools of shadow in her white, white face. "Shall we begin?"

"*Ahai*," they agreed in unison, and the Nightingale smiled and began to sing as she set before them the bitter cup, and the sweet, and the blooding cup of binding vows. That summer night, in the four hundred and ninety-ninth year of Illumination...

...as his beloved lay frowning in her sleep, one arm flung over her belly,

...as his mother walked restless by the moons-lit sea,

...as some few among his Bloodsworn lay with saiku, drowning their loneliness in lust.

Jian Sen-Baradam, the pearl diver's son, declared war upon the emperor of Sindan.

"Truth is treason in the eye of a tyrant."
——General Yu Fengui, on the day of his death

Long they drank into the night, loath perhaps to stand and depart. It was as if they believed that as long as their budding plans were contained in one room, to one group of men and women, it would remain a perfect floret nurturing beautiful possibilities.

Once they stood and made their goodbyes, once the door was opened, and the breath of the world let in, the tree of their dream would be shaken. What manner of flower might that unblemished bud reveal, once it was kissed awake by the hot sun? Would it be a shining thing, fragrant and whole? Or might it reveal instead petals of pestilence and rot, fated to kill the branch upon which it grew?

❖

Just as the first light of dawn touched the peaks of the Mutai Gonyu, igniting the mountains with violet flames, a house-servant hurried wide-eyed and quaking with fear into the room where the Sen-Baradam sat, playing cards and drinking. She fluttered like a little bird to Giella's side.

"Mistress!" the girl cried. "The emperor's own soldiers are come!"

"Of course they have come," Giella said, "you silly thing. Fetch more peach wine—we wish to make the emperor's soldiers feel welcome!"

Jian would have leapt to his feet but for Mardoni's hand on his arm. "Be still," the older man said. "You are Sen-Baradam, playing cards with friends in a comfort house, nothing more. You have nothing to fear."

Even as he spoke, the guards at the doors folded as rice paper in the hands of an artist, swiftly and silently, and the saiku fell to the ground like petals in a storm, pressing trembling lips to trembling floorboards. All, that is, except Giella, the White Nightingale. She laughed and threw the windows wide, letting their plans loose into the dying of the night.

"We will meet again, you and I," she promised, blowing Jian a kiss. "My brothers." With a flutter of robes and a whisper of song, she was gone.

Mardoni shrugged and poured himself another glass of peach wine. "Three," he said, discarding two cards and drawing new ones.

"Hold," Kouto said. Latukhan made a face and tossed all his cards in. "*Bu sing dai.* Luck is not with me tonight," he complained.

Jian drew a deep breath and willed his trembling hands to be still. "Hold," he said, even as the doors burst open and Xienpei blew into the room before a storm of imperial soldiers, broad-shouldered and horn-helmed and with the white bull of Daeshen Tiachu emblazoned upon their breasts. Their swords were long and long-blooded, folded a thousand times over in the House of Steel Prayers, and their eyes were hard as diamonds.

The King of Seas smiled up at him from the cards in his fist, and Jian washed the fear down his throat with a mouthful of peach wine. The King of Seas, if played at the right time, was a powerful card. With cunning, and courage, and a bit of luck, Jian might yet win this game.

"I am most disappointed in you, Daechen Jian." Xienpei drew her mouth down into a sorrowful mask. The expression did not reach her eyes any more than did her false smiles.

We are still playing games, Jian thought, but he knew they were playing with her deck now, her dice.

"I cannot fathom why," he said, and tugged at the neck of his blue-and-silver robes, as if the fit were not perfect, or the fabric less than the finest spidersilk. "I was winning. Unless you were disappointed to find me enjoying such low entertainment as a comfort house?" This last was a deliberate barb. Xienpei, herself, was known to have… exotic… tastes.

"You think you hold the winning hand," she told him, striking a blow to his heart, "but you do not even know what game you are playing. You are a Yellow Road prince who fancies himself a warrior, yes? A noble hero from the old stories, come to topple the evil empire, and set the sky alight with the fire of a new dawn." Xienpei reached up to his face and drew her sharp nails across his skin, making him shudder. "Oh, to be so young again, Daechen Jian, so sweet, to think that one might play the game without cheating, and still win." Her laugh was a cold storm, blowing in the window and scattering his cards.

"Jian *Sen-Baradam*," he reminded her, as if she had spoken no other words. He bared his teeth at her. His sharp teeth, so like those of his sea-bear father. "Lest you forget… Yendaeshi."

"Of course, Sen-Baradam," she replied, bowing low. "A thousand apologies to you and your house. Speaking of which, and lest you forget, I have a gift for you." She dipped her clawed hand behind her wide silk belt. "From your beloved wife." Her jeweled smile was wide and brilliant. It reached her eyes, and Jian's blood ran to cold seawater. He accepted a small scroll from her, and let it unwind.

"Ah," he cried out, stricken, as a severed finger fell to the floor. He knew, before he bent to snatch it up, he knew.

"You see, Sen-Baradam," Xienpei crooned, "I hold the winning hand, after all. The cards are mine, and the dice, and the cups." She touched her fingers lightly to his chin, forcing him to look up and meet her eyes, filled with malice and mirth and murder. "The game is mine, and you are nothing more than a playing stone. Do you wish to live to see the end of this game? Do you wish Tsali'gei to see the end of this game?"

"Yes," Jian whispered, and bowed his head. Let Xienpei think him defeated. If she believed he still bent to her will, Tsali'gei might yet survive.

"Yes *what*?" Her voice was a whip.

"Yes, Yendaeshi. I wish her to live."

"Then you will do exactly as I say, Jian Sen-Baradam, or I will carve your beloved wife into pieces." She smiled. "And feed them to you myself."

FORTY-FOUR

The hem of Ismai's touar whispered mournfully as he walked through the burnt remains of his people. Like the sky at twilight, the fabric of his robe and trousers grew heavy and dark, sliding from bright indigo to violet and finally, at the very edges, the mute and angry black of funeral ashes.

For that is what Aish Kalumm has become, Ismai thought as he bent and sifted through what little remained of the City of Mothers. *A funeral pyre.* Not a proper funeral pyre, either, meant to send the beloved dead on their way with songs and flowers and memories of sunlight. This was a cold, nasty, stinking hole in the ground filled with bones and the end of everything. His sandaled foot struck something small and light that skittered across the ground in front of him. Unthinking, Ismai picked the thing up and held it before his eyes. Half a jawbone, charred to a feather's weight, studded with tiny teeth like pearls, with bigger teeth just beneath them.

A child, he thought, horrified. His fingers tightened on the bone and some of it crumbled away into dust. *A little child.* He put it in the basket at his waist, along with the other bits and pieces, and then bent back to his task. Ismai was a warden, sworn to serve the people, and the only service he could render now was to find what little the flames had not devoured, that these innocent ones might be properly laid to rest.

Most of the residents of Aish Kalumm had been herded away from the city before that snake woman and her priestesses burned it to the ground. Most... but not all. Those who were too ill, too elderly, or too unworthy to be allowed to live—by Mah'zula standards—had been left to perish. *"To strengthen the pride,"* Ishtaset explained to them all as they stood watching their home burn. *"A hard sacrifice, but necessary."* No few of the people had cried out at that, had broken away toward the city or had thrown themselves at the Mah'zula. Those people were thrown back, beaten senseless, or killed.

A handful of others, Ismai had noted with horror, had nodded thoughtfully at Ishtaset's words. *"To strengthen the pride,"* they agreed. *"A necessary sacrifice."*

Istaza Ani would have had an apt reply.

"Fuck that."

The crepuscular robes of another warden shushed along the ground ahead of him. "Monstrous," someone said in a low voice. Ismai glanced up and met Jasin's eyes, and they both flinched back.

"You look terrible," Jasin offered. His own face was streaked black and gray and white, as if he had been trying to emulate the warriors' paint, and his eyes were pools of bitter water.

"You look like you were dragged ass-backward through the seven gates of Yosh," Ismai countered, and he sighed. "What are we doing here? How is this helping our people?"

"We are doing what we can… for now." Jasin pointed with his chin toward the Mah'zula and their vash'ai who stood watch along the edges of the ruined city. "Helping those we can help… for now."

"For now," Ismai agreed. "But when we can—"

"Sssst," Jasin cautioned. "Trust no one, at least for now. Too many agree with the Mah'zula and think we should return to the old ways. Too few think this was wrong." He gathered spit in his mouth, looked at the ashen ground, and swallowed instead. He lowered his voice further. "How is your Ruh'ayya? Is she still safe?"

Trust no one. Ismai took a deep breath through his nose and bent to pick up a shard of rock, avoiding Jasin's eyes. "I do not know," he lied. "She does not speak to me. Perhaps she has gone back to the wild vash'ai." He stood and looked at the stone, shrugged, threw it over his shoulder.

Jasin nodded so slowly that Ismai knew he had not been fooled. *"A necessary sacrifice."*

Wait—*had* that been stone? He turned to retrieve the pale bit of rubbish, turned it over in his hands. *Bone*, he decided, and

349

bent again to peer at the dirt and ash. Where had he picked it up? *There*, he thought, just by his sandal print. A charred piece of door lay there. The wardens turned it over and stared in horror. The jawless skull of a child stared up at them, hopeless and lost, and the tiny bones reached up with one good arm as if Ismai had come to save him.

Jasin looked at his face, looked down, and bent to gather up the child's bones as gently as if Sammai were only sleeping.

"Ismai," he whispered, and his voice broke. "Ismai, I am so sorry."

Ismai took the boy's skull from Jasin, kissed the paper-thin forehead. The ashes burned on his lips, and tears unshed burned his eyes. He cradled the skull to his breast for a moment before placing it into his basket with the others.

"They lied," he said at last.

"The Mah'zula?"

Ismai knelt to gather up Sammai's bones, careful not to miss the tiniest fragment, careful in his words. "First Warden. First Warrior. My... my mother. All of them." The words were foul black soot, and he choked on them. "*Ehuani. Saghaani. Mutaani.* Where is the beauty in truth? In youth? Where is the beauty in death? Where is the beauty in any of this—Ja'Sajani?" In fury and in grief, he tore the touar from his head and threw it upon the ground. "They *lied* to us!"

"*Sssssst*," Jasin hissed, whites of his eyes pale against the filth of his skin. "*Sssssst*, Ismai, keep it down. They are coming for you now."

"Let them come." Ismai groped at his waist for the golden shamsi and nearly howled with rage to remember that it had been taken from him. "Let them come! What else can they do to me? What else can they take from me? Everything I had has been taken. Everything I loved has been lost. Let them come!"

Jasin grabbed his robes. "Ismai, Ismai, do not do this," he begged. "I know you have lost—"

Ismai's heart was dead as ash, brittle as charred bone. "You know nothing of what I have lost," he ground out. "Nothing."

He tore himself free of Jasin's grip, and turned toward the sound of approaching hoofbeats. Ishtaset herself was riding toward him, a fist of her Mah'zula—and no few Ja'Akari—close behind. They looked like the heroes out of one of Daru's books, before the Mah'zula had destroyed them. They looked like a painting that might have hung in his mother's rooms, before his mother's rooms had been burned to ash.

He reached into the basket at his hip, and stroked the sad little, brittle little, dead little skull.

"Let them come," he said again. "It is a good day to die."

Ismai clung to Ishtaset's back for the ride to the Madraj, denied so much as the dignity of his own Ehuani. She was slim and muscular, and rode her mare as if the two of them were a song made of wind. He was dismayed to find his body reacting to hers, and dismay turned to anger so that when they reached their destination and she soothed her horse to a prancing, snorting stop, Ismai slid off the mare's back and stalked away stiff-legged and bristling like an angry cat.

I do not stomp like that.

Ismai froze. *Where are you? Are you safe?* Then the thought, *You should not be here. They will catch you.* And kill her, likely as not. The vash'ai who ran with the Mah'zula were bigger and stronger than those who ran with the Zeeranim. Any who opposed them had been slain.

I am stronger than they, she protested. *But they will not catch me. I am Ruh'ayya, and my sire's brother has taught me well.* With that, her voice faded, leaving the faintest impression of her presence. It fluttered in the back of Ismai's mind.

"Ah, you speak to your Ruh'ayya." Ishtaset's voice came from behind him, a warm purr of approval. "A fine young queen, clever and strong. A jewel to be treasured—as are you, my handsome young warden."

351

Ismai froze, but he did not turn and look at her. "Leave her alone," he demanded, and filled with shame and fury as his voice betrayed him with a crack. "Let her be."

Sareta strode past him with nothing more than an amused sideways glance.

"We are not her enemy, young warden," Ishtaset replied, "any more than I am yours. We are your people."

"My people are your captives. My people lie dead in the ashes of Aish Kalumm."

The beads and bells braided into her pale mane sang a sorrowful tune as she shook her head. "You will see, young Ismai. You will learn." Her vash'ai joined her and she strode toward the arena, surefooted and tall as any conqueror. Ismai glanced behind. The Mah'zula had taken Ishtaset's mare away and stood there, a half-circle of hard faces not unlike his own.

If I ran now, they would cut me down, he thought, *and this pain would end*. He groped again for the shamsi that was not at his hip, and clenched his fists.

No, Ruh'ayya urged, her voice the shadow of a whisper in his mind. *You will serve no people by dying here. These sands are thirsty. All the blood in your body would not slake their thirst. Also, I would miss you. A little. Do not spend your life so easily, Kithren.*

No, he agreed. Ismai turned and followed Ishtaset, with the Mah'zula at his heels. *Not so easily. Not yet.* They walked through the wide tunnels and into the arena. When Ismai would have turned and walked upon the sand, one of the Mah'zula nudged his shoulder.

"Ah-aat," she warned. "Follow her." So he did, around the edge of the sands, in front of the seats. He was shocked to see how many of the seats were filled, row upon row upon row of Mah'zula and Ja'Akari and ordinary citizens, the latter huddled together like tarbok being stalked by vash'ai. He continued up the steps to the dais. It was strange to stand on high, when all his life had been spent craning his neck to stare up at the people whom life had set so far above him.

Stranger still to see so many seats filled which once were empty. The air, once redolent with scents savory and sweet, thick with laughter, heavy with anticipation, now rang silent with the hollow bellies of hungering shadows, and smelled of ash and anger. Ishtaset stood in the very center of the high dais where not so long ago his mother had reclined on cushions of silk and dined on figs and honey. The Mah'zula leader raised both arms to hush the silent crowd, and the air around them clotted in anticipation.

"My sisters," she said. "My brothers. Proud people of the Zeera. My people." A low moan rose from the crowd. Like a sandstorm on a windless day it danced among the watchers, and died without becoming much of anything.

"I come before you today as a *rajjha* among the Mah'zula, the First Women. We are descended from those who rode and fought—and died—beside Zula Din, in the long ago. We were the first to ride, the first deemed worthy by the vash'ai, the first to lay down our lives for the people. We were here before the Sundering, before Kal ne Mur laid waste our world—and we will be here long after the kings of Atualon are dust and shadows.

"In the long ago," she continued, speaking to a Madraj gone silent, "the Zeera was a fertile land, a land of meat and mead. The banks of the Dibris were green, her waters sweet and so filled with fish that it is said they would all but leap into our boats. Tarbok ranged in herds by the thousands and our kith the vash'ai, sleek and well-fed, lived among us, freely sharing their skills and knowledge. And the Ja'Akari…"

Ishtaset's voice broke and she took a deep breath. As one the Zeeranim in the stands, in the arena, leaned forward and took a breath with her. He frowned and looked from his people, to Ishtaset, and back to the people.

Have they forgotten our dead so soon?

The golden warrior cleared her throat, straightened her back, and continued. "This dream was stolen from us, even as our children are stolen by slavers every year, as our fish are stolen by the giant fleets that dock in Min Yaarif, as our magic is stolen from us whenever *Ka Atu*"—she spat the title—"takes a fancy to perform tricks for his people. Even now, though sa and ka returns to our lands, our minds, it returns slowly. Who here can sense the presence of prey, or of water, or of enemies, without feeling the strain? Who here can no longer feel the land about them at all?

"And though it returns, as I have said, who here believes it will return to its former strength? The magic in our land is like mead in a pitcher of gold, poured into a golden cup for the Dragon King. His thirst is never satisfied, and though the pitcher is refilled there is never as much as there had been—is there? Who here believes that some day the dragon kings will drink the world dry, and leave the pitcher empty?"

A dark storm gathered among the people, clouded faces and the distant thunder of angry words. Ismai bit his lip when he saw Mastersmith Hadid, whose own mother had perished in the burning of Aish Kalumm, stroking his chin thoughtfully.

Our dead are not yet buried, their ashes are not yet cooled, and the people stand here listening to her lies as if they were dying of thirst, and she has promised to bring the rain. Why are they listening to her lies?

"I believe—the *Mah'zula* believe—that the Dragon King, if left unchecked, will be the death of the Zeeranim. Look how our lands have already been spoiled, our people left impoverished by the greed of Atualon. And for what? So Ka Atu may keep the dragon from waking?" Ishtaset put her hands on her hips like a kitchen-mother scolding the younglings. "What proof do we have that this song of Atualon benefits any land but Atualon? Perhaps this song drains the dragon's magic, as it does ours, and perhaps some day the dragon's pitcher will be emptied..."

The world would rot from the inside, Ismai thought with a start. Like an egg with a dead chick inside. *We would all die.*

This is why they listen to her lies, Ruh'ayya whispered inside his mind. *She weaves them into a fabric of truth and dazzles them with the pretty colors.*

"...cannot let this happen. *Will* not let this happen. In the days of my grandmother's grandmother's grandmother, we Mah'zula saw what was happening to the lands, and to the people we love. People we vowed so long ago to protect. We saw how the people had begun building houses, then towns, then a city of stone, crouched on the banks of the Dibris like a toothless old woman hoping to catch fish. How the magic was leaving us, and the vash'ai, and how little our leaders were doing to prevent it. Instead they squabbled and schemed among themselves like outlanders, gathering wealth and power for themselves even as the people faded and died away, until you are as we see now. A remnant. A *remnant* of a remnant, shadows and sad reminders of your former glory."

"What have you done to stop it?" a woman shouted from the stands, a stout older Mother with gray in her hair and anger flashing in her eyes. "Where have the Mah'zula been?"

"A fair question." Ishtaset smiled. "Long ago it was decided that we would remain pure by remaining apart from the people, and keeping to the old ways, the path of *ehuani*. We have been watchers in the night, guarding your sleep. The riders in the morning, driving slavers back to their forsaken lands and filthy cities. We have been the sword at dusk, slaying the greater predators as they came to devour your flesh. We have been the song in your bones, reminding you of what you were, what you might become once again, if only you would wake to the sun of Akari. And we would have remained so, perhaps indefinitely, had it not been for this woman."

There was a commotion at the back of the arena and a fist of Mah'zula emerged from the crowd, dragging a bound and gagged woman between them.

Ismai shivered as his blood ran cold.

Sareta Ja'Akari Akibra.

"The Zeeranim have withstood the Dragon Kings, raiders and slavers who would steal your children. You have survived droughts and famines, plagues and predators, but you would not have survived this. An enemy in your midst, one whom you clasped to your breast and called sister. *Friend*."

The Mah'zula reached Ishtaset and hauled Sareta upright. The golden warrior spat into her face. "First Warrior. False Warrior, I name you. *Kha'Akari.*"

"Kha'Akari," the Mah'zula echoed, and it seemed to Ismai as if the sands trembled with their fury.

"Many of you would look upon me, upon my riders, and call us murderers. Is this not so?" An ugly murmur came from the stands. "Yet I have, *we* have not done anything here that Akari himself would not have done. The Zeera is no place for the weak, and it never has been. The people are only as strong as the weakest among us. In the days to come, my brothers and sisters, we will need to be *strong*.

"Dark winds born of foul magics sweep down upon us from atulfah-clouded Atukos. Bloody winds born of a longing for war sweep down upon us from the shining walls of the Forbidden City. Scorching winds boil down upon us from the cursed peaks of Jehannim and the Seared Lands beyond. Do any of you think the Zeeranim will stand a chance of survival in the times to come, if we wield our shamsi with shaking hands? If we hide in cities of stone, like the outlanders, and if we allow our hearts to grow soft and our blood thin, the Zeeranim will be no more.

"My sisters and I have taken vows—as did our mothers in the long ago—to do whatever it takes to protect the people. Whatever it takes, no matter how bitter the task, no matter how it stains our own hearts and souls. We will kill for you, my people. We will die for you. It is a woman's duty to protect her people, no more and no less, and we have suffered this burden alone, unseen and unsung and alone in the long, cold night. For honor. For love.

"You spit at our heels and call us murderers. This burden, too, we shall bear for you, and yet this… woman… this woman you have embraced as a sister, loved as a mother, upon whose brow you have set a crown of high honor, and into whose hands you have pressed the sacred shamsi, this woman alone among us has committed murder most foul. In shadow and secrecy she has whispered with the sworn enemies of the people. She has conspired against you and committed crimes without count. Not least among them is conspiracy to murder your First Mother and her family, in a wicked attempt to seize power by ending the line of Zula Din."

The world around Ismai roared with silence, as if he had been swept into the eye of a storm. Blood thundered in his ears. It blinded him and sucked the breath from his lungs, and the world twisted and lurched. He staggered and would have fallen, but a pair of Mah'zula warriors grasped his arms and held him upright. Ishtaset's words rang.

"Do you deny these charges, Sareta of the Zeeranim?" The Mah'zula pushed Sareta to her knees, but she had not been First Warrior these many years because her veins ran with water.

"*Kha'ehua*," she spat at Ishtaset's feet. "I deny them. I deny you."

"Very well," Ishtaset said, and a hard smile played at the corners of her mouth. "In that case, I invoke *Raqs eh Shamsi*. Pray to Akari that he might have mercy upon you—because I will not."

Raqs eh Shamsi... the Dance of Swords. Ismai felt sick to his stomach. He looked down at the gray-haired woman, tall and proud even as she swayed upon her knees before him, and his heart was torn. If Ishtaset spoke true...

"So be it," Sareta whispered. Her face had gone pale, exposing the shadows of bruises on one cheekbone and under her eye, but her gaze was as strong and proud as a First Warrior's must be. "I am ready."

FORTY-FIVE

The Dance of Swords was always performed at midsun, the better for Akari to see. It was not a dance of naked young men, sweating and laughing before the admiring eyes of potential lovers, nor yet a harvest-dance, meant to give thanks to the shades of the animals and plants that sustained the people's lives. It was a dance of justice, of blades bared under the sun, and that meant death.

The lower seats of the Madraj were nearly full. It was this sea of faces, more than the lack of food and drink, or his seat upon the high dais, that made Ismai dizzy. As the son of Nurati and brother to his murdered siblings, he had fasted since the previous day, and took the seat of the accuser. The arena itself was filled edge to edge with Mah'zula and Ja'Akari, naked and painted and grim so that they resembled the vash'ai more closely than he could remember. Cats and warriors stood ready, row upon row of them, swords and claws gleaming in the bright sunlight, breathless-still as statues.

To the east of them, and the west, stood the two women who sought through blood to prove the worth of their words. Ishtaset and Sareta were naked and painted as the rest of them, but they were blindfolded, as well, and their arms bound behind their backs.

From the tunnels and caverns beneath the Madraj came a low *thud-thud-tharrrrrum, thud-thud-tharrrrrum*, as drums in the deep called the swords to dance. As one the Ja'Akari and their sister Mah'zula raised their arms and lowered them again, raised and lowered. Shamsi flashed in the harsh light as swords cut through the air, just as the gaze of Akari would cut to the truth of the matter. Swords were caught, thrown, twirled around the women's heads in a dance so ancient, so sacred, that no man was allowed to watch it. Raqs eh Shamsi…

Ismai had never seen anything so beautiful.

Nor had he ever wished for anything so much as he wished, in that moment, to close his eyes and shut it out. Yet as Sareta and Ishtaset stumbled forward, driven by the drums into the shining, whirling maelstrom, Ismai straightened his spine and hardened his heart. He sat alone upon the dais because his family had been murdered. He would not turn away from his duty to them.

Not alone, Kithren, Ruh'ayya whispered in his heart. *Never alone.*

Ismai let the tears fall from his eyes. *Thank you, my friend.*

Ishtaset reached the dancing blades. She cocked her head as if listening, and without hesitation strode into the storm of death. Neither did the women pause in their dance, not to slow or deflect the course of a single blade. They allowed the Rajjha to glide between them, graceful and sure. Ismai held his breath as a shamsi whirled just in front of her face, and another just behind her head as she passed.

She was not so fortunate the third time. A sword sang through the air and licked her skin as a hungry child might lick honey from a platter, carving a deep gash into her flesh from one shoulder and across her back. The blade stuck point-first deep into the sand, and the Ja'Akari who had wielded it sank to her knees, head bowed. For her, the dance was over.

For Ishtaset, it had only begun.

She twisted and ducked, graceful as a young girl, and even from such a distance Ismai could see a wide and delighted grin upon her face. The hilt of a sword hit the point of her jaw with an audible *crack*, and Ishtaset laughed aloud. She shook her head as if to clear it, then whirled around light and careless as a sand-dae, to roll beneath a flurry of sharpened steel before leaping to her feet again.

"Yeh Atu," Ismai breathed. What sort of woman, faced with Raqs eh Shamsi, would dance with the swords, in truth? *She is mad*, he decided.

Mad, and beautiful.

A gasp from the crowd drew his eyes to the other side of the arena. Just as Ishtaset had done, Sareta was joining the dance.

Her face showed no more fear than that of the Mah'zula, her feet were no less sure, her movements no less swift or graceful, but her story, written in blood upon the sand, looked to have a very different ending.

Even as Ishtaset reached the very center of the arena, where a ring of unarmed warriors stood ready to embrace her and kiss her cheeks, Sareta wove and twisted, ducked and came up again—directly into the path of a thrown sword. It struck high and hard, deep into the flesh just below her collarbone so that it stuck fast. A flap of skin hung down and a smell like a butcher's tent hit Ismai as blood poured down her front. The Mah'zula whose blade had struck sank to her knees, smiling.

Sareta grunted, but did not go down. Her movements became slow and clumsy, less a dance of life than a lumbering, staggering fall toward death as another blade, and another, tasted her blood and found her unworthy. Ismai swallowed hard as a shamsi plowed into the First Warrior's gut. She bellowed in agony through gritted teeth, but staggered on. The sword fell from her belly, leaving a hideous wound from which loops of pale intestine slipped like pale snakes, and someone in the lower seats screamed.

Ismai could only stare. He felt numb, and strange, as if he might float free of his body and up, up into the sky.

Sareta had managed to stagger perhaps two-thirds of the way across the arena when the final sword slicked across her upper thigh. Blood spurted thick and bright across the faces of Ja'Akari and Mah'zula alike, naming her Kha'Akari before the eyes of the people.

Liar. Traitor.

Murderer.

Sareta sank to her knees and then toppled to one side, kicking weakly as her life poured forth and pooled beneath her. The women nearest Ishtaset removed her blindfold and the bindings from her arms, and one of them pressed a shamsi into her hand. No longer smiling, she strode to where her enemy lay dying, leaving a trail of bloody footprints in the sand behind her. When she reached Sareta's side, Ishtaset looked up, up to the high dais, and met Ismai's horrified stare.

"Akari has spoken," she said, and though she did not shout, her words were as clear as if not a hand's space lay between them. "It is done."

She raised the sword high, and brought it down in a single, clean cut. Sareta's head rolled face-down into the sand, and Ishtaset bent to cut off one long, bloodied braid as Mah'zula and Ja'Akari alike threw their heads back and roared.

Ishtaset held the shamsi off to one side, without looking at it, and it was taken from her. She did not watch as the head of the former First Warrior was placed upon her chest, and the body carried away. She did not respond when the lower stands burst into a cacophony of shouts, screams, and ululations, as the Zeeranim watched the world they had known come to an abrupt and bloody end.

Holding out her arms to either side she allowed the victor's mantle to be draped across her shoulders. The thin linen stuck to her wounds, soaking up blood, and light played along its beaded edges. Two of the older Ja'Akari emerged from the tunnel bearing the First Warrior's headdress between them, and they raised it as if they would crown Ishtaset.

They would make her First Warrior, Ismai thought as he watched the rapt faces that surrounded them. *She burned the City of Mothers to ash, and still the people would crown her queen as the outlanders do, did she but wish it.*

Ishtaset frowned and waved the headdress away.

She does not wish to be First Warrior, after all, any more than she aspires to live in a city and sit upon a golden throne like the Dragon King of Atualon, he realized then. *What does she want, I wonder?* As if drawn by his thoughts, Ishtaset's face tilted up just so, and her eyes met his again. Her face softened for a moment, as if she were smiling on the inside.

Oh, Ismai thought. *Oh, fuck.*

Ishtaset stalked across the bloody sand like a vash'ai queen sure of her prey. She mounted the stairs, climbing to the dais, and

Ismai sensed every eye upon them when she stopped at the foot of his high chair and stood before him, hands on her hips, mantle billowing out behind her, stained with old blood and new. There was blood in her hair, he noticed. Blood streaked the paint across her face, and a promise of blood swam deep in her eyes, like the shadow of a greater predator more sensed than seen.

She kissed the long gray braid and handed it to him. What could he do but accept, and bow his head? Akari had spoken. It was over. Ismai accepted the token and pressed his lips to it, masking his dismay at the smell of death. He had spent half the night rehearsing the words, and they flowed from his lips as easily as wine.

"Well done, O warrior, and well met. Justice has been served, and the truth laid bare for all to see. What boon do you seek, O warrior, for your service? For your blood has blessed us in the eyes of Akari, and you shall have your reward." He had been instructed to give the victor whatever she might desire, from what little had been salvaged from the ruins of Aish Kalumm—precious stones, hides, swords. Horses, of course, or salt.

Ishtaset's grin was as wide and bright as the midsun sky. She stepped closer—too close—set one bare foot upon the bottom rung of the witness chair, and hauled herself up so that her face was even with his. Ismai held his breath and would have pulled back, but she laughed again, buried both hands in his hair, and kissed him so hard Ismai could feel her teeth mashing against his lips.

Releasing him at last, she stared at his face with a hunger that had nothing to do with Ismai, and everything to do with the blood that ran in his veins and smeared his mouth.

"I choose you," she answered, in a voice meant to carry. "Ismai son of Nurati, last of the line of Zula Din, I claim you as my prize."

"No," he whispered, "No. I do not want this."

Ishtaset looked deep into his eyes, and in her gaze Ismai could see the flames of Aish Kalumm.

"Sweet boy," she told him. "What you want—what I want— these things do not matter. We are but pawns in a greater game." And she kissed him again, to thunderous applause.

FORTY-SIX

Rage and terror coiled in her gut as Hannei waited her turn to die.

Screams and sand rained down upon her bowed head with every *thud, thud thud* of the heavy drums, every attack by the pit beasts against the slaves sent out to die, all for the entertainment of people who had not—yet—fallen so low. The crowd roared hungrily as a blacksmith's furnace each time the pit slaves' door opened and disgorged yet another victim into the arena. They roared again with each death, stoking the fire inside her till Hannei felt it might wake like a dragon and sear the world to ash.

Her hair had been bleached and stiffened with lye, dyed with saffron and henna and woad so that it stood up from her head in a riot of color like a lionsnake's plumes. Her ears and nose had been pierced and hung with gold. Gold dust had been pinched into her cheeks and lips and nipples. Dressed only in a loincloth of garish red and yellow, she was as garnished and tasty a dish as ever the hearth mothers might set out before a hungry crowd.

Hannei cut her eyes to the side, but at the sight of Noura—dressed as she was dressed, in vile imitation of Ja'Akari—she closed them again. The other warrior's tears were no shame, she supposed, though her own had been baked to salt in the heat of her lover's pyre.

The blood-maddened crowd reached its frenzied climax, shrieking and chanting and jeering as yet another life ground to an inglorious halt, and the pit slaves' heads turned to the small arched door to bear witness as the most recent of their number was dragged from the arena. This last one had been Mamouk, a bright-eyed youth from a northern land, with skin dark as good coffee and hair like a sunset. Now he was so much offal, red-black meat and white bone, his lower jaw torn so that it flopped against his chest as they dragged his sad corpse away. A fine meal for the sea serpents, payment for safe passage of some merchant's ship.

Perhaps he was meant to sustain what few of them remained that evening. Hannei had long suspected that the pit slaves' meat came from the very bodies into which it was fed. No mind. It was sweeter than goat, and more tender.

A shadow moved in the corner and laughed with the sound of teeth on old bones.

If you cannot save the living, the voice of old Theotara said, *soothe the dying. Send their spirits off with a drink, a song, and fragrant smoke… and never forget to loot the bodies.*

Or eat them, Hannei thought.

For a full two-moon now, maybe more, Hannei had been plagued by visits from those who should have long since traveled down the Lonely Road. Ani would have scolded her to pull in sa and ka, lest the shadows feed upon her spirit. Dreamshifter would have burned her with those golden eyes and demanded to know how she had drawn the attention of the dead, but neither of those women was near, to chastise or to save her. Even the voice of a ghul was welcome when it spoke of home. So Hannei let sa and ka roil around her like blood in hungry waters, and quietly longed for a glimpse of her lover.

Tammas would touch me, though he has no hands. He would hear me speak, though I have no tongue. He is not long dead, there is hope…

Where there is life, there is hope, the shade of Theotara hissed. *But there is no life here. There is no hope for you,* ehuani.

Ehuani.

Entanye stood with the other rehazot by the big wooden door, arms folded across her chest, face utterly expressionless. The pit mistresses and masters waited, Hannei knew, for the crowd to quiet and digest their last meal, then to grow restless again. The noise would grow again, like an insatiable monstrous child demanding the bloody teat. More lives would be tossed out to assuage that hunger. It was an art form, Entanye had told them, laughing. She was not laughing now, however. Rehaza Entanye frowned as she stared at Hannei, eyes darting from her to the corner and back again.

She sees them, Hannei realized, chillflesh raising along her arms and the back of her neck. *She sees the shadows.*

Though the crowd was still somnolent, mumbling and growling, Entanye jerked her chin at the two men who stood ready, gloved hands on the thick ropes. They heaved and pulled, jaws set and muscles bulging as the great wooden doors began to move. Sated or not, the crowd roared to life at the prospect of new death.

"That one," Rehaza Entanye said, voice bored and hand waving languidly toward Noura. "And that one. Let us see how well the Zeera fares against the Sear." Hannei stared at the pitmistress, but the woman turned her head away, eyes slipping past like a serpent through cold waters. The once-warrior realized two things, in quick succession.

The pitmistress meant her to die.

At that, Hannei felt nothing.

Noura straightened her back and gave the outsiders a last haughty glance. She was a queen among swine, that one, despite the collar and gold and rouge, a vash'ai among goats, and they shied back as she passed. Hannei followed, and the shadows came after, whispering excitedly of the feast to come.

Akari soared high, indifferent to his daughters as they stepped out to meet their doom. Slavers' gold flashed upon their faces, their bodies had been painted and adorned for the amusement of lesser peoples, but still they were daughters of the Sun Dragon, tall and proud beneath his blind eye. Noura turned to Hannei and smiled so wide and bright and beautiful that the shadows fell back.

"Sister," she said. "Come… it is a good day to die."

Just like that, the shadows fell away from Hannei. She returned the smile, and took her new sword sister's hand.

A good day to die, she agreed. *None better.*

Swords had been left for them, outlander-forged shamsi thrust into the sand. They took these, tested the weight and length of them. The swords were passable, if ugly. Shoulder-to-shoulder the warriors faced the far corner of the arena, waiting to see what form their deaths might take.

The crowd hushed as the red doors drew wide.

A small figure stepped out onto the sand.

Hannei blinked as Noura grunted and jostled her shoulder. *What...?*

It was a small girl, no older than the dreamshifter's little apprentice Daru. Her skin was dark as night, and glittered all over as if she had been rolled in gemstones. She drew near and they could see that her eyes were pale yellow, slit like a cat's. Those eyes were wide with terror. She shook with it, she stank of it, even as she walked across the sand to meet them. She was naked, rouged and gilded even as they were, and her hands were empty.

Hannei turned her head and met Noura's shocked gaze. *Are we to kill an unarmed child, then?*

No, Noura mouthed, shaking her head.

No, Hannei agreed. There was no beauty in this.

They held out their shamsi at arm's length, ready to drop the blades into the sand and die at the hands of the pitmistresses rather than murder a child...

Then the child began to dance.

Her expression changed. She threw her arms wide, head jerking back so that her throat was exposed and the cloud of hair about her head bobbed. Small feet beat rhythmically upon the pounded sand, *rum-bum-ba-bum*, as her body undulated. She whirled, eyes fierce, thin arms and legs whipping around her like weapons. She was a tiny warrior defying their swords, and it was glorious.

Sword still held at arm's length, Hannei gaped first at the child and then at her sword sister. *What?* she mouthed. How were they to fight this, this dancing child? Noura shrugged, round-eyed as their sword arms dropped to their sides.

"A warrior does not murder children..." she began.

Then the shadows woke.

They rose around the little girl's feet, faint at first as if they were dust kicked up in the wake of her frenzied dance. Shadows twined about her ankles, legs, and hips like snakes, thickening to opacity, till the child's form could scarce be seen in their midst. The arena darkened, and shadows drew like a black touar across the face of Akari Sun Dragon.

The Ja'Akari crouched, swords readied. Hannei, who moments before had cared so little whether she lived or died or was thrown down the throat of a dragon, felt the blood pounding in her ears in time to the child's movements.

What is this? her mind cried. *What is this?* Though she had been sword sister to a dreamshifter's daughter, Hannei had never much liked magic. Belatedly, she drew in sa and ka, lest the roiling clutch of shadows strip the soul from her body and leave her deathless.

The dancing girl faced them, body twisting this way and that, yellow eyes and star-studded skin gleaming within the patch of night sky she had woven about her body. Hands no bigger than a bird's claws clasped before the thin chest. She raised them to point…

…and the shadows struck.

A thick maelstrom formed about the child's body, faster and thicker, till a swaying column of black rose from the arena and their opponent was entirely obscured. Hannei's neck prickled as she looked up, up… There were voices in that shadow storm, voices as soft and hateful as the whispers that fell from her own tongueless mouth in the dead of night as she wept of vengeance and loss. The voices tore at her, at the edges of her so recently raw and unprotected, as the column grew in weight and depth. It took on the form of a massive black hooded viper with a belly full of dancing malice. Great yellow eyes, bright as stars, turned toward them as the thing *hisssssss*ed and readied to strike.

"*Ai yeh*," Noura breathed, and her voice shook. "It is a good day to die. I am sorry, Sister."

I am sorry, child, the night snake echoed, laughing with Sareta's voice. *Thus perishes the line of Zula Din.* Then it struck.

Shocked or no, the Ja'Akari were no easy meat. They whirled

367

back-to-back, facing toward and then away from each other, even as the passing of shadows kicked dust up into their faces. Sunblades rose and fell and rose again. As her blade struck the thing's flesh, though it was insubstantial, it seemed to pull against Hannei's palm as if she had tried to cut into a swift-moving river. The thing shrieked, a whisper of sound half-heard and half-imagined, and it drew back from their dull blades, rearing high and swaying stark against the sunlight.

Best to cut the taint out now, it hissed, still mocking Hannei with the voice of the First Warrior who had killed her. *Cut it out. Bones in the sand.* It prepared to strike again.

Cut it out, Hannei thought, and the sky cleared as Akari Sun Dragon smiled his approval. *Of course.* She hissed between her teeth to catch Noura's attention, gestured with a sweep of her empty palm and a flash of sunlight upon her soulless blade.

That way. Noura nodded, eyes flashing, and took off running toward the crowd. The shadow snake narrowed its eyes, gave a long hiss, and struck. Its snout collided with the front row of seats, raising a chorus of bloody screams from the audience as the monster shook its head and sought its prey. *Deer leaps away* became *dancing sand-dae*, and Noura Ja'Akari spun in a cloud of sand.

Hannei scarce spared the Zeerani warrior a second glance. She ran, sword tucked tight to her hips, chin tucked against her chest as she prayed to the uncaring sky. She prayed for her life, not because it was worth living, but because the voice of Sareta had reminded her of her purpose.

Let me live, she prayed to Akari Sun Dragon, to the bloodied sand beneath her pounding feet, to the uncaring lapis sky. *Let me live, and I will bring your wrath upon them. Let me live, and I will shed such blood that even you might be satisfied.*

Let me live.

Even as the shadow snake caught its prey's scent and struck out at Noura, Hannei reached the far end of the arena, and the dancing child. This close, she could see through the dark veil to the small girl, sweating and weeping with the effort it took to dance her magic. Thin arms trembled, thin legs shook. She was younger than Hannei had thought, a child of eight perhaps, and her face was wet with tears. No doubt she had been taken from her family by slavers and lived a life of misery. No doubt she had vengeance of her own to wreak.

Hannei did not need to brace her heart. It was long gone to dust and ash, a cup of poison spilled upon the sand. She raised her blade high and brought it down in a sweeping motion, catching the child just above her neck and cleaving the small body nearly in two. The child fell to the ground without so much as a whimper, taking the false shamsi with her. Behind Hannei the shadow snake burst in a silent explosion, shadows fleeing in terror from this new truth.

The crowd was silent.

Akari take you all, Hannei thought, and sprayed spit at them. *To the hells with you.*

Noura jogged over to her. Her face was grim, eyes bleak as Hannei wrenched her sword from the child's hacked corpse. When she wiped the blood off on one thin leg, the warrior grimaced.

"Ja'Akari do not kill children," she said, voice low and hard. "There is no beauty in this."

No, Hannei agreed, as she slid the blade between Noura's ribs. *But I am Kha'Akari. The only beauty left to me is vengeance.* It was a clean death, a good death. It was, as Noura herself had admitted, a very good day to die.

Hannei picked up the sword of the Ja'Akari. She kissed it, and she kissed the blade newly blooded, and thrust them up toward Akari Sun Dragon. It was a promise, no less true for being silent.

The crowd went wild.

FORTY-SEVEN

His feet hurt.

His feet hurt, his back hurt—Leviathus was so tired his hair hurt. Life as a pirate, he was beginning to suspect, was not as glamorous in true life as it was in his books.

Perhaps nothing is, he mused. *Perhaps one who has experienced life mostly through books is doomed to be disappointed by the real thing.*

He sat crosslegged upon the deck of the empty ship, examining the roughened skin of his knuckles by the light of a small lantern. He winced at the little red crosshatch marks that made a bloody map there. Mahmouta had insisted that he train as a fighter, and so far that training consisted mostly of pounding a burlap-wrapped board until his skin was raw, then plunging both hands into salted, scalding water. It was too early to tell yet whether the technique would be successful in toughening the skin, but it had certainly inspired him to foul language.

Leviathus turned his hands over and winced again at the sight of his blistered palms. It was too much, he supposed, to hope they might be healed by morning.

"Five years," he grumbled. That was the time he had promised Mahmouta, in exchange for food, lodging, training, and a share of booty. So far the only booty he had realized was the sight of his fellow pirates' bare bottoms as they shat over the side of the ship. "Five years. Sixty two-moons. One hundred and twenty small-moons. Not that anyone is counting, mind you."

"Counting the moons does not help," a high, sweet voice chided. "Neither does picking at your blisters—they will just hurt worse tomorrow. Let it be. Blisters heal, and the moons roll across the sky, and it is better to just let things be as they will be."

He turned to see Totoua standing barefoot on the deck behind him, grinning and holding a pot of salve. "Hey, little man," Leviathus said to the boy. "Why are you not asleep in your mother's tents? You should not be on the ship at night. There are serpents, remember? If your mother catches you here, she will likely beat us both."

"My mother is no more likely to beat me than I am to eat a serpent," Totoua said, laughing. He handed Leviathus the pot, which smelled of cool mint. "I would rather face the serpents than your na'iyeh—but I think they have lost your scent. I have not seen them in some time. Maybe you do not need to sleep on the boats anymore? Maybe they got tired of chasing you? Anyway, it is a beautiful night, and I like sleeping on the ship." Grinning, he hopped up to sit on the railing.

Leviathus rubbed the salve into his blistered palms, shaking his head. He could scarce keep up with the child's words as they skipped like pebbles across the surface of his thoughts.

"I was told that once the na'iyeh have a scent, they do not stop hunting until they catch someone or unless they are killed. I do not know where they might have gone, but as they have not yet managed to catch me, and as I am fairly certain that I have not managed to accidentally kill them, I will sleep on the ship as often as I can. You are right though, my friend—it is a beautiful night."

The sands were singing, and the serpents as well, far enough away that it was a lovely thing to listen to. Moonslight danced upon the Dibris. It was a good night not to have been beheaded, or eaten, or dissolved and turned into a nightmare plant. A very good night to be free. Leviathus took a deep breath of the clean night air, and closed his eyes so that he might better listen to the songs of the night.

Free.

A thump sounded from below, a deep shuddering sound like someone striking a wooden drum with a hammer. *Thud. Thud-thump.* Leviathus leaped to his feet, staggering as the ship rocked violently.

"Serpents!" Totoua shouted. He clung to the ship's railing with

371

his arms and legs, eyes rolling white in terror. "'Ware serpents!" The ship lurched and the boy screamed, arms flailing as he lost his grip and slid over the side. Leviathus only just managed to catch the back of the boy's trousers with one torn hand as he fell.

Please, Divines, no, he begged, more fervently than he had ever asked for himself. *Not the boy, not the boy, please. Take me, take me, only leave the boy.*

Totoua, skinny as a brown eel, began to slip out of his trousers. Leviathus flailed with his other hand and was able to get a handful of hair. Cussing, straining, and praying, he hauled the lad to safety. They collapsed together upon the wooden deck.

The ship shook one final time, timbers squealing in protest. His lantern toppled over, sputtered, and went out. Then the world went still, as if the lonely shepherd girl in the old stories, who played the song of life, paused to draw a breath. Totoua curled into a tiny, shivering ball. Leviathus shielded the boy's body with his own, turning his face so that he could see the constellation Bohica, she who guided soldiers safely home.

Divines, help us, he prayed. *Help him.*

A shadow deeper than prayer, darker than the night, spread across the sky like ink, blocking all light and hope of salvation as an enormous sleek head rose dripping from the river. Two eyes, bigger than his head, pale as moons, peered down at Leviathus as he lay curled around the terrified child.

The giant head wove back and forth, back and forth, glistening in the light of the moons and stars. The serpent opened its maw and a tongue flicked out, flicking through the air like a whip as it tasted the air. Scaled lips pulled back, revealing row upon row of jagged white teeth. It blinked again. Air hissed through its teeth and the beast's throat swelled as it sucked in a long, slow breath. Leviathus flattened himself upon the ship's deck, his only wish that the thing would eat him and leave the boy.

Let him be, he prayed. *Let him live.*

The serpent closed its mouth, closed its moons-pale eyes, and two enormous nostrils on top of its head quivered as the thing let its breath out in a watery canticle so pure, so weirdly beautiful that tears pricked Leviathus's eyes, even as he braced for death.

Moments later the song ended, and the eyes opened once more to stare at Leviathus. The serpent's mouth gaped open in an enormous, deadly grin.

Well, little two-legs, it greeted in a familiar voice. *I see you have finally figured out who you are.*

Leviathus rolled away from the boy and stood, staring at the serpent, shocked to the marrow of his bones.

What? he thought. *What? Who? What?*

Laughter half-heard, half-felt, rippled through the air.

I am Azhorus Ssurus az Lluriensos, First Scald, killer of men, poet to the deep, the black waters, the voice crooned. The night sky further receded as that great head loomed close, tongue whipping out, *sssst-sssst*. Azhorus Ssurus az Lluriensos nudged Leviathus with his snout, very gently so that he only staggered a little bit.

And you are mine.

FORTY-EIGHT

On the first day Ani rested. She ate and drank, fussed over Talieso as his leg healed and he set about cropping every blade of grass in their small oasis, and watched Akari chase his own anger across the sky.

On the second day she readied herself. She shook the sand out of Askander's tent, and discovered that he had secreted much of his gear and supplies into her bags before they parted. Cursing him, she sharpened her sword, and became friends with the bow Askander had left her. It was an old bow, one with which she was very familiar but had never shot.

Ani expected some awkwardness, since the bow was longer than she was used to using and had heavier draw weight. Whatever healing Inna'hael had performed upon her body, though, seemed to have given her arms a new strength. She drew, loosed, drew again as if she held a child's bow. She smiled at the ease of it, then scowled to think of how she had been manipulated.

Males, she told herself. *Such a pain in the arse.* Still, she could not deny that she would have need of these things. She had shelter and food, weapons and a sound horse. Perhaps it would be enough.

She spent the remainder of that day and most of her strength singing a circle of protection around the small island of dry grass and sour water. Step by slow step she paced, making painfully sure that not so much as a grain of sand might find its way between her footprints as she revealed her intentions to wind and sky and sand. She woke the felldae lord, and felt his song slither and coil through her bones. She called him to this place, but did not intend that he should feed upon her flesh, nor wear her bones.

On the third day, he came.

The song of Khoroush-Il-mannech remained with her from

the moment she raised him from the long dark, so Ani was not surprised when Talieso tossed his head, nostrils flaring, and screamed. She laid both hands on his neck, feeling his flesh shudder and flinch at the touch, and closed her eyes.

I am sorry, she told her oldest friend. *I am so sorry.* Then she did a forbidden thing. Ani sang his bones, his mind, his soul to somnolence. She might have argued that this was necessary, that it was a kindness, even, but such magic was forbidden for a purpose, and she felt stained with shame beneath the gaze of Akari as she drew back from the drowsing stallion.

So quickly the high are brought low, a laugh gargled in the back of her mind. *How easily seduced is the heart of a human.*

Stay back, she warned him, even as she walked to the very edge of the circle she had made. *I am no easy meat.*

Oh, but I have feasted upon you already, he mocked. *So tender your mind. So sweet your soul.*

Come to me, foul thing. Ani planted her feet in a stance that any of her younglings would have recognized, and heeded. *Show yourself.* Then the ground trembled at the coming of Khoroush-Il-mannech.

As you wish, little bonesinger. As you wish.

She felt him first as an itch beneath the soles of her feet as his vile laughter trembled beneath the earth. Just beyond her circle the earth roiled as the desert turned itself inside out in an effort to disgorge the felldae. A churning hill of sand rose before her eyes, sticks and bones and foul bits of carrion thrust into the sky triumphant as a warrior's fist. Khoroush Il-mannech shook himself free of the clean sand and let his foul stench roll forth. With his bulk between her and the sun, Ani stood in a dark shadow, and for a heartbeat her world came to an end.

For a heartbeat only.

Little meat-bag, Khoroush-Il-mannech crooned. A ripple ran along his length and he swayed back and forth. *I have come for you.*

"No," Ani replied aloud, ignoring his presence in her mind. "You have come *to* me, at my bidding. You are here by my will, and mine alone."

Half-taught youngling, he snarled. *Lost child of an insignificant tribe. I will suck the flesh from your bones and wear your ribs as a crown. I will—*

"You will shut the fuck up and do what I say, you ridiculous sack of goat turds," Ani replied, surprised at how calm she was able to keep her voice. "Or I will sing you all to pieces."

Khoroush-Il-mannech howled and reared up, blotting the sun from the sky. His cavernous mouth writhed open wide, wider still, a slick red well lined with teeth and chunks of rotting prey. The vast bulk of him rippled across the sand, closing the distance between them with breathtaking speed and surprising grace.

Suddenly he stopped short, held back by a magic old and simple as sand and stones. Had she wished, Ani might have reached out and touched the sticky, stinking daemon. She most decidedly did not, however, wish to do so.

I will have you, meat-sack! Khoroush-Il-mannech began to writhe and howl, beating against her barrier with his bulk, beating against her mind with his red wrath. *I will—*

"Enough," she said, bringing her two hands together in a symbol that would have seen her skinned, drowned, buried alive in any of the four corners of the world. Khoroush-Il-mannech wailed and flinched back at the sight of it and began rapidly burying himself in the sand.

Noooo…

Before he could disappear, Ani raised her two hands, still twined together, over her mouth… and blew.

A whistle, low and thin, breathed from her lips into her cupped hands. It became… more. Bigger, wilder, *more*. Ani had watched for more years than she cared to count as the people of the prides drew back in fear from Hafsa Azeina and her dream-crafted instruments. Had they known she could do this, using no more than her hands and her breath and the music in her bones, they would have stoned her and set her out to die, friend or no, youthmistress or no.

Dropping her hands to her sides, Ani took a deep breath and

began to sing. Khoroush-Il-mannech shrieked, twitching and dancing upon the sand, caught in the snare of her magic. His vast gray-green hide undulated with her music and even his cries of agony took on the flavor and cadence of her chant.

Eyes half closed, Ani sang in a language older than rivers, older than flowers, older than fish or beast or man. Zula Din herself might have recognized these words, might have thrown her head back and sung along.

> "Ghar-mah qarc-ap-teh domma'esh et ghar-mah batasoreh,
> Ghar-mah batasoreh domma'esh et ghar-mah kat-pat-a'a!
> Be-me-lath-u'on sa'otani-noa ah-Sajani'oa-e leka'a! Leko'a!
> Ghar-mah kat-pat-a'a domma'esh et ghar-mah bad-rae-a'a…"

The bonelord's shrieks reached a fever pitch as bones began to push their way to the surface of his hide. The skull of a giant tortoise emerged and rolled free, and the large clawed foot of some enormous beast—

Enough! he squealed. *No more! I yield! I yield!*

Ani hesitated. The act of destroying a bonelord might balance the debt her soul had incurred by raising him in the first place. She drew another breath… and remembered her need, a need so great she had traded everything she held dear for this hellish moment.

"I have a boon to ask of you," she told the weeping, twitching bulk that loomed before her. "A small enough favor, for one such as yourself."

Name it, the bonelord begged. *Anything*. But even as he pleaded, Ani could see that he was gathering himself to strike.

"Do not play games with me, daemon," she warned. "I have no love for you, and less patience. Do I so much as think you are going to try something, I will sing you to pieces here and now, and burn whatever bits are left without the whisper of a song."

As you wish, Dzirani. Khoroush-Il-mannech drew in upon himself and became still. *Name your price, and I will pay it.*

377

"Ehuani," she agreed. "I ask little enough. All I need from you are the bones of an Atualonian male, hale and whole."

That is... all? The mass of eyes bobbed in surprise.

"It is enough for now, bonelord."

He twitched. *And what do you offer in return?*

Ani smiled. "Your continued, miserable existence. Is that not enough for you?" She raised her hands before her as if she would bring them together again.

Enough, Bonesinger. Khoroush-Il-mannech burrowed further into the sand. *Enough. It will be as you say.*

"Good. You will deliver these bones to me by sunset—"

Impossible! The bonelord protested. *This is no easy—*

"By sunset," she continued. "Then you will return to Jehannim whence you came, and to the long dark. If you do not..." She brought her hands the rest of the way together. Twice she had done this, now. Once more would seal her fate.

It will be as you say, the bonelord replied in a petulant voice. *On your bones it be.* He writhed and twisted, burrowing into the sand until there was no sign that such a thing had ever been.

Ani sank to her knees upon the sand and let the tears flow freely. On this day she had done the unthinkable. She had turned her back upon Akari, upon the people, upon every promise she had ever made, for one thin chance.

There was no choice, she wanted to cry. *No other way.*

Yet she would not lie to herself, even now.

FORTY-NINE

Warm water sluiced down between her breasts, washing away the blood and sand of another day spent killing at her mistress's command. Salt stung a number of shallow cuts, the worst of which had been stitched and poulticed by her own physician.

I have my own physician, Hannei thought, *to stitch my body back together when it gets too damaged. Girls to wash this body, boys to please it should I so desire.* As she stepped out of the bath, the salted water pooled warm and fragrant around her feet, ruining the fur upon which she stood. It was khallas-fur, rare and precious, and would be thrown away after this. She wriggled her toes in it as a breeze rose from the river to dry her own hide, nearly as scarred now as that of Askander Ja'Sajani.

Thoughts of the First Warden and his lover made her smile. *What would Ani say, if she saw me like this?* she wondered. *These rooms—my rooms—are finer than those of the First Mother. What would she say if she knew every meal I am served here in Min Yaarif is as good as a feast in Aish Kalumm?* Her smile faded then. If the youthmistress could see Hannei now, if she knew what had become of her former charge…

She would kill me, and I would not raise a hand to stop her.

A terrified squeak from the young girl at the door announced the presence of Sharmutai, who owned them all. Sharmutai crossed the room, chuckling as Hannei pretended to ignore her presence.

"Fair afternoon, my prize," she purred. "I see that Talis has done a passable job of keeping you in one piece for me. And look—you did not let them hit your pretty face this time. Well done." She stopped before Hannei, cupped her face in both hands, and kissed her full on the mouth. Hannei stood stiff and unresponsive as the mistress's tongue invaded her mouth, as those hated hands caressed her flesh, torn and bathed and torn again for pleasure and profit.

"You are so beautiful," Sharmutai murmured against her mouth, "my wild one. So beautiful. Do you have any idea how much I have been offered for one hour in your presence? Women would give me their first-born daughters for a chance to invade this body of yours. Men would pay mountains of salt for a chance to lick your feet. And *Ovreh*." She laughed, hands still caressing Hannei's body. "Ovreh has offered me an asil mare for the opportunity to whip you one more time. He is the laughing-stock of Min Yaarif, for having sold you to me at such a low price."

Hannei stiffened, and the breath hissed between her teeth. *An asil mare, in the hands of that goat-fucker?*

Sharmutai laughed again, low and throaty, and bit Hannei's lip. "I could take you now, you know. I could have you any time I wish, but it is more fun to seduce you. One day, you will beg me for this…" her hands slid down Hannei's throat, to her breasts. "And this." Her hands slid lower. "You will beg me, and perhaps I will say 'yes.' Perhaps. Perhaps not. I would have you wet for me in any case, not dry like your beloved desert." She gave Hannei a pat between the legs, winked, and stepped away, reaching up to give her left nipple one last pinch.

"Your breasts are growing, had you realized?"

Hannei froze.

"I thought not." Sharmutai strode to a low table, picked up a linen towel, and tossed it to Hannei. "Surely, I told myself, surely she has been too busy working for me to notice the changes in her body. Those luscious breasts. That adorable little belly. Such pouty, red lips… you had not noticed? Had you noticed that your moons-blood has not flowed once since I bought you? No? No," she said, staring at Hannei's face intently. "No. You are a good and faithful pet. I will not punish you for this. You may thank me." She stepped out onto the balcony.

Hannei stood on the ruined and sopping fur, clutching the linen towel to her breasts. They *had* grown, she realized, and they had been sore, come to think of it, though the daily hurts her body suffered had caused her to miss it.

Tammas, she thought, and tears prickled in her eyes. *Tammas.*

"Did Ovreh do this? Because if that pig sold me tarnished goods, after all…" The slavemistress's voice tapered off, and Hannei shook her head. "No? No. Good, then, because if the spawn was his, I would not be offering you a choice in the matter." She sighed deeply. "I am a fool, my prize. A soppy, sentimental fool, too softhearted for my own good. Come, pet, sit. Speak with me a bit." She laughed at her own joke. "Better yet, just sit and listen to me. I know you love the sound of my voice nearly as much as I do."

Hannei wrapped herself in the linen and joined Sharmutai on the balcony. The women sat for a while in silence as slaves removed the basins and soaps and the wet fur. More slaves brought plates of meat and cheese, and water, and wine. Children played in the gardens below. Slave children, all of them, born to slave mothers and attended by slave aunts, in a beautiful garden grown of salt and blood and misery.

At long last, the mistress spoke. Her voice was all hard edges now, without a trace of sultry purr. This was the real Sharmutai, a woman who wanted more than the world had to offer, whose hungers could never be satisfied by meat or wine or soft, warm flesh.

"You are pregnant. You carry a child in your belly."

Hannei took a long draft of wine, and her hands shook so badly that it sloped down her front.

This will be the end of it all, she thought. *I will die today, with a belly full of child.*

"It happens, soon or late, to every slave girl who lives long enough. You had a lover, I suppose, out there in the sand?"

She nodded. *A lover, yes.*

"Does he live?"

Hannei closed her eyes, and the moons cast a shadow over his face. Opened them again, and met Sharmutai's gaze.

"I thought as much. What man, having tasted such a lovely dish, could but love you? And what man, loving you, would let you fall so low, while he yet lived?" She shook her head. "This makes it all the more difficult for me, you know. A lover, and of course you loved him back. I suspect that is the story that led to your... present circumstances.

"Lovely girl, I am going to give you the choice I never had. You may bear this child, if you wish."

Hannei's jaw dropped open. For a moment, the whole world stood still. Akari Sun Dragon paused in his flight overhead, Sajani Earth Dragon paused mid-dream, and not a soul in the whole world so much as breathed.

A child. His child.

"You may bear the child, if you so choose." Sharmutai nodded, but she did not smile. "This much I will give you. This much— and no more. The law of the slave is absolute. You may earn your freedom by earning back, in the pit, thrice what I have paid for you. If you earn the price of your freedom before this child is born, you are both free. If your price is earned back even one day after it is born, the child belongs to me... and I do not willingly give up what is mine. Not ever. And, my prize—no pit-slave with a belly full of child has ever earned her salt. Not once."

The world started turning again, cruel as it ever was.

"I was a slave once, did you know that? Of course you did not. Everyone who might remember is dead." Sharmutai held out her wine glass, and a trembling slave refilled it. "Most of them I killed myself. Oh, I was not a slave like you—I was never talented with the sword—but I had weapons, all the same, and I used them. By the divines, I did. It took a river of blood and a ship made of bones to carry me here, to my little palace by the river.

"You think your life is over. You think your dreams are dead, long gone to dust and ash and shadow. I tell you now, it does not have to be so. You may yet walk upon the skulls of your enemies, little one, just as I have. Just as I *will*. Your story is not over yet— and neither is mine."

Hannei met Sharmutai's eyes and was caught, trapped as in a dreamshifter's web.

She smiled.

"Yes," the slavemistress whispered. "You see it. I knew you would. There is a chance for you, a chance for both of us. It is a slim chance, but I was a slim girl, not yet ten years of age, when I was first sold down by the river. My first master took me there, in front of all those cheering, laughing men, then he sold me over and over... and over again." She drank. They both drank, washing away the ugly taste of truth.

"He is dead now. I hung his head from the walls of my first palace, until all the skin and flesh had rotted away, till nothing was left but a skull with no smell, then I smashed his bones to powder and had them mixed into my wine. It is good, is it not? Wine mixed with the bones of your enemies."

It is very good wine, Hannei thought. *Better than the mothers ever made. Better than usca, maybe.*

"Perhaps some day you will have your own vineyards, and slaves to make your own wine. On that day, we may raise our glasses together and toast the shades of our fallen." Sharmutai smiled. "That would be a good day, but if you want to get there, my pet— if you wish to walk a path cobbled with the skulls of your enemies and eat meat salted by their tears—you must make sacrifices.

"I have a dream, sweet one," she said, "a dream so close I can almost, *almost* reach out and touch it." She did reach out then, and stroked Hannei's shoulder. "The false king in Atualon has raised a fighting pit of his own. 'The Sulemnium' he calls it, an arena like your own Madraj, only ten times as big, with columns of gold and ivory, and silken pillows upon which the elites park their powdered asses as they watch your kind die. A world wonder, they say, as beautiful as that hulking fortress Atukos, but it is just another fighting pit, to those who spill their blood into the dirt. It is just another whorehouse, to those who are raped before a cheering crowd. One of my masters had a chamber pot made of gold. It still smelled of shit." She smiled at the memory. "I caved his skull in with it, one night, as he lay snoring in a puddle of my blood."

Hannei was almost glad for her missing tongue. What could she say to that?

"The false king and his false heir have begun holding tournaments, pet. Champions from every land are invited to fight to the death before the silk-clad arses of Atualon, and their patrons to sit at the feet of the Dragon King himself. Champions such as you may become, if you fight hard enough and stay as lucky as you have been. Patrons such as I, if I salt enough palms and grease the way with the blood of a few more rivals.

"Were I to sit at the foot of the Dragon King..."

The wineglass shattered in Sharmutai's hand, and the lesser slaves fled. Blood and wine dripped from the slavemistress's hand, to pool upon the floor.

"...were I to sit at the foot of the Dragon King," Sharmutai continued, "I would be so close to this thing I want that I might reach out and throttle it with my bare hands." Sharmutai's chest heaved, the air hissed between her clenched teeth, and her eyes had a hot, glazed look. Hannei knew that look well. It stared up at her from her washbasin every morning.

"Now, my pet, you know more of my desire than is entirely safe for you." Sharmutai glanced at the ruined wineglass, grimaced, and set it aside. A brave slave lad crept from the shadows, carrying soft linen cloths, and began to wrap her wounded hand. "You will be my champion, dear one, with or without a brat suckling at those lovely teats. So much easier for you—so much safer for you—without." She waved the lad away, withdrew a folded scrap of parchment from a pocket, and held it out.

Hannei took the packet and sniffed it. As she had expected, there was a strong smell of lemons and mint and dust... "stillborn tea" the Mothers called this. It was given to a woman whose child needed to be expelled.

"I am a foolish woman, with a heart of sand," Sharmutai whispered. "I could force you to drink this, as I was forced, but I will not. The choice is yours, such as it is, as the choice was never mine." Her laugh was brittle, edged with blood and wine. "I have given you a choice, and now I will give you some words of wisdom. You should heed them, because I own you and can have you killed for no reason at all.

"Lose the child, my little two-blade killer. Lose the child, win your freedom. There can always be another lover, another child. There may never be another chance for you to get what we both want."

Vengeance, Hannei thought, clutching the deadly packet in her fist. Sharmutai held out a hand, and took another goblet of wine from the slave lad. She held it out to Hannei, and their fingers twined about the thick glass stem.

"Vengeance," she said as Hannei drank deep of the sweet wine, and the sun cast a shadow over her face.

Hannei stood upon the balcony long after the slavemistress had left, staring upon the gardens and fountains, and the miserable laughing slaves. Akari Sun Dragon disappeared behind the Jehannim, and the world grew cold.

At long last, she picked up the goblet that lay waiting at her elbow, and dumped the packet of herbs into the pale wine. Some of the herbs sank to the bottom, while others floated on top.

Had I a dreamshifter, she thought, *I could ask her to see my future in these patterns. Had I a Mother, I might ask her for advice.* She had neither of those things, however, and had to choose her own way. She lifted the goblet.

I am sorry, she told the child of Tammas, as it slept deep beneath her dead heart. *I have been given a choice, but it is no choice at all, not for me.*

Hannei poured the wine out onto the cold stones.

F I F T Y

For so long Ismai had been invisible, the awkward younger brother of Tammas, underfoot bratling to an embarrassment of sisters, favored son of Umm Nurati.

He had been born too early, so early that the midwives had at first despaired for his life, and later that he would ever grow into so much as the shadow of his handsome brother. How he had craned his neck to see those members of his family as they stood on high, and longed with all his heart to be seen as they were seen. To have his voice heard, and his deeds matter.

How foolish I was, he thought now, his eyes wet. *It would have been better if I had been born three moons early instead of two, and not survived at all.*

You are foolish to think so, Ruh'ayya scolded. She remained hidden away from the people, but never from his mind.

You are foolish to think I am foolish, he responded irritably, and allowed himself a small smile. Ruh'ayya alone, of all his friends, had not abandoned him to his fate.

Yet, she said.

Yet, he agreed.

Ismai's smile faded as Ishtaset's chestnut mare powered up a steep dune, its powerful hindquarters bunching and thrusting so that he was thrown against the woman's back. Ishtaset was a beautiful woman, but he wanted no part of this, no part of her, and the feel of her hot skin against his belly made him feel like sicking up the breakfast they had stuffed down his throat before dawn.

There will be a lot more physical contact than this, before the day is done, he knew. They made it to the top of the dune, and Ismai leaned back as far as he was able.

"I hope you are not thinking of running away again," Ishtaset said, barely turning her head. "It would not go well for your mastersmith, were you to attempt it. And wipe those tears from your face. I will not have my husband standing before all my sisters looking like a sullen child."

With one corner of his touar Ismai dashed the tears from his cheek, and his face scrunched into a scowl. "Sand in my eyes." He bit the words off short, angered, near tears again by the petulant sound of his own voice.

I am not a child.

You are no cub, Ruh'ayya agreed, and the tender concern in her voice was almost his undoing. *You are stronger than they know. Stronger than* you *know, even.*

Like Daru, he thought, struck with a longing to see the boy. *I wonder how he is faring, far away in the golden city? Better than me, for sure. He is probably chin-deep in books and scrolls and magic, and I am about to marry the First Arsehole of the Arsehole Mah'zula.*

Ishtaset had announced her intention to claim exclusive rights to his body and his seed. *Azuage*, she called it, an "ancient and blessed covenant between woman and man." Ismai knew another word for it. He was being given over to slavery no less than Hannei had been. Then, he had thought he was showing Hannei mercy. Now he wondered whether it would have been kinder to let her die.

The chestnut mare crested the dune and flew down the other side. All around him Ismai could hear the whoops and wild ululations of Mah'zula and Ja'Akari, and others besides as they plunged deeper into the heart of the Zeera. Screaming like the wind across the sands, beautiful beneath the eyes of Akari, uncontained, unhindered, free. His fondest dreams, he realized, had come true.

All it had cost him was… everything.

They came at last to a midsize oasis which in days long past, Ishtaset explained, had been a large oasis and a favorite gathering spot of the prides. The Madraj, she had determined, should be used only rarely for high feast days. The people had grown too fond of stone walls and false comforts. For lesser ceremonies such as the unwilling sacrifice of a lowly boy to the Rajjha of Arseholes, the oasis would suffice.

As soon as the mare halted, he pushed away from his captor. Ishtaset dismounted more gracefully and turned to smile at him, and Ismai was overwhelmed by the urge to grab that pretty throat in both hands and squeeze the very life from her eyes. He clenched his fists and glared for all he was worth.

"Better than tears," she purred, patting his cheek. "I will make a man of you yet, young Ismai."

"Fuck you," he growled, and he spat at her feet.

She laughed at him, of course. Ismai might not be invisible these days, but he was still insignificant. Ishtaset led him to the edge of the water, a wide and mirror-still pool thick with reeds and ringed by date palms heavy with fruit. At the edge of the water stood a great pyre of fresh-cut palm logs, built some days earlier by riders and warriors and wardens.

My funeral pyre, Ismai thought, and almost he wished it was true.

The Mah'zula joined them, and Ja'Akari, some of whom had chopped their braids and stiffened their hair with lye in the manner of the wild riders. After these came no few of the mistresses and masters of craft, including Mastersmith Hadid, whose life was hostage to Ismai's good behavior. Jasin was there, and Ghabril, and Daoud. None of them would meet his eyes, and Ismai curled his lip in contempt.

The ashes of the elders still sting our eyes, and yet here come the Zeeranim, willing as goats led to slaughter. He looked away, unwilling to gaze upon the shame of his people even as they witnessed his. *We thought ourselves a free people.*

The snake woman, Hassetha, swayed across the sands to join them. Her eyes were yellowed from long use of poisons and potions, she was thin-lipped and slender as the vipers she kept as pets.

She even moves like a snake, Ismai thought. He met that cold unblinking stare, though it raised chillflesh along his spine and turned his bowels to water every time. *Never show an enemy that you are afraid*, his mother had taught him. *The greater your fear, the harder you must appear.* Ismai turned his face to wood, his heart to stone.

Hassetha flicked her tongue at him.

"He reeks of fear," she said.

"He is a boy." Ishtaset reached to ruffle Ismai's hair, and laughed when he pulled away. "But he is my boy, now."

"Are you certain?" That unblinking gaze weighed Ismai and found him wanting. "His blood is as water. Too long have we been away. The hearts of the people have grown pale and weak."

"His blood is true," Ishtaset insisted. "You have tasted his salt. Is this one not of the line of Ishmalak, for whom he is named? What says your god?"

"The blood is true." Hassetha flicked her tongue at Ismai again. "He is of the line of Ishmalak, but even that line has grown... less." She turned away. "Thus speaks Thoth, son of Eth and Illindra."

"The line of Ishmalak has grown weak, but we will make it strong again." Ishtaset smiled at Ismai, though he knew she did not see him. "Thus speaks Ishtaset, last of the line of Iftallen. We will join that which was sundered—we will mix the blood of Iftallen with that of Ishmalak, son of Devranae, daughter of Zula Din, and in so doing we will mend what was broken in the long ago." As she spoke a crowd gathered and stood rapt. Akari Sun Dragon glared through the red dust, bathing their world in fire and blood.

Ishtaset continued, raising her voice for all to hear. "With this marriage, and through our children, the destruction brought upon the people by Davvus and Devranae will be healed, and the people will be restored to their rightful power and glory. Once more will we raise our people up, that they may find favor in the eyes of the Four. Once more will the skies tremble with the thunder of our warriors' hearts. Once more will the Zeera sing with the voices of our priestesses and priests. The Dragon King is not the only one in this world who can wield magic. The Daemon King is not the only one in this world who can raise an army."

"*Ehuani,*" Hassetha hissed, thin lips stretched wide in a killing smile.

"*Ehuani*," the people muttered more fervently than Ismai might have hoped. He looked upon the faces of his friends and elders, and realized with a sinking heart that he was a sacrifice they were willing to make.

Hassetha held up her arms. The world held its breath.

"Let us begin."

Ismai had no idea what to expect as Hassetha took her place before him, Ishtaset to his left, her riders beyond her. To Ismai's right hand stood the rider Adalia, and with her stood Hadid. The mastersmith gave Ismai an inscrutable look. Ismai nodded to the older man, trying to convey his apologies with a look.

I will not let them harm you.

A shame the Zeeranim had never made that promise to *him*.

"People of the Zeera," Hassetha cried out, and a hush fell upon them. "My sisters and brothers, my children. Even as sa and ka are bound into atulfah, even as Akari Sun Dragon and Sajani Earth Dragon are bound to the earth beneath our feet, even as Eth and Illindra are bound to the skies above our heads, we bind together this woman and this man to join the ancient bloodlines of Iftallen, priest of Thoth, to Ishmalak, son of Devranae, daughter of Zula Din. Let that which was sundered be mended. Let the halves become a whole, let that which was wounded be healed. Let the fire in our hearts—the hearts of those who live and ride and die beneath the gaze of Akari—once more rage across the land."

Even as she spoke these words, the snake priestess of Thoth unfastened a small yellow bottle from her robe and brought it to her mouth. She tipped her head back and drank some viscous liquid, and then whipped around quick as a snake, quick as death, and hissed as she spat a fine spray of—whatever it was—onto the waiting pyre. The logs, green as they were, exploded into flame. Streaks of red and black reached upward.

"Aaaaah," the crowd breathed, as if they had never seen fire before. Ismai stared in open-mouthed horror.

This is how they burned Aish Kalumm so quickly, and with no warning, he thought. *This is how they killed my people.* Hassetha turned back to them, a look of satisfaction upon her sanguine face, and met Ismai's furious stare with a tiny smirk, there and gone again in half a breath.

I am going to kill that woman.

'Ware, Kithren, Ruh'ayya warned. Her voice cut through the flames like a cool wind. *Do not rush blindly down the red path.*

"By Sammai's bones, I will kill her," he whispered, giving his promise to the wind, making it real.

As you will.

"Fierce cub." Ishtaset's eyes flicked to his face as if she had heard the promise, and her smile was indulgent. "Only do not think to try your claws out on *me*, little one."

Hassetha returned the empty yellow bottle to its place and addressed Ishtaset. "This man is giving his life to you, the hours of his day, the children of his body, should Sajani so bless this union. What do you offer in return?"

"I offer him the comfort of my fire, the protection of my blade, and these few humble gifts." The riders behind her parted, and a handful of women emerged, arms laden with gifts, to parade before them. One held a stack of books—his mother's, Ismai saw with a pang—another led a brace of spotted goats, a third presented a fine touar with horses embroidered all along the hem. They were shown to him and then whisked away again, but one last item—his own shamsi—was handed to him with a flourish.

They trust me with my sword, Ismai thought, then, indignantly, *she would offer to give me things that are already mine.*

Hassetha turned to Ismai. "This woman is giving her life to you," she intoned. "She will listen to your words, consider your interests, bear children by you at the risk of her own life, should Akari so bless this union. What do you offer in return?"

Ismai gaped. He was supposed to offer gifts to the woman he was being forced to marry?

They can kiss my—

Adalia spoke, so loudly that Ismai jumped. "This boy offers stud-rights to the stallions Ruhho and Zeitan, pride of the prides."

"What!" he shouted. Stud-rights to those stallions, stolen by Hannei and Sulema, had reverted to him as part of Hannei's blood-debt, and were more precious than salt.

The Mah'zula rider ignored him and went on, gesturing toward Hadid. "He offers the skills of this man, a mastersmith in his own right, whose life was deemed forfeit by his own actions. He offers this fine mare." At these words, Hadid was given a shove so that he stumbled to his knees at the feet of Ishtaset, and Ehuani—beautiful, beloved Ehuani—was led before them, snorting and rolling her eyes at the people, the fire, and the red, red sky.

Hassetha turned to Ishtaset. "Are these things agreeable to you?"

The Rajjha of the Mah'zula gazed upon Ehuani, and upon Ismai, and she smiled.

"They are."

"And to you, boy?" Hassetha's eyes glittered hard and cold.

"I… I…" he stammered. *No*, he shouted with everything he was. He looked over his shoulder at his people, and it seemed to him that their eyes had all turned to snakes' eyes, cold and hard and filled with spite. Where was Jasin? Where were Ghabril and Daoud, his friends? Surely they would not allow this to happen?

His friends were nowhere that he could see them, and the people stared back at him impassively, waiting for him to bind himself to the woman who had murdered their kin. Mouth filled with a taste of bitter ash, heart heavy as stone, Ismai turned to the priestess of Thoth.

"Are these things acceptable to you, Ismai son of Nurati?" she asked again through clenched teeth. Adalia, standing just behind Mastersmith Hadid, placed her hand lightly upon the hilt of her shamsi.

"They—"

"—are *not*," Hadid finished. The older man leapt to his feet, knocking Adalia to the ground. He grabbed Ehuani's reins from the startled Ja'Akari who held them, and threw them to Ismai.

"Go!" he shouted, and again, "*Go!*" Adalia, red-faced and bug-eyed with fury, grabbed Hadid by the shoulder and brought her shamsi perilously close to his throat.

Ismai stood for a moment gaping like a fool, reins clutched reflexively to his chest.

"I cannot—"

"You can," Hadid said, as calmly as if he were discussing the best way to put a fine edge on a sword. "You must. We both know that things are only going to get worse here. This venom which has been brought into our midst cannot be healed from within. Go, find help. Do not give them what they want, Ismai."

All around them people began shouting, but it was as if they were far away and speaking another language. Ismai ignored them completely. In that moment, only the mastersmith and the Ja'Sajani truly existed.

"If I do not, they will kill you."

"No," Hadid smiled, the sweetest smile Ismai had ever seen. "They will not kill me. *Go.*" With that, he grabbed Adalia's wrist with both of his hands and, still smiling, thrust her shamsi through his own neck.

Ismai screamed.

The front of the blade sliced neatly through the front of Hadid's throat and the mastersmith toppled backward, hot red blood spurting from his neck, spraying a fine red mist over Ismai, his touar, his horse, his whole world.

Go, Hadid had urged.

So Ismai went.

He grabbed Ehuani's reins in one hand, her mane in his other, and pushed himself up onto her back. Her silver hide was so slick with blood that he nearly slipped off the other side, but he clung as well he could. Leaning far forward onto her neck he kicked his beloved mare harder than he had ever kicked any horse in his life.

"*Het het!*" he called, giving Ehuani her head.

Even as the pale mare gathered her strength, even as her front lifted light as silk and her haunches bunched behind him,

Hassetha grabbed for Ismai's leg and nearly unseated him. He had a moment—only just—to see that she held in her other hand a small black bottle. The snake priestess tilted her head up, her nostrils flared wide, and she spat full into his face.

The world went red.

Ismai's face exploded in pain. It burned. He opened his mouth to scream, but instead of drawing breath he sucked in fire so that his insides burned, too. There was pain. It stretched across his life like the red sky stretched across the Zeera. Deep in his mind, Ruh'ayya roared, but he could not understand her words, drowned as he was in agony.

My eyes, he screamed at her. *My face, my eyes, I am burning—*
Then Ehuani launched herself into the air, and they *flew*.

FIFTY-ONE

The blooms of spring had long since died, withered and fallen and lost. Tender petals once woven into garlands for a lover's neck, or tossed with laughing wishes into the Kaapua, were crushed into dust beneath the soldiers' feet, their fragrances lost to rot. But the trees were still the same, and the blackthorn. Roots reached deep and limbs stretched wide as tender green leaves burst forth to lick hungrily at the sky, eager for the Sun Dragon's power.

The Yellow Road prince, Daeborn, sea-born, cursed and blessed by men, stepped mindfully through the low brush, careful lest he step wrong on a tussock and twist an ankle, or snap a twig beneath his boot and startle the hunters' prey. It had been less than a two-moon since he had last seen these trees, their bare branches, less than a six-moon since he had left his mother's home in Bizhan to walk the Yellow Road. Yet it seemed to Jian that he had walked a lifetime, that he had set foot upon an endless road with neither sleep nor death at journey's end.

Well... maybe death.

He stopped at the edge of the woods, where the willow trees and the birch gave way to the old forest, and the world went dark and green, and signaled to Perri, first and most beloved of his dammati.

Pig tracks, he signed as if they were still villagers, as if pig was the reason he had sharpened his sword that morning. Though Perri carried three spears, fine and steel-tipped, they did not have the men for such quarry, nor raptors. Three spears, two youths, and a quiescent sword—hardly preparation to hunt a young sow, much less the bristle-backed, tusked beast whose spoor they followed.

Perri followed him, trusting, without question. They were bloodsworn, closer than brothers. Jian's hand closed on the hilt of his sword and he closed his eyes, wishing he could deny the vision of his heart as easily. He felt Perri step close and opened his eyes to his friend's calm face, his one eye deep with trust and sorrowing.

"It is as good a place as any," Perri said. "I am ready, Sen-Baradam." He dropped his spears to the ground.

"Perri?" Jian's breath left him as his chest clenched shut.

"I know as well as you," his dammati said, "that you have not been sent here to kill pig, Sen-Baradam. Xienpei has commanded you to kill me, has she not?"

Jian's hand fell away from his sword. "She has," he admitted. "I am to kill you and return to her with your heart, as a test of my loyalty. And if I fail—"

"She will kill Tiungpei."

"Yes. I am sorry."

Perri was silent for a long moment, then he shrugged. His one eye was dry and cold. He had not cried since the Inseeing, nor would he cry ever again.

"I am not sorry." He reached up and began to unbuckle his breastplate. The issuq emblazoned across his chest flashed cobalt in the afternoon sun.

"What are you doing?" Jian was stunned.

"You are my friend. My brother." Perri's breastplate fell away. He wore a white silk shirt beneath. "You are my Sen-Baradam, and I am sworn to you. My life is yours, my blood a coin for you to spend as you wish."

An image came to Jian's mind of three blood pennies, now tucked safely away with his childhood treasures. A book, a handful of pearls, the tooth of a shongwei. *Mine to spend as I wish*, he thought, *but is this how I choose to spend it? Is this the darkest wish of my heart?*

Perri raised his arms to either side. His face was still and cool as sea-glass.

I think not. I think… He drew his sword. Perri nodded and

closed his eye, waiting for death. Jian gripped bare steel sharp as death's kiss just below the hilt until the blue steel was slippery with his own blood, and then he drew back and slapped Perri hard, leaving hot streaks of blood across his face.

The dammati staggered back, touched his cheek, and then stared without expression at his bloodied fingertips.

"What of the test of loyalty?"

"I pass the test." Jian wiped his bloodied sword on Perri's white silk tunic, sheathed it again, and smiled. "Come, brother, put that armor back on and hand me one of those spears. It is time for us to go hunting."

The shadows were long, the ground cooling, and his feet were dragging by the time Jian returned to the Yellow Palace. He was ushered without comment through the bronze doors, up and through the wide, winding hallways, into the presence of Xienpei.

The yendaeshi sat before a small fire, her eyes half closed in apparent bliss as three lashai combed and oiled her long, dark hair. Jian glanced idly around the room. He had never set foot in the yendaeshi quarters, and was surprised to find them as bare and comfortless as any whore's.

Fitting, he thought, *considering the role Xienpei plays in the emperor's court.* Jian went to one knee and presented his offering to her. The heart of a young pig, wrapped in Perri's white silk shirt. After some time, Xienpei slid her eyes toward Jian. She did not turn her head, nor smile, nor beckon him closer.

"Ah, so you have decided to return at last, Jian Sen-Baradam," she said in a mild voice. "I had wondered whether you became lost."

He dipped his head in obeisance, and the heart he held in his hands was not nearly so dead or cold as the one in his breast. Still, he held his voice steady and answered.

"I have done as you commanded, Yendaeshi."

"Have you?" she asked. She waved the lashai aside, and her hair fell about her shoulders like a mantle of night as she sat forward, eyes hungry, mouth cruel. "I ask so little of you, boy, and I offer you so much." She shook her head and sighed in mock sorrow, but her eyes were hot coals in a face white with fury.

Jian held the pig's heart higher, thrust it toward her, hoping that he did not sound as desperate as he felt. It had all seemed so easy, out in the woods.

"I have brought you—"

"The heart of a *pig*," she spat, nostrils flaring, jeweled teeth flashing in the firelight. "You take me for an idiot."

"I—"

"*Enough.*" Xienpei's calm was worse, much worse than her fury. She smiled a little, leaned back in her chair, and the lashai resumed brushing her hair as if nothing had happened. "Enough. I have warned you, little prince, against playing games with me. Apparently you believe my words to be as empty as your own head." She snapped her fingers. Jian tried to rise up, but strong hands on his shoulders pushed him down, down onto both knees, back bent, as the pig's heart fell from his grasp and rolled across the floor, leaving a trail of cold gore. "Perhaps this will convince you that I mean what I say, Sen-Baradam."

The hands gripped harder and Jian winced as Naruteo's red and black boots strode past him. The bull-shouldered youth was dressed in fighting leathers made for sparring, and he smiled a tight smile of triumph as he took his place by Xienpei's side.

"You called for me, Yendaeshi?" His eyes never left Jian's face.

"Yes, Sen-Baradam." She reached up a languid hand and stroked the side of Naruteo's face. "I sent a boy to do a man's job. Would you be so kind as to finish this small task for me?"

"Of course, Yendaeshi."

Xienpei smiled as four of Naruteo's dammati strode past, dragging a bloodied and nearly unconscious Perri between them. Jian cried out and tried to struggle free, but one of the lashai who held Jian's shoulders drew back and kicked him in the jaw, so that he collapsed with a groan.

"Attend, Daechen Jian," Xienpei sang out in a voice like a young girl's laugh. A boot crushed his head to the floor and someone sat on his legs, pinning him, as Perri was dragged before his face. Naruteo met his eyes, spat, and drew his bright sword.

"Watch and learn, little Issuq," he said, curling his lip in disdain. "This is how one bloods a new blade, and rises to power in the emperor's court."

Naruteo's bloodsworn dragged their prisoner upright by the arms. Perri's face was swollen, cut, and bloodied almost beyond recognition, but his one eye stared straight into Jian's heart, and his cut lips pulled up into a bloodied and fearless smile.

He *winked*.

"Sen-Baradam," he croaked. "Jai tu wai, my friend. I will wait for you beside the Lonely R—"

Perri's last word was cut into pieces by a high, thin shriek as Naruteo's treacherous blade flashed and fell, biting into the soft flesh and nearly severing his head from his shoulders. Naruteo grunted, placing one booted foot on Perri's back and pulling his blade free so that Perri fell facedown to lie twitching on the floor, blood spraying from the terrible wound in crimson spurts. The air thickened with the smell of blood and shit and the sharp tang of death. Then it rang with laughter and the sound of Perri's feet scraping across the floorboards.

Three names twice shall slay him—
"Jai tu wai, my friend"
—and Perri's had been the first.

A growl rose in Jian, deep in the pit where his heart had been. It rose like a wave and drowned the sounds of the end of his world. His fingers dug deep into the soft wood, tearing deep furrows as he launched himself up at the lashai who had held him down. The pale face showed no shock, no fear even as Jian's hand shot forward and slapped the man's head so hard it flopped backward onto his spine with a *snap*.

Naruteo opened his mouth to shout, but his voice was drowned in the raging of Jian's soul. He lowered his sword to point at Jian, but it was as if he and his dammati moved through water, through mud, crawling so feebly and so slowly that it was a simple thing for Jian to blow through them, drawing his own blade, scattering swords and men like fish torn from the sea.

Jian raged at the death of his bloodsworn. Naruteo raised his sword to parry but it was too little, too late. Not even thousand-folded steel sung to life by the light of the moons and quenched in the body of an innocent could stand against the wrath of the sea king's son. The bright steel shattered as Jian's blade whispered its dark song down, down, through the air, through the ties of blood and bone and broken promises.

It cleaved Naruteo's helm and the skull within it.

Xienpei shrieked, and Jian looked up, chest heaving, still growling low in his throat. The yendaeshi still sat upon her chair, but one wooden arm had been severed neatly, and she clutched at her own arm as blood blossomed bright through her yellow silk robes. The bodies of the lashai lay piled about her, along with those of Naruteo's bloodsworn and the bullish youth himself, not nearly as impressive now that the top of his head was missing.

He had a brain after all, Jian observed. *Pity he never learned to use it.* The room trembled as the doors behind Jian crashed open. Yellow Daechen in robes, in armor, in their underrobes—a few in nothing but their own skins—filled the room.

"Seize him!" Xienpei shrieked, jeweled teeth bright and bloody in the dying light. "Stop him!"

Strange eyes—round eyes, slit eyes, sloe eyes, and hawkish—stared at her, then turned to Jian. One by one the yellow Daechen fell to their knees, wrists bared and held upward as they offered fealty. He took a step toward Xienpei, and another, flicking Naruteo's blood from his blade. Oddly enough, there was no sense of anticipation, or victory. Rather he was calm, as if every step he had taken in his life had prepared him for this moment.

"Daechen Jian," Xienpei said, "stop this at once."

Jian raised his sword high. It trembled, as if hot with the rage he could no longer feel.

"Jian Sen-Baradam," she pleaded, soft voice breaking like waves upon the rocky shore. "Please. Please—"

"Jai tu wai," he told her, and his blade bit deep.

There was silence after that.

Somewhere in the dark, a nightingale sang.

FIFTY-TWO

Hafsa Azeina crept through the Dreaming Lands quiet as the memory of an ordinary day. Bereft of her instruments of death, no longer assisted by her young apprentice or strengthened by her bond with a vash'ai, she was more naked here in this land than she had been at the moment of birth. More naked, perhaps, as then she had been covered in the blood of innocence.

I am not here, she told the strange green grass as it bowed beneath her weight. *I am not here*, she told the low trees as she ducked and dodged between the leafed branches. *I am not here*, she told the wind, *I am most certainly not here*.

So the grass sprang up behind her, unmarred. The trees' branches snapped back into place unbowed, unbroken. The wind carried no scent of her blood, for the land believed her. As for the one who had breathed this land to life in the long ago, whose flesh was the earth, whose hair was the trees, whose breath was the very air—she was not deceived.

Even as the dreamshifter hunted these forbidden paths there came to her dreaming ears the hollowed-out and desperate cries of the hounds as they bayed *hungry, hungry*, and the sound of drums beating *thrrrrum thrrrrummm thhhhrumble—doom, thrrrrrum thrrrrummm thrrrrrumble—doom doom*.

Hafsa Azeina stepped more lightly still. She made no more noise than the shadow of a shadow, and walked so deftly upon the land that she no longer had to beg the forgetfulness of grass or tree or wind. They never dreamed she was there.

But the one who had blooded this land in the long ago, who had dreamed it to life from song and sorrow and shadows—she was not deceived. Even as the dreamshifter opened her waking eyes, the better to see her way in this dark place, there shivered through the air a single golden note, long and low and lovely as the first dawn of time, and the world stood still. The dreamshifter, trembling with exertion, wove for herself a hiding place from fugue and shadows and the cobwebs of old dreams.

I am not here, she told herself, *I was never here.* So convincing she was, so sweet her song, that she believed with every fiber of her being. Deep within her concealment she began to fade from the Dreaming Lands, to unravel and drift away back, back to the land of waking and sunlight and harsh truths, but the one who had hunted these lands for ages unmourned was not deceived.

Her hounds bayed *ouuuuu-ouuuuuu*, her steed's hooves threw sparks where they struck the rocky path, and the *tooooook-tooooook-tooooookiaaaahhhh* of her horn blasted through the dreamshifter's hiding place, bursting it asunder and leaving her exposed to the eyes, the hounds, and the arrows of the Huntress.

Hafsa Azeina stood still while the hounds flowed around her, red-eyed, red-tongued, and slavering. Black as a starless night, no two were the same. Some of them were long creatures, lean and clean-limbed, with ears long and silky. Others were hunch-backed, strong and thick as bulls. And there was a third kind, twisted and wretched to look upon, hairless, pitiless things of hide and bone and spite. None of them came closer to the dreamshifter than the edge of the clearing in which she made her final stand, but neither did they need to. They had been commanded not to kill, but to seek, and to hold.

This kill belonged to the Huntress.

Courage, Annu.

Hafsa Azeina looked down in surprise. There at her feet sat Basta, more beloved than self, whom she had murdered and who, apparently, had decided not to stay dead after all.

Annu no longer, she told her kima'a. *I am Hafsa Azeina, and that is all.*

Ahhhhh, Basta purred. *But will that be enough?*

It has always been enough, Hafsa Azeina answered even as she turned to face the hounds. *It was enough when I bound the Dragon*

King to my will, using only the natural magic of young girls. It was enough when I took his fire into my belly and used it to create a daughter who will be more powerful than either one of us. It was enough when I used fear, and love, and the magic in my bones to defy his will and escape Atukos.

Before ever I was the Queen Consort, before I was Dreamshifter, Dream Eater, Annubasta... it was enough. I was enough. I was just too foolish to see it.

Too foolish and, I think, too deeply in love with death.

Hafsa Azeina did not answer, but brought the golden shofar to her lips and blew. The first sounding of the shofar akibra was the *tookiah*—three long, low notes which were meant to stir the human heart to thoughts of music and beauty, poetry and dreaming. When the dreamshifter sounded this call she felt a stirring, as those in the Dreaming Lands woke and those in the waking lands were drawn forcefully into their own, deepest dreams.

The hounds bayed, white-toothed and red-mouthed, eyes gleaming in the underbrush as they swept round the place she had chosen for her last stand.

The second sounding of the shofar akibra was the *neshamsha*—two sharp, trilling notes that trailed off in an upward curve, meant to waken the human soul to its own beauty. It was a call to duty, to higher power, to the realization of her own place in the Web of Illindra. The dreamshifter sounded this call, and those who had ears to hear were stirred in their hearts to be better than they had been, before. Or worse, depending on the color of their dreams. Beauty would be created, and murder committed.

The hounds ran faster, closer, a storm of death and bloodlust, whining in their eagerness to devour her dreaming soul.

The third sounding of the shofar akibra was the *sut ah'sud*, and to play this note was khutlani to all people in all worlds, for this was the voice of the golden ram—a call to judgment, a call to the final battle, and this note was meant for the gods alone.

The hounds fell still and silent, a black fog full of mad red eyes, and faded deeper into the strange woods, away from the one who dared fling such a challenge at their Mistress's feet. Basta leapt up, back arched, hair standing stiff, and hissed her displeasure.

I cannot believe you would have the temerity, she spat, furious beyond words. *Even you. Even now.*

All roads lead to death for me now, Hafsa Azeina responded as she lowered the horn. *I might as well choose the swiftest way.*

Death, certainly, but this… this! Basta faded away, leaving only her lovely emerald eyes. *You will rue this day long after your death, Dreamshifter.*

So be it. Hafsa Azeina's hands shook even as she stuffed the shofar back into its bag at her hip. *To save my daughter, I will pay any price.*

The price will be high, Basta said as her eyes winked out. *Too high, perhaps. Would you sacrifice the world to save your daughter?*

If Basta's words had been meant to urge her to despair, or to sanity, they missed their mark. Hafsa Azeina smiled. Despite the hour of the day, despite the hounds and the hunt and the horror of this never-ending twilight, she saw clearly now the path her own heart had set, long years ago.

Would I sacrifice my daughter to save the world? she countered. *I think… not.*

One of the hounds, a hulking beast three times as big as most, threw his head back and screamed. Hafsa Azeina, who had once disemboweled a lover and strung her lyre with his guts as he hung dying, thought that she had never heard anything so horrible. Her flesh prickled with a painful chill.

So it is true, she thought, *that some hounds are fashioned from men. For such a scream as that could never come from the throat of a true beast.*

The hound fastened his tortured eyes upon her, pleading for—*something*—but before she could react, he flew apart in a bloody mist, leaving his final shriek to hang in the dreaming air, forever unfinished. The ground where he had stood was rent open, revealing a doorway to some twilit hell from which rose a dark and fulsome smoke. The hounds cowered and quailed, wailing upon the ground. Then with a flash of blood and fire a dark horse surged through, and into the clearing. It was a fell beast, wild-eyed, gape-mouthed, nostrils flaring red, and upon its broad back it bore the Dark Lady, the Whisperer of All Souls, whose arrows had tasted the heart's blood of countless victims. The Huntress.

Tall and slender as the supple willow, pale as a new dawn, deadly as life the Huntress sat laughing astride the great black mare. In one hand she held a bow fashioned like a rearing lionsnake, and in the other a blood-red shamsi, its hilt fashioned from the jaw of a horse. She was dressed crown to ankle in a black-and-gray touar fashioned from burned funereal rags said to have belonged to dead heroes. Hung at her waist was the horn of a ram, a shofar akibra, twin to Hafsa Azeina's own. A brace of ravens flew in her wake, screaming with rough glee.

"Effective," Hafsa Azeina said, "if a bit melodramatic."

The Huntress pulled up her mount at the very edge of the clearing. Bright, even teeth gleamed from beneath the charred touar.

"Do you call me to dance at last, Annu?"

"No," Hafsa Azeina replied. "I come to make a bargain."

"A *bargain*?" Had she a heart left for mirth, Hafsa Azeina might have laughed outright as she imagined the look on the Huntress's face. "Do you think to mock me, human?"

"I would not *dream* of it," Hafsa Azeina answered. She opened the pouch at her waist and drew forth the traditional small loaf of flat bread, flask of sweet water, and tablet of red salt. "Shall we begin?"

The Huntress swung one leg over her horse's back and leapt to the ground, landing easily, and then crossed the clearing in quick, fluid strides. Sheathing her blade, she put away her bow and reached up with both hands to push the cowl back from her face as she reached the dreamshifter's last stand. She smiled a wide, predatory smile as their eyes met—golden eyes set in faces as alike as moonstones.

406

It is like looking into a mere, the dreamshifter thought in shock, *and seeing my own dark sister.*

"The trap is sprung," the Huntress intoned in a voice much like Hafsa Azeina's own. "Now let us see which of us is the prey."

"So," the Huntress said at last. She sat almost knee-to-knee with the dreamshifter, smoking a long-handled pipe made from the rib of someone who had been—perhaps—less fortunate than herself.

Hafsa Azeina stared, bemused, as Breama—such was the name she had given—blew perfect rings of blue-gray smoke into the air, one after another. The hounds stood watch, the dark mare cropped the strange grass, and the two deadliest hunters ever to set foot in the Dreaming Lands chatted as amiably as old friends over a game of bones and stones. Yet a promise of death hung in the air between them.

"We have shared bread, and salt, and water, as allowed by the new laws. Now let us to bargaining. I can guess what desire coils within your sweet human heart—long have you hunted the golden wyvern, and long has he mocked your efforts. A candle against a great roaring flame, *ta*? Those were your words, *ta*?"

"Yes," Hafsa Azeina agreed. "Those were my words."

"You seek my aid in hunting this… great roaring flame of yours, so you can singe him with your little candle." She grinned, and smoke poured between her pointed teeth. "I am right, *ta*?"

"Yes," Hafsa Azeina said, "and no. May I?" She held out her hand. Surprised, Breama handed over her pipe, and doubled over with mirth as Hafsa Azeina attempted a smoke ring of her own, with no success whatsoever. "I always wanted to try blowing smoke rings," she admitted. "And this is probably my last chance."

Still chuckling, the Huntress took her pipe back. "If you do not need my help in finding your *husband*"—she emphasized the word cruelly—"then what do you wish, and what do you have to offer that you think I might possibly want? Besides your own sweet heart, of course." She licked her lips. "Certainly you do not think to offer me this… abomination." She pointed at the dragonglass dagger hanging at Hafsa Azeina's waist.

"Of course not," Hafsa Azeina replied. "I would not offer insult in such a way."

The Huntress grunted, satisfied. "What, then?" She tossed the heel of her bread to the ravens, who clacked and gabbled in delight as they stabbed it to death with their sharp bills. "What do you have to offer that I might possibly want? Besides your own pretty skin, of course." She licked her lips.

"Oh," Hafsa Azeina said. "Well, I had thought to offer you this." She pulled the golden shofar from its bag. The Dreaming Lands went still and silent at the Huntress's wordless wrath.

"You!" she said at last, in a voice hard enough to shatter rock. "You. You did this. You killed him. You!" She leapt to her feet, eyes blazing, teeth bared in a feral snarl. "I will—" But she froze in the middle of her lunge, prevented from murder by laws that held much more sway in the Dreaming Lands than ever they would in the world of men. Her hounds threw themselves flat upon the ground, wailing, as the air about their mistress shimmered red with her impotent rage.

The trap snapped shut.

"Yes," Hafsa Azeina said, "I killed the golden ram, I took his horn. From it I fashioned this, my first instrument of death, and now I offer to return it to you… for a price, of course."

The Huntress trembled, wide-eyed and taut, fists clenched so that her knuckles shone white. Her face, in those few moments, had grown markedly less human. If possible, this made her look even more like the dreamshifter than she had before.

"You know full well that I cannot refuse you," she said bitterly. "Not for this. Name your boon, human. If it is mine to give, you will receive it. But be warned—"

Hafsa Azeina held up the horn. It glittered in the strange light of Shehannam, and the Huntress stared at it hungrily, longingly.

"My price is not high," she assured Breama. "Neither is it low, for to ask such would be an insult. I ask only that you give to me a weapon powerful enough to kill... to kill..." Much to her own shock, Hafsa Azeina choked on the words. *Idiot girl*, she fumed, *still in love with a dream.*

"You wish a weapon fit for a queen," the Huntress said. "More than that, a weapon fit to slay her king."

"I do."

"He is the father of your child." The Huntress's rage shifted itself into something more malevolent and a slow smile, wry and wicked, stole across her face. "The only man you have ever truly loved."

Hafsa Azeina inclined her head. "It is true."

"Such a murder will make you a monster in the eyes of those you love." The smile burst as the Huntress threw back her head and laughed. "All in vain, as by killing the Dragon King you doom your world—and your daughter with it. I *love* it. Such drama. Such tragedy! Ah, Dreamshifter, such a gift you have given me. I could just kiss you." She winked. "But doing so would kill you, and so, alas! I am forbidden." Her eyes fixed on Hafsa Azeina's, and her smile hardened as she went on, "Long have I sought the missing piece, the lost horn of Guruvred. And now at last it comes to me. You come to my lands—*my lands*—and offer it to me freely. I cannot deny that my heart has longed for this day, and yet..."

Hafsa Azeina drew a shallow breath as the hounds, still on their bellies, inched closer. A low growl rose about the two women like a dirge, a warning.

"Yes?"

"Your offer, while tempting, lacks substance. His horn is nothing to you. A trinket." Though the Huntress's face remained still and cold, the ground beneath them trembled. "It costs you nothing to part with this... this thing. You cannot buy the death of a king with nothing, Dream Eater. Pain may only be bought with pain." She held both hands palm-up and shrugged. "It is law."

No, Basta's voice whispered, far away and flat as an old dream. *No.* Hafsa Azeina closed her heart and took a deep breath.

"Name your price," she said.

The Huntress gestured to her sorry, mad beasts. "Your soul,

of course. Hafsa Azeina, Princess of the Seven Isles, I offer you a weapon powerful enough to slay your greatest enemy. In return, you will give to me the horn of the golden ram, and your eternal soul. When you die, you will hunt with me till the end of time." She licked her lips again and smiled, a real smile this time that lit her eyes and stopped the wind. "Do you swear it?"

The hounds wailed, a sound like the death of all hope.

"I swear it," Hafsa Azeina said, "I swear."

Three times, making it true

"I swear."

Breama took an arrow from her quiver and, quick as lightning, drew the flint head across the palm of her own hand. A line of blood, ruby-red, glistened in its wake. She handed the arrow to Hafsa Azeina. The dreamshifter repeated the ritual, wordlessly, and they clasped hands, mingling salt and water in an oath of blood.

Dark lightning hissed and burned through Hafsa Azeina's veins. Her hand clenched, her back arched, and her mouth opened in a wordless scream as agony engulfed her from scalp to sole. When at last the Huntress released her grip, the dreamshifter staggered back panting and shaking her head as the world spun around her. The arrow she had been gripping fell to the ground between them, blackened and smoking.

"I may not be able to kill you here," the Huntress grinned, "but I never promised not to hurt you. Now..." She held her hand out, and all trace of mirth vanished. "*Give him to me.*"

Hafsa Azeina did not hesitate. She thrust the golden horn into the Huntress's eager hands, then she sat down, hard, all of her strength gone.

"Ah," the Huntress said, staring at the horn as if she expected it to disappear. "Ah." She clasped it to her breast, and closed her eyes. "At last, oh my dearling, at last."

She went to the dark mare and took a thick leather bag from her saddle. Hands trembling, she unfastened the laces which held it closed, and placed both horns—the one she had gotten from Hafsa Azeina, and the one she had worn at her own waist—into the bag. There was a rattling, as of old dry bones, when she closed the bag fast again and shook it hard. Once, *rattle-rattle*, twice, *rattle*, *rattle*, three times she shook the bag. The third time there came a crack, the ground shuddered, and Breama dropped the bag at her feet.

The bag fell open and a golden ram leapt free, shaking his great horns and bellowing with fury. The Huntress screamed and fell to her knees, throwing her arms around his throat and sobbing so hard it seemed as if her ribs might burst. Hafsa Azeina stared. She had always heard that the Huntress was fond of her ram, but this—

A light bright and angry as a fallen star burst from the animal, enveloping them both. Crying out in surprise, Hafsa Azeina shielded her eyes against the glare. The light winked out as suddenly as it had burst forth and she blinked away the tears to see—

Oh.

Oh.

For the Huntress stood weeping with her arms draped across the shoulders of a beautiful, if somewhat sullen youth. She stroked his downy cheek, though hers were the ones wet with tears, and buried her face in his golden hair. The young man stared angrily at Hafsa Azeina for a long moment.

"You killed me," he accused.

"I did," she admitted. "I thought you were a ram."

"Stupid human." He turned to his mother, and Hafsa Azeina saw that he was younger than she had first assumed. "Mother," he said, "let us go home. I am so tired." He swayed where he stood.

"See?" Breama's eyes were hot as coals as she turned to face the dreamshifter. "See what you have done. My boy has been gone so long he is nearly grown. My only boy!"

"I am sorry," Hafsa Azeina snapped, trying to sound sincere. "If I had known he was your son, I would not have killed him in the first place. I thought he was a *ram*."

"It does not matter," the Huntress replied. "I will kill you, in this life or the next, I vow it. Come, Guruvred, let us go—"

"What of our—" Hafsa Azeina began.

The Huntress howled, her hounds howled with her, and with a clap of dark thunder and a smell as of cinnamon and sulfur, they were gone.

"—bargain?"

But the Twilight Lady was gone.

Hafsa Azeina staggered forward angrily, determined to chase them to the Twilight Lands if need be, and tripped over the arrow she had dropped.

Ah, she thought, *I should have known.* It was not in the nature of the Huntress, after all, to go back on her word. She stooped and retrieved the arrow. Its shaft was black, black as the hounds.

The hounds... but her mind shied away from that load of horse shit. *First let me destroy the Dragon King—and the world with him, like as not—and then I will worry about whatever is left of my soul.*

The fletching was black, but the flint arrowhead had been stained a deep, rich, heartsblood red that glowed in the dim light and whispered of death, and the nock was pure, soft gold. It was heavy, heavy as a soul full of guilt, born as it was from a promise of murder.

She clutched the arrow to her breast much as the Huntress had clutched the golden shofar. It was a fell thing, filled with a single dark purpose, but it was her last, best hope. She reached into her pocket and drew forth a trinket, a treasure, the last possession of a happy childhood.

For a moment Hafsa Azeina, long ago a moons-haired princess of the Seven Isles, looked upon the miniature portrait of her long-lost love. With one finger she traced the curve of his cheek, and her heart ached at the laughter in his eyes. Then she took up the worn blue ribbon that had been fastened around her neck for those many years, and tied it around the shaft of the black arrow.

"Find him," she told the arrow. "Find him, find my love and take me to him." She kissed the miniature one final time, and tears washed the cut on her palm. "Find him," she said a third time, making it true. Sealing her fate.

Sealing all their fates.

The black arrow heard. It understood, and in its wicked dark heart it wanted nothing more than to do as it had been asked. It glowed with a fell, dark light, then it twitched in her hand, and pulled.

This way, it whispered in a hideous little voice. *Thissss wayyyy.*

"Yes," the dreamshifter agreed. "Let it be done." She dropped the image of her body and became a shadow, a shadow of herself with murder in her heart and an arrow in her hand. She rose up, up, into the strange flat sky...

...and flew.

FIFTY-THREE

ake up, little mouse. Wake up and live.

Khurra'an's voice sunk its tusks into Daru and dragged him, screaming, from a sleep so deep not even the Huntress could have found him. He jerked awake and cried out in pain and fear to find himself bound shoulder to knee with some sort of thin rope. It clung and burned his skin, and seemed to clench like the coils of a snake as he struggled.

His head was muggy with too-hard sleep, and Khurra'an's scornful laughter still clutched at the back of his neck, so it was some time before he could wake enough to calm himself and stop flopping around like a fish in the bottom of a boat.

"Pakka!" he cried out, his voice tremulous and soft, a weakling laid out for the shadows' supper. "Pakka!" She did not answer, but the shadows did. They crept forward, eyes shining red like moonlight on blood.

At lasssst, they hissed, *at lasssst*.

"Have you learned nothing, boy?" Dreamshifter's words fell against his ears hard as stones. *"In all your years with me, nothing?"*

"Stop your sniveling and act, boy!" He could see Ani frowning at him.

Help me, Daru. Hannei's voice was last. It sounded as if she had been crying. *Help us, we are lost.*

Daru's heart turned to hot stone at the thought of Hannei's tears. He stopped fighting against his bonds—*like spiders' webs*, he thought with disgust—and drew as deep a breath as he could manage.

"I am coming, Hannei," he promised. "I will save you."

How will you save her, little mouse? You cannot even save yourself.

Khurra'an's voice was more real than the others in his head, and that gave him pause. Was the vash'ai speaking to him in this world, then, and not through the Dreaming Lands?

I will find a way, he answered, pushing the thought out as Dreamshifter had taught him. *I will.*

Find your way home, then, little mouse. The great sire laughed. *I will be waiting for you.*

With that, he was gone.

Out of the dragon's belly and into the vash'ai, Daru thought ruefully, but the conversation—dream or no—served to still his mind. He gathered up his thoughts and his wits like a farmer harvesting jiinberries, and rinsed away the foam.

First things first, he thought. *Do I know where I am?* He blinked in the dark. *Yes.* All those years of training with Dreamshifter, all the nights spent finding his way back to his own body, had not been in vain. He knew precisely where he was in space and in time, which was something. His heart warmed a little as he thought of Dreamshifter's approving smile, there and gone again, quick as shadows.

Second things second. If Daru was to save Hannei, or the exceptional children, or even himself, he was going to have to do it on his own. He was not certain he wanted to save the children, though, as those butt-heads had gotten him caught in the first place. Still, he should probably at least try.

I can do this, he realized. *I can do this.* His lungs cleared as he imagined Ani's approving nod, and he took a deep breath. *I am stronger than they know.*

You are stronger than you *know*, Hannei chided. In his mind's eye she looked up to him, and not the other way around. In his dreams he was whole, and unafraid, an older, stronger version of Daru.

Struggling against the spider-rope did more harm than good, and though he still wore his knives, he could not reach them. Nor could he reach the rope with his teeth, though he tried mightily, tucking his chin down on his chest as far as it would go and sticking his tongue way out, as if that would help.

"No good," he said aloud, then he sucked air through his teeth in alarm as one of the shadows darted forth to sip at his breath.

The result was a faint whistle—*wheeeee*—and the shadow jumped back in alarm. *Aha*, he thought.

Wheee-wheee-wheeee, he whistled through his lips, and the shadows retreated until the dark was just dark-dark, not stifling-death-dark.

I can do something about that, too, he realized. *Goat-brained idiot.* He opened his dreaming eyes. The shadows were still there, of course, but they had drawn back a little at the sound of his harsh music, and drew back even more to see the dreamshifter's apprentice remembering.

"I am no easy meat," Daru reminded them, and again he began to whistle. It was a simple tune, a sleeping-song, a lullaby that Hannei had sung to him when he was little, and not expected to live. He had thought her beautiful even then, and his love for her had been a light for him in dark hours. It was the best magic he knew. He closed his eyes as he whistled, imagining as he did so that she sang to him:

> *Look to the stars, little one,*
> *Do you see me smiling at you?*
> *Listen to the wind, little one,*
> *Do you hear my voice?*
> *Feel the wind, little one,*
> *Do you remember my touch?*
> *Though I am long away, far away,*
> *I will come home to you,*
> *I will come home to you,*
> *I will come home.*

Daru filled his lungs with darkness, and sent it out into the world as magic so pure and bright and powerful that the shadows fled from that room. To his dreaming eyes the song painted a picture, of a striking young warrior stroking her moon-round belly and singing. She looked up and saw him, and her smile was wide as the midday sky.

4 1 6

Little one, she sang in his dream, and dimples showed at the corners of her mouth. *I will come home, I will come home… I will come home across the Zeera.*

Though he did not know why, Daru's heart squeezed so painfully in his chest that the breath failed him at last. His music faded, and his magic, and the vision faded with them slowly, slowly.

It was just a dream, he thought, choking on a sob. *Just a dream.*

Ah, but love is a dream worth having. It was a new voice, feminine and strong as the stars. That startled Daru so that he stopped weeping.

"Who is there?" he asked, for that voice—the Dreamer, as he thought of her—had not been born of his own imaginings. "Who are you? Will you help me?"

There was no answer but a warm feeling around his heart.

No, wait. Ow! A hot feeling across his chest, and his belly too. Daru tucked his chin down again and stared with his dreaming eyes in disbelief. His mother's knives were glowing red hot, white hot, blue hot, and if he listened very closely he could hear the faintest echo of her voice, singing to him from their sharp little hearts.

Now if only I could— He wriggled against the spider-ropes, hoping the knives might burn him free. *If I could just—* It was no use, he was caught fast and the knives were fading again into sleep.

"Oh, come on," he yelled in sheer frustration. "Shit! Fuck!" At this rate, his tongue was going to be sharper than Istaza Ani's.

"*Peeeee-oh!*" The answer came from deep in the tunnels. "*Pip-pip-peeeeeee! PEEEEE-OH!*"

"Pakka!" Daru shouted, heedless of the shadows or the Nightmare Man or whatever had spun the webs that held him tight. "Pakka!" He saw a dim glow in the darkness.

"*PEEEEE-OH!*" she shrieked again, her bright light illuminating the little room as she came around the corner. She danced midair, so happy to have found him, swooping and swirling till Daru's head spun.

"Stop!" he laughed. "You are making me dizzy. Oh, Pakka, you came back!"

417

We will come home, his knives sang in their tiny little metal voices. *We will come home. We will come home across the Zeera.*

"Pakka, can you—?"

Before he could finish she lit upon him and began chewing through the rope, making unhappy little noises at the taste. *Snip-snip-snip* went her sharp, clever little mandibles, and in no time at all his arms were free. Daru drew one of the knives, the one that was carved to look like an owl, good for seeing in the dark, and cut away the rest. Then he sat for a long moment. The darkness was not so dark to his dreaming eyes, and he breathed.

I am grateful, he told the stars, though he could not see them. *For breath, for life, for my good friend Pakka. Thank you.*

You are welcome, that strange voice replied, warm and approving. Daru shook his head, sheathed his knife, and called Pakka to him. There were enough mysteries in his life already, he decided, without chasing this one down. At least for the moment.

"A little light, if you please," he said. Pakka chirruped, and settled herself primly on his shoulder, and glowed like one of the moons come down to keep him company. "Thank you." He reached into his pocket for his bird-skull flute, and sighed with relief to find it unbroken. "Shall we dance?"

With that, Daru played his bird-skull flute. His knives heard, and sang of longing, while Pakka chirped and chirruped and lit their way. The shadows danced behind them, not daring to get close, but hungry for that music. He knew their dark hearts, just a bit. Music cut all the way down to their core. It made them *feel*. How could he deny them that, when it cost him so little?

He could not.

So he did not look back, and neither did he stop. Daru played his music and danced his way up the tunnels and out of the belly of the dragon. As he passed the passage that would lead to the Chambers of the Exceptional Children, Daru paused, music faltering in the cold, dark breeze that seemed to breathe down that fateful path. There was nothing he could do for them today, but—

"Worry not," he whispered into the darkness. "I will find a way to help you... somehow. I swear it."

The shadows giggled at his innocence, but it seemed to Daru that the Dreamer, whoever she was, approved.

He ducked through a little round doorway and could see a faint light ahead. He could smell the fresh air, and oh, how his belly grumbled when he realized he could smell air wafting thick and warm as soup from the kitchens.

Almost there, he thought, and his soul wept. *Almost there.*

A shadow bigger than all the rest stepped into the tunnel ahead of him, barring his way to freedom. Daru yelped, his bird-skull flute shrieked, Pakka bit his ear in fright, and the shadows nearly ran up his tunic before they realized that he had stopped.

"Stop," it commanded in a voice so deep and resonant it made Daru's broken arm ache. He heaved a sigh and nearly collapsed, so overwhelming was his relief. This was no greater shadow after all, but the Loremaster of Atualon.

"Bones and ashes, I am so happy to see—"

"Stop," the Loremaster said again. His eyes were dark as the night sky and, it seemed to Daru, as sorrowful. He held out one hand as if he would push Daru back down into the belly of the dragon. In his other he held something strange and wonderful.

Like the Bones of Eth, Daru thought, curious despite his pain and weariness and the strangeness of everything. *If they were shrunk down so that a man might hold them.*

"What?" he asked.

"What what?" Loremaster Rothfaust echoed, and he smiled through his great beard, though his eyes were still sad. "What am I doing here? What am I holding? Or perhaps you mean to ask, what are my plans for you?"

"All of those, I suppose," Daru answered. He slipped the bird-skull flute into his pocket, and Pakka peered out from behind his ear.

"*Pip-ip*," she scolded.

"Ahhhh," the Loremaster breathed. "What a lovely friend you have there."

"Thank you," Daru replied, but all he could think was how strange it seemed to be talking to another person as if the past few days had not happened, and as if nothing were amiss in this place and time. He wondered if the Loremaster had any food about him, and if Dreamshifter had sent the man to look for him. The thought of Hafsa Azeina set his pulse to racing.

"If you will please excuse me, Loremaster, I must—"

"No," the Loremaster shook his head slowly, "you must not, young man."

Daru began to tremble, then, and the corners of his vision started to go dark, his limbs grew weak and watery.

No, he told the shadows. *No*, he told his body. *Not now. No.* And for the first time in his life, the shadows obeyed. His vision cleared, his knees stopped shaking, and he drew a whole breath. "I have to go," he insisted. "I have been lost in these tunnels for... a long time. Dreamshifter must be looking for me." Even as he said the words, a longing to see his mistress clutched at Daru's heart so that tears were wrung from his eyes.

"She is not," the Loremaster replied. "I am afraid, dear boy, that the only one who has been looking for you... has just found you."

Nobody was even looking for me. Daru closed his eyes against a pain greater than the ache in his arm. *I was lost and all alone, and nobody cared.*

"They care," the Loremaster said softly. "The great minds of the land are turned to more important matters at the moment, that is all. What they think of as more important, in any case. And this is a good thing."

"Good?" Daru all but shouted. Pakka squeaked. "Good? My people have forgotten me. They might have left me to die... how is that *good*?" His voice broke, and he hated it. He hated the Loremaster for telling him what he did not want to know. He wanted, very much, to hate Dreamshifter for not caring enough to look for him, but he burst into tears instead.

"Oh, they will remember, young dreamshifter, and they will come looking for you, but you will be long gone. Long gone, and far, far away. This is a good thing, a very good thing for you. Because you are in Atukos, young man, and Atukos is no place for an exceptional child such as yourself."

Daru stared, open-mouthed. "You know?" he asked. "I saw them. In the Downbelow, in the belly of the dragon. I saw them."

"Then you know." Loremaster Rothfaust stroked his beard with his free hand. Daru's eyes darted again to the strange thing that rested upon the man's outstretched palm. It really did look just like the Bones of Eth.

"What is that?" he asked finally.

"This?" The Loremaster brought the strange miniature close to his face, and smiled at Daru through the thin, twisted pillars. "This is your door out of here, my boy. Have you ever wanted to see the stars?"

How did he know? Daru thought, so startled he forgot that he was supposed to be crying. "What?"

"Come, Daru, it is time for us to leave this place. It is not your fate to wear a golden mask, to have your magic drained by this Dragon King, or by *any* king. There is a much kinder fate in store for you, kinder and greater than even you might imagine." He held out his free hand. "Come with me, and I will show you."

A kinder fate. Daru wiped his tears on the back of his good hand, and shook his head. "No," he said. "No thank you. My fate is here."

Without warning the Loremaster pursed his lips and blew upon the miniature Bones of Eth. They began to spin, slowly at first, but then faster, throwing off little red sparks as they did so, and opening like the petals of some weird and exotic flower. Daru gasped as the air between the petals darkened and opened with a crackling pop and a smell like burnt metal.

It is a door, he thought in panic, *like a door to the Dreaming Lands.* He tried to back away, to run away.

"I am sorry, child," the Loremaster said, as the darkness opened up to swallow them both whole. "I am so, so—"

"No," Daru cried, "I have to help Dreamshifter. I have to help

Hannei." But it was too late. The world beyond the door had been flung open, and he was pulled through and up, and then he was falling, falling, falling through the song and dreams of an alien sky.

Or was he flying? The stars were singing to him, welcoming him home.

He was *flying*.

FIFTY-FOUR

She found him in the mountains, in a corner of the Dreaming Lands that was nearly devoid of life, if not charm. It was a lonely place, the loneliest she had ever seen, all bare rock and scorched earth and the jagged ends of dead trees thrusting up through the flesh of the earth like broken bones.

The wind sang, even here, and the light shone, and she could see why he had chosen this as his heart's home. It was lonely, yes, and sorrowful in its loneliness—but there was power, and a kind of stark beauty that was almost love.

It is the perfect home, she thought, *for a wyvern.*

For a king.

The golden wyvern had dug his cave into the side of a sere and pitiless peak, leaving a dark hole staring from the ashen precipice like the jealous eye of a blinded king brooding over the lands he had claimed. He lay upon a narrow ledge barely wide enough to accommodate his bulk, curled round and round himself and seemingly asleep. As she drew nearer, the dreamshifter could see that the golden wyvern—kima'a of the Dragon King—was bound as Sulema was bound—as she herself was bound—by magic and by choice.

The wyvern's bonds had been grown and nurtured and strengthened through debt and obligations in the waking world, as well as by those who held claim to his heart. Here was the white-hot chain of Akari Sun Dragon, the dragonglass links of Atukos. Strands of the Web of Illindra and the Shroud of Eth— no surprise there, as he had long had dealings with the shadow-sorcerers of Quarabala. Vines of green and gold, webs of intrigue and the shadowy, sticky stuff of lies held him fast in sleep even as they held him in life.

As she drew nearer, the dreamshifter's song faltered as in the waking world she caught her breath—nestled and imprisoned within the wyvern's coils lay the white fennec, small and forlorn in this terrible place, trembling in the wyvern's shadow. The wyvern was bound to his daughter, tied by bonds of loyalty, of love, of treason and deceit, and of blood.

Her chest tugged painfully, and Hafsa Azeina looked down in surprise to see strands of moonsilk reaching out, yearning toward the great golden being that lay before her.

Love, she thought, *even now, even here.* Tendrils of red and gold reached up from the wyvern's heart to meet hers, and her spirit was torn by his warm regard. *Even here... even now, we are both of us bound in love.*

It changes nothing.

Hafsa Azeina let her song fade, let her awareness of self dissipate like mist scattered upon the winds. This was his place, not hers. She had hunted the wyvern to his very lair, and what little flame she held in her heart was almost nothing compared to the inferno of his glory.

Almost nothing, she told herself as she hovered too close to the sleeping wyvern, *is still something. And perhaps it will be—yeh Atu, let it be—it* must *be enough.*

I must *be enough.*

Scarce daring to breathe in the waking world, Hafsa Azeina nocked the black arrow and drew back. She aimed high, as the miniature of her love would slow the arrow's flight and drag it down, even as her love of him dragged at her resolve. She aimed, and it broke her. She aimed for his heart, the path to which was laid clearly before her by the strands of moonsilk, and in doing so broke her own.

She drew back, and the string of the bow burned against her fingers as, trembling, they touched her cheek.

Even as she loosed her arrow, Hafsa Azeina cried out in pain, a cry that shook both worlds to their core. The golden wyvern reared with a scream, eyes blazing. When he beheld her hovering before him, his cry of grief was so profound, so true, that it broke into pieces the magic of *ehuani*. Hafsa Azeina watched in horror as the golden wyvern flicked his tail, hurling Sulema's fennec deep into his cave.

He rose up, wings outflung, to take the black arrow in his heart.

The golden wyvern screamed. His wings wide as dawn beat, twice, three times, and he launched himself into the sky. For all his bulk, the wyvern was quick as sudden death. He caught up the dreamshifter's spirit-mist form, clutched her to his hot bright breast with talons like swords, and held her there as if she were the last treasure in all the world. Up, up he shot past the trees that clung to the mountain peaks, past the clouds, past any thought of salvation, into the sky and out of memory.

The wyvern's claws were an iron prison, and Hafsa Azeina clung to him, to the kima'a soul of her enemy and lover. It was not out of fear for her life. She pressed her face against his warm hide, stretched her arms as wide as she could, and sang herself into the Dreaming Lands. As her song grew thin and weak, she knew her dreaming self would grow more substantial, while her body in the waking world would grow cold and stiff.

There was no apprentice in the waking world to sing her home, and for this she was grateful. She belonged in this place, at this time.

With him.

The wyvern's heart labored, faltered, and as his wings skipped a beat they hung suspended so far above everything that they might have been a single golden leaf upon a vast and colorless ocean. All that had been, all that was, all that would ever be between them ceased to matter in that moment, leaving nothing but love and a faint aftertaste of regret.

Give me this death, Belzaleel whispered. *Give me this death, and free yourself.*

Ah, she replied, *but I am free.*

Life is pain, Wyvernus whispered into her mind, infinitely sad. He allowed himself to be drawn unresisting into his kima'a, even

425

as Hafsa Azeina sang herself to sleep. *Only death comes easy. I am sorry, my moons-haired princess.*

I am not sorry, Hafsa Azeina answered. She closed her waking eyes, then closed her dreaming eyes, and held on tight. *I am free at last... and I am with you.*

Free, he said, and his voice caught as his great heart slowed. *At last.*

Slowed...

...and stopped.

Hafsa Azeina did not weep, did not cry out as they fell, locked tight in a last embrace, blazing through the pale sky like a dying star. She had killed her love, and in doing so she had doomed the world. In the end, however, her daughter was close, her daughter was safe.

That was all that had ever mattered.

FIFTY-FIVE

The scents of leather and horses, and of women and sweat, were sweeter to Sulema than any perfume sold in a merchant's stalls. She took a deep breath and held it in, as the shadowmancer and his apprentice might when smoking their spirit-herbs.

Sensing her rider's momentary distraction and fresh from spending too much time idle, Atemi crowhopped a bit to one side and made a half-hearted attempt at unseating Sulema with a series of sassy little bucks. Sulema laughed and rode out the ill-mannered display.

"You need to teach that filly some manners," one of the Draiks called out, even as he yanked his mount's head around. The shaggy gelding stuck its tongue out, rolling its eyes in displeasure at such rough handling.

"Watch your tongue, lest Her Radiance teach you some manners," Iyezabel replied as she flashed by in her Divasguard robe and mask of blue-and-green. "Ja'Akari know how to ride without beating their mounts silly." She gave her own horse—a long-legged bay—his head as they raced for the dead sheep.

"Maybe," the Draik called, "but Herself is ne Atu now, not some barbarian wench."

Wench, indeed. Sulema encouraged Atemi's tantrum and the young mare complied, spinning about so that her hindquarters collided with the ill-treated gelding, sending its rider flailing and yelling through the air. Sulema grinned as she flew past the disgraced guard. Any apology he made would have been a lie, anyway.

Because she was warrior enough to cling to the beauty in truth—even ugly truth—Sulema had to acknowledge the verity of the guard's words. Though her place as heir to the throne was no more than a fool's mummery, her future as Sa Atu more than suspect, neither was she wholly Ja'Akari. The fox-head staff belied her claim to that title.

Even as guards and warriors alike galloped shrieking toward the sheep's head, Sulema opened her dreaming eyes. It was child's play when compared to the voice exercises Aasah had given her. She watched the game of aklashi as if from a very great distance. If she reached out, just so, she might turn this rider away, might swing the sheep's body that way, and so affect the outcome of the game. She did not, but her joy in the day was somewhat diminished.

One of the Divasguard rode past at a controlled canter. Her face was flushed with pleasure and the morning's chill air, and her eyes shone. She wore three white ribbons on her helm, signifying that she had captured the target thrice.

"My thanks for teaching us this game, your Radiance," she called out as she passed. "Truly, it is a sport fit for a queen." Even as she said the words, her eyes lingered covetously upon Atemi. The asil were still and always forbidden to any but the Zeerani, and no few of the Atualonians resented this.

Beware the one who wants what you have and they do not, the voice of Istaza Ani whispered. *Such poison turns even a friend's heart to wickedness.*

Sulema sighed. She had just wanted to play aklashi in the sunlight, but there was no escaping the long game of Atualon. Though she was surrounded by her own Divasguard, and by a few remaining Ja'Akari, though she was ringed about with her father's guards and the Salarian salt-cloaks and by citizens who smiled and paid her all manner of courtesies, still she was alone in a hostile land. She would do well to remember it.

There are no few people in this world, she thought, *who would rather see me dead. I would prefer to disappoint them.*

The Diva with ribbons on her helm streaked past again, this time in the other direction, screaming in triumph. The sheep's head was clutched tight to her chest. Sulema dropped her worries, spun her mare around, and gave chase.

It was a good day to die. It was a better day to *live*.

When they had finished the game of aklashi—the sheep had lost, as usual—Sulema and the rest of her entourage rode back to the city proper at a leisurely pace. Saskia had her back, as always, and Sulema had long since outgrown blaming the girl for the attack on her mother.

If a viper strikes, one should blame the fool who stepped into their nest, not the fool who let them do it. Neither can I rightly blame the viper, for it is simply following the way of its kind.

She smiled to realize how much she had begun to sound like her old youthmistress. *I wonder where Istaza Ani has gone*, she thought wistfully. *Probably raising another crop of younglings to be warriors, by sending them to clean churra-pits.*

She had never thought she might miss *that.*

"Salt for your thoughts, your Radiance?" The Draik who had lost his mount—with a bit of help—smiled indulgently at her as if she were a Mother in child. Sulema kept the irritation away from her face.

"Nothing of import." She had long since learned that any word of hers could become fertile soil for speculation. Atualon was a land of beauty, but its beauty did *not* lay in truth. Sulema had heard enough wild fancies to fill volumes of stories, had she the time or the will to write them down.

From what she had heard, her father was a pretender to the Dragon Throne, and the real king was biding his time until he could reclaim his rightful place. Her mother had taken a lover, young and antlered like a stag, from among the Salarians, and they had conspired to kill the king. Her mother's lover was the king's old concubine, and they had conspired to kill the king. Sulema, herself, had conspired to fill Atukos with her barbarian warriors and kill the king.

The king, it seemed, would suffer many deaths.

For all these conspiracies against my father, she thought with a wry smile, *the old goat is surprisingly alive.* Then her smile departed. More disturbing were the rumors that surrounded the king's intentions toward Sulema. It had occurred to her, some time past, that her own chances of survival would be considerably better were she not in Atukos, and seated at the feet of its Dragon King.

Atemi snorted and tossed her head, still fractious. Sulema reached forward to stroke the silken, sweat-damp neck of the one friend she had in Atualon.

I know, she told her good mare silently. *I want to go home, too.* With her entire heart Sulema wished to leave Atualon and return to the winds-blasted desert, but freeing herself from Atukos was a more difficult task—and a dirtier one—than cleaning churra pens could ever be. Sulema had sussed out her father's security at the four main and twelve minor gates of Atualon, and what she had learned did not inspire her to confidence.

Her father's guards knew her by sight and by reputation, enough so that even a casual disguise would not allow her to pass unnoticed. People were allowed to come and go through the Sun and Moon gates as they wished, but each person was stopped and questioned, more or less respectfully, Sulema had observed, depending on their dress and apparent social stature. Bags, carts, and packages were carefully searched, more so since the Salarians' stunt at the Sulemnium.

The Sunrise and Sunset gates would open only to those who had a writ of passage from the king or his shadowmancer, and the smaller gates were, to a one, closed and barred except for certain times, and to certain people. None were ever left unguarded. Sulema would have been pleased, were she not trying to leave the seven-times-damned place. If she could just get past the gates, Sulema thought, she would give Atemi her head and never stop until they were back in the Zeera.

The Zeera is mine, she thought. *My own. I would be safe among my people, free to ride once more with my sword sisters beneath the gaze of Akari.* She had dreamed of fleeing over the mountains, but indeed to go north over the forbidding mountains meant to fly, and Sulema had neither wings nor an amenable wyvern to carry her.

While possible, escape by sea was less likely still. Without a

430

Baidun Daiel on board to dazzle and confuse the river serpents and sea serpents, any vessel was doomed to be torn apart, its passengers gobbled up like minnows, before its crew had lost sight of land. Thus Sulema remained in the land of her enemies, smiling and nodding at them and biding her time.

Ani would tell me to be patient. Yet her old youthmistress, she was certain, would have found her way to freedom by now.

The Draik was still making eyes at her, and Sulema resisted the urge to roll her own in exasperation. His name was Seamus, she thought, or perhaps Theamus? He had been flexing his calves and batting his eyes in her direction for a handful of days now. When finally it became apparent that she had no interest, another would take his place, and another. Using both men and women—some too young to be taken seriously, others old enough to know better— they had attempted this ruse repeatedly. She needed neither her youthmistress nor her mother to tell her that it was a trap.

One lover is enough of a pain in my arse, she thought, *and at least I know I can trust Mattu Halfmask.*

In truth, she knew such a thing, but Sulema had decided not to spend the entirety of her life weighed down with suspicion. There were few in Atualon she trusted. Her dream-eating mother, her sword sister Saskia, her good mare Atemi. Her lover, Mattu—and not because he had shed his clothes, delightful though that was to behold—but because he had first shed his mask.

As they neared a pasture near the Sunrise Gate, where the asil were kept, the Ja'Akari gave a series of war whoops and began to race. Much as Sulema longed to join them, she did not. She had attempted to maintain a camaraderie with her sword sisters, joining them at mealtimes or for a game of stones and bones, but the drawn-out silences and abrasive looks had grown as thick and stinging as a sandstorm. As a result she had learned to shield herself by shunning their company.

"Sulema…" Saskia began.

"Yes, Diva?" Sulema responded, not turning her head.

There was a long, heavy pause.

431

"Nothing, your Radiance. Never mind."

A hawk wheeled overhead, screaming into the silence.

It is better this way, Sulema thought. *For both of us.* She considered ordering the warrior to return to the Zeera, but Saskia would doubtless refuse to leave her side. Again. *Churra-headed brat*, she thought with a smile. *Reminds me of—*

Sulema, her mother whispered. *Open your Dreaming eyes.*

After a moment of startlement, she opened her Dreaming eyes, and what she saw made her pull Atemi up short. Even as the Ja'Akari reached the pastures, the pasture guards and horse-minders sprang to life. Bows appeared as if from nowhere, and the hapless riders fell beneath the rain of arrows like sheaves of wheat to the farmer's scythe. Horses screamed, riders screamed.

Saskia screamed.

A lone rider broke away from the mass of gold-and-white cloaked imperators at the Sunrise Gate. He raced toward them low to his horse's neck, a shield over his back, and gave his mare her head as if all the winds of Yosh were behind them. Indeed, he was pursued by a hail of arrows, all of which fell short, and then by a wedge formation of white-cloaked Salarian guards, golden-antlered, bull-horned, and armed with the bright white blades of the il Mer.

"Salarians," Sulema hissed. She stood in her stirrups, heart pounding in her ears. "What are they doing here? And who are they—"

"Davidian!" Saskia cried. She flung herself forward and her mare leapt away, toward the fleeing figure. "Dav—"

A red flower bloomed, impossibly, upon the pale leather vest on Saskia's back. She toppled from her mare and fell to the ground, a dagger protruding from between her shoulder blades. She was crushed beneath the hooves of Sulema's guard.

"Saskia!" Sulema screamed. She would have leapt from her saddle, but was prevented by a strong grip on her arm. Strong, and cruel. Sulema looked up, shocked, into the face of the Draik who had offered salt for her thoughts.

432

"Saskia!" she heard Davidian cry, as all around her Divas and Draiksguards unslung bows from their backs, nocked their arrows, and drew. "Saskia!" Three times, making it true. "Saskia!" Even as the arrows struck him, struck his horse, struck the blood-soaked ground at their feet. He fell as his love had fallen, pinned to the ground by the weight of betrayal.

Sulema went cold and numb all over. Her hands, gripping the reins, were heavy, clumsy. The brown-eyed conspirator in a Draik's helm took them from her grasp with ease.

"Why?" she asked him. "Why?"

"I am sorry, your Radiance," he said as he lifted his drawn sword high above his head. "But it is better this way. For all of us."

The blow fell, and she fell.

Into darkness.

Sulema did not know for how long she remained lost to the world, or how they got her into Atukos, but when she came to her senses she was bound and kneeling on the stone floor in front of the Dragon Throne.

The cold, dark, angry stone.

The fury of Atukos returned before her own pain. Deeper than blood, deeper than bone, deeper and colder than the heart of the world it ran, and the world trembled and knelt before Atukos even as she trembled and knelt before the man on the Dragon Throne. A man who, though he held the Mask of Akari and wore the golden robes of the Dragon King, was not her father.

My father... Sulema blinked back the tears, bit back the pain and heartbreak, and dug her fingernails into the palms of her hands, bound tight behind her back. *Focus, Sulema*, she told herself. *Think, girl. Think, and look.* For the second time that day, she opened her Dreaming eyes. This time she was trampled beneath the dark hooves of pain.

"Ah, ah," Aasah scolded in his gentle voice. "Do not try that again, girl."

433

Girl. Not your Radiance, or even Endada. Heart sinking, Sulema dropped her eyes. There, at the very bottom of the steps leading to the Dragon Throne, she saw them.

Her father was laid out upon a golden bier, his head on a golden pillow, his body draped chest-to-toes in a shimmering golden shroud. His hands were folded neatly atop his breast, eyes closed, face as peaceful as that of a sleeping child. But he was most certainly *not* sleeping. Wyvernus, the Dragon King, her father, was dead. Sprawled upon the floor at his feet, broken and torn, her beautiful face mutilated as if they had wished to erase all memory of her from the world, lay Hafsa Azeina, foremost dreamshifter among the Zeeranim.

Mother, Sulema thought. *Mama.* A wail rose in her heart. It flew up her throat and burst from her mouth in a single, clear note of purest agony. Again she sang out, and again, putting power behind it this time so that the cold dead walls of Atukos flashed a sullen red, so that the floor shook beneath her.

"*Wake!*" she called, though to her father, her mother, or to Sajani herself, Sulema did not know. Nor did she care. In the depth of her grief, she wanted nothing more than to see the world burn. "*Wake!*"

Far below her, in the darkest depths of a dreamshifter's nightmare, something old and cold and inconceivably huge began to stir.

A third time she sang, thrice to make it true.

"*Wa—*"

She froze, the last note caught in her throat. She was unable to breathe or move or so much as blink. An icy paralysis spread through her body like a spider's web, binding her fast, freezing her into a moment of time that stretched out infinitely in all directions.

"Enough." Aasah's voice rolled out at her from everywhere, it seemed, and echoed in the bright chill of her injured shoulder. The red walls of Atukos dimmed, and flickered, as if uncertain, before once more falling cold and dead. The ground rumbled and rolled for a moment longer before it, too, fell into quiescence. The air around her went dark as Sulema, starved for breath, began to slip away.

"Breathe." It was Aasah again, commanding her to live, bending her will to his. Her lungs pumped air in, out... Blood rushed through her heart and into her body... in, out. Still she was frozen in that moment, hunched on the floor beneath the Dragon Throne, unable to move or call out, unable to so much as look away from the desecrated body of her mother.

Fuck this, she thought, as a red rage blossomed within her, a dark music of the soul unlike anything she had ever felt or heard. Sulema raised her chin fractionally, raised her eyes to the king's dais. A man she did not know, but whose name she could guess, sat upon her father's throne.

Pythos, she thought, and let his image be burned into her memory. *Son of Serpentus. Not dead, after all.* Mattu had spoken truth, in that.

The man, who looked much like an older and unblemished Mattu Halfmask, held the Mask of Akari in his lap as if it were a toddler, and her father's robes of state pooled about him in a lake of gold. Ninianne il Mer stood behind the throne and to one side, a proud woman as beautiful as Nurati had been, head high and proud, eyes flashing in the dim torchlight. She wore upon her brow a diadem of diamonds and salt, and her robes were thickly crusted with precious salt.

Pythos was flanked on the other side by a woman in a demure gown of rose and cream, which left as little flesh exposed as a warden's touar. Her gaze was downcast, but when she raised it for a moment and met Sulema's stare, her fleeting smile was venomous.

Standing upon the steps beneath the throne were the matreons and patreons of Atualon, mistresses and masters, men and women who just that morning would have happily licked sand from the sole of Sulema's foot. A few were notable in their absence. Loremaster Rothfaust was nowhere to be seen, nor Matreon Bellanca, nor—and this last surprised her—Master Santorus. The twins Matteira and Mattu were there with all the rest, dressed in the white-and-gold robes of the ne Atu, with thin circlets of gold

435

upon their brows. Mattu did not wear a mask, nor did he meet Sulema's eyes, though she thought she might burn a hole in his heart with her wrath.

Liar, she thought. *False heart.* She would have torn hers from her chest and thrown it at him if she could, so great was the pain of his betrayal.

Heralds all around the room raised golden trumpets to their lips and blew out a series of long, quavering notes so unlike the powerful sound of her mother's shofar that Sulema curled her lip in disdain.

Even their horns are weak, she thought.

They may be weak, a laughing voice sounded in her head, *but they are strong enough to have defeated you, Sulema Firehair.* The blood chilled in her veins. She knew that voice.

Nightmare Man.

As the heralds lowered their trumpets, and the last feeble notes faded away into nothing, the man who had stolen her father's throne sat up straight, twisting the golden mask in his lap back and forth and letting it catch the light for all to see.

Why does he not wear it? Sulema wondered. *Surely that would make him seem more kingly, more powerful.* For she had no doubt as to this man's intentions.

Pythos raised a hand, and smiled, and spoke. "I am Pythos ap Serpentus ne Atu, Ka Atu, and your rightful king."

People behind Sulema began to cheer, to laugh, to cry out in horror. As the women behind the throne raised their hands in unison, the crowd quieted just enough for Pythos to raise his voice and begin again.

"I am the firstborn son of Serpentus, who as you know was Ka Atu until… until Wyvernus murdered him and stole his throne. His soldiers were supposed to have killed me, but as you can see"— he flashed a bright and charming smile at the crowd—"rumors of my death have been slightly exaggerated."

There was laughter at this.

They laugh, Sulema thought. *My father, my mother lie there dead, and they laugh.* The walls flickered red, and the crowd gasped, but Pythos ignored it and went on, raising his voice yet again, beating the crowd into submission.

"Moons ago, the man who betrayed my father realized his error. Upon learning of my continued existence, Wyvernus sent envoys to Taz Merraj, where I had long lived with my mother as an honored guest of our friend, Ninianne il Mer. We did not believe these envoys, in truth, being somewhat wary of the false king's intentions." More laughter. "But as I am echovete, able to control the atulfah that keeps us all safe from a wakeful dragon, and as he had no *proper* heir"—he glanced meaningfully at Sulema—"we did, at last, reach a resolution to our many differences. Wyvernus agreed to make me his heir, and I, in return, agreed to marry his daughter. His *virgin* daughter," he went on, "raised though she was by barbarians."

"Lies!" a voice called in the crowd. "Lies!"

"Why would I lie to you, my people?" Pythos smiled that charming smile again. "The truth is ever so much more entertaining. Though if you should doubt your king, and I suggest you do not do so out loud again..." He winked. "...my ministers would be happy to educate you in the matter."

"He speaks truth." Master Ezio's voice was heavy, as if he spoke through a mouth full of mud. "Hard though this is for me to hear, I have read the truth in the king's, in Wyvernus's own hand, sealed with his own seal." There was muttering in the chamber, but none raised further protest. Pythos let the smile fade from his face, and continued.

"As I said, an agreement was reached. An agreement that would have meant a peaceful transfer of power in time, and the continued safety of all, but Wyvernus was betrayed, even as he had betrayed my father. He faced a worse treachery than his own, if such a thing is possible. In the end, he was betrayed by his own blood." He stood slowly, raising the Mask of Akari in front of him so that it stared down upon Sulema. The mask glittered, as it always had, and it was beautiful, as it had always been, but it was just a thing of gold, quiescent, as dead as Atukos herself. Sulema would have laughed, had she been able to do more than breathe and glare.

"He was murdered," Pythos declared, "by his own daughter."

No…

The crowd gasped. Somewhere behind her, Sulema heard a woman cry out, and the sound bounced round and round the walls. Aasah, the king's shadowmancer, came to stand beside Pythos. His eyes were wide blue pools, cool and deep as the dragon's lake, and filled with liquid sorrow.

"Sulema an Wyvernus," he intoned, staring at her. "You have been accused of the crimes of regicide, and patricide. Of killing your father, your king."

No, she wanted to scream, *no no no*. But she could not move.

"Sulema an Hafsa Azeina," Aasah continued, damning her before the world, "you have been accused of the crimes of regicide, and matricide. Of killing your mother, the Queen Consort."

Sulema jerked within the magical web that bound her, but managed no more than a weak and muffled "*nuuuuuuuuu*," which was swallowed whole by the crowd's ugly moan.

"Sulema of the Zeeranim, daughter of no one," Aasah finished in a voice of steel and stone, "how do you answer?"

Sulema was jerked upright, as if held by a puppeteer's strings. Her eyes bugged out and her throat was a fiery agony as words were forced from her well-trained lungs, through her well-trained throat, to fall from her well-trained lips at the feet of the man who had taught her to sing.

"Guilty," she heard herself say. "I am guilty."

The crowd behind Sulema erupted into a storm of fury. There were cries of pain and the *thud-thump* of fists on flesh as the Draiksguard beat them back. Aasah, her teacher, her *friend*, stared at her with his pale blue eyes, and nodded.

The golden mask glittered in her enemy's hands.

And the Dragon swallowed her whole.

FIFTY-SIX

The Grinning Mymyc was destroyed and rebuilt, but not as it had been. Where once the inn was warm and welcoming, now it was a grim, sere fortress, all sharp edges and ugly, undressed stone. Gone were the wide windows overflowing with laughter and the smells of fine food. In their places were arrow-slits scowling over a small army of guards. Even the sign had changed. The grinning, dancing, merry mymyc had been replaced with a fell red-tongued beast snarling defiance over a disemboweled enemy.

Charming, Ani thought. *I wonder if I will find Aish Kalumm so changed, if ever I return. Likely I would not recognize my old home.*

As she shifted her weight from foot to foot, the bag she had slung over her back rolled to the side and she heard the soft, sad clatter of human bones. *Then again*, she admitted, *it is likely that Aish Kalumm would not recognize me, either. Istaza Ani is as dead and gone as the man in my bag. In her place…*

She was spared further thought when the heavy iron-bound doors of the Grinning Mymyc swung open, revealing a dark interior and disgorging a pair of imposing figures. Bretan wore his helm set with bull's horns, while the other… Even from such a distance, Ani could feel the heat of the smaller man's eyes. It was Soutan Mer—but only *just*, she thought. He had the look of a sword that had been forged in pain.

Everything is changing.

The doors thudded shut and the men approached her, hands at their hips, with the cautious low-centered glide of fighting men who sense a serious threat. As they drew near, Ani held up her free hand, palm-out, and smiled as charming a smile as she could manage.

You will scare the skin off them with that grimace, Askander would have said.

Shut up, she replied to the dream of her lover. *To them I am only an old woman with a bag full of bones. What might they possibly have to fear?* The changes she had experienced were hidden beneath loose-fitting clothes, and she hoped that would be sufficient.

She could tell the moment Bretan recognized her. He looked at her curiously, as if uncertain, then straightened, mouth dropping into an "o" and flattening in a stern line, and his step quickened so that his companions had to scurry in order to catch up.

"Istaza Ani," he said, and she could have wished his voice had been warmer. "I had not thought to see you again, not here." His eyes narrowed as he stared at her.

"It is Ani only, now," she replied, "and I am very glad indeed to find you alive. What happened here?" She gestured to… everything. "Where is your Eleni? I have brought her a visitor." Talieso whickered. The city may have changed, and the demeanor of these people as well, but her stallion remembered a warm welcome and plenty of food. *If only humans were more like horses,* she thought, *the world would be a better place.*

Bretan and Soutan exchanged heavy glances. Soutan shook his head, but Bretan stared at him hard till he relented with a sour shrug.

"As you will, brother," he said. His mouth was a sour twist. "On your head it will be if this woman brings further trouble to the family." Ani regarded the youth steadily, wondering what had happened to quench his bright and mischievous flame.

No more than has happened to any of us, I suppose, she thought. Aloud she said only, "Well met, Soutan Mer, once again. This time I find you better clothed, I see." One of the guards coughed a laugh, but Soutan did not even flick his eyes in her direction. He turned on his heels and left.

Bretan shook his head. "I will not apologize for my brother's behavior," he told her. "Much has happened since last you came to the Grinning Mymyc, Meissati. Much has happened to sour our attitude toward outlanders."

"Much has happened to me and mine, as well, salt merchant," she snapped, out of patience. She needed food, water, a bath, feed

440

and shelter for her horse. She did not need a pair of broody young men and their heavy words. "As well you know. You hardly left me in safe circumstances, despite your pledge of honor."

He stiffened at those words, dark eyes flashing.

"That is not fair," he growled.

"Life is not fair," she tossed back. "Surely your mother taught you that. Are we going to stand out here under the sun, kicking words back and forth like a goat's head? Or are you going to invite me inside your... charming establishment?" Her heart pounded in her ears even as she flung the challenge in his face, and she more than half expected him to turn her away. Or worse, to attack her. It had been a long road and hard, and she was not in the mood for a fight.

He frowned at her a moment more, and she frowned back twice as fiercely. *I was playing these games for years before ever they placed you at your mother's tit*, she thought. Finally the young man grunted, much like the bull whose horns he wore.

"Come then," he told her, "and on your head be it if you have come to cast shade upon our hearth once again." He turned his back and stomped toward the inn, expecting her to follow.

"Is Eleni here?" Ani asked his retreating shoulders. "I had hoped to..."

"Eleni is dead," he replied without slowing. "If you want your horse fed and watered, you will have to do it yourself."

The new stable was much less to Talieso's liking than the old one had been, and he communicated his displeasure by kicking at his stall door.

Ani felt much the same about the new inn. Gone were the serving girls and boys with their colorful clothes and bright smiles. Gone was the warm hearth piled high with sweetbreads, the dark ale, the salt-crusted fish. Piss-pale ale was set before her by dour-faced servants, followed by a shallow bowl of stew as thin and unenthusiastic as her welcome had been.

Ah well, Ani thought as she grimaced around a swallow of

ale. *At least I have not had to kill any of them yet.* Still, the night was young.

"Your hospitality is somewhat meaner than it was, the last time I sat beneath your roof," she remarked in a mild way as Bretan sat down across from her.

"And yet it is warmer than the welcome I was shown by your warriors," he countered.

Ani picked up the mug again, considered it, and set it down without drinking.

"It is not poisoned," Soutan Mer said, as he took the bench beside her.

"Poisoning this ale would be a kindness." Ani pushed food and drink away. She would rather subsist on her remaining pemmican and stale water. "Mariza was none of mine," she told Bretan. "Her false warriors are nothing more than Kha'Akari—exiles."

"Was?" he raised his brows.

"I killed her." She smiled. *And they killed me, in return.* But she saw no need to tell him that.

"And the king's son?"

She held out both hands and shrugged. "Alive, last I saw him. I wish him well." *And luck,* she thought, *if he is still alive.*

"There have been rumors that he is dead."

"I heard that he was sold as a slave in Min Yaarif," Soutan interjected.

"There are more rumors in the Zeera than there are grains of sand," she said, and she snorted. "Only a goat-brained idiot would listen to half of them."

"Only a goat-brained idiot would admit to having been with the son of the Dragon King just before he disappeared," Bretan said in a hard voice, bringing both hands down upon the table between them. "And with the king dead…"

Ani grabbed the edge of the table as the world spun around her.

"The king is…" she said, gasping. "How?"

"You did not know?" Bretan blinked at her. "How could you not have known?"

442

She staggered to her feet, grabbing her bag and clutching it to her chest as a child might cling to her blanket.

"Where is Hafsa Azeina?" she demanded. "Where is my Sulema?"

Soutan stood too quickly, too close. He grabbed for her shoulder. "Do not act innocent, you—"

She struck him down hard. He flew from the bench, ass-over-helm, to lie in a crumpled heap near the wall. Ani backed away from the table still clutching the bag of bones, which had begun singing to her.

Bretan was on his feet, shouting. The entire room was on its feet, roiling like a kicked spider-hill.

"Soutan! My brother!"

"He will live, Meissat," a guard cried, kneeling next to the prone youth. "He is just—"

"Where are they?" Ani roared. "Where are they? *Tell me!*"

Heat flashed through the room, through all their bodies, as the fire that was in all their bones crackled through her voice. The serving girls, the serving lads, every guard and patreon and cook in the room went still as stone. Then they all collapsed like heaps of ash. All except Bretan, who stood and stared at Ani as if she were a monster.

As well he should. Ani walked carefully back to the table, set her bench upright, and took her seat with slow and gentle ease. She set one hand upon the table, but when the wooden surface began to smoke beneath her touch, she put it in her lap instead.

"Tell me," she commanded. "Tell me everything. Now."

Bretan again took the seat across from her, staring at the smoking handprint on the table between them, and took a deep breath.

"The king is dead," he began.

Ani tightened her grip on the bag.

"He was found slumped before the fire in his chambers," he continued, "as if he had fallen asleep. But there was… there have been rumors that…"

She knew. "What was missing?"

"His heart, they say. Burned out from within."

443

"What music might a dreamshifter make, with the heart of the Dragon King?" Ani did not know whether to scream, or laugh, or cry. She felt as if she might puke up every meal she had ever eaten. "What might she not do, with that blood upon her lips? Has she gone mad?"

"Truly you do not know," Bretan whispered. He lifted his gaze from the charred table to look into her eyes. "How could you not know? She was your friend. Do you Zeeranim have no souls?"

The breath stopped in her chest and Ani hunched forward, shaking her head in denial.

"Know what?"

"The queen is dead, as well. Dead, in her chambers, just like the king. Nothing was missing," he hurried to add as she raised her hot eyes to his. "She was just... dead."

"And Sulema?" *My Sulema, oh my child. Oh daughter of my heart, not you too...*

Bretan hesitated. "Gone, they say. Gone, without a trace."

"Dead," she whispered. "Murdered." The bones in their bag were singing to her again, a song of ash and fire. *I could kill them all.*

"Well..." Bretan pursed his lips, looked at her carefully out the corners of his eyes. Around them, those who had been laid low by Ani's fire had begun to stir. "Maybe not. Not many people know this, but her horse disappeared, too, and many of her belongings. Zeerani things, mostly. Her bow, her sword... it is said that perhaps Sulema killed both her parents, that it was a Zeerani conspiracy all along."

"Who says these things?" Her heart had begun to beat again, crippled and painful and slow.

"Pythos and his folk, mostly. He put it about that Wyvernus was to name him heir, and since the king's death..."

"Pythos? Heir?" Now Ani let the bag drop to the floor, and the bones within chittered angrily. She set her elbows on the table, her head in her hands, and closed her eyes against the dim light. "I leave my girl alone in this city for half a year, and everything goes to shit."

The fire in her bones burned low, and Ani began to weep.

FIFTY-SEVEN

Soutan handed her a nondescript bundle. "As you requested, Meissati. Though I fail to see how even these can help get you into Atukos. You hardly look like a Draik." He cupped his hands before his chest, puckered his lips, and batted his eyes. The boy seemed to have found some of his missing sass, though none of his quick smiles quite reached his eyes.

"Impertinent brat," she said, but her heart was not in it. Her heart was not in *anything*. Still, Ani drew aside the top rag—an old kamish, far from home—and tossed it aside. Air hissed through her teeth as the gold of a draik's helm winked up at her. "How did you... Never mind, I do not want to know."

"Ah, but it is a grand tale of bravery and derring-do," Soutan protested, striking a dramatic pose. "Are you certain you do not wish to hear it? A tale to tell your grand-brats, for sure."

"I am certain." There would be no grand-brats for her, however.

"Ah," he said, disappointed. "Well, to tell you the truth, I am fucking one of the wash maids."

"Only one?" Bretan asked. He had entered the room and was shaking his head at the youth. "You are losing your touch, brother."

"Well, one at a time, anyway. I—"

"Sssst," Ani hissed. She drew the bundle open and laid out everything it contained. A complete draik's uniform from helm to smallclothes, and a sword besides, short and ugly but serviceable. She nodded, satisfied. "I do not wish to hear your tales of sexual conquest, cub. I do need you to leave. Both of you. Now."

"What are you going to do?" Soutan's eyes were ripe with curiosity. "Magic?"

"I am going to undress," she snapped. "Now, unless you wish an eyeful of my scarred old tits...?" She had not seen young men

445

scurry so quickly since the last time russet ridgebacks had gotten loose in the wardens' quarters.

In truth, it was not her scarred old flesh Ani had wanted to hide, but the whole, strong flesh of youth that she still kept concealed beneath loose clothing. Not of *her* youth, either. Ani could not remember a time when her own skin had been so smooth, unmarked by lash or blade or hard living. The little finger of her left hand no longer canted out at an odd angle, neither of her knees hurt, and both shoulders swung as freely as if they had never been dislocated.

Damn Inna'hael, what has he done to me? Who am I, now, in this strange new body? If I ever get hold of that louse-ridden cat—

She pushed the thought aside and finished dressing herself in the uniform of a Draiksguard. In order to confront Inna'hael, she would first have to find him, out in the vast wilds of the vash'ai pridelands. Before she could do that, she would have to survive this day. Neither was likely, and so there was no use fretting over it.

The uniform was loose and ill fitting, likely meant to cover a frame much larger and more male than her own. Ani needed no polished glass to tell her that never in a fucktillion moons would she pass for a member of the Draiksguard.

She smiled a small and secret smile.

Ani would not pass… but *he* might.

Taking the bag of bones, she spilled its contents onto the table, then caught the skull as it would have rolled away. She brought it up before her face, waggling a finger in admonition as if this were one of the pride's cubs she had been tasked with raising.

"Ah, now," she told it, "there will be none of that. You have work yet to do, my boy." These bones, the bones she had sent Khoroush-Il-mannech to fetch for her, had not been long without flesh. Istaza Ani would have demanded to know whence they had come, and what had happened to their owner—and how she, herself, could condone such a thing. Was she now no better than Hafsa Azeina?

Bonesinger Ani dismissed the thought with an impatient flick of her fingers. Hafsa Azeina was dead, and who else might dare to chide her? As she laid the bones out in their places, Ani began to sing, just as she and her mother had done so many times, so long ago.

Ghar-mah qarc-ap-teh domma'esh et ghar-mah batasoreh,
Ghar-mah batasoreh domma'esh et ghar-mah kat-pat-a'a!...

The skull laid just so, and the delicate clavicle—which for some reason had always been her favorite. Sternum and vertebrae, long bones and short, and every tiny bit of his fingers and toes, she laid them each out in their turn, in the proper order, and she crooned to them with as much love as any mother might sing to her child.

"Be-me-lath-u'on sa'otani-noa ah-Sajani'oa-e leka'a!"

"Leko'a!" She shouted the last word, and as she did her voice broke. It grew deeper, much more resonant, so much so that she coughed at the strange feel of it in her throat. She pounded her hairy chest with a hairy fist and laughed a harsh, masculine laugh.

Akari above, that feels so strange. She squeezed her big fists, wriggled her big toes, and peeked inside the waistband of her kilt. *And that feels more than strange.* She let the waistband fall shut again and decided to pretend she had not seen such a thing. She had done murder and worse, now, but murder at least was a natural thing.

This was just plain *wrong.*

Bretan and Soutan burst into the room, short swords drawn, alarmed no doubt by the sound of male laughter. At the sight of her—him—standing there, they raised their swords and charged.

"Aat-aat!" Ani shouted, and coughed again. She held both hands up, palms out. How did men ever accomplish anything, with these hams stuck on the ends of their arms? "Give me a minute to get this shit figured out, before you go killing me."

Bretan stopped so abruptly that his brother ran into him and they both almost fell over. His jaw dropped halfway to his chest.

"Ani?"

"In the flesh." She cleared her throat and spat. That worked, at least. "Though whose flesh, I am not entirely certain."

"You are a bonesinger?" Soutan's voice climbed to a squeak. "A *bonesinger*?"

"Impossible," Bretan said. His eyes had gone wide and round and white about the edges. "The Dziranim are gone, long gone."

"I am the last," Ani said, folding her arms across her hairy chest. It itched. "The last of my tribe, the last of my kind."

"The lost tribe," Soutan whispered. He punched his brother on the shoulder. "Show her. Show her. You have to... Mother would wish it." Bretan turned his head to stare at the youth, then back to Ani. His eyes were dark and strange.

"When you return, Bonesinger," he said at last, "my mother will wish to speak to you. We have much to discuss, we small people of the world. Much to offer one another, perhaps." He reached up and took hold of his bull's horn helm.

"What—" Ani began, but her deep voice choked off as the enormous young man removed his helm.

His helm, but not his horns.

"Ohhhhh," Ani breathed. "Oh, *shit*."

"Exactly," Soutan agreed. He smiled, and as he did so he dropped the glamour that had hidden his too-sharp features, grinned at her with too-sharp teeth. "Yours is not the only lost tribe, Dzirani. You are not as alone in this world as you think."

"Daeborn," Ani acknowledged. Her massive new heart pounded in her hairy new chest, and she inclined her head toward the two brothers. "Long have our people been allies. We shall have much to discuss upon my return, ehuani. If I return."

"If you return," Bretan agreed, bowing his horned head to her. He smiled. "As the worlds meet, Dzirani, so shall we again. Of this I have no doubt."

As the brothers had given her a disguise in which to enter Atukos, so too did they give her an excuse. The brothers were well known to the fortress guards, and it was not unusual that a member of the Draiksguard might escort them as they brought a gift of fine liqueurs and cheeses to tempt the palate of the new Dragon King. As they neared the kitchens, Ani raised her head and took a deep, appreciative sniff.

There is always time to stop and smell the bread, she thought. *Even on the last day of your life.* Especially *on the last day of your life.*

"Do you remember the way?" Bretan whispered.

"I do."

"We could go with you," Soutan offered. "At least one of us."

"No, but thank you for the offer." She was impatient to be off, truth be told, and they would simply slow her down. "The absence of either of you would be noticed. I will see you again, if I return—"

"When you return." Bretan touched his bull's horn helm, and winked. "Until the worlds meet again, Dzirani."

"Until then," she agreed, and watched the two young men continue down the hallway, bearing their bottles and casks. Theirs was a heavy burden to bear. *But not nearly as heavy as my own.*

The bones of the Atualonian man whispered to her of the ways and roads of Atukos till she could have navigated the fortress in her sleep, yet still she stepped gently, carefully. It was likely that she would die this day, but it was not *quite* certain—at least so she hoped. In any case she very much wanted to carry out this final duty before she was slaughtered.

Bretan and Soutan had told her of the rumors, that the Dragon King's body lay in state in a secret room, and would soon be interred with the bones of the kings who had gone before him. The body of Hafsa Azeina, that outlander queen who was accused of his murder, was another matter entirely.

Her corpse had been set upon a high wall, impaled upon an iron spike, subject to wind and weather and whichever birds of prey might wish to feast and shit upon her flesh. There she would hang until every bit of her had rotted away, unmourned, unsung, unloved, despised in death even as she had been in life.

Ah, but there was one who loved you, Ani thought, *one who loves you still.* She turned a corner and nearly ran into a young woman

449

clad in maroon and gray, with hair the color of sandalwood and eyes gray as a stormy sky.

"Oh!" the girl cried, and a hand fluttered to her mouth. "You gave me such a… Jennet? *Jennet??* Where have you been, you two-timing goat-assed whelp of a—"

Ani held one hand up to the girl's face and began to sing. *I am sorry*, she thought, as the slow, cool words wound round the girl's bones and dragged her down into unwilling slumber. The lass would wake confused and sick, wondering why she had dreamed of her absent lover… but she would wake. *I am so sorry.*

The way was long, but her victims mercifully few. Atukos was dark, dead as true stone and nearly empty. Those who were forced by duty to brave those brooding halls scurried about with their heads down and with no wish to speak to anyone. Soon enough she reached the high walkway, the narrow path lined on either side with unspeakably crusted iron spikes. Three bodies rotted here, in this sky chamber, beneath the harsh gaze of Akari. One was a man, naked and without legs. One was a half-grown person of indeterminate gender. And the last…

Oh, thought Ani, and her massive man's heart crumpled. *Oh, my beloved. Oh, my friend.*

Sheathing her short sword, she reached up and lifted what was left of Hafsa Azeina from the cold iron that pinned her fast. Never minding the stench, the gore, never minding the sight of her friend's smashed face and half-flayed corpse, she held close the body of her dearest and oldest companion, and kissed her blood-matted, gore-matted, moonsilk hair.

"Oh, my love," she intoned, and the voice that issued from her throat was her own. Not even a bonesinger's magic could deny the power of a broken heart. "Oh, my friend. What have they done to you, what have they done…"

She shrugged out of the armor and removed the silk undershirt she wore, so that she could wrap her friend's body in it. Most of the blood was dried, and it hardly bled through at all as she cradled the pale bundle in her arms as once she had cradled her child. A new song rose in her heart, the song of the Zeera, slow and mournful and vicious, and as she gathered the too-light bundle and began the long trek upward she began to sing. Soft it was at first, this song, but it rang true in the silent chambers of her heart, the silent chambers of Atukos. These angry echoes lent a strength and breadth to the notes that had waves of red-gold power rippling along the path before her.

Never in her life had Ani felt so powerful. Never had she wished for it, for any part of it. She strode up and through the fortress Atukos like a daemon queen from the old stories, baring her teeth in a feral grimace, and the dragonstone walls wept as she passed.

First there were hallways, and bridges, and walls. These she climbed with the featherlight body in her arms, half wishing that someone might try—*try!*—to stop her. None came. She stepped free from the overlarge sandals, the studded skirt and underkilt of a Draik, and let them lie where they had fallen. Let those who came upon the tale of her passing pause to wonder. Let those who noted the absence of this defiled body raise a cry. She did not care.

Let them come, she half wished. *Let them come.*

Ani walked on, ever on and ever upward. The stone hall and stairs of Atukos grew rough and wild till at last they merged with the living rock from which they had been called by Kal ne Mur in the long ago. Even as the mountain shed its glamour of civilization, Ani did the same, letting the bones and flesh she had stolen from an Atualonian man melt away so that she was herself again, a Dzirani dark-skinned, dark-eyed and dangerous, bloodying her feet upon the forbidden path. This narrow way meant death for any save the Dragon King and his kin, but no shout was raised as her bare feet touched the black rocks, no arrow was loosed to find her heart, and Akari did not swoop from the heavens to punish her for this trespass.

Let them try. She sang on, clutching the mutilated body of her friend. *Even Akari. Even he, for I will strike him from the sky, if he dares try to stop me.*

451

Tough as her feet were, dragonglass shards sliced at her flesh with each step. It seemed fitting to Ani that she would leave a trail of blood and tears, a warning to any who might follow. Still none came. Thick white fog rolled down from the peak of Atukos as if the mountain herself offered them cover. Soon nothing in the world existed but the mountain, the sky, and two women—one murdered, the other broken.

As night crept upon her, the song of Ani grew in volume and power with each step, wave upon wave of it rolling outward from the marrow of her bones till she itched with it, burned with it. It had a color, this song, a taste. A scent, of rot and flowers and salted clay. Almost, it had a name. Such a thing was forbidden, of course. It was the darkest of dark magic. Of such songs were nightmares born... but Ani sang on. This world had murdered her, had murdered her friend and stolen the daughter of her heart, and she did not care on this day whether her song raised bonelords, or daelords, or an army of the dead. Let this song wake the dragon, for all she cared. Ani was done with this world.

You were supposed to sing my bones to sleep, she thought as she paused and cupped a hand behind the silk-bundled head, pressed her lips to the cloth. *It was not supposed to end like this. Never like this.* The song, her grief, and her bloodied feet carried her up, up, up till she had reached the very summit of Atukos.

Ani stood for a moment at the very peak of the world, overlooking a lake of purest magic, the dreaming breath of Sajani herself. But there was no beauty left to her, not a song in her heart to hold the love of earth or sky or the reflection of starlight. The moons bathed in the lake even as they danced across the sky, and Ani would not have minded watching it all go up in flames.

Her burden had grown heavy, and sticky, and it dragged the last ragged notes of song from Ani's soul, leaving her speechless and empty.

"Come," she croaked. "Come, sweetheart, let me take you home." She walked down the gentle slope of black sand. When she had reached the very edge of the lake that was not a lake at all, Ani set her burden down gently, gently. There were songs for this, too, she knew, proper songs of mourning and leavetaking, songs meant to release the soul of a loved one so that it might find peace and joy in the next world, songs meant to appease the vengeful dead and soothe the vengeful living.

Ani had no wish for further song on this day, and peace was the very last thing her heart desired. She knelt upon the black sand, unwrapped the poor, torn body of Hafsa Azeina, and wept anew over each hurt, each mark of abuse and defilement. She used the last of her water, the scraps of silk, and her own hands to wash her friend's face and hands and feet as best she could, and pressed her lips to the cold, torn cheeks.

If only I could look into your eyes once more, she wept. *Just once more. If only I could hear you laugh. You had the most beautiful laugh in the world, my friend, and it has been far too long since I have heard it. I am sorry. I am sorry I did not make you laugh more. I am sorry I let them do this to you, my sister-in-heart.*

My dearest love. I am sorry.

Dzirana Ani, the last bonesinger, gathered the naked body of Hafsa Azeina to her heart one last time, staggered to her feet, and walked straight into the magic of Sajani's dreaming, breaking every sacred law in the world.

Let them kill me for it, if they can. The world had killed every thing, every person she held dear, one by one, and she was done with it. *Let the dragon wake, if she wills. I am sending my friend home, and I do not care what happens after this.*

The dragon's magic did not feel like water, not at all. It was warm, uncomfortably so, and stung her flesh like nettles. Ani waded out into the lake until she was waist deep, ignoring the discomfort and the strange numbness that made it feel as if the lower half of her body no longer existed in this world at all. She closed her eyes and hugged her friend tight, wishing that she might carry her for all time close to her heart.

"But that is not the way life works," Hafsa Azeina had explained

to her, when they were young, and had hearts new to breaking. *"You cannot have life without pain. Life is pain, my friend."*

"Life is pain," Ani agreed. "Only death comes easy." She let her arms drop, let the body of her friend slip beneath the still and waveless magic. She let go of everything she had ever loved.

Then she screamed.

FIFTY-EIGHT

The world was red, and mad with agony.

Ismai clung to Ehuani's blood-slick hide till the blood had dried and flaked away, till Akari Sun Dragon rose high in the sky, breathing a hot sand wind to scour and torment him. He clung to her when the world went cold, though his hands and feet went numb and his body shook so that the water-filled ruin of his face sloshed like a skin of wine.

He held on until time no longer mattered, till heat and cold blurred into an endless buzz of torment, all the while his heart pounding in his ears like a war drum, *tha-rump tha-rump tha-rumble*, until he knew nothing but pain and thrumming, pain and throbbing. When he could no longer hold onto Ehuani he held onto stubbornness, and when he could no longer hold onto stubbornness he clung to Ruh'ayya.

I am here, Kithren, she told him, more than once, more than a hundred times, and *We are nearly there*, and *I love you*. Vash'ai, he knew, held a deep disdain for the word love. Had Ismai been capable of thought, he would have known by her words that he was dying.

The wind ruffled his hair and scalded his face, and Ehuani surged and jogged beneath him. On a subconscious level Ismai understood that they rode through the Zeera, over lands that were known to him, but all of his being was centered upon drawing one agonized breath after another into his lungs and pushing them out again, in and out, in and out. He was past caring about such trifling matters as when and where.

Thus it was that two days and two nights after his doomed marriage to Ishtaset, Ismai son of Nurati, last of the line of Zula Din, came at last to the Valley of Death. It was not a victorious homecoming, as storytellers might sing of it, nor was it an arrival heavy with portents. He came blind and unknowing as a babe born too soon, and when Ehuani at last came to a nervous stop he fell from her back to lie unmoving upon the sand, scarcely breathing.

Ehuani gave him the gentlest of nudges with her delicate muzzle, tickling across his stinking, dying skin with her whiskers, and pawed at the ground beside him with a careful hoof. Ruh'ayya shoved her way between them and the mare retreated.

Kithren. The vashai's voice was a balm, a cool wind. *Kithren.* That was all. She did not beg him to wake, or to live. Still, her regard was a rope that bound him unwilling to the land of those not yet dead, and Ismai loved her even as he resented her for it.

Let me go, he thought.

"Ismai." The voice was softer than a horse's breath, deeper than the love of a vash'ai. Stronger than death. "Oh, Ismai."

Char lifted him as easily as he might lift a one-armed child. As gentle as she was, still her touch was pain, a storm of pain that sucked the last breath from his lungs in a thin, rattling scream. From a great distance Ismai watched his own body tremble and convulse as it tried to draw another breath—

Oh, he thought, *I can see again, how wonderful.*

—failed, and tried and—

Why did I never notice how beautiful...

—failed.

"Ismai." She called to him, and "Ismai," and three times, binding him, condemning him to agony. "Ismai!"

Air seared his lungs, exploded from his mouth, splitting the skin of his face so that it wept blood. Ismai found himself wracked by a fit of coughing and consumed by pain so intense that it could only mean one thing.

He was alive.

"Curse you," he rasped. "To... seventh circle of... Yosh."

"I have been there and back again," she told him in all seriousness. "The Red Gate holds no fear for me. Here, drink this."

A cup—a bowl?—was held against his lips. Too weak to push it away, too dazed to refuse, Ismai swallowed some cool liquid and grimaced at the taste.

"What—?"

"Do not ask, Ismai. You do not want to know, but it will help you to heal." Indeed, a numbness spread from Ismai's scorched throat to his stomach and even his lungs, a tingling relief from pain that had him sighing and sinking back into some soft, furred bedding.

"You should have let me die," he said at last.

"I know," she answered. "I am sorry, Ismai."

There was nothing to say to that, so Ismai allowed himself to be swept away into the dark, sweet oblivion of sleep.

The smell of burned flesh wrenched Ismai from the blessed darkness of sleep into the wretched darkness of living. At first he thought that it was his own burning flesh he smelled. He sat up with a cry of alarm, hands going instinctively to his eyes, and yanked to a stop. His wrists had been bound as he slept, and he jerked in panic against his bonds.

"Ismai. Ismai, stop." Char's voice, close and growing closer, low and soft as if she would soothe a spooked horse. Char, the scarred guardian of Eid Kalmut, the Valley of Death. "Stop, you are going to hurt yourself. Here, let me." He felt a light touch upon his arm, a tug at his bonds, then he was free. He waved his hands experimentally before bringing them back to his face, but was prevented again, this time by her hands on his. "No touching," she scolded. "The skin is delicate and must be left to heal."

He thought she was moving away again, and was seized by a sudden panic.

"Where are you going?"

"Just here." Light, soothing. "I have a rabbit on the fire."

Fire. He whimpered.

I am here, Kithren.

Where? I cannot see you. I cannot see.

Not far. I am at the oasis, with your horse. I have caught a tarbok. His mind was filled with the scent of fresh blood, red meat, steaming and delicious in the cool night air.

Is it night? I cannot see. Then, sounding pathetic even in his mind-voice, *Can you come here?*

I cannot. The Valley of Death is—she struggled to translate her next thought into a word that humans might understand.

"*Khutlani*," Char whispered. "It is forbidden for her to come here, but she will not leave you."

"You can hear her?"

"I can hear you, and you can hear her. It is much the same." Her voice was close again, startling Ismai so that he jumped. She touched his curled fists, coaxing them open, and he flinched at the feel and smell of hot charred flesh as she pressed meat into his hands. "Eat."

"I am not hungry." That was a lie. *I do not wish to eat* would have been closer to the truth, and *I would rather die* closer still, but Ismai no longer cared nor had the energy to tell the difference.

"Eat," she insisted. "We have much to discuss."

After another moment of doubt, Ismai ate. It hurt so badly to move his face that he shredded the meat into tiny bits with his fingers, and scarcely chewed at all. Still, by the time he had finished his small portion he was drenched in sweat and shaking with exhaustion. Char helped him to lie back on the soft pile of... furs? Clothing? She arranged his arms comfortably before tethering his wrists again.

"So that you do not claw at your face as you sleep," she explained, "and undo all my healing." Then she spread a cream or salve of some sort over his skin. She started low on his chest—which Ismai had not realized was burned, till then—and up toward his face in small, circular strokes. Though the salve was cool and her fingers light, Ismai whimpered at the touch, and would have pulled away if he could.

"Be still," she told him, and he thought she was weeping. By the time she reached his face, Ismai's cries had joined with hers into a

458

long, low wail of misery. When she pried his eyes open and dropped the cream into them as well, it burned so much that he screamed.

"I am sorry, Ismai," she told him as she knelt over him, and her tears fell onto him like liquid fire. "I am sorry."

Later—much later, he thought—Ismai turned toward the little sounds Char was making as she tended the fire.

"Is this what it was like, for you?" he asked. "When you were… hurt?"

There was a long, slow, heavy silence. "Yes," she answered. "Very much like this."

"I am sorry." He meant it. *No child should suffer like this*, he thought. "Will I be—will my face—"

"Will you be scarred as I am scarred?"

"Yes." His voice was so small and afraid he could hardly hear it over the *tha-rump tha-rump tha-rumble* of his drumming heart. "Yes."

Ismai swallowed his pain, and with it a lifetime's worth of hopes and dreams. "Well," he said finally, "I guess I will never be as handsome as my brother."

"Oh, Ismai." Char touched his hair, lightly, and he jumped again. "You were handsome, before… but now you will be *beautiful*." She took his hands in hers, and settled down beside him. When she spoke again, it helped to calm him.

FIFTY-NINE

"In the long ago," Char began, "when the land was whole, and the dragon slept soundly, and the earth was rich and dark with her dreaming, there lived a little girl named…"

"Charon," he guessed. *Tha-rump tha-rump tha-rumble* thundered his heart.

"No," she told him, and he thought she smiled. "There was no Char then, no Charon, there was no Valley of Death and so no need for a guardian. Now hush.

"There was a girl, and her name was Naara."

Naara, the winds mourned overhead. *Naara.*

"She was the beloved and only daughter of a woman with seven sons. Born on the back of a horse, as was customary in the long ago when women were stronger and babes more plentiful, and rumored to have been planted in her mother's belly by Sai ne Nar, son of the Middle Sea. Her mother encouraged this idea and went so far as to bathe the babe in salted waters, but there was no truth in it. Her father was no sea god, but a being more powerful and terrible than even the Four.

"Her mother, First Rider of the Mah'zula, had lain with Kal ne Mur, and from this ill-advised pairing the child was born. Her secret name, known only to mother and child, was Naar-Ahnet, an ancient name meaning 'fire upon the dark water,' but the people knew her only as Naara, or 'pearl.'

"Her father, once he learned of her existence, called her by yet a third name. He called her Sa Atu, the Heart of Atualon. Kal ne Mur invited his daughter to Atualon, to the great fort Atukos, there to abide with him for a season. The girl's mother was loath to let her leave, but the girl begged morning and night to be allowed to go, and even in the long ago it was folly to anger the Dragon

460

King. In the end, and with great reluctance, she sent the girl off with blessings, and fragrant smoke, and these words, '*Remember who you are.*'"

"Wait… wait! This is you? The girl in the story is you? But— but—how—" *It is Sulema's story all over again*, he thought, and his mind scattered like a herd of frightened horses. *I have to go save her.* In the next moment, he remembered that he was blind, and probably dying, and unlikely to be rescuing anybody. Ever.

"Hush, you. It is rude to interrupt a story." That soft touch again, on his shoulder this time. "Listen. *Listen.*

"These were dark times in Atualon. Many of the people resented their foreign-born king with his foreign ways and Daeborn looks. No few of the women and men in power encouraged this animosity, using the people's fear and hatred as a wedge between the king and his people. They did this in a bid to attain more of his influence for themselves. War hung like a cloud over all their heads. Then, as now, there was great power to be found in Atukos, and power draws the ever-thirsting hearts of men as a watering hole draws predators. Like predators snarling at one another over a puddle, Ismai, our kind *never* share power. It is only ever taken with force and bloodshed.

"Still, for a time the girl was happy. Her father adored her, showering her with gifts and affection, and she was the darling of the Bitter Court. Though she was too young to think it was anything but disgusting, the leaders of the land sent their sons to win her favor. Learned women and men strove to teach her. Atualon at that time had a great library, buildings and rooms and tunnels filled with books and scrolls and maps. Naara was delighted, for she was one of those girls who find books and horses more enthralling than boys and pretty clothes.

"Her father, being an indulgent man and smitten, gave her leave to roam as she liked, read whatever she liked, and so it was that she came to know the keeper of these books, one of the most powerful men in all Atualon, one of those they called the Baidun Daiel because of their sleepless dedication to the realm. On a day like

461

any other, she was reaching for a book on a high shelf, and it was plucked down for her by none other than the loremaster himself."

Her voice turned hollow and sharp at the edges. A chill swept over Ismai as if some greater predator had flown between him and the sun.

"The loremaster?" he whispered. He found himself clutching at his soft bedding, despite the pain it caused. Knowing Char meant this story would not have a happy ending.

"His name was Ahruman, but nobody ever used it," she continued. "He was chief among the Baidun Daiel, if they can be said to have any chief besides Ka Atu. All of the gathered knowledge in the known world was given over to his care—and there is power in knowledge, just as there is power in magic."

"Or in swords," Ismai said, thinking of the Mah'zula.

"Or in swords," she agreed. "The girl's father, as Dragon King, controlled all three. Naara grew to love the loremaster as he showered her with attention and books, and shared his knowledge freely. Behind his smiling mask of office, however, Ahruman hid a sinister purpose. He coveted the Dragon Throne and all it represented, and saw the dragon's daughter as a weapon he might wield in order to seize the power of Atukos for himself.

"Now, the loremaster of Atualon, in those days long gone, was responsible for more than the care of books and scrolls, maps and records. The real power he wielded, the most important and secret duty of his office, was as the Keeper of Masks. Each of the Baidun Daiel—men and women sworn first to serve the interests of Atualon, then to Atukos, and finally to the Dragon King himself—wore a golden mask of office. To an observer these masks seemed faceless, as the people who wore them were supposed to be devoid of all but pure servitude. On the inside, however..."

Her voice broke.

"I have seen the Baidun Daiel," Ismai murmured, and he barely repressed a shudder.

"You have not seen them as I have, as the girl saw them," Char replied. Her voice was soft and harsh as sand driven by dark winds.

"Though each mask seemed like any other from the outside, on the inside they were very different. *Very* different. There was a ritual—"

Her voice broke again, and for a long moment there was silence. Ismai waited in the dark. Caught up as he was in Char's story, he half wished she would not go on.

It does not end well, he remembered.

No, Kithren, it does not end well. He had never heard Ruh'ayya's voice like this, full of fear and ancient sorrow. *Better you had not come here at all.*

If I had not, he reminded her, *I would have died.*

Ruh'ayya said nothing.

"There was a ritual," Char continued, gripping his hands so hard he gasped with pain. Hearing this, she eased her grip. "Words were inscribed inside each mask," she said. "A vow, I think, some sort of spell or poem. Nobody knew for sure except the loremaster. Most did not even know there was a spell, but he told—he told Naara this secret. Because they were friends." She spat the last word so hard Ismai flinched.

"Before receiving the mask, she or he who would become Baidun Daiel had a spell tattooed into the skin of their back, between the shoulders. Once the skin healed, the person would be strapped to a cross, and flayed. The spell was peeled away, slowly and carefully, all in one piece. This piece of skin was worked into leather, and the leather was used to line the mask. In this way each woman or man was bound to service, bound by words and magic and their very flesh. If any put aside the mask…"

"They were killed?" Ismai asked.

"They were destroyed." Her voice was flat. "Wiped from the world's memory as if they had never been. When a child is selected to become Baidun Daiel, she is stripped of her old life. Friends, family, home, all are taken from her. She becomes nothing more than the promise she has made, the promise she has been *forced* to make, and wears it upon her face till the end of endings."

"Forced to make?"

"Surely you do not believe that any child would choose such a life

463

willingly? The Baidun Daiel are chosen. It used to be a great honor. When a child was selected for service, their family would be paid thrice their worth in salt. Mothers would hire tutors in painting, in music, in poetry as soon as the darling child showed the slightest artistic talent. These children, you know, are the ones most often selected by the Baidun Daiel. Artists, leaders, geniuses, the best and brightest. So, too, those whose minds are not quite… usual, are set aside. The ones who never learn to talk, but who count pebbles, or clouds, or who have imaginary friends. Those gifted ones are nearest and dearest to the heart of the dragon, and so to the Dragon King, who ever lusts for power. They are most beautiful.

"No child, once selected, may refuse the call of duty. No parent, no matter how powerful, may withhold an exceptional child from the Sleepless Ones."

"No child?" Ismai asked. He was thinking of Char's face, and of Sulema. "No parent?"

"No parent," Char said, and she patted his hands. "Though the Dragon King controls the Baidun Daiel, even he is bound by their vows. It is a bitter magic, Ismai, bitter and without end." She lapsed into silence.

"That is horse shit," Ismai said at last. He pulled his hands away from Char's touch and would have wept, had his eyes not been burned away. "This is all horse shit. You, me, the Mah'zula, the Baidun Daiel…" His voice broke, and he slapped his hand weakly against his bedding. "Horse shit."

"Yes," Char said. "That is true. It is horse shit."

"And there is nothing you or I can do about any of it."

"Ah," she said, and her voice became urgent, "this is not true. Ismai, there *is* something we can do. You and I, together. A power we might wield—"

Kithren! Ruh'ayya's thoughts clawed at his mind. *Kithren, 'ware! She is not—* Her voice cut off abruptly, or was cut off.

"Ruh'ayya!" Ismai tried to sit up. Tried, and failed. Char's fingers pressed lightly against his chest, and Ismai found that he could not move.

"Your Ruh'ayya is unharmed. I would never hurt her, Ismai, for in doing so I would hurt you… but I do not like being interrupted, and I am telling you a story."

"Go on, then."

"Once upon a time, there was a little girl. She had a mama who loved her, a mama as fierce and beautiful as the red winds." Impossibly, a gust blew through the Valley of Death, moaning like a woman. "She had a papa who loved her, too, and he was as powerful and terrible as the earth itself." The ground beneath Ismai trembled and bucked, and he heard a smattering of rocks fall from the high walls, their voices hard and angry. "She was taken from them, taken from everything, and when she tried to run away…"

Yet again her voice broke, and Ismai groped toward the sound.

"Oh, Char. I am so sorry." Her hands caught his, squeezed. *Such power in her little bird-bones, such heat.*

She squeezed back, and then pulled her fingers gently from his grasp. "It was long ago, Ismai, and I am a child no longer. That child died, long and long and long ago, and the world she loved died with her, but her father lived on," she continued.

"In his rage and loss he did terrible things, terrible things that he came to regret and in the end he was betrayed. Led to a dark place by those he loved best and trusted most. They told him that there was a chance for peace with the Quarabalese, with the Sindanese, and he leapt at the chance to put an end to the bloodshed—an end to the need for the Baidun Daiel. But it was a lie, Ismai.

"Those whose houses are built upon war will never agree to peace. Kal ne Mur knew that, he saw that, but so desperate was he for an end to the endless wars that were destroying his world that he ran where he should have trodden with caution. On a dark road, under the dark moons, Kal ne Mur was ambushed and stabbed in the back by a man he had called 'friend.' One who has no heart, himself, who can neither sleep nor die."

"Ahruman," Ismai whispered.

"He was called so, then. In this time he is known by another name, one I will not utter so close to the dead who hate him. You know him only as the one who can neither sleep nor die—"

"Nightmare Man," Ismai said, and shuddered.

"Nightmare Man," Char agreed, and spat into the river of death.

"Those who witnessed the murder of Kal ne Mur turned blind eyes, and deaf ears, and dumb mouths. They shuttered their windows and turned their faces, and left their king—their foreign, hated king—to die alone in a puddle of piss and blood. And that, they thought, was that. The Baidun Daiel would wield atulfah as best they could, for such was their bond with Sa Atu that some remnant of his magic flowed through them. In time a new echovete king or queen would be found, a proper Atualonian with the proper bloodlines, not some antlered interloper from the bitter lands."

"Did this happen in Min Yaarif?" Ismai guessed. "In Bayyid Eidtein? I have heard—"

"Oh, Ismai, you silly. No, the place where it occurred no longer exists. Do you think I—do you think the girl would let a city survive, that had stood by and watched and done nothing while her father was murdered? No, no. That place is gone, long ago gone, burned to ashes and dust and the laughter of shadows."

"I thought they had killed the girl?"

"They thought so, too, Ismai, but they were mistaken, and it killed them. It killed them all. The girl's father had found her, much as she found him, later. Beaten and burned and... and mutilated beyond all hope of healing. When he found her he wept over her body as it cooled and stiffened. He did not allow her flesh to be burned, or preserved, or eaten by wyverns. He did not allow her bones to be sung. He did not allow any of those things we do to the dead to make sure their journey into darkness is comfortable and swift and, most importantly, that it is a one-way trip. It would not do, you understand, to have the dead realize they can step off the Lonely Road and retrace their steps."

Char laughed, and in her laugh Ismai heard that which had sent the bonelord Arushdemma fleeing into the desert.

"The Dragon King wrapped his daughter's poor little body in

his own golden robes, and he laid his own golden mask upon her breast. He carried her in his own arms, all the way to the Valley of Death, where for generations of generations people of all lands had interred their best, their brightest, their most beloved. He sang as he rode, and as that sad procession neared the Zeera, the girl's mother joined them and added her fine, soft, sad voice to his. They dug a tomb deep in the valley, and there they sent their beloved child off to sleep as they had made her. With love.

"But their song did not soothe the girl's sleepless spirit. It did not quench her thirst for vengeance, and when later she tasted the salt of her father's blood upon the red winds she rose, and gathered his body up in her arms, and she carried him home. And here they wait, as they have waited since the Sundering."

"For me," Ismai whispered.

"Well, not for you in particular." Char laughed a little. "But we will make do."

It stung. "So I am not… uh…"

"The Chosen One? The Boy of Prophecy? No," she told him. "Those are silly stories, told by silly people, but you are here, and I am here, and we are friends, are we not?"

"We are." Of that much he was certain. Ismai relaxed, and shushed Ruh'ayya as she scrabbled at the edge of his mind. *Not now*, he told her. *I am fine. It will be fine.*

"And friends help one another, do they not?" She stroked back his hair, exposing his ruined face to the bitter air.

"Yes. They do."

"I can help you, Ismai. You say that we are powerless to change the things we do not like about our worlds. Your world, seized as it has been by the Mah'zula. My life, my *not*-life which has for so long been confined to this tiny place, this tiny piece of time. We could be free, Ismai, you and I. We could be free to go wherever we wish, to do whatever we wish to do. None could deny us, withstand us. I could go and see the sea, if I wished. I have heard it is glorious. You could free your people. We could—"

"How?"

"You are willing?" Char sounded, he thought, surprised. Ismai did not hesitate.

"Yes," he said. "Whatever you wish of me, if by doing so I might free my people..." *And keep Sulema from sharing your fate*, he thought without saying it. "I am willing."

"Ah," she sighed. "Ah, walk with me, Ismai."

He opened his mouth to protest, but Char took his hands in hers and drew him to his feet.

"Oh," he said instead.

"Mind your feet," she told him. "You do not want to bathe them in this river, Ismai, not while you are living."

"River?" Ismai was puzzled. "There is no—" Then he heard it. The rushing water. It called to him, and he swayed toward that sweet, cool song.

"Ah-ah!" Char warned sharply. "None of that, not for you! There, step up into the boat. Yes, just there, very good." Ismai let himself be led, felt wooden planks beneath his feet, the sway and lurch of a boat as it was pushed into deep waters.

"There was no river, was there?"

"Of course there was a river," she chided. "It was always here, it has always been here, though it cannot be seen with living eyes."

"My eyes are dead."

"They are."

"And if I open them?" The very idea of peeling his burned lids back caused a spasm of pain, but Ismai was curious.

Kithren, Ruh'ayya wailed from far, far away. *Kithren, no no no no...* But Ruh'ayya, beloved as she was, had not been able to save him. Had not been able to help him. Char offered him another way.

"If you open them?" she said. "Open your dead eyes, and look upon the Valley of Death? What is seen cannot be unseen, Ismai. I do not think you are ready for this, not yet."

"I am," Ismai insisted. He knew it was a bad idea, but that had never before stopped him from tumbling head-first into disaster. He took a deep breath, steeling himself against the pain, and forced his burned lids to open wide, wider. He would have shed

468

tears of pain, but of course that was impossible.

At first there was nothing. Not the thick blood red of light through closed eyelids, nor even the soft of darkness. It was like trying to see with his fingers or toes. There was nothing.

Then there was something.

Then there was… everything.

Ismai cried out in terror and fell back. He could see the boat now, the sickly green-black of decaying wood. He could see the river, red and pale as watered blood, and he could see Charon, the Guardian of Eid Kalmut, as she used a long pole made of white, white bones to push their boat down this river of the damned. He turned his face from the sight of hers, and wept in terror.

"I told you that you were not ready," she said, in a voice edged with hurt and anger. "I told you."

"I am sorry," he wept. "I had no idea. You are so—so—"

"Hideous," she spat, thrusting her pole into the water so that the bloody water sloshed against the side of their vessel. "Ruined."

"Beautiful," Ismai told her. He wanted to cover his eyes, to shield himself from her terrible bright face, but she was right. What had been seen could not be unseen.

"Beautiful?" She laughed, and the water rippled outward, away from the boat. "Beautiful. You are silly, Ismai." She smiled, and it killed him. She laughed, and it tore his soul to pieces. "Come on, then, help me. He has been waiting for far too long, and we should hurry."

Ismai frowned to find himself standing upright, a pole grasped in his hands, twin to the one Char was using. He shrugged the confusion away and pushed. Their little boat skimmed across the turgid waters, and a lively breeze played upon his skin.

"Hurry where? Who has been waiting?"

"You are *such* a silly boy." Char turned her face away from Ismai, casting its light instead upon the waters before them, and his heart ached. "We are going to see the Lich King, of course. It is time for you to meet my father."

S I X T Y

asy meat, the slave raider thought. *It is almost as if she does not know she is being hunted.*

For three days they had tracked their prey, as the sword-tusked cats to the east might stalk a wounded tarbok—leisurely, laughingly, making no effort to conceal their presence or their purpose. A young woman on an old horse—stolen, no doubt, since the stallion had the look of the Zeera about him. Friendless and alone.

She was a dark stranger, lost in a golden land under a golden sky. Easy prey, worth a bag of salt or two at least. It had been a pleasurable hunt, and their prey had made it easy for them, fleeing down the very roads they would be taking after she was theirs. Why feed another mouth one day too soon? If the silly little hare would run straight into the cooking pit, it would be folly to stop her.

But their water was stale to the point of bitterness, and the shit-tasting dried flesh and berries they had taken from some dead barbarians were little more than dust in the bottom of a bag. At last they raised their weapons and their voices, and the five of them rode their prey down.

Or would have, had she had the sense to flee.

The girl halted her old horse at the bottom of a ridge of dunes, lacking even the sense to choose high ground for her final stand. As they drew close, Farak the bandit leader could see that she rode with her body curled protectively around some small object.

A babe, he thought. *That explains a great deal.*

"Two for the price of one, lads!" he shouted, laughing. "Red salt to the one who brings me that brat, alive and unharmed. Fetch a pretty price, it will."

Then they were upon her. They made a loose ring about the girl, hooting and shouting, calling out obscene suggestions to frighten her. Strangely, she sat there wrapped head to toe in robes as bright and gaudy as a merchant's stall, hands curled around the babe at her breast. She acted as if they were not there at all. Her stupid old horse was just as bad, letting its head droop and cocking a hind leg to doze in the sunlight.

It pissed Farak off.

"*Girl*," he shouted to her, "hand over the babe and come easy with us, and you have my promise that I will let you live."

"You will let me live?" A laugh, low and throaty, made him want to tear those veils away and see the face behind them.

Her form was nice enough. Was her face as comely?

Laugh at him, would she? *I will tear those veils away, and make her scream.* He kicked his horse closer. "I will let you live," he said through gritted teeth. If he overpowered her now, the babe might be hurt or killed, and a brat would bring thrice its weight in salt. "My word on it."

"The word of a slave raider." Her shoulders shook beneath the colorful robes. "Worth nearly as much as a handful of goat shit. And I suppose you promise not to touch me."

He laughed at that. They all did. "Girl," he said finally, wiping tears from his cheeks. "Do you have any idea what your life is about to become? This road leads to Min Yaarif."

"All roads lead to Min Yaarif," she said, "or so I have heard." She shifted in the saddle. "Are you certain you want this babe? It is no easy burden to bear, I can tell you that. You might do better to turn and ride back to whatever shit-hole spawned you."

"Mock me one more time, whore," Farak spat, "and we will see who is still laughing when the sun goes down."

She threw her head back and laughed. She *laughed*, pulling her veils aside with one hand as she did so, raising the other before her face, revealing the treasure that she had been cradling close to her heart. The marrow of Farak's bones turned to ice as he beheld a skull, a *child's* skull, crusted in gemstones and gold and salt, winking at them in the dying light.

"Bonesinger," he shouted, his voice as thin and high as that of a frightened boy. "*Bonesinger!*" He yanked his horse's head around, ready to flee, but the gelding screamed and reared, throwing him to the sand. Its hind hooves flashed beside his head, so close he could feel the wind of death against his cheeks, then the damn beast was gone.

From the ridge above them came a series of deep roars. Farak nearly wept to see three of the great desert cats—*vash'ai*, the barbarians called them—cresting the ridge. They were enormous, big as horses it seemed to him. The broken-tusked bastard in the middle stared him straight in the eye and roared again.

"Easy meat," the woman said, and he gaped. "It is almost as if you did not even know you were being hunted."

"Please," Farak begged. "I have a woman… a child. Please. I want to live."

"It is a good day to live," she agreed, and smiled. "It is an even better day to die."

With those words, she brought the child's skull to her mouth, and pursed her lips over a small hole drilled into the top.

Then she blew.

472

SIXTY-ONE

Long they poled down Ghana Kalmut, the river whose name meant "Songs of the Dead." In the long ago, Char had explained to him, this river filled the whole valley and gave life to the surrounding lands, and was called Eid Kalnassa, the River of All Peoples. Then when Davvus fled the wrath of Zula Din, journeying across the wide and lusty waters, so many of his people died in the attempt that it became known as Eid Kalmut, the River of the Dead.

When Zula Din in her fury smote the waters that had let her enemy escape, the very river shrank back from her, dwindling and dying so that the land around it dwindled and died, as well, until only the song was left—this shadow, pale and sullen, red as the baneful flowers that crowded its bank. No living eyes had looked upon Ghana Kalmut in so long that it had passed from memory to legend, and from legend into shadow. People eventually came to call the valley itself Eid Kalmut, and avoided it when they could.

"It is my belief," she told him, "that the river can no longer be seen by living eyes, at all."

"Certainly not with you as its guardian," Ismai said. Instantly the pain made him regret speaking.

She only smiled at his words, and thrust her bone-white pole into the water, sending them deeper into death. Ismai gripped his own pole and bent to the task. The muscles in his arms, his shoulders, his back ached but it was a good ache, the kind of ache felt when the body was young and the work worth doing. Less wholesome was the jagged burning in his mouth and throat that made every breath a struggle, every word an agonized rasp.

Kithren, Ruh'ayya wailed, but it was the ghost of a thought and required no answer. Ismai hardened what was left of his heart,

473

tightened his grip on the bone pole, and pushed, pushed, pushed.

The going was not difficult, traveling as they were with the current and in no particular hurry. The walls of Eid Kalmut grew steeper and darker till the sky overhead was a blistering white-blue sear. Ismai craned his head to look up once, and it seemed to him that what he saw was not the sky at all, but another river, blue and pure and sweet as in the songs of old. It seemed as if he were a dead shade floating up and away into oblivion.

It hurt his eyes to see it.

It hurt his heart to think of it.

"Do not," Char cautioned, her voice heavy with compassion. "Ismai, do not wish for such a thing. That is the land of the living, and the way is shut to you now. To both of us."

Ismai rubbed the tattered and dirty hem of his once-fine touar across his dead eyes, though there were no tears, and returned his gaze once more to the river of death.

The walls of the valley were steep and pale, striated with the ages of man and before-man. They were rippled and fluted as if shaped by a delicate and playful hand. The dead were here, too, keeping their long and peaceful watch from their thrones of wood or bone or precious metals, gazing down upon the travelers with eyes as dry as Ismai's own. As they passed beneath those faces, those great women and men of long ago days, it seemed as if they might have smiled.

"This is not so bad a place," he remarked as they made their slow way past one low and particularly splendid tomb in which a warrior-woman clad in bronze and obsidian sat on a mound of furs, cradling a clay mug between her dark and bony hands.

"No," Char agreed, and a smile flitted across her face. "Not so bad at all."

The walls of the valley drew close, then receded to the point that Ismai had to squint to see either side, and closed in upon them once more. The harsh light of the living world grew softer, kinder, throwing shadows flesh-pink and purple across the faces of the waitful dead so that their eyes seemed to move, their mouths to smile or frown or yawn. Night fell, though almost imperceptibly so. The sky changed, the walls changed, but ever the river stayed the same, slow and cool and smelling of copper and the cinnamon-rot scent of the crimson flowers all along its banks.

Ismai pulled his pole up, firming his grip on the cool rough bone as the river tugged and played with it, and then pushed down, feeling the end catch sometimes in weeds or reeds, and the good solid feel of the river bottom as he pushed against it, sending them ever onward. He and Char worked together, silent except for their breathing—hers soft and barely there, his own raggedy and jaggedy—until the moons rolled away, and the stars as well, and all there was in the world were a boy, a girl, and a river that sang with the voices of the dead.

"I am not tired," he remarked at one point, and grimaced at the raven's caw of his own voice.

"No," Char agreed, and he waited for her to go on.

She did not.

The air about them grew subtly brighter, and at first Ismai reacted as if Akari had begun his ascent. He tugged the veils of his touar around his face, but it was not the dawn of a new day at all. Rather, the blood-red blooms on the banks of the Ghana Kalmut had begun to glow from their centers, a pale and pretty light like the first blush of dawn, and the perfume they sent out into the night grew stronger, sweeter. Ismai breathed deeply and imagined, as he did, that the essence of these flowers soothed the pain of his burns and kept fatigue from settling into his muscles. He shot a suspicious glance at Char, but she hid a smile behind her hair and layers of strange clothing, and said nothing.

The flowers crowded ever more thickly against the river's banks, spreading out into a soft mantle like a Mother's robes sewn with precious stones. They clustered most densely upon the northernmost bank, fading away to the south and west, and Char pointed with the top of her bone pole to where they glowed brightest.

"There," she said, and her voice was light and soft with unshed laughter. Ismai bent into his pole, nearly falling over the side of the boat as their craft shot eagerly as a fresh horse towards the ruddy bank. They pushed through a mat of flowers and reeds and soft mud, and shoved together, grunting with the effort, until they were well and truly grounded.

Char stepped from the boat onto shore, and Ismai followed. He watched nonplussed as she drew their craft high up onto the bank. When he offered to help, she shook her head and laughed.

The flowers crowded round the landing, cobbled with pale round stones stained a faint red in the flower light. They bordered a short path overgrown with goatfoot and mint, and grew in a scattering around the mouth of a tall, wide cave. Char pattered on ahead, her little bare feet barely skimming the ground, but Ismai dragged some distance behind. That cave was dark—darker than the starless sky so far above, darker than the emptiness behind his own dead eyes when he closed them. He imagined that a cold wind breathed forth from that gaping maw, full of voices and fell laughter—

"Ismai," Char called, dancing on the balls of her feet. "Come on!" She disappeared into the cave.

Ismai shook the dread from his shoulders and followed.

There was nothing. Only a few steps in and there was no light, no sound, no movement in the air. He tried reaching out to Ruh'ayya, to no avail. He tried stretching his arms out in front of him and felt nothing, saw nothing. He turned his head this way and that, trying to catch the faintest sound or smell—

"Ismai," Char said again, her voice at once exasperated and full of mischief. "Come on."

She touched his arm, and Ismai screamed like a little boy, jumping half out of his skin. She laughed at him and he frowned.

"That was not—oh." He stopped and stared in surprise. "I can see."

Char snorted a laugh, turned, and trotted away down a narrow path. Ismai shook his head and trotted after.

What choice do I have, after all? he thought. *And what have I left to fear?*

The path wound on and on, angling steeply down so that Ismai had to skip in an attempt to keep up with the fleeing Charon and not fall on his face. He angled this way and that, so abruptly that several times he narrowly avoided smashing into the walls. The air grew cool and dry so that it burned his throat and lungs and his poor dead eyes, and the ground beneath his feet was soft as pounded sand. Char's laugh and the sight of her tattered skirts urged him on, so he ran, legs pumping faster and faster, heedless of the dim light and the narrow way.

The path dropped away beneath his feet, and Ismai yelled as he tipped forward into oblivion, arms pinwheeling, death opening its hard maw to swallow him whole.

A hand grabbed the back of his touar and yanked him away from the edge. Ismai turned on her, heart pounding fit to burst, breath thundering in his ears. Then anger's flames flickered and died at the sight of Char's face.

Her eyes were lit with joy, and her ruined face was wreathed in a wide smile of delight. Those dark eyes, wide as the desert sky, dark as the deepest wish of his heart, sparkled with life.

"Ismai," she said, reaching out to tug at his sleeve, and dancing with excitement. "Ismai, we are here!" She swept her arm in a wide arc, and Ismai, obedient to her every whim, turned to look.

"Oh," he said.

"Oh."

A cavern opened before them, deep and wide as the Madraj, and like the Madraj it was wound round and round with tier upon tier of stone seats. Upon these seats sat warriors, stern and upright even in death, with golden swords laid across their knees. Ismai's heart leapt.

Many of these warriors were men.

"It is just like in the old stories," he said, wondering. "Or like the dreams I used to have, before…"

"Before they killed them," Char whispered. "Your old dreams. This is a new dream, Ismai, one we can share."

"I do not understand."

"You will." She tugged at his sleeve, laughing again. "You will."

Char led the way down a steep ridge, a narrow ledge of rock that was not quite stairs. Ismai breathed a sigh of relief when at last they reached the bottom, but scarce had time to draw a breath before the girl took off running and he was forced to chase after her once again. He laughed, as well, and his throat did not hurt as much as it had.

Running across the pounded sand floor of the arena, they laughed as if they were not lost in the shadowed heart of the world. As if they were not pinned beneath the gaze of a thousand thousand of the ancient dead. As if they had not come to the end of everything. They laughed as if they were alive, and young, and flush with friendship.

Coming to the foot of a high stone dais, Ismai looked up. The laughter died in his lungs so that he choked on it.

In the middle of the dais sat a massive beast of a man, crowned and antlered and clad in gold-chased armor that gleamed even in the dim light of the arena of the dead. Beside him sat the statue of a woman as fierce-eyed as Sareta, as beautiful as his own mother. It was not difficult for Ismai, raised on stories of past glory, to guess who that woman must be—and, by her presence, the identity of the long-dead man, whose eyes seemed to glitter beneath his crown.

"Ahsen-sa Ruh a'Zeera," Ismai breathed, "Spirit of the desert wind. First Rider of the Mah'zula." She who had raised the armies of the Zeeranim from obscurity and propelled them into legend.

"Kal ne Mur," Char said. "The Dragon King. The one *true* king." She started up the steps, and half-turned toward Ismai as he stood staring at the seated figures, frozen with awe. "Come, Ismai. It is time."

His feet dragged him all unwilling up those last few steps, taking him to the feet of the man who broke the world, and there they stopped. His soul and his heart fluttered like birds in a cage and urged him to fly, to fly, yet he stood rooted in fear and an odd, cold anticipation as Char turned her back on him. She stood on tiptoe and whispered into the ear of the long-dead king, as she placed her small, ruined hands on either side of his face and kissed the dead lips.

Still Ismai stood without moving as she came to him, eyes bright with some fell and eager light, as she pulled him down to her and pressed her mouth to his in a long and passionless kiss.

This is wrong, Ismai thought, waking from his stupor too late. *Wrong, wrong, wrong.* He tried to pull back, to pull away, but Charon clamped her small hand onto the back of his neck with all the strength of the river, of tree-roots and sinew and bone, and she forced his mouth to open with hers. Ismai gasped and choked as something hard and round and cold passed from her mouth into his. He fought and flailed as she pulled back, stared into his mouth, and breathed. The sweet-rot scent and taste of the red flowers filed Ismai's senses and he bucked, he thrashed—

He swallowed.

A cold wind rose around Ismai's heart, sucking the breath from his lungs and the sight from his dead eyes. It swept all memory from him as a sandstorm sweeps away all trace of a dead warrior, covering him in layers and layers of hot red memories not his own. He pushed the girl away from him, frowning as she staggered and fell to her knees. Ismai then—

Ismai? No, not I.

—lifted one hand in front of his face, and flexed it, frowning at the smooth young skin. A good hand, big and strong, not yet grown to manhood but large enough to hold a sword.

"Where is my sword?" he asked, and he frowned again at the youthful rasp of his own voice. "Where… am I?"

The girl child, still kneeling, looked up at him. At the sight of her face, so small, so wounded, his heart kindled to fury.

"Who has dared do this to you?" he roared, and then, "Who are you? *Who am I?*"

"Do you not remember?" The girl's voice caught in a sob, and she struggled to rise. "I am Charon… Char. I am your—"

"Daughter," he finished, and he held out a hand to raise her up. He looked deep into those wide, dark eyes, so beautiful, so like her mother's. "Not Charon. Not Char. You are, you are…" He groped for the memory like a blind man in the dark.

"Naara," she whispered.

"Naar-Ahnet," he said, sure that it was so. He reached out to touch her face, and as he did so, the skin beneath his fingers took on the flush of health, of youth. Even as he watched, the charred and ruined mess of her face began to knit together, to heal.

Char—*Naara*—closed her eyes and sighed.

"Father," she said, and a tear slipped from beneath her dark lashes.

"Yes, my darling child," he said, "it is I." *Kal ne Mur. The Dragon King.*

The Lich King.

He gathered her up into his arms, and kissed her weeping face, as all around them the dead began to stir.

SIXTY-TWO

Perri had been of the air, and to the air he would return. They rubbed whale oil and dragonmint into his skin and hair until he glowed with a false blush of health. Stitching and binding his wounds, they hid them beneath fine robes and the silver-and-blue lacquered armor of a bloodsworn soldier.

They built a pyre made of sandalwood and sant, agarwood and pine. Upon this high and precious bier was placed a bed of fragrant herbs, soft grasses, and such flowers as blossomed into summer. Daechen Perri, born of a son of twilight and a daughter of man, was laid to rest beneath the stars, beneath the moons and the wide, wide sky. Jian Sen-Baradam himself brought forth a torch, touching it to the oil-soaked straw and bits of yellow silk which bound the structure together.

The wind blew in from a faraway sea, rousing the fire to wrath. Flames like oulo dancers wreathed in smoke danced across Perri's empty shell as he had once danced with a pretty girl at Nian-da, both of them laughing and leaping higher, higher as the red-robed monks tossed firecrackers at their feet. Then the boy was gone, meat burned from bone and bone to ash, borne up by the wind as a babe in its mother's arms, up up up to dance with the distant indifferent stars.

Jian peered in rage and longing through the smoke at the sea, and the sky, and the pale sands, wishing for a wind to blow his friend home. But the sea was still the same, and the sky was still the same, and his friend was still gone, a streak of soot, a scattering of cinders scarring the night's lovely face.

The wind was heavy with salt, and the dreams of dae princes, and the tears of lost boys. It struck at the burning pyre, tore at Jian's hair where it whipped free from his helmet. The wind howled at the moons like the voices of a thousand Issuq lost on the waves, lost to their own kin, lost, lost, lost.

The howling, the smoke, and the dancing flames woke something deep in Jian's breast, because a bond of brotherhood sealed in blood could never be truly broken, nor could the smile of his friend be forgotten. He stepped through the smoke and into the sea, the wide and welcoming arms of his homeland, and in the starslight and moonslight he beheld with eyes neither truly human nor truly dae the edge of a shimmering veil, that gossamer border between the world of men and the lands of twilight, thin as a caul between twins.

The wind tore at the veil, at weft and warp of daekin and man. It tore and howled just as his heart stormed and raged, but the stars could not be bothered to care, and laws older than the moons forbade his crossing. He could not pass. He could not, it was forbidden…

Then the halfkin child, grown now, strengthened by song and longing and the kisses of a lost wife, held both hands before his face. There was blood beneath the nails, his own or that of another. There was ash upon his sleeve, the remnant of blood and bone and promises broken before they could become anything.

Deep in their dungeon the Sisters stirred. They screamed and gnashed their broken teeth, and black tears streaked their faces like soot.

"He burns," the first sister wailed. "Do you see him? Do you see?"

"He sings," the second sister cried. "Do you hear him? Do you hear?"

"Aaaahhhh," the third sister moaned as she thrashed against their common bonds. "Aaahhhh, ahhh, aaaahhhhhhh!"

They fell silent again, still and dead as old meat.

Far away, long away Jian Sen-Baradam brought the pad of his thumb up to his mouth and bit down, hard. His blood dripped thick and crimson into the rising tide.

Drip…
Drip…
Drip…
Three drops thrice shall bind his heart
Lest that heart betray him.

The son of two lands looked through the veil with his father's eyes, Issuq eyes, born of sea and longing and the loneliness of a twilight lord. He saw upon the water a path made of moonslight and mer-dreams, a wide and shining road upon which he might walk to the land of his father's people, to find an army fit to break the Forbidden City, and steal an empire.

He rubbed hands together till his fingers were bloody, and then seized the fabric of the Sundering Veil.

Grasping it, he tore.

DAMNED

He followed her from the Dreaming Lands to the road he could not take. As she walked, barefoot and naked and bereft, her soul shed its cares like a living woman might shed clothes. Weapons she left behind, dagger and staff and lyre. Love and hate fell from her skin like winter's mantle grown too warm to bear. Her little feet left no impression upon the sand, her moonsilk hair did not stir to life in the harsh winds of summer, but she cast a faint shadow upon the ground.

This penumbra whispered as she passed. It stroked the face of a well-hidden hare. The creature, frightened into stillness, crouched low, so the hawk overhead never saw it, never stooped for the kill.

Well, he thought, *that is interesting*. He had thought this woman, this Eater of Dreams, might be the one to finally bring him peace. In the end, however, she only brought death to herself, her love, and her world. He should have known better than to cling to hope.

The Nightmare Man, the Bad-Luck Man, the Man of Many Skins… these names he bore, these faces he wore, all of these and countless more. He stopped short when he came to the crossing. He could see the easy way and the difficult, the steep way and the narrow, the paths of endless possibilities. Running through them all, binding them as the Web of Illindra bound all worlds to the heavens, was the Lonely Road.

The ways were shut to him, just as rest was denied him. The cares of a mortal life, the brief bright respite of death, none of these were for him, not until the end of all days.

His black-clad hand tightened on the haft of his great hammer, till the fell-iron glowed hot with rage and the air shimmered before his ruined eyes, his ruined face. The mask chafed, it burned, and he let go the hammer, reached up, and removed his mask.

The Nightmare Man, the Trickster, the Shadow King turned his broken face up to a broken sun, daring the light to warm his skin, daring the wind to bring him relief.

The hare, sensing a danger more imminent and complete than any hawk, twitched her whiskers, looked up, and *saw*.

Instantly the heart in her little breast stopped beating.

Even so much as this, I am forbidden. He replaced the mask, and once more took up his hammer.

So be it.

APPENDICES

THE LANDS OF THE PEOPLE

From the Notes of Loremaster Rathfaust

ATUALON

The mightiest kingdom in the Near West, Atualon is the seat of Ka Atu, the Dragon King. Fabled to be built on the back of a sleeping dragon, Atualon is the wellspring of a deep and ancient magic.

This magic is known as atulfah, and is comprised of sa and ka, female and male, heart and spirit, the Song of Life. Only those born echovete—able to hear the magical song of creation—have the potential to manipulate this magic, and only an echovete child born and raised to the throne may be trained to wield it.

SINDAN

The Sindanese empire stretches from the pearl-choked waters of Nar Kabdaan in the Middle East, over the ice-tombed peaks of Mutai Gon-yu, to Nar Intihaan in the Far East: End of the Bitter Lands, End of the Great Salt Road, End of the Known World. The story of Sindan stretches far beyond written memory and into the misted memories of the First Men, before the thickening of the veil. The Daemon Emperor of Sindan rules absolutely from his throne in Khanbul, the Forbidden City, though his thoughts turn ever westward. He is covetous of atulfah, for its power is the only thing greater than his own.

QUARABALA

Once a place of beauty and art, high learning and gentle culture, the Quarabala was scorched clean of life and hope during the Sundering. Few now survive in the dead lands west of the Dibris. Occasionally a story will turn up in the slave-trading town of

Min Yaarif, rumors of wicked beasts and wickeder men driven to desperate acts as they struggle to survive on the Edge of the Quarabala. Even more rarely an Illindrist, a shadowshifting sorcerer, will emerge from the smoking ruins, night-skinned and demon-eyed, leading a trader or three with packs full of the precious red salt and eyes full of waking nightmares.

THE ZEERA

A land of silk and honey, great warriors and greater predators, the Zeera is a vast golden desert and home to the desert prides. Once a proud and prosperous nation, the Zeeranim are now a remnant of their former glory. The Mothers live in mostly empty cities along the banks of the Dibris, the Ja'Sajani take census and record the final days of a dying people, and the Ja'Akari guard the people against enemies within and without the prides. Too few are born, too few survive, and too few are chosen to become Zeeravashani, bonded to the great saber-tusked cats with whom they are allied. The wardens write, the warriors fight, and the Mothers sing lullabies against the coming darkness, but their struggles are like the notes of a flute, lost and forgotten in the coming storm.

THE PEOPLE

From the Notes of Loremaster Rathfaust

Aadl (Istaz Aadl): Zeerani youthmaster

Aaraf (Loreman Aaraf): Zeerani storyteller and bard

Aasah (Aasah sud Layl): priest of Illindra, shadowmancer and advisor to Ka Atu

Adalia: Warrior of the Mah'zula

Ani (Istaza Ani): Zeerani youthmistress; also the last known Dzirani

Annila (Annila Ja'Akari): young Zeerani warrior, peer to Sulema and Hannei

Annubasta (*see* Hafsa Azeina)

Ashta: journeyman mantist studying under Loremaster Rothfaust

Askander (Askander Ja'Akarinu'i): First Warden of the Zeeranim

Bardu: Daechen prince

Bashaba: former concubine of Ka Atu; mother to Pythos (deceased), Mattu, and Matteira

Basta (cat): kima'a to Hafsa Azeina

Bellanca (Matreon Bellanca): Matreon of Atualon

Belzaleel the Liar: an ancient, wicked spirit, currently trapped in a dragonglass blade

Boraz (Boraz Ja'Sajani): Zeerani warder

Breama: the Huntress

Bretan Mer (Bretan Mer ne Ninianne il Mer): salt merchant and liaison from Salar Merraj to Atualon; son of Ninianne il Mer

Brygus: member of the Draiksguard

Char (Charon): Guardian of Eid Kalmut

Daeshen Baichen Pao: the first Daemon Emperor, ruler of Sindan
Daeshen Tiachu: the current Daemon Emperor, ruler of Sindan
Daru: young apprentice to Hafsa Azeina
Davidian: Imperator General of Atualon
Davvus: a legendary king of Men
Dennet: a daughter of Nurati
Devranae: legendary daughter of Zula Din; abducted by Davvus, king of Men
Deyenna: a young woman who seeks to escape Atualon
Douwa: bathhouse attendant in Atualon
Duadl (Duadl Ja'Sajani): Zeerani warden and churra-master

Eleni: attendant at the Grinning Mymyc in Bayyid Eidtein
Ezio: Atualonian Master of Coin

Fairussa (Fairussa Ja'Akari): warrior of the Zeeranim

Gai Khan: Daechen prince
Gavria (Gavria Ja'Akari): Zeerani warrior
Ginna: Atualonian maidservant

Hadid (Mastersmith Hadid): Zeerani mastersmith
Hafsa Azeina: dreamshifter of the prides and Queen Consort of Atualon. Rarely: Annubasta
Hannei (Hannei Ja'Akari): Sulema's peer and good friend
Hapuata (Istaza Hapuata): Zeerani mentor to Theotara Ja'Akari
Hekates: Draiksguard of Atualon
Hyang: village boy from Bizhan

Ippos: Stablemaster of Atualon
Isara (Isara Ja'Akari): Zeerani warrior
Ishtaset: Mah'zula warrior
Ismai: Zeerani youth; son of Nurati
Istaza Ani (*see* **Ani**)

Jamandae: (deceased) youngest concubine of Serpentus, deposed Dragon King of Atualon

Jasin (Ja'Atanili'I Jasin): Zeerani youth and would-be warden

Jian (Daechen Jian, Tsun-ju Jian): young Daechen prince

Jinchua (fennec): kima'a to Sulema

Jorah: Zeerani craftsman

Kabila (Kabila Ja'Akari): Zeerani warrior

Kalani: Zeerani maiden

Karkash Dhwani: powerful Daechen prince, advisor to the emperor

Lavanya: Zeerani warrior and peer of Sulema

Leviathus (Leviathus ap Wyvernus ne Atu): Sulema's half-brother, son of Ka Atu, Leviathus is surdus—a princeling without magic

Makil: Zeerani warden

Mardoni: Daechen prince

Marisa: maidservant in Atualon

Mariza: Renegade Ja'Akari. Once banished and declared Kha'Akari, she now rides with the Mah'zula

Matteira: daughter of Bashaba, a former concubine of Ka Atu. Twin sister to Mattu, and sister to Pythos (deceased)

Mattu (Mattu Halfmask): son of Bashaba, a former concubine of Ka Atu. Twin brother to Matteira, and brother to Pythos

Naruteo (Daechen Naruteo): Sindanese youth. Daeborn and yearmate to Jian

Neptara (Umm Neptara): daughter of Nurati

Ninianne il Mer: Lady of the Lake, matriarch of the clans of Salar Merraj, city of the salt merchants; mother of Bretan Mer, Soutan Mer

Nurati (Umm Nurati): First Mother of the Zeeranim; mother of Tammas, Neptara, Ismai, Dennet, Rudya, and an as-yet unnamed infant daughter

Perri: Sindanese youth; daeborn and yearmate to Jian

Pythos: (deceased) son of Serpentus, deposed Dragon King of Atualon

Rama (Rama Ja'Sajani): Zeerani warden and horsemaster from Aish Arak

Rheodus: young Atualonian man, member of Leviathus's Draiksguard

Rothfaust (Loremaster Rothfaust): loremaster of Atualon, keeper of tomes and tales

Rudya: daughter of Nurati

Sammai: Zeerani child

Santorus (Master Healer Santorus): Atualonian patreon and master healer

Sareta (Sareta Ja'Akarinu'i): ranking warrior of the Zeeranim

Saskia (Saskia Ja'Akari): Zeerani warrior and peer of Sulema

Soutan Mer (Soutan Mer ne Ninianne il Mer): son of Ninianne il Mer

Sulema (Sulema Ja'Akari): Zeerani warrior, daughter of Hafsa Azeina and Wyvernus

Sunzi: Daechen prince

Tadeah: (deceased) daughter of Bashaba and Ka Atu

Talilla (Ja'Akari): Zeerani warrior

Talleh: young Zeerani boy

Tammas (Tammas Ja'Sajani): Zeerani warden, eldest son of Nurati

Teppei: Daechen prince

Theotara (Theotara Ja'Akari): honored Ja'Akari

Tiungpei (Tsun-ju Tiungpei): a Sindanese pearl diver who took a lover from among the Issuq; mother of Jian

Tsa-len: Yendaeshi to Naruteo

Umm Nurati (*see* **Nurati**)

Valri: warrior of the Mah'zula

Wyvernus: Ka Atu, the Dragon King of Atualon
Xienpei: Yendaeshi to Jian

Yaela: apprentice to Aasah
Yeshu: Atualonian weaver

Zula Din: trickster/warrior of legend, daughter of the First People

TERMS AND PHRASES
OF INTEREST

From the Notes of Loremaster Rathfaust

Aish Kalumm (the City of Mothers): Zeerani river fortress

Akari (Akari Sun Dragon): according to legend, Akari is a draik (a male dragon) who flies across the sky bringing life and light to the world as he seeks to rouse his sleeping mate, Sajani the Earth Dragon

aklashi: a game played while on horseback. It involves a sheep's head and quite a lot of noise

arachnist: a human mage, who worships and does the bidding of the Araids

Araid: massive, intelligent spiders that live deep in the abandoned cities of Quarabala

Atualon: a western kingdom founded upon the shores of Nar Bedayyan; home to the Dragon Kings

Atukos (City of Dreams, City of the Sleeping Dragon): dragonglass fortress of the Dragon King, named for the living mountain into which it is built

atulfah: sa and ka combined to create the song of creation

Ayyam Binat: a period of time in the spring during which young Zeerani women vie with one another for the sexual favors of men

Baidun Daiel (also known as the Sleepless, or Voiceless): warrior mages who serve Ka Atu

Baizhu: a religious order of Sindanese monks

Bayyid Eidtein: trading town near the mouth of the Dibris, a known den of miscreants and rogues. The southernmost trading post along Atualonian-maintained roads

Beit Usqut: the Youths' Quarter in Aish Kalumm

bintshi: an intelligent flying animal with some natural affinity for psionic manipulation; carnivorous; considered kith

Bohica: patroness divine of soldiers

Bonelord: one of the greater predators, bonelords are massive carnivorous creatures that rely on camouflage, speed, and mind-magic to capture prey

bonesinger: Dzirani medicine man

Bones of Eth: an ill-reputed ruin or monument in the Zeera, formed of a rough circle of tall, twisted pillars of red and black stone

churra (pl. churrim): a hardy desert omnivore prized by the Zeerani as a pack animal, and seen as a suitable mount for outlanders

craftmistress/master: Zeerani women and men who have been trained in and work at their particular craft—blacksmithing, painting, building, weaving, etc.

Dae: a race of magically gifted people who reside in the Twilight Lands

daeborn: of dae descent

daemon: commonly used to describe any wicked thing (also daespawn)

Daechen: half-Dae, half-human Sindanese warrior caste (male)

Daeshen: half-Dae, half-human, member of the Sindanese imperial family

Daezhu: half-Dae, half-human Sindanese ruling class (female)

Delpha (Big Sister): one of two moons; has a twenty-eight-day cycle

Dibris: a river that runs through the Zeera, supporting a wide range of life

Didi (Little Sister): one of two moons; has a fourteen-day cycle

Dragon King: Ka Atu, the monarch of Atualon (currently Wyvernus)

Draiksguard: elite military unit assigned to guard members of the Atualonian royal family

Dreaming Lands: *see* **Shehannam**

dreamshifter: Zeerani shaman who can move through and
manipulate Shehannam

Dzirani: wandering storytellers, healers, and merchants

Dziranim: a member of the Dzirani clan

echovete: one who can hear atulfah

ehuani: Zeerani word meaning "beauty in truth"

Eid Kalish: trading town, a stop on the Great Salt Road, known for
its thriving black market and slave trade

Eth: Quarabalese destruction deity, he whose breath creates the
darkness between stars

Great Salt Road: trade route that stretches from the edge of the
Quarabala in the west to the easternmost cities of Sindan

Hajra-Khai: Zeerani spring festival

hayatani: a Zeerani girl's first consort

hayyanah: Zeerani couples who are pledged to one another and
remain more or less monogamous

herdmistress/master: responsible for the health and well-being of a
pride's horses and churrim

Illindra: Quarabalese creation deity, an enormous female spider
who hangs the stars in her web of life

Issuq: twilight lords and ladies who have a clan affinity for the sea
and can shapeshift into sea-bears

istaza/istaz: youthmistress/master of the Zeerani prides

Ja'Akari: Zeerani warrior, responsible for keeping all the pridelands
safe from outside threats

Ja Akari: Zeerani phrase meaning "under the sun"; loosely translates
to being completely open and honest, hiding nothing

Ja'Sajani: Zeerani warden, responsible for maintaining order and
security within his local territory

Ja Sajani: Zeerani phrase meaning "upon the earth"; loosely translates to being present in the moment

Jehannim: a mythical hellish place of fire and brimstone; also the name of a mountain range west of the river Dibris and east of Quarabala

jiinberry: a water-loving berry that grows along the banks of the Dibris during the flooding season

ka: the male half of atulfah, known as the breath of spirit. It manifests to most as an expanded awareness of one's surroundings

Ka Atu: the Dragon King of Atualon (currently Wyvernus)

Kaapua: a river in Sindan

Kha'Akari: Zeerani warrior who has been exiled from the sight of Akari

Khanbul (the Forbidden City): home of the Sindanese emperor

khutlani: Zeerani word meaning "forbidden"

kima'a: avatar spirit-beast in Shehannam

kin: intelligent creatures descended from the first races and considered relatives of dragons—vash'ai, wyverns, and mymyc are numbered among the kin

kith: term used to describe creatures that are more intelligent than beasts, but lack the awareness of kin or humans

kithren: Zeerani person bound to a vash'ai, and vice versa

Ladies/Lords of Twilight: Dae lords

lashai: modified half-human servants that wait upon the Daechen and yendaeshi

lionsnake: an enormous, venomous, two-legged plumed serpent that lives in the Zeera

the Lonely Road: in Zeerani mythology, the road traveled by the dead

Madraj: an arena and gathering place of the Zeeranim

Mah'zula: a society of Zeeranim who live a purely nomadic life and abide by the ancient ways of the desert, seeking to return to the glory days of the First Women

Min Yaarif: trading and slavers' port on the western bank of the Dibris

Mutai Gon-yu (The Mountains that Tamed the Rains): mountain range in Sindan

mymyc: one of the kin, mymyc live and hunt in packs. From a distance, mymyc strongly resemble black horses

Nar Bedayyan: a sea to the west of Atualon

Nar Intihaan: a sea to the east of Sindan

Nar Kabdaan: a sea east of the Zeera and west of Sindan

ne Atu: member of the royal family of Atualon

Nian-da: a ten-day-long festival in Sindan. Any child born during this time is assumed to be fathered by a Dae man during Moonstide, and without exception is taken to Khanbul at the age of sixteen

Nisfi: Zeerani pride

outlanders: term used by the Zeerani to describe people not of the Zeera

parens: heads of the ruling families in Atualon

pride: Zeerani clan. Also used to describe all prides as a single entity

Quarabala (also known as the Seared Lands): a region so hot that humans live in cities far underground

Quarabalese: of Quarabala

reavers: insectoid humans that have been modified by the Araids. Their bite is envenomed

Riharr: Zeerani pride

russet ridgebacks: large (five-pound) spiders that live in underground colonies. Harmless unless they are disturbed. Their eggs are considered a delicacy in the Zeera.

sa: heart of the soul. An expanded sense of empathy and harmony

Sajani (Sajani Earth Dragon, the Sleeping Dragon): according to legend, Sajani is a diva (a female dragon) who sleeps beneath the crust of the world, waiting for the song of her mate Akari to wake her

Salar Merraj: city of the salt miners built upon the shores of a dead salt lake. The Mer family stronghold

Salarians: citizens of the salt-mining city Salar Merraj

sand-dae: shapes made of wind-driven sand

Shahad: Zeerani pride

Shehannam (the Dreaming Lands): the otherworld, a place of dreams and strange beings

shenu: a board game popular in the Zeera

shofar (pl. shofarot): wind instrument made from the horn of an animal

shofar akibra: a magical instrument fashioned from the horn of the golden ram

shongwei: an intelligent, carnivorous sea creature

Sindan: empire that stretches from Nar Kabdaan in the west to Nar Intihaan in the east

Sindanese: of Sindan

Snafu: patron divine of fuckups

Sundering: cataclysm that took place roughly one thousand years before the events of this story

surdus: deaf to atulfah

Tai Bardan (Mountains of Ice): mountain range in Sindan east of Khanbul

Tai Damat (Mountains of Blood): mountain range in Sindan on the Great Salt Road, north of Khanbul

tarbok: goat-sized herd animal, plentiful near rivers and oases

touar: head-to-toe outfit worn by the Zeerani wardens: head wrap and veils, calf-length robe, loose trousers, all blue

Twilight Lands: a land at once part of and separated from the world of Men; home of the Dae

usca: a strong alcoholic beverage popular in the Zeera
Uthrak: Zeerani pride

vash'ai: large, intelligent saber-tusked cats. Vash'ai are kin,
    descended from the first races

Wild Hunt (also the Hunt): deadly game played by the Huntress, a
    powerful being who enforces the rules of Shehannam
wyvern: intelligent flying kin

yendaeshi: trainer, mentor, and master to the Daechen and Daezhu
Yosh: name of the wicked spirit or deity that rules Jehannim
youthmistress/master (istaza/istaz): Zeerani adults in charge of
    guiding and teaching the pride's young people

Zeera: a desert south of the Great Salt Road, known for its singing
    dunes, hostile environment, and remote barbarian prides
Zeeranim: people of the desert
Zeeravashani: a Zeerani person who has bonded with a vash'ai

ACKNOWLEDGEMENTS

I would like to give a nod of thanks to...

My readers. I love you guys.

My rockstar agent, Mark Gottlieb of Trident Media.

My Dark Editorial Overlord, Steve Saffel of Titan Books.

Alice Nightingale, again, for initially acquiring *The Dragon's Legacy* and applauding my every success.

Nick Landau, Vivian Cheung, Paul Gill, Miranda Jewess, Ella Chappell, Samantha Matthews, Julia Lloyd, Chris McLane, Lydia Gittins, Katharine Carroll, and Polly Grice of Titan Books, for believing in my story.

My high-school English teacher, Deane O'Dell, who against all odds kindled the love of literature in the heart of an ungrateful young barbarian.

5/12/19

Newport Library and
Information Service

ABOUT THE AUTHOR

Deborah A. Wolf was born in a barn and raised on wildlife refuges, which explains a lot. As a child, whether she was wandering down the beach of an otherwise deserted island or exploring the hidden secrets of bush Alaska with her faithful dog Sitka, she always had a book at hand. She opened the forbidden door, set foot upon the tangled path, and never looked back.

She attended any college that couldn't outrun her and has accumulated a handful of degrees, the most recent of which is a Master of Science in Information Systems Management from Ferris State University. Among other gigs, she has worked as an underwater photographer, Arabic linguist, and grumbling wage slave. Throughout it all, Deborah has held onto one true and passionate love: the art of storytelling.

Deborah currently lives in northern Michigan with her kids (some of whom are grown and all of whom are exceptional), an assortment of dogs and horses, and two cats, one of whom she suspects is possessed by a demon.

Newport Community
Learning & Libraries